Praise for L. E. Modesitt, Jr.

"Independent science-fiction consciousness-raiser, from the versatile and dependable Modesitt."
    —*Kirkus Reviews* on *Haze*

"Satisfying from a science-fictional perspective, with its discussions of Hawking effect displacements and intergalactic conflict; from a conceptual perspective as the reader must follow complicated reasoning processes; and from a literary perspective, as Modesitt reaches a new stage in the intertwining of plot and character."
    —*SFRA Review* on *The Elysium Commission*

"Modesitt's prose is lively, and there's enough sense of wonder here to satisfy even the most jaded. . . . A must-read for Modesitt fans, as well as those of Jack McDevitt and Arthur C. Clarke."
    —*Kirkus Reviews* (starred review) on
    The Eternity Artifact

"Modesitt's work shines with engrossing characters, terrific plotting, and realistic world-building."
    —*RT Book Reviews* on *The Eternity Artifact*

"If you're seeking space battles and diplomatic intrigue within a well-thought-out universe, then Modesitt delivers."
    —*Vector* on *The Ethos Effect*

TOR BOOKS BY L. E. MODESITT, JR.

*Forthcoming

HAZE

L. E. Modesitt, Jr.

TOR®

A TOM DOHERTY ASSOCIATES BOOK
NEW YORK

HAZE

A Tor Book
Published by Tom Doherty Associates, LLC
175 Fifth Avenue
New York, NY 10010

www.tor-forge.com

Tor® is a registered trademark of Tom Doherty Associates, LLC.

ISBN 978-0-7653-6290-2

First Edition: June 2009
First Mass Market Edition: May 2010

Printed in the United States of America

0 9 8 7 6 5 4 3 2 1

For Hildegarde and her mistress

Some call the planet Haze
for its gray shield of sky;
But Doubt of other ways
Is what refutes that lie.

HAZE

1

The man in the drab pale blue Federation shipsuit sat inside the oblong cubicle just large enough for the chair and hood that provided direct sensory-reinforced information—useful for everything from maintenance data to in-depth intelligence briefings. After thirty standard minutes, he removed the hood, rose to his feet, pushed back the screen as he stepped out onto the dark blue of the third deck. The bulkheads were an eye-resting blue, close to the shade of his shipsuit, and devoid of any decoration or projections. That was true of all bulkheads on the *WuDing,* and of all Federation deep-space vessels. He eyed the three datastations for a moment, now all empty, then shook his head.

He stood 193 centimeters and massed 104.4 kilograms, and under the ship's single grav, mass and weight matched. His hair was nondescript brown. His eyes were silver gray.

He frowned for a moment, still trying to ignore the residual odor of burning hair that remained trapped in his nostrils. The odor was a side effect of the suspension cradles in which he and much of the *WuDing*'s crew had spent the transit out from Fronera, and it would pass. It certainly had on his missions to Khriastos and Marduk.

He just wished the odor had already departed. He remained motionless, trying to organize the mass of information he had been mentally force-fed.

ITEM: The planet was too close to the K7 orange-tinted sun to be habitable under normal conditions, although the system was older by at least a billion years than the Sol system.

ITEM: The planet had a mass of 1.07 T-norm, with an upper atmosphere that suggested optimal habitability.

ITEM: The planet itself was impenetrable to all forms of Federation scanning and detection technology.

ITEM: The planet presented an image of feature-less silver gray haze to normal human vision and remained equally featureless to all forms of observation technology.

ITEM: It had no moons or objects of significant individual mass in orbit.

ITEM: Identical objects massing approximately .11 kilograms orbited the planet in at least three differing levels. The number of such objects in each orbital sphere could not be quantified, but estimates suggested more than two million per sphere.

ITEM: The planet radiated nothing along any known spectrum. No electromagnetic radiation, no gravitonic waves, no nothing . . . except a certain amount of evenly dispersed heat and radiation consisting of energy reflected from the planet's sun.

ITEM: He had to find out what lay below that silver gray haze.

He nodded slowly, then stretched. He disliked info-feed briefings. He always had. He turned and began to walk toward the *WuDing*'s Operations Control. His shipboots were silent on the plastiform deck.

Major Roget, to OpCon.

Stet. On my way.

There was no response. The colonel disliked unnecessary communications, particularly on the shipnet, and particularly when he had to deal with an FSA agent transferred into his command at the rank of major. The other four FSA agents accompanying Roget were lieutenants and captains, though he'd known none of them before boarding the *WuDing*.

An Ops monitor tech, also in a pale blue shipsuit, hurried in Roget's direction. As she neared him, her eyes took in his collar insignia, and she averted her eyes, just enough to display the proper respect.

Roget inclined his head fractionally in response and continued to the first ladder, which he ascended. Two levels up, he headed aft.

The hatch to Colonel Tian's office irised open at Roget's approach and closed behind him. Roget took two steps into a space four times the size of the briefing cubicle and halted. The office held two chairs. The colonel sat in one.

"Sir," offered Roget.

"Please be seated, Major." The colonel gestured for Roget to take the other chair. The thin operations console was folded flush against the aft bulkhead. Hard-connected systems worked far better in battle than broadband links, although no Federation warship had been in a pitched space battle in centuries.

Roget sat down and waited.

The colonel steepled his fingers, his eyes looking not at Roget, but through the major. He was a good half a head shorter than Roget, but slender, almost willowy despite his age, and his black eyes were youthfully ancient. Finally, he spoke. "According to the report forwarded by FSA, you are most capable, Major, especially when acting alone. Your accomplishments on Marduk and on system station Khriastos appear particularly noteworthy." Tian paused. "Independent action, in particular, may be needed on this assignment, and that is why the FIS requested assistance from FSA."

"Yes, sir."

"What do you think lies behind that haze-shield, Major?"

"An alien culture. Probably Thomist, but that would be speculation, sir."

"You consider the Thomists as aliens?" The colonel's tone suggested raised eyebrows, but his face remained serene.

"Alien to the goals and aims of the Federation, certainly."

"How would you define alien?"

"Not aligned and unfathomable," replied Roget easily. He'd reported to more than enough hard-eyed and unnamed FSA colonels over the years that an FIS colonel was hardly anything to worry about.

"Unfathomable?"

"Theoretically intellectually understandable, but not emotionally comprehensible."

The colonel offered the slightest nod. "Analytics calculate the probability at 73 percent for the likelihood of a Thomist world."

Again, Roget waited. Even for a Federation Interstellar Service security officer, the colonel was being casual, if not blasé, about the discovery of a human splinter culture or an alien world. Unlike Roget, he had to have known of the world long before Roget's briefing.

"Do you have any questions?"

"How long have we known about this world?" Roget asked the question because it was expected, not because he anticipated a meaningful answer.

"If it's Thomist, we've known about the possibility for quite a time."

"How long might that be, sir?"

"Long enough. We're not absolutely certain it is a Thomist world. That's your task. You will, of course, wear a pressure suit until you confirm that the world is not environmentally hostile, and your dropboat is configured with some additional survival features to deal with that eventuality, although the scientists believe such is unlikely."

The colonel's response confirmed Roget's feelings. The senior officer wasn't about to answer the questions Roget would have liked to ask, and the ones he would answer had already been addressed by the console briefing. The issue of a hostile environment had also been touched upon and dismissed, as if the colonel knew far more than he was revealing.

"Any other questions?"

"No, sir."

"Your outward complacency exemplifies your inner arrogance, Major."

"Yes, sir."

"Inscrutability behind an emotional facade. The heritage of failed Noram supremacy." Tian's short laugh was humorless.

"As opposed to inscrutability behind inscrutability, sir?"

"There is a difference between inscrutability and deception, Major. It's called honesty, I believe."

"Yes, sir."

"If you're successful, Major, you'll doubtless end up in a position similar to mine, if within the Federation Security Agency."

That was a large "if," Roget knew. So did the colonel.

The senior officer looked at Roget. "You won't like the entry."

"You don't expect most of us to survive it." Roget's silver gray eyes never left the colonel's face.

"We do hope you will. We'd rather not lose the investment, and we'd like some confirmation of what lies beneath that haze. The dropboat and your suit are designed to handle everything engineering could anticipate."

That didn't reassure Roget. The Thomists had left the Federation with enough high tech that they'd only been rediscovered—if the planet called Haze was indeed theirs—by accident more than a millennium later. But if what lay beneath that silvery shifting shield happened to be nonhuman alien, then matters would either be far better . . . or far, far, worse.

He wasn't certain whether he would rather face the Thomists or nonhuman aliens.

"That is all, Major." The colonel's smile was cool. He did not stand.

"Yes, sir." Roget stood, smiled politely, turned, and walked from the small office.

He couldn't help but wonder what surprises this mission held. In one way or another, every mission had provided something he hadn't anticipated, and often had revealed matters that even the FSA had not expected. Not that he had ever revealed all of those.

2

Roget and Kuang sat on the balcony. The only hint of the snoopblock was the slightest wavering in the night air, an almost invisible curtain that extended upward from the pewter-like circular railing. The multicolored towers of Taiyuan rose around them, glittering and gleaming with lines of day-stored and night-released light. The air was warm, but not uncomfortably so, and held a fragrance Roget could not identify, doubtless one specified by Kuang and released from the railing and dispersed as a side effect by the snoopblock.

"Beautiful, is it not?" asked Kuang, setting down his near-empty glass on the table between them.

"It should be. It's the heart of world culture and the capital of the Federation." Roget offered a polite smile.

"It's been a capital before. Capitals come and go. They've done so here for more than sixty-five centuries." Kuang's voice was matter-of-fact above the whine of some form of ground transport, muted by the snoopblock, that rose from the street some eleven levels below. A mock lightning bolt flashed across the top of a tower bordering the river.

"Taiyuan has lasted longer than any other . . . and in greater glory."

"So has its intrigue."

"If there are people, there's intrigue," Roget said, taking a last sip of the amber brew. He would have preferred a true lager, but Kuang had once mentioned that a preference for western lager was a sign of less than discriminating taste, and Kuang was the senior officer-agent in the team. He'd also report on Roget's performance, and that would determine whether Roget would remain a team member . . . or head his own team or be given an independent assignment. Either of the latter options was preferable to reporting to Kuang . . . or anyone else, Roget felt.

"True, and, like most people, the intriguers never learn."

"I wonder," mused Roget, setting his beaker on the table. "Is it that the intriguers never learn, or is it that the ones we catch are the ones that never learn?"

"You're suggesting something." Kuang offered a thin smile. "You often do."

"We never catch anyone involved in the Federation government, but we all know that there's intrigue there. We seldom catch anyone in the upper levels of the multilateral corporations, and we all know that they're not always pure."

"Purity doesn't have much to do with legality," said Kuang. "We aren't given a choice. Our job is to uphold the law, not to monitor personal ethics."

"That's right. How could it be otherwise?" asked Roget. "But the most skillful intriguers know how to operate within the law, and they do. Then there are the misguided idealists like the ones we're pursuing. They believe the laws are corrupt. Because of that, they never learned how the laws operate. They couldn't use them if they tried."

"They're not idealists. For all their rhetoric about the lack of freedom in commerce, and their protestations that they're only trying to restore full freedoms, they're antisocial thugs. Full freedom is another word for chaos and mob rule. You should remember that." Kuang's voice was calm.

Roget managed another polite smile at the veiled reference to the fall of old America, a reference that Kuang managed to make more than infrequently.

"It's time to go." Kuang stood. "You have the datacard?"

Roget rose as well, nodding.

"Make sure you get them to say that you'll be paid."

"I can do that." Roget followed the senior agent from the balcony through the living area to the front door, then out into the corridor. The dull polished metallic composite of the corridor wall reflected but vague image of his dark blue singlesuit and light gray vest—the standard garb for a midlevel datager or multilateral proffie.

The two FSA agents walked without speaking to the center of the tower, waiting for a descending lift car. Two passed, presumably full of residents, before a third, half-filled, stopped. No one in the car spoke as the lift continued downward. Once they stepped out of the lift at the concourse level of the residence tower, Kuang headed north. Roget continued straight ahead, toward the Chiacun Tube station. At close to ten, the evening was still young, and people streamed to and from the underground transport. Most were couples, but some of the groups were either of young men or, more frequently, of young women.

Roget held an open-link, but neither Kuang nor Kapeli pulsed him. As the most junior member of the team, Kapeli was tasked with the routine tailing of the targets, but he'd have contacted Roget if anything looked out of the ordinary, and that meant that Sulynn's group had headed to the rendezvous.

When Roget reached the Chiacun station, he swiped a dayproxy Cred-ID past the scanner at the entrance, then headed down the moving ramp. Once he was on the concourse level, he joined the queue for the southbound riverside express. According to his internal monitors, the wait was nine minutes and twenty-one seconds.

Once the tube train doors opened, Roget moved with the crowd into the nearest car. He took a position with his back to the silvered train wall, just to one side of the doors, his hands apparently loosely folded over each other as he surveyed the others nearby, taking in the pretty dark-haired schoolgirl with her parents, the three female clericals chatting amiably, the off-duty space-forcer with the eyes that seemed veiled, and the groups of datagers who had clearly just left work.

Twelve minutes—and roughly seventeen klicks later—Roget stepped from the train at the Shengli station, brushing through others, his internal monitors registering so many energy sources that they might as well have been useless. Amid the crowds, energy weapons were unlikely, knives or muffled projectiles far more probable. Keeping with the fast-moving crowds, he walked swiftly up the moving ramp and then out into the chill evening air. He strode across the Plaza that opened onto the River Fen.

Not more than fifteen meters into the crowded Plaza, from his right, he sensed the quick movement. He turned, his hand stiffened, and struck, hardly moving his upper body, as his movement fractured a lower arm. Then he slammed his boot heel down on the top of the would-be lifter's foot. "So very sorry." His Mandarin was impeccably polite as the youth half-crumpled, half-cringed away. While Stenglish was the official Federation language, Roget had found that in some circumstances Mandarin was preferable.

The others in the crowd parted just slightly, hardly altering their paths or changing their verbal or comm-net conversations. Another youth turned and hurried away from his wounded partner.

Stupid, thought Roget. The vidcams would note it, and the patrollers would have both members of the lifter team in custody in moments. While the patrollers could stop him, legally, that was highly unlikely. They had more than enough to do than to detain someone who'd acted to prevent being assaulted or robbed.

On the far side of the Plaza, Roget turned north on the promenade that overlooked the River Fen. His destination was the LeClub Henois, some three tower-blocks from the Plaza. Strains of plaintive and perfectly repitched kaluriolk—*perfectly boring,* thought Roget—drifted through a night lit with piped sunlight split into monobeams that played across the walkways as if at random.

Once he passed the first tower, the crowds thinned. Even so, he had to step aside to avoid a commlinked-couple, their eyes blank, who walked automatically southward toward the Plaza.

Two youths ran down the walkway, dodging pedestrians as they exchanged long passes of virtie dirigibles that morphed into miniature spacecraft far sleeker than the real vessels.

At the door to LeClub Henois, Roget again flashed the proxy, triggering the reservation code. The broad-shouldered Sinese doorman barely nodded in acknowledging his presence, despite the fact that a good third of the proffies in the capital were Euro. A whisper projected in Stenglish to Roget's ears announced, "The corner table to the northwest."

Roget turned to his right and continued. LeClub Henois was furnished in fifty-first century—or twenty-fifth century by the western Gregorian calendar—Vietnamese decor, which was, in turn, an offshoot of earlier French colonial. Roget doubted that many knew or cared about that, not after more than a millennium of Federation one-worldism. Those who might care, in the still radio-active and glassy ruins of TransIslamia or in the scattered eco-isolates of Afrique, were in no position either to object or to do anything about it.

Few people looked directly at him as he wound his way through the tables toward the northwest corner. From below the low stage, under the shifting multi-images, some of which were real, and most of which were not, a small combo played, and scents and sounds wafted across the club. Roget winced as bitter lime clashed with pepper cinnamon and oversweet bergamot, amplified by three wavering and atonal chord lines playing through each other.

As he neared the corner table with the two couples—and the two vacant chairs—he glanced around casually. He didn't see Sulynn, and that wasn't good. Yet he hadn't heard anything from Kapeli.

Roget slipped into the chair across from Huilam. "Very lively place."

"It will do," replied Huilam. "It's not authentic in the slightest, but any orbit in a flux. It is amusing, in a degrading sort of way."

"Degrading?" Roget raised his eyebrows. "Isn't imitation the sincerest and noblest form of flattery?"

"Good imitation is, but that is infrequent. The Sinese merely absorb, without true regard for the subtleties of other cultures, while demanding full respect for all the meaningless subtleties in their own."

"That's been true of all dominant cultures in history," Roget replied.

"Except for your own. When the old Americans had power, there was no subtlety at all. That was refreshing at first, until the world realized that the lack of fine distinctions reflected a corresponding lack of depth and an innate contempt for true culture."

"That's what history says, but it's always written by the winner. Look at Ramses the Great."

"Ah, yes. Part of the longest-lived imperial culture in history, the most stable, and the one with almost no technical and scientific advancement from beginning to end. Your American ancestors redeemed themselves for a time by their scientific advances, many of which they stole but made available to the world. Then, conformity and that contempt for true education stifled even their science. That always happens in empires."

"Even the ancient Sinese fell prey to that," Roget pointed out.

"But of course. One expects that of empires, without exception. That is why they should not last forever." Huilam's lips twisted into a momentary sardonic smile. "You have the entertainment card?"

The "entertainment card" meant the specs and keys to certain proprietary economic accounts in the Federation Bank of Taiyuan. Theoretically, use of that information, as planned by Huilam and Sulynn, would cripple banking functions, if not disable them permanently, until the entire system's architecture was restructured and reformulated. It would also allow them short-term access to billions of yuan to fund their "revolution."

Roget slipped the thin leather folder onto the table, making certain it was in plain sight of whatever monitors Kuang had arranged. "Both hard-copy and molecular-key. You should be able to enjoy yourselves immensely and most profitably with the subjects appearing there. They're absolutely without cover. Quite amazing." Roget smiled, not quite lewdly. "I expected to see Sulynn here."

"You just missed her," said Pryncia, from beside Huilam. "I'm most certain she'll catch up with you."

"She had something to tell you," added Moriena from across the table.

Huilam nodded, half-smiling.

"Payment?" asked Roget.

"You'll be paid, just as agreed. We have the proxy-drop." Huilam lifted his goblet and sipped, as if to dismiss Roget.

"Within the day," Roget emphasized.

"Of course."

Roget stood. "If you need any more special entertainment, you know how to reach me." He did not move, letting his greater height emphasize the point.

"That we do," Huilam nodded. "We will be in touch."

"Until then." Roget inclined his head, then turned and began to wind his way back through the tables. Once he left the LeClub, he'd have to be most careful. Leaving a drop was one of the most dangerous parts of any operation, and especially of this one, he feared. But what choice did he really have? What real choices had he ever had?

The doorman didn't even look in his direction as Roget stepped back out into the moderate warmth of the late summer evening . . . and under the shifting lights of the promenade. He'd taken less than ten steps, deftly avoiding close contact with anyone, still mulling over Huilam's point about how empires stifled scientific advances, when he heard a voice.

"Keir!"

Roget recognized Sulynn's voice. Should he ignore her? He'd completed his immediate part of the operation. That would be the safest, but it would also make her more suspicious, and the rest of the team could use more time to round up all the terrvert group.

He turned slowly to his right, as if trying to locate the caller.

Sulynn stood alone, a good ten meters away, between

one group of young women and another of two couples, her black hair up in a stylish twist.

As a young man hurried past leaving the space between them open, Sulynn offered an embarrassed smile, then shrugged.

Roget saw the glint in her left hand too late.

Blackness slammed into him.

3

15 MARIS 1811 P. D.

Roget scanned the controls one last time, then nodded, before triggering the link.

DropCon, this is three. Checklist complete and green.

Stet, three. Estimate one seven to release.

Even through the link, Roget could sense the warmth of Major Zhou. Too bad more of the Federation officers weren't like the scoutship's pilot. She was also far and away the best pilot on the *WuDing*, certainly better than he was, he had to admit.

DropCon, two here. All green.

DropCon, four here. Green.

DropCon, five here. Green and good.

Waiting, his dropboat in the exterior cradle, Roget nodded as Fierano reported, the last of the five survey operatives, and the only woman. All he could do was wait. The dropboat's systems wouldn't kick in until it was clear of the scoutship.

One five to drop one.

Roget swallowed. All he could do was wait . . . and review the drop procedures. He tried not to think about his options *after* he completed his survey evaluation of Haze—*if* he completed it. If the landing boat survived the transit of all the objects in the three orbital shells, he could take off and attempt to reach low orbit where a scoutship could retrieve him. Or he could program the boat to climb as far as it could, far enough into or beyond the haze to burst-send his report. Or he could commandeer local transport, assuming any such existed. None of the options were optimal. But, after his last two missions, his situation had been anything but ideal. Not because he had failed, but because he had been expected to fail, and had managed at least limited success. The FSA had been forced to take over governing Khriastos station because of the degree of corruption when all the colonel had really wanted was the removal of Station Administrator Sala-Chung.

Roget took a long slow breath. In a fashion, all of his independent assignments had ended that way. Was it because the FSA hadn't wanted success? Or because they'd only defined success in limited terms.

Roget forced his mind back to the drop.

Dropboats, stand by.

Standing by.

Another five minutes passed. Then the scoutship shivered once. Another five minutes passed before the second shiver. Then another interval passed, not quite five minutes.

Drop three, stand by . . . ten, nine, eight . . .

With the linked *one!*, Roget was pressed back in the half-cocoon for a moment before weightlessness took over. He swallowed to keep the bile in his stomach, rather than let it creep into his throat, then used his implants to link with the dropboat—now fully powered.

The farscanners showed no ships above the planet—
except for the scoutship returning to the *WuDing* and the
five dropboats, spaced far enough apart and with enough
difference in course, velocity, and trajectory so that they
would not land all that close to each other.

Roget gave the steering jets a quick squirt to orient
the dropboat to the planned courseline.

"You won't like the entry." The colonel's words went
through Roget's thoughts as he waited for the dropboat
to encounter the outer orbital shell. Theoretically, the
first shell shouldn't be too bad, because the scoutship
had dropped all the boats on trajectories that would
ensure they entered the shell at a velocity only slightly
slower than that of the outer level of orbiting objects—
whatever they were.

After that, it was up to the operative and the dropboat's nav systems and shields . . . and luck.

The farscreens showed nothing but the other dropboats . . . and the grayish haze. Was that haze something totally alien, perhaps even alive? Or was it a form
of technology that comprised the planetary defense
system? And what lay below it? Were the readings correct in assuming a breathable atmosphere, or was the
whole operation a way to remove him and the other FSA
agents?

It couldn't be the last. Cold as they could be, even the
upper-level Federation Mandarins wouldn't have sent a
battlecruiser and its escorts across the stars and dispatched five operatives and dropboats to their death to
remove one operative whose attitude had been less than
exemplary. Nor would they have forced the FIS and
FSA into a semicooperative joint effort.

Colonel Tian's nonanswers suggested much more was
at stake, and that the Federation regarded the Thomists
as far more than an historical curiosity.

Roget continued to watch the closure with the planet below looming ever closer. All he could do was wait until the outer fringes of the atmosphere began to impact the shields. The screens and systems still registered nothing in any energy spectrum except some reflected light and emissions from the boats.

Then . . . what could only be called noise appeared, concentrated in the orbital layers, creating three levels of smokelike spheres. That was how his implants registered the data.

The dropboat neared the outermost sphere, the one whose shardlike components appeared to orbit from polar south to north, unnatural and implausible as it was. As the dropboat entered that outermost layer, angled to go with the apparent flow, the outside temperature sensors went blank.

The dropboat seemed to skid sideways, then drop, slewing sideways to the courseline.

Roget *knew* that couldn't happen, but the instruments confirmed what he felt, and the system pulsed the port steering jets. When nothing happened, Roget overrode the controls and then fired them full for an instant. Sluggishly, the dropboat returned to courseline and orientation.

The dropboat shivered, and a chorus of impacts, like metallic hail, reverberated through the craft. Cabin pressure began to fall, and Roget closed his helmet, letting the direct suit feed take over.

The EDI flared. Drop one was gone.

More impacts battered Drop three, and Roget eased the nose down, adding thrust. He'd pay later, but there was too much of a velocity differential between the dropboat and the orbital shards or whatever they were.

The intensity of the hammering decreased. But even

inside his sealed suit, Roget could feel the heat building in the dropboat.

The hammering vanished, and the screens showed that the dropboat was below the outer orbital layer. They showed nothing except Drop three and the two layers, one below and one above.

The nav system, as programmed, increased the thrust and began a course correction to bring the dropboat onto a courseline at right angles to the previous heading. Roget watched intently, ready to override again if the dropboat did not complete the heading and orientation change before it entered the second orbital shell.

Heading, course, orientation, and the smokelike shell all came together at once.

This time the hammering was louder. Was that because there was some atmosphere or because the dropboat and its shields were being punished more? Roget couldn't tell. He was just glad when they dropped below the second level. By then he was sweating heavily inside the pressure suit, and he hoped that he didn't fog the inside of his helmet.

The third level was worse. By the time the dropboat was clear, the shields had failed, and the craft had no atmospheric integrity. The automatics had dropped off-line, inoperative, and Roget was piloting on manual. The dropboat shuddered and shivered.

Roget eased the dropboat's nose up fractionally to kill off more speed and decrease the rate of descent. That might bleed off some of the excess heat that was close to cooking him, even within his suit, and the dropboat's remaining functional systems.

His entry and descent had to have registered on every planetary tracking system. Yet the screens showed no aircraft, no missiles, and no energy concentrations.

Roget concentrated on maintaining control of the systems and holding as much altitude as possible, especially given the ocean directly below. The waters were silver green. He thought the screens had shown small islands, but he was still too high and too fast to try a landing there. Besides, getting off an island might be more than a little difficult, given the failing state of the dropboat.

Before long, the screens registered a mountainous coastline ahead. In moments the dropboat was approaching a coastal range and passing through twenty thousand meters in a gradual descent. Less than five minutes later, the dropboat had descended to twelve thousand meters and was passing over the tallest of the peaks, less than three thousand meters below.

Roget's scans showed that the mountains were the center of a peninsula. To the east water stretched as far as the screens could show. He immediately banked to the north, paralleling the lower hills because of the short distance between where the hills ended and the ocean began.

With that sharp a turn, the dropboat's glide ratio began to approximate that of a flying brick hurtling downward toward the forested slopes below. Roget hurried through the landing checklist while scanning the terrain ahead, finally settling on a long brushy area some three klicks ahead.

When the radalt alerted him at five hundred meters AGL, he eased into a partial flare, using the dropboat's lifting body form to trade off speed to kill his rate-of-descent—but not enough to stall.

Less than a hundred meters above ground, the dropboat shivered with a sudden crosswind. Roget corrected, angling the nose to the wind and easing the nose up just a trace.

The power levels were at less than 7 percent when the dropboat's tail touched the ground. Roget let the nose drop slowly, and the boat skidded and bounced across the uneven ground. It came to a stop less than a hundred meters from the tall evergreens to the north.

The farscreens were fading. They showed no one and no large animals anywhere nearby. Given the sonics that had preceded the dropboat, that didn't exactly surprise Roget. The diagnostics did tell him that the atmosphere composition was T-norm, or close enough that it made little difference. He doubted that the dropboat would be useful for much of anything after the descent and rough landing. Still, he went through the standard shutdown checklist before he unstrapped his bruised and sore figure from the pilot's couch and eased himself out through the narrow lock hatches, one after the other. Once he was clear of the still-warm hull, he cracked his helmet. He could smell evergreens and charred vegetation. For all that, there were no fires around the craft. That suggested that the area wasn't all that dry.

For several moments, Roget stood beside the dropboat. All his implants and systems checked, despite the rough entry. There was one problem. They registered nothing beyond himself and the fading residual energies within the dropboat.

No emissions. No signals. Nothing. Was there no intelligent life on the planet? Or had all his implants failed, despite the internal telltales that indicated they were functioning? That couldn't be. He was getting indications from the dropboat.

He shrugged.

One way or another, he had a mission to complete. He needed to retrieve his gear from the sealed locker and get on with it—preferably before any locals showed up. If there were any.

After a last set of scans of the area around the drop-boat, Roget moved quickly, stripping off his pressure suit and helmet, then retrieving his gear and the modest backpack to contain it, and finally locking the boat. If the locks were forced, certain key parts of the controls would melt down. Since the screens and shields had been tried to their limits on the descent, the boat didn't have enough power to carry Roget more than a few klicks, let alone return to orbit.

He checked his equipment a last time, then paused, taking a deep breath. The air was heavy and damp and carried a faint scent, somewhere between a sultry perfume and the clean dankness of a virgin forest. He had a feeling that the sea-level atmospheric pressure was higher than T-norm, possibly as much as 10 percent. The oxygen content was a bit higher, and that might offset the slightly higher gravity.

Finally, he strode into the forest, heading north. There certainly hadn't been any signs of technology or habitation farther south on the peninsula. He decided against powering up the camouflage capacity engineered into his singlesuit. That burned power, and he saw no reason to drain his limited supply, especially since the background melding capability was only useful for optical detection. Even had he used the camo feature, the last thing he wanted was to be caught in the open. The tall pines, while spaced in a way that suggested a natural and mature landscape, provided enough cover that an attack from something like aircraft or even an advanced flitter would be difficult. If there happened to be a local culture with nanotech capabilities, they wouldn't need anything that crude to deal with him.

That was what he hoped.

4

Wearing a dark gray proffie singlesuit, like any number of young professionals, Roget sat in the reception area, a space with shimmering dark gray walls and green accents. The chairs and the couch were a muted dark green. The piped sunlight added a note of cheer to the semicircular chamber that could have been one in any multilateral's headquarters. It wasn't. It was one of a number of similar reception areas in the Federation Security Agency's Taiyuan headquarters.

Roget did not read, nor did he access, any of the entertainment nets. Instead, he amused himself by tracking the energy flows everywhere, although he couldn't discern the purpose of most, except for those designed to locate explosives, metals, and other potentially lethal objects. Some were doubtless merely routine dataflows. A polite-looking young man sat at a console, occasionally glancing indifferently in Roget's general direction. Behind the receptionist/guard and the console, three wide corridors fanned out into the north half of the tower.

Roget had been waiting for sixteen and a half minutes when a tall Sinese with silver gray at his temples emerged from the left-hand corridor and walked past the receptionist. Another seven minutes passed before the receptionist looked up.

"Agent Roget . . . the colonel will see you now. Take the left-most corridor to the second door, also on the left. Just open the door and enter."

Roget stood. "Thank you." He walked past the reception desk, noting that there were no open screens behind it. The reception agent was direct-linked, another simple security procedure. If anything happened to him, hidden gates would doubtless seal the corridors.

When he reached the door, he touched the entry screen. The door slid into its recess, and Roget stepped into the office. He stopped and offered a slight bow. The door closed silently behind him.

"Agent-Captain Keir Roget, do come in." The man behind the desk console did not stand. To his right was a wide window that offered a sweeping view of the silvered side of another tower. "Please be seated."

"Yes, sir." Roget bowed, then took the seat across the desk from the Agent-Colonel, whose name he did not know . . . and might never, not unless he encountered the man in another setting, and that was unlikely in a capital city of ten million plus, surrounded by satellite cities that each held millions.

A long silence followed as the colonel scrutinized Roget.

"Your last assignment left you in some physical difficulty," observed the colonel.

Two weeks in the medunit hadn't been easy, but there was no point in saying so. Roget waited.

"The other members of your team were successful in apprehending the terrvert group. All but two. One was killed in the operation. Because the weapon used on you was tracked to Huilam, they all will face capital assault charges."

Capital assault meant intelligence reduction and locality restriction—usually to an isolated marginal community. It also suggested that there wasn't enough evidence to prove more than conspiracy to commit cyberterr.

"And the other?" asked Roget.

"The other is still at large, but not for long."

"Sulynn?" asked Roget.

The slightest hint of a frown appeared above the colonel's black eyebrows. "You have something not in your report that would shed light on that?"

Roget wasn't about to comment on the most obvious point—that Sulynn had left the weapon solely in order to implicate Huilam. "No, sir. She was the smartest and most wary. That's all. If anyone might have escaped, she would have been the one. There was a caution in my reports about her." For all the colonel's assurances, Roget doubted that security would soon locate her . . . or that her identity had ever been Sulynn. He had his doubts that she'd ever even been a cyberterrorist.

What he didn't understand was how they'd managed to miss her, when she'd been the one who'd nerved him— unless she'd disabled Kuang or Kapeli. Even with his internal backups and contingent blocks against neural cascades, Roget almost hadn't made it. That was what the Security doctor had told him. But . . . if she'd been a plant, why had she almost killed him? Or had she either used too much power or too little? He withheld a wry smile. That was something else he doubted he'd ever know.

"Just so." A pause signified that the comments on Roget's previous assignment were at an end. "You are being given a single-agent assignment in St. George in Noram District 32. The local community is primarily Saint. . . ."

Saint? It took a moment for Roget to place the locality and the culture. The Saints were a religious community that had been founded by an old American prophet and, against all logic, had survived the Wars of Confederation. He should have known that. His sister lived only a district away, but then, they'd been raised in the American southeast, and she'd moved there after the southern climatic disasters had forced her and Wallace to relocate.

". . . Your cover will be that of an E&W Monitor. No additional technical training will be necessary. The previous agent died of heat exposure after a fall. While it is unlikely his death was natural, he was merely a data-agent. You're aware of the possible dangers, and you should be able to handle the situation. It should be far less stressful than the assignment you just completed, and it should allow the additional time for your nerves to heal before you return to more . . . strenuous duty."

Another not-so-subtle reminder of his failure to exercise adequate caution in dealing with Sulynn, Roget thought. Yet . . . if she had been a plant . . . He pushed the thought away. He couldn't do anything about the past. He'd just have to be even more careful in the future.

"Your briefings will begin at eight hundred tomorrow morning. Kuyrien has the details, including your cover and travel schedule."

"Yes, sir." In short, he was supposed to conclude that he'd been a good boy, and he was getting an easy and relatively straightforward investigation as a reward. He didn't believe it. Officer-agents never got easy assignments, especially non-Sinese officer-agents who were neither junior nor senior.

"That is all, Agent-Captain."

Roget rose. He'd never understood the reason for the short and summary assignment process, since what the colonel had conveyed didn't require any personal contact, unless it was to remind him that he had flesh-and-blood superiors—even if their names were never disclosed. Or to remind him that all agents lived on sufferance of one sort or another. He inclined his head politely, then turned and left the office.

5

On the first day, Roget walked a good fifteen klicks before the daylight died away into a deep twilight that was not quite night. With the higher humidity, he'd had to put the all-weather jacket in his pack. Even so, he'd sweated a lot, and he'd had to stop and refill his water bottle several times. His treatment tabs would likely run out far sooner than he'd anticipated. With only the silver gray haze overhead, he had been able to make out only in a general fashion where the sun was. For some time before twilight, the western half of the sky appeared slightly brighter, but that might have been his imagination. The twilight had lasted longer, and that hadn't been just what he believed.

He'd seen tracks of animals that might have been deer or elk, or something similar, and paw prints of what could have been any type of large canine or non-hoofed mammal. All were quadrupeds. The leaves and needles of the trees were similar enough to those on earth, if a far darker green that verged on black, that the trees had to be Terran-derived, or some form of parallel evolution too alike to be coincidental. Those facts alone tended to confirm the colonel's suggestion of a Thomist world, but the ecology looked far too settled to have been established in a mere thousand years. There was also the fact that, while the colonel had paid lip service to the possibility of a hostile environment, the entire mission had been set up on the tacit assumption that Haze wasn't environmentally hostile.

He'd keep that in mind, but he just didn't know enough, not yet.

In setting up his camp, he decided on the hammock, although it took him some time to find a tree with branches high enough to be well above ground predators, low enough for him to be able to reach the branches, and strong enough to bear his weight. Although the not-quite-perfumed air was pleasant, there was something about it, the slightest of subscents, that nagged at him, and he didn't sleep that well. He also thought he heard movements, but whenever he woke, he saw nothing in the dimness that was as bright as a starlit night.

After Roget woke under a gradually brightening light, he surveyed the area around him from within the hammock. He could hear various sounds, from insects to bird calls, but he did not see any larger creatures. Again, his implants revealed no broadcast signals or power.

He struggled out of his hammock and then climbed along the stronger and wider branch closest to his head until he could swing down to the ground. Underneath where he had swung in his hammock were large paw prints. While he was carrying a sidearm, and a limited shot stunner, he was just as glad not to have had to use either.

Breakfast was not immediate because he needed water for the small self-heating ration-pak, and he did not find a stream for several klicks. After treating the water in the bottle he carried, he started the ration-pak, then refilled the bottle before he ate. Once finished with his mostly tasteless meal, he began to walk northward at a quick but comfortable pace.

He'd traveled less than an hour before the first butterfly fluttered down from the overhanging branches, swooping by his face so closely that its wings actually brushed his cheek. Its wings were a brilliant blue with swirls of gold. Then, there were two, and three, and then a handful, all swirling around his face and neck, and all with similar wing markings.

He half jumped at a needlelike jab on the back of his neck, then swatted at the swarm, which retreated. He spent the next klick waving off the butterflies, until they finally lost interest. He hadn't expected biting butter-flies, but they were definitely a reminder that Haze was not just another exact earth-type world.

Sometime before midmorning he finally found a trail. He'd actually been paralleling it for more than a standard hour without knowing it, but it was higher on the slope by almost a klick. He caught sight of it from a large clearing stretching both uphill and down—a burned out area that had likely been the target of a lightning strike several years back, judging from the regrowth. Hiking uphill wasn't that bad, although his legs ached some by the time he reached the trail, not much more than packed earth stretching north and south under the predominantly ever-green canopy. The trail was of an even width, though, with a covering of wood mulch, and that suggested both continual use and maintenance.

As he hiked north, he studied the trail. In several places, he could make out relatively recent boot prints. They seemed no different from those left by any other human. In one place, the entire print was clear in the dried mud. Regular studded tread, the kind that was most likely produced by at least a midtech culture. So . . . where were the people? Could they have all been evacuated? How? There had been no sign of any broad-cast comm. Or was he walking the trail at a time equiv-alent to midweek, when few were out and about?

As he kept walking and watching, he tried to review what he'd learned about the Thomists. Initially, they had been a loose movement scattered throughout the Federation in its early years. Their slogan or watchwords were simply, "Doubt it." Their initial political activities had revolved around providing factual information that cast doubt on the statements and policies of politicians, administrators, multilaterals, and others in positions of authority and trust. Later statements and papers suggested scientific skepticism as well. A number had been detained or sequestered in the second War of Confederation, but a larger number had obtained an early jumpship and had begun to ferry followers and equipment out of the Sol system. After a cat-and-mouse game lasting several objective centuries, the jumpship had been intercepted by a Federation flotilla and destroyed when it refused to surrender. The High Command had never been fully convinced that there was but a single renegade ship, but the ships of the Federation Interstellar Service, which patrolled all of the systems that held Federation worlds—not that there were any other kind, to date—had never found any trace of any other worlds that had ever been inhabited by intelligent life—until Haze.

So why were the colonel and the High Command convinced that Haze held Thomists, as opposed to some other unknown splinter group that might have fled during the disruptions that had surrounded the establishment and consolidation of the Federation? Roget didn't know, but the boot print, the empty trail, and the lack of power and broadcast emissions all left him with a most uneasy feeling.

He kept walking and watching . . . and shooing away the carnivorous, or at least biting, butterflies.

By what he felt was late afternoon, he had the definite

sense that the planet had a quicker rotation than T-norm. From his implants and senses, he had a general sense that the local "day" was around twenty-one or twenty-two stans, but without a sun directly in the sky, it might be several days before he could pin it down exactly. The other matter was that of clouds. He'd seen a few, although they were thin, almost stratuslike. Was that because the planet didn't have spots of more localized heat created by the direct rays of the sun?

Another standard hour passed, according to his own internal clock, which was clearly out of synch with the rotational pattern of Haze. Ahead of him, on the downhill side of the trail, he saw something. Something unnatural.

He froze, then stepped sideways and into the widely spaced trees.

Step by step, Roget moved over the carpet of pine needles, a sign that there were no earthworms in all likelihood, passing from tree to tree, taking time and care. After he had covered the first fifty meters, he could make out the stone building set into the hillside so artfully that it was almost invisible. Even the slates of the roof had been cut irregularly and were of differing shades of gray and black.

When he finally got within twenty meters of the building, he was largely convinced that no one was there. The brown shutters on the two windows flanking the east-facing door were fastened shut. The gray brown door was closed.

Roget sensed no one, heard no one. He moved closer, edging along the side of the small building. In the clay in front of the door, there was one set of boot prints that seemed to match the one he had seen earlier, and they showed someone leaving. A paw print over part of the boot imprint suggested that it wasn't that recent.

With the stunner in one hand, Roget pressed down on the smooth, dull gray metal door lever. To his surprise, it depressed under the pressure of his hand, and the door opened inward.

There was no one inside. A wooden table that might have been oak stood in front of the shuttered window on the south side of the single room. Four armless wooden chairs were set around the table. In the middle of the west wall was a stone hearth. Behind it was a stone wall. A radiant heat pipe ran up one side of the wall, across the top, and down the other. In the middle of the hearth was a small iron stove with two heating elements. Roget suspected all were light powered, with some sort of concentrator. On each side of the hearth were built-in double bunks, one over the other, simple wooden shelflike spaces.

The roof slates were clearly more than they appeared to be. That, or the heating elements were geothermal in nature. He eased into the building, leaving the door open. Was he under observation? If he happened to be, that observation was all passive, because he could sense no energy flows.

There was a small metal plate set at eye level in the stone wall on the right side. The plate was of the same pewterlike gray metal as the door lever. Protruding from the plate were two studs and a dial, also metal. Roget stepped forward and pressed the left stud, then the right one. Within moments he could feel warmth flowing from the dark gray heat pipe—made out of some sort of composite, he judged. He turned the dial to the left, and the heat flow increased. Immediately, he turned it all the way to the right, and the heat flow died away. The building was warm enough. Then he stepped back and in front of what he had taken to be the stove. On the thin angled surface between the stove top and the front were three inset dials but only two elements. He looked down at the front and shook his head. A sliding panel provided the entry to an oven of some sort.

In the end, after all his prodding and investigating, Roget could detect nothing except what he had observed. What he saw disturbed him a great deal. The cabin was simple, but it had heat and a power source for cooking. But there was no source of artificial light. It was spotless, as if it were scarcely used, yet there was no sign of recent construction. The exterior looked to be years old, and it was situated on a trail that had been traveled regularly, if infrequently, for years.

Roget was tired. The last two days had been long—very long. He decided to spend the night in the building. The back of the door did have a sturdy metal bolt that could be slid into place to lock the building. While the cabin might be a trap, that didn't make sense. But then, he had the feeling that not much about Haze was likely to make sense. He did know that anyone who could build such a structure wouldn't have much more trouble running him down in the forest than cornering him in the building.

That, too, was disturbing.

Still, after he'd eaten and was ready to go to bed on one of the bunk shelves, he locked the door and wedged a chair behind it. He hoped he'd be able to get some sleep.

6

Roget wore the white singlesuit of an energy and water monitor, if without insignia. He sat alone on the aisle in the second double seat on the left in the electrotram that ran down the center of the boulevard, flanked on each side by lightly traveled lanes. Back in the glory days of the United States of America, St. George had once been a small city. Now it was just a large town, an old, old town that had baked in the sun of Noram District 32 for the millennium and more since the founding of the Federation.

Almost all the neat stone dwellings were roofed with solar arrays designed to resemble ancient ceramic tiles, and most had shaded rear courtyards. Beyond the town limits, red rocks and sand and dry mountains stretched in every direction, with a towering bluff on the immediate west end of the town proper and a ridge along the north side of the town, with a gap in it to the northeast, a gap blasted out in the old days that had allowed expansion to the northeast. Coming in by the single maglev line that ended on the northeast end of St. George, Roget had noted the track of the old highway where it deviated from the maglev route, and he'd wondered why the maglev hadn't been extended through that gap. It hadn't, though.

As the tram neared 200 East and the stop there, Roget glanced to the south, taking in the shimmering white of the ancient Temple. Close as it was to a thousand years old, it was still a replica. The original had been destroyed in the first War of Confederation, but once it was clear that the violent hostilities were over, the local Saints had rebuilt it faithfully, although it had taken some thirty years because times had been so difficult. But then, they'd rebuilt their original temple at Nauvoo twice.

They'd also cleared the ground so that a hundred-yard-wide greenbelt ran the nine blocks between the boulevard and the Temple. Similar greenbelts ran from the Temple to the south, east, and west. The ground cover was desert green, good at retaining water, but off-limits to pedestrians or anything else weight-bearing. The Saints didn't seem to mind, and there hadn't been many tourists since the Federation had imposed regional energy curbs and geometrical incremental pricing nearly a millennium before. Not that there had been that many once the Virgin River dam had been completed and blocked the old overland route through the gorge to Mesquite. Only scholars in clean-suits visited the still-radioactive ruins of Las Vegas or the giant concrete ruins of the Hoover Dam. Other scholars visited the Saint Genealogy Center on the south side of the Temple. The Saints had an interest in all aspects of genealogy that bordered on obsession.

Peaceful as it looked to Roget, and notwithstanding the colonel's assurances, he had his doubts. The previous Federation Security agent—acting as a nature photographer—had died in an "accident" while hiking. The accident had been a loose boulder that had knocked him unconscious in the midday summer heat. His body and equipment had been found three days later, and his death had been reported as heat dehydration. One agent-captain Keir Roget had been assigned to investigate. Roget didn't think it would be the almost-vacation the colonel had promised after Roget's efforts against the Taiyuan economic terrorists. Not that he could do anything about it, but he still wondered exactly what had happened to Sulynn and who she really was.

His cover in St. George was as a regional E&W water monitor. The man holding the position—an actual monitor—had been promoted and transferred to Colorado Springs. Roget was listed on the payroll and everywhere else as a temporary replacement.

The only information Roget had was a list of four names: Brendan B. Smith, Mitchell Leavitt, William Dane, and Bensen Sorensen. He'd run searches on all four. Smith managed the local data/print center that specialized in Saint-oriented religious and entertainment material. Leavitt was a collateralizer. Dane was the assistant manager of the Deseret First Bank's local branch. Sorensen operated a guesthouse complex for Saint pilgrims and the infrequent tourists.

When the tram halted at the 200 East station at a quarter to eight, Roget exited by the front door, along with the other men, and one couple. Only a handful of unaccompanied women left by the rear doors. The station platform was of hardened and polished native Navaho sandstone. So were the columns supporting the roof that held the photovoltaic arrays. Of necessity, such systems topped all public structures in southern Noram that did not have historic significance.

He stepped from the shade of the platform onto the stone sidewalk that stretched northward toward the Red Hills Bluff and the Federation Services Station. A bronze plaque on a sandstone pedestal offered a local map. Prominent on it were the Temple and the summer home of the second Saint prophet, the one who had laid the groundwork for the Saint faith to become a world power before the wars of consolidation and federation.

Just beyond the station was a small shop. A woman had just unlocked the door and was raising the blinds. Her blond hair was French-braided, like that of most married women, at least those older than twenty-five whom Roget had seen over the past day in St. George.

The window featured mannequins displaying female attire, mainly below the knee dresses in subdued shades with brilliant flashthreads. There was one feminine singlesuit set in the corner, as if as an afterthought. Except for the shimmer of those threads, the dresses would not have been out of place in ancient Deseret or the state of Utah that had followed that short-lived Mormon dominance of the Noram southwest.

Ahead on Roget's left was a small café. "JOHN D. LEE HOUSE" proclaimed the modest sign above the windows that were already darkening in response to the intensifying sunlight. Most of the tables were taken by men. He only saw one couple—both white-haired.

He glanced westward across 200 East at another restaurant—Lupe's. There, two Sudams with their darker skins emerged from the doorway and hurried toward the tram. They wore the darker blue denims of manual workers. Another man walked toward the café from a battered electrocoupe parked at the curb behind a small lorry. A shaggy brown dog was tied in the open bed of the lorry, and it was already panting. Roget frowned, but he couldn't do anything. The dog wasn't being overtly abused, and it wasn't running free, something not allowed in environmentally fragile areas like St. George.

Roget took his time walking the four long blocks uphill to the Federation Services Station on the north side of where 200 East ended at Red Hills Boulevard. Already the temperature was over thirty. Even on fall days such as the one he was beginning, the afternoon temperature was often above forty-five degrees. He didn't want to think about how hot it would be in the height of summer.

The vent-weave of his singlesuit kept him from getting too hot. He was still sweating when he stepped into the cooler air of the FSS entry hall. There, a single guard sat behind a gray synthstone-fronted stone desk. Roget's implants sensed the energy fields around the man and around the screening gate beside the guard position.

Before Roget reached the gate, the scanners picked up his imbedded ID. Many had tried to counterfeit Federation IDs. A very few had succeeded. The rest had vanished.

"Good morning, sir," offered the guard. "What can we do for you?"

"I'm Keir Roget. Reporting for work as an E&W monitor."

"Last door on the left at the end, sir."

"Thank you." Roget stepped through the gate without any alarms being triggered and walked down the long corridor.

At the end he opened the door on the left and stepped through it. He closed it behind himself. The man who rose from the wide console filled with datascreens had silvering black hair and an oval face. His skin was an olive tan that minimized the blackness of his eyes. He smiled but did not speak.

"Keir Roget, sir. Are you head monitor Sung?"

"Elrik Sung, and we're not all that formal here, Keir. St. George is smaller than it looks, and formality wears thin when you're a minority. Those of us who are Feds or multis are a very small minority."

That was something Roget had been briefed on, in far

more depth than a standard monitor would have received. So he nodded again. "Is fraternization a problem?"

"Yours. Not theirs. Everyone will smile and be quite polite and friendly, and you'll be fortunate to have been invited to two Saint houses in the course of a year. Both of those, if they happen, will be to determine whether they think they can convert you." Sung motioned. "Over here. Let's get your ID into the system."

Roget stepped toward the chief monitor.

Sung lifted a tube scanner, then turned to the console. "Enter. Personnel. Code follows." He straightened, gesturing to the wall display with the shifting views of St. George and the various data-drops. "There. Now the guards won't question you every time you come in. Here's the main console, not that you'll spend all that much time here after today and tomorrow. It's like every other one you've seen. The system analyzes what it finds and offers a set of prioritized options. Then it sends you out to verify what's happening. You never inform or confront the offender. If asked, you just say that you're checking systems. I'm certain your training has emphasized that, but I want to reemphasize it. You just confirm and document the situation and enter the report. If it's a criminal offense, the local security patrollers will deal with it. If it's merely a civil offense, the power board will issue the requisite compensatory levy. Our job is strictly to verify and certify any excessive use of energy or any escape of water beyond the minimums. I'm not sending you out on verification immediately. They're a little old-fashioned here. I'd prefer that you have at least a basic familiarity with the local geography and usage patterns first. Also, it won't hurt if you're seen around town for a few days."

Roget nodded. He'd almost said, "Yes, sir." Instead,

he asked, "You want me to take the console and learn what I can?"

"That's right." Sung pointed to a pair of narrow built-in desks with small screens and two drawers inset into the wall. "When you're not on the main console or out on verification, the one on the left is yours."

"Thank you."

"Go ahead and take the main console. You'll get better visuals there."

Roget slipped into the thermacool seat. Following Sung's indoctrination protocol was fine with him. The more quickly he learned about St. George the better. He glanced up. "Is there any area or sector where I should start or where I need to be wary?"

"The Temple complex has a 10 percent variance under the religious leeway provisions. That includes the Tabernacle. Also, there's a history of faint geothermal activity to the east of Middleton Ridge. You won't notice that, if at all, except on cool winter nights."

"They haven't tapped it?"

"According to the old surveys, there's not enough volume for consistent power, and it's right along the fault line. No one here has the yuan to do that kind of speculative exploration and development, and no one elsewhere has any reason to fund such a low-yield project."

Roget nodded once more.

"I'll leave you to get yourself familiarized, and I'll check back in a bit. I need to attend the weekly supervisors' meeting." Sung stepped through the side door into what had to be his private office, then returned almost immediately and departed.

Roget linked to the system through his implants, using only those standard for an energy and water monitor. He had no idea who had betrayed the previous agent, or what systems had been compromised. He did know that any new Federation employee in St. George would be scrutinized closely.

In less than half an hour, he had a solid overview and understanding of both energy and water usage patterns, along with daily and current comps. The inputs came from hundreds of thousands of minute sensors across and within St. George, all integrated and tabulated by the systems beneath the FSS building. Energy and water use defined a culture, from those who were a part of it to those who wanted to change it or overthrow it. Even with a stable planetary population of three billion, there weren't enough resources for the kind of profligate squandering that had marked the last days of the Saint-dominated Noram Confederation.

The Sino-Fed mandarins had learned the lessons of history. Let the market system allocate resources, and make sure everyone has the minimum for bare comfort, but ensure that excessive uses or waste required extraordinarily high recompense. Equally important was the understanding that whoever controlled energy, communications, and water controlled society. Food could always be found, made, or stolen, and the same was true of weapons. Industrious and inventive humans could turn anything into a weapon.

The Federation understood that most people just wanted to live their lives, to work at what they could, enjoy what they could, and live without fear or insecurity. Anyone could follow any belief system or religion he or she wanted—but only where those beliefs did not conflict with the rights and health of others or contradict Federation law.

For those who didn't want to follow the laws, FSA had very simple rules. Concentrate on the top, and eliminate those few who ignored or flaunted Federation law. Keep the eliminations to an absolute minimum and do it without publicity or notice. Relocate and reeducate all others involved, especially the flunkies of the law-breakers, wherever possible, and send them to locales and situations where they had to work to follow the rules. If that didn't convince them, implant location monitors and nerve-blocks that did.

Roget began to manipulate the board to learn all the local coordinates and match them to the scanned images and maps. He wondered whether the dead agent had been killed by some Saint underground or because he'd uncovered commercial corruption.

Roget would find out.

In time. He was in no hurry, not with intermittent residual nerve soreness.

7

17 MARIS 1811 P. D.

Roget woke early and uneasily, sore from lying on the hard bunk shelf, barely cushioned by his jacket. For a moment, he had no idea where he might be because the cabin was pitch black. He eased halfway off the bunk shelf where he sat and pulled on his boots, then sealed them. He walked to the door, unbolted it, and opened it a crack, listening intently, and letting his internal systems scan the area.

He could sense no energy radiation of any sort, and he heard nothing except insects—or their equivalents. He opened the door more widely. It was before what passed for dawn, but the sky still held a hint of amber radiance, and to the east he could see a faint brightening. With a nod, he turned back, leaving the door open for light. For breakfast, he drank the last from his water bottle and chewed field rations. He had enough for another three days at full diet, but he had the definite feeling he wouldn't go undetected for anywhere near that long. He supposed he could, if he headed out into the wild, but that wasn't what he'd been sent down to do. He couldn't really assess the culture without getting into it—and that meant he had to meet the locals . . . and risk internment or incarceration.

He stretched enough to loosen tight muscles. After that, he left the cabin as he had found it, the small amount of trash he had created tucked into his pack. He covered close to two klicks before the sky brightened fully and amber light filtered down through the dark-needled pines and onto the needle-covered ground and the trail. Twice he glimpsed something that looked to be fast and yet rodentlike. It wasn't a rabbit but resembled a miniature kangaroo, except with shorter legs and tail. He also saw more of the large pawprints in places beside the trail. One set looked to belong to a creature larger than a wolf. Possibly much larger. He checked his sidearm and stunner. He didn't see or sense anything like squirrels or ground rodents, but he did see a few small holes that looked like possible burrows. He also caught sight of a number of large raptor-looking birds from a distance and got a close look at a flock of tiny gray and brown birds that could have been ground-feeding bushtits.

About an hour after what might have corresponded to dawn, he walked over a low rise in the trail and saw what looked to be a small pile of blue and gold leaves a meter or so to the right of the path—scores of the butterflies, their wings moving slowly. Did they sleep or gather in piles?

He stepped toward the pile. The butterflies rose in a cloud that split into lines and then vanished into the overhanging branches. Roget looked down and swallowed. Lying on the carpet of evergreen needles were the remains of a ratlike or squirrel-like animal. What little fur remained was shiny, but mostly all that was left were bones. Were the butterflies carnivorous or scavengers, or both? He couldn't help but wonder what else lay in and around him in the trees. The heavily scented air didn't seem quite so much perfumed as holding a hint of sickly-sweet decay.

By late midmorning he had covered close to ten klicks along the trail. He'd seen no aliens or people, but he had found a small fountain. It was simple enough, just a spout in the middle of a circular stone basin forty centimeters across from which water flowed over a lower section of the rim into a stone drainage sluice that fed a stream perhaps half a meter wide. The stream looked clear, although it was hemmed in by low brush and grass.

A small splash downhill caught Roget's attention. He watched the area for several moments but couldn't tell what had made it—a fish, an amphibian, or an oversized arthropod. He filled his water bottle from the fountain and returned to the trail.

Less than an hour later, passing through a small clearing, Roget glanced uphill. He thought he saw another trail, just below the top of the ridge line. That might give him a better view. In any case, higher was probably better.

He started uphill through the trees. It was pleasant walking on the needle carpet, and the trees were far enough apart. There was also very little brushy undergrowth—

only in places where there was a break in the evergreen canopy.

The distance uphill was farther than he'd thought, and after a time he paused to catch his breath. He judged he was still half a klick below where he thought the trail might be.

"Hello, there!" The voice came from higher on the slopes.

Roget froze. He couldn't see anyone through the pines, widely spaced as they were.

"Did you have difficulty coming through the shields?" came the second inquiry. "Your descent was steeper than optimal."

Then he smiled wryly. The words were in Federation English, and well-pronounced, with a feminine tone. That implied continued observation of the Federation and considerable technology. If whoever she represented had detected his dropboat coming down, there wasn't much point in trying to evade her. Not obviously. He didn't want to walk right up to her . . . if the caller were even female . . . or human. But he didn't see any realistic alternative. While he couldn't sense any broadcast emissions, that didn't mean that she didn't have reinforcements. Or that she or it or they were friendly. On the other hand, it didn't mean they were unfriendly. Her words did suggest that there was little use in activating the singlesuit background blending camouflage.

"Some," he called back.

"I'll meet you up ahead at the rest stop. When you get to the trail, turn to your right. It's about half a klick ahead on the trail."

Should he take the caller's word? He could attempt to escape, but they'd found him in the middle of a forest, and not even on a trail—and they knew standard, including measurements. Thomists? That was looking to be the most probable conclusion, but anything was still possible.

He continued making his way uphill. He came to the trail after less than a hundred meters, although he hadn't been able to see it until he was almost upon it. Again, it was a manicured and wood-fragment-mulched walkway. Roget stopped, then looked north and south. He saw no one. He turned north, walking at a deliberate pace.

The rest stop was little more than two benches on the uphill side of the trail, with another stone fountain on the downhill side. A woman wearing a long-sleeved green shirt, gray trousers, and gray hiking boots sat on the bench nearest Roget. There was no one else in sight except the two of them.

She stood as he approached. She was a good thirty centimeters shorter than Roget, and muscular, but neither slender nor stocky. Her hair was white blond, and her face was oval with deep gray eyes, wide cheekbones, and a jaw that was just short of being square. Her skin was either lightly tanned or that shade naturally. With the planet's shields, how could he tell?

He stopped a meter short of her but did not speak. He saw no obvious weapons.

"I'm Lyvia. I'll be your guide to Dubiety."

"That's what you call the world?"

"Officially and unofficially. What does the Federation call it?"

"Haze."

"You haven't told me your name. Or the cover name you've adopted. Either will do." Lyvia smiled.

Her expression was fractionally warmer than polite, and slightly amused, Roget noted. "Keir. Keir Roget."

"We have a hike ahead of us, Keir. It's a good twelve klicks to the trailhead station. I'll explain a few matters along the way, and you can ply me with questions. Some I'll answer. Some will have to wait, and some you'll be able to answer yourself in time."

"All your responses will be Delphic, I'm certain."

"Only if you take them that way. We try to be factual. Oh, and I'd ask that you be careful with the weapons and those powerpacks built into your suit. Matters could become difficult if you hurt anyone." She turned and began to walk.

Roget had to take three quick long steps to catch up with her. The trail was wide enough for two to walk comfortably side-by-side. As he matched her pace, he couldn't help but think that she'd shown no surprise meeting him, and no fear and no hesitation in turning her back to him. It hadn't been a bluff. Nor had it been naiveté. Haze—or Dubiety—knew where he'd come from and had been prepared to meet him within a day and a half of his landing in what appeared to have been a relatively remote area . . . or at least an area removed from easy transport access. That raised the question of how much more the Federation knew than he'd been told. It also suggested just how expendable he was.

"This is one of the Thomist worlds, I take it?" he finally said.

"Thomists settled Dubiety. You should be able to tell that once you've seen more."

"What sort of commnet do you use?"

"There's a full planetary net."

"You don't care much for the standard broadcast spectrum. Why not?"

"Broadcomm has definite physical and physiological effects. We've avoided those."

"Such as?"

"Both implants and hand-held devices have adverse impacts on brain physiology. That's especially true for certain genetic profiles. Overall, the economics don't work out, either."

What did brain physiology have to do with economics? Roget was getting the feeling that all her answers might hold the same sort of non sequiturs. "Would you mind explaining that?"

"Any answer I give," replied Lyvia, "would be either simplistic or wrong. It's not my field."

"It might give me an idea, at least," said Roget mildly.

"That's exactly the problem in too many high-tech societies, even in some that are not so high-tech. Simplistic and wrong ideas lead to simplistic and wrong public opinion and wrong-headed public policies. That retards progress far more than is gained by so-called open dialogue by those who don't understand. Generalizations breed misunderstandings, and misunderstandings lead to greater problems in maintaining an orderly society."

"But most people don't want long and technical answers to simple questions."

"That's their problem."

"How do you keep people from giving those simplistic answers?" asked Roget.

"Personally, in conversation, and privately, they can say what they want. Anything meant for public communication falls under the libel and slander laws." She laughed. "That's what keeps most litigators in business."

"They can get damages if someone says or writes something factually inaccurate?"

"Exactly. One of the factors in governing the award is the number of people to whom the inaccuracy was conveyed."

Roget was both intrigued and appalled. "What about the use of accurate facts or figures to misrepresent?"

"If it's by a public figure, either a representative of an

organization or elected official, and it's bad enough, it's a criminal offense."

"How can anyone determine that?"

"The test has to do with relevant information withheld or omitted."

"In a noncriminal case, what if they can't pay?"

"We have a great number of public service positions, both for criminal and civil offenders. We've found that well-compensated litigators, solicitors, business directors and managers, and elected officials have a great aversion to maintaining trails such as this one or handling sanitary duties in the subtrans system or working land reclamation and enhancement . . . or any other number of equally necessary and not always tasteful tasks."

Roget kept a pleasant expression on his face and asked, "You mentioned elected officials. What's the governmental structure?"

"Nothing too unfamiliar to you, I'm certain. Representative democratically elected lower House of Tribunes. The upper chamber—that's the House of Denial—consists of those with specific areas of expertise. They're elected from nominees from various occupations and subjected to denial by the House of Tribunes."

"Do you have political parties?"

That brought another laugh, one more rueful. "Oh, yes. At the moment there are seven."

"Proportional voting of some sort?"

"It's not quite that simple. I'll have to get you a copy of the constitution."

For roughly three hours, Roget asked question after question. The answers provided by Lyvia were as satisfactory as her first replies. That is, they answered almost none of his real questions. Dubiety was sounding more and more like a fascist state run by environmentally-oriented lunatics. Yet, he reminded himself, lunatics didn't create orbital shields that could shred dropboats and keep the Federation at bay.

As the trail came to the top of a low rise, the trees ended abruptly. Lyvia gestured at the low circular grassy depression ahead. "There's the trailhead station."

A columned portico with a domed roof some fifteen meters across stood in the center of the grassy swale. Trails radiated from the circular stone walk that bordered the structure. All the stone was of a pale gray that was probably almost white but looked faintly rosy in the amber light that filtered through the orbital shields.

As they walked nearer, Roget could see two ramps under the low domed roof, each slanting into the ground— one on each side of the portico. A couple wearing hiking gear emerged from the ramp opposite the one immediately in front of Lyvia and Roget. Neither hiker so much as looked in Roget's direction.

"This way," Lyvia said pleasantly.

The mouth of the tunnel holding the ramp was encircled by a deep green band. On each side, waist-high, protruded four black squares, each some ten centimeters on a side. Lyvia raised a black tube and pointed it at one of the squares.

"Paying the fare?" asked Roget.

"Paying yours. Mine is deducted automatically."

The tunnel beyond the entry formed an oval with a flat base, roughly three meters wide, and the top of the ceiling was about four meters above the ramp. The flooring looked to be a deep green composite that offered a certain amount of give, combined with enough roughness to provide easy traction. The walls were a deep greenish gray, except for the two curved lighting strips some thirty centimeters wide set three quarters of the way up from the ramp surface. The light from the strips was slightly whiter than the amber that filtered through the atmospheric shields.

As he walked down the curving and sloping ramp, Roget asked, "You don't have any aircraft, flitters, that sort of thing?"

"We don't use them. They're energy intensive and excessively hard on the environment. They also create unrealistic expectations."

"Don't use them? That's an interesting way of putting it."

She smiled. "It's accurate. You'll see."

"Unrealistic expectations?" asked Roget.

"I'll explain once we're on the subtrans."

Roget started to protest in exasperation, then just smiled politely.

The ramp descended in a semicircle, then straightened for the last few meters before emerging onto a simple concourse that stretched some twenty meters to Roget's right. The walls of the concourse curved slightly, suggesting that they were but a fraction of a larger arc. A series of four archways punctuated the straight wall facing Roget. A half-transparent, half-translucent light green substance filled each archway.

Lyvia walked briskly to the third archway, halting there. "It shouldn't be long now. Not too long anyway."

Two older men stood talking several meters away, right before the last archway. While Roget thought he heard some familiar words, clearly language on Dubiety had diverged from the Federation standard. Yet Lyvia spoke Federation standard perfectly.

"If you listen closely for a while, you'll begin to understand," she said. "It's more a matter of cadence and localisms."

Roget hoped so. He could feel a gentle but persistent

breeze, and he glanced to his right, taking in the slots in the end wall of the concourse. Even straining his senses, he could detect no sounds of machinery.

"About expectations?" he asked.

"Later, after we're on the subtrans," she repeated.

Roget decided not to push her. A good fifteen standard minutes passed before the translucent green doors slid back to reveal the interior of the subtrans. Again, Roget had been unable to detect the approach of the underground conveyance.

Lyvia stepped through the archway, and Roget followed her. The subtrans's interior was simple enough, two individual seats on each side of a center aisle, set in groups of four, two seats facing two others. The flooring and walls flowed into the graceful seats, a deep green, with a brownish amber "trim." There were no windows, just a featureless wall.

Lyvia took a wall seat and gestured for Roget to take the seat across from her. He eased his small pack off his back, then settled into the seat, expecting it to be excessively firm, if not hard, since it looked to be the same material as the walls and flooring. Surprisingly, the seat was yielding and comfortable. His pack went between his legs.

The platform door closed, leaving a wall as blank as the one facing it.

"That's a great deal of wasted space." Roget pointed to the open area between the doors.

"That's where large packs, luggage, and sometimes freight get placed. There are concealed and recessed tie-downs."

The acceleration of the subtrans was gentle but continued for a time.

"Air travel? Expectations?" pressed Roget.

"Oh . . . that. Letting people travel by air creates a

whole host of expectations. One expectation is the feeling that they ought to be able to go when they wish and exactly where they want. After all, there's nothing like a maglev tunnel or the obvious limitations of one train at a time to reinforce the idea that not all things are possible. The expectations are even higher for those with resources and power, especially if the society allows them private aircraft of some sort. They believe their time is more valuable; they're more important. That reinforces the feeling that anything can be bought, regardless of the cost to others."

"That sounds like old-style socialism, even communism."

Lyvia shook her head. "We're very capitalistic, extremely so. We just price things at their total value. We don't allow people to buy privileges at the cost of other people's health or future, or life expectancy. Those are real costs. Most so-called market systems don't include them." She smiled. "At least, they haven't in the past. We don't always either, but we keep trying."

Roget didn't believe a word. "What about other expectations?"

"There's the expectation that immediate travel at comparatively low costs is a right, rather than a costly privilege. There's also the expectation that personal freedom of movement is a right, regardless of what it costs others."

Roget decided that he was getting nowhere. "Where are we headed?"

"To Skeptos, of course. It's the capital. Isn't that where you wanted to go? To find out our weaknesses?" Lyvia smiled warmly.

8

By the time Roget arrived at the FSS on Friday, his first four days on the job had given him a very good understanding of the routine of an E&W monitor in St. George. Immediately after reporting each morning, he went over the status reports and reviewed all the anomalies reported by the system. Then he'd set up a preliminary prioritization of the anomalies, with recommended observation points. He'd offer those to Sung. Once the head monitor had approved his plan for the day, Roget was free to head out with his portable official E&W monitor. The monitor held all the data for the day. That way, no one could hack or razor transmissions because there weren't any, and it kept down unnecessary energy usage.

Unless there happened to be an urgent surge in excess energy or water usage, Roget was free to arrange his observations to minimize his travel time. Since he was limited to public transport and his feet, he'd learned after the third day to be most careful in planning his route. Even so, his feet had ached by Wednesday evening, and Thursday night hadn't been that much better.

He actually was in the office on Friday before Sung. The anomaly list was short—four shops; two residences in the historical district—probably poor insulation or equipment that needed maintenance; and an increase in ambient temperature in the Virgin River that couldn't be accounted for by weather or solar radiation intensity.

The river had to come first because there was no tell-ing how long that anomaly might last. He also might have to take several readings over the course of the day. He'd just finished his proposed priority listing when Sung appeared and settled himself before the main console.

"The list is up," Roget said.

"Good." After a moment, Sung turned in his swivel. "You've got the Virgin first. That's right. But you need to move your first observation farther north, out east beyond the Green Springs tram terminal." Sung called up a map on the console and motioned for Roget to join him.

Roget did.

A red triangle appeared—a good klick to the east of the station. "There," announced Sung. "Don't forget to check to make sure nothing's coming down the Mill Creek wash, either. A reading there will determine whether it's natural, or whether it's coming from a source in town."

Roget thought about the long walk ahead.

"Oh . . . you can sign out a bicycle if you don't want to walk it." Sung grinned.

"I don't believe you mentioned that."

"Supply keeps one for us, down on the lower level. They fold and fit in the carriers at the rear of the tram cars."

"Thank you. I could use it today."

Sung smiled. "I thought you might. You'll need three locations on the river and three different intervals at least an hour apart."

Roget had planned on that. He just nodded. "I'd bet-ter get going."

Sung returned his attention to the console, and Roget finished loading the data into his duty monitor. Then he left the office and took the ramp at the end of the corridor down to the lower level. He had to walk the entire length of the corridor on the lower level to reach the supply office—a small cubicle with a door behind it, presumably to a storeroom.

The supply clerk was a black-eyed and black-haired woman. She looked up with a cautious smile. "Yes?"

"Keir Roget. I'm the new E&W monitor."

"Caron Fueng."

"Monitor Sung said that there might be a bike I can sign out?"

"There is." The clerk smiled. "Sung must like you."

"Oh?"

"He didn't tell Merytt about the bike for close to a month. I'll get it for you."

Roget laughed. But as he waited for Fueng to return with the bike, he wondered if the head monitor suspected what he really was.

The bike that Fueng wheeled out was the compact type with wide balloon tires. Not the speediest on paved surfaces, but much better on trails and lanes or unpaved surfaces.

"Just a thumbprint, please." She gestured to the authenticator on the corner of her desk. "I checked the tires. They're fine."

Roget thumbed the authenticator panel. "Thank you."

"If you don't bring it back before five, you'll have to keep it in your office. You can't take it home." She shrugged. "That doesn't matter to me, but accounting doesn't like it. Rules." She shook her head.

"I appreciate the warning. I should have it back by then." He offered a smile as he took the bike from her.

He wheeled it up the front ramp and managed to get it through the security gate and the front doors without banging anything. Once outside the FSS, he rode down to the tram station. The morning was already warm and

clear, more like late summer than late fall or early winter. Then, he doubted that there was really any season
besides summer in St. George.

His ID implant allowed him entrance to the platform
and train—but only during working hours. The carrier
in the rear of the second car was empty, and the bicycle
did fold—if not as easily as Sung had suggested. He sat
down in the seat next to the carrier.

A young man scurried onto the tram just before the
doors closed. He wore the white short-sleeved shirt and
dark trousers that all the Saint youths affected. As soon
as his eyes took in the white monitor's singlesuit, he
looked away and slipped into a seat two rows forward
from the one where Roget sat.

Three rows forward on the other side sat two white-
haired women. After the tram left the platform, they
began—or resumed—their conversation.

". . . still think it's a shame the way the Federation
limits missions . . ."

". . . say it's to reduce energy spent on travel . . . don't
want us converting people . . ."

". . . Jared's oldest is in Espagne . . . says it's hotter
than here . . . and almost as dry . . ."

"What do they have him doing?"

". . . building a new stake center there . . . they can't
offer their testament, except in church or on the premises . . . just show faith by example . . ."

"So much for freedom of speech . . ."

Roget wanted to snort. He didn't. Why did so many
people think that freedom of speech meant the ability
to harangue other people when they didn't want to be
bothered? True believers had the idea that once someone understood what they were saying, the listeners
would be converted. Understanding didn't mean accept-
ing, and that was why, under the Federation's freedom

of speech provisions, people could harangue all they wanted, but it had to be on their own property, or in their own dwellings, or with the consent of the property owner. Public thoroughfares or property were to be free of any form of solicitation, ideological or commercial, and soliciting others in their dwellings or on their property, without their permission, was also forbidden.

". . . how can anyone learn the Way if no one can tell them?"

". . . time will come . . . the Prophet says . . . after the great tribulations . . ."

". . . not too soon, if you ask me . . . had enough tribulations . . ."

"How is Jared?"

"Doing mission duty this year . . . Wasatch reclamation team . . ."

By the time the electrotram came to a halt at the Green Springs platform, the northeastern terminus of the system, and across from the maglev terminus, Roget was the only one in the car. He lifted the bike out of the carrier and carried it onto the platform, just before a large group of young women entered on the other side of the car. All of them looked to be fresh-faced and far younger than he was—and yet all had the braided hair of married Saint women.

Were they all headed to the Tabernacle or the Temple? For what?

He smiled faintly and snapped the bike together. Then he wheeled it down the ramp from the platform to the street, where he swung onto it and began to pedal eastward along Green Drive South, past white stucco dwellings larger than any he'd seen nearer the center of town. Like the others, though, they had walled rear courtyards. Only a handful of small electrocoupes passed him, all headed westward.

Roget stopped where Green Drive South ended at Riverside Parkway West—on the west side of the Virgin River. It scarcely deserved to be called a river. While the reddish clay, sandbars, and low vegetation of the riverbed varied from a good fifty to a hundred meters wide, the water itself was less than three meters wide, and certainly less than a meter in depth in most places. It was the largest watercourse between the Colorado River and Reno. No wonder the old American republic had left the place to the Saints.

For several moments, Roget looked at the thin line of water that effectively bordered the east and southeast of St. George. Generally, building was limited to the ground inside the borders of the Virgin River and the Santa Clara wash, which had once been a stream of some sort. Then he leaned the bike against the low sandstone wall that marked the edge of the protected area of the riverbed and studied the ground.

Several minutes passed before he determined the approach to the water that would disturb the vegetation the least. He walked north almost forty meters. There he walked along a line of mostly buried black lava, and then picked his way from rocky point to rocky point until he stood on a flat boulder that overlooked the water. He flicked out the microfilament probe and let the stream flow over and around it until the monitoring unit flashed. Then he stored the data and retracted the probe.

After carefully retracing his steps back to where he had left the bike, he looked back out over the river. He certainly hadn't seen any sign of gross thermal or other pollution, but the master systems would compare the water temperatures and composition to the river's environmental profile, once he returned and linked the monitor to the system. He continued to study the riverbed for several minutes longer, but nothing changed, and there was no one nearby. To the north he thought he'd seen a heron, or some sort of crane, but he wasn't certain.

Roget took the bike and rode southward down Riverside Parkway West. He didn't want to go through the process of riding back to the tram station, folding the bike, going two stations, then unfolding the bike, and riding back out east and south again. It wasn't that hot yet.

The parkway wound more than he'd realized. He rode close to five klicks before he reached the second monitoring point, just east of where River Road ended at the parkway. Reaching the water was easier there because there was a nature overlook.

Just as he had finished his monitoring and was walking back to his bicycle, a group of youngsters appeared. They were escorted by a young woman—a teacher, Roget thought.

"Good morning," he said politely.

"Good morning," she replied with a smile.

After he had passed the group, behind him, he heard the teacher.

"Who was that, class?"

There were various answers, all politely framed, before the woman's voice replied, "He's an environmental monitor. You can tell by the white uniform and the monitoring unit at his belt. He was checking the river. That's to make sure everything is as it should be. . . ."

Roget mounted the bike and rode farther westward on the parkway and then continued south until he reached the point where the dry Santa Clara wash joined the river—close to another six klicks. There he repeated the monitoring process.

After he finished, he took a long swallow from the water bottle at his waist and looked out to the south. It was still hard to believe that the blistered expanse of red clay and sand, dotted with scattered cacti and occasional tufts of some sort of desert grass, had once held thousands of dwellings and other structures. Or that hundreds of thousands of Saints—as many people as some main Federation locials—had populated the area. That had been before the wars and the Reconstruction, of course. St. George hadn't been funded for reconstruction by the Federation. All the work done in the area had been by Saint volunteers, and the Federation had only grudgingly accepted the environmental results, and only because the outcome had been to keep the Saints, who had been a quiet but destabilizing factor in the fall of the American republic, somewhat more isolated. That wasn't exactly what the briefing materials had said, but Roget had read between the lines.

He replaced the water bottle, then checked the monitor for the map and coordinates of the other sites he needed to check and verify. Three of the shops were north and slightly west of him along Bluff Street, in the area reserved for commerce. He was getting hot, and he decided to ride the bike to the south station and let the tram carry him north to the station closest to the southernmost shop on his list.

The station turned out to be only a quarter klick or so from the river, but he found himself sharing the rear car with fifteen youngsters—all about ten—being chaperoned by two large and jovial-looking young men. Yet none of the seventeen said a word during the time Roget was on the tram. He was almost relieved when he carted his bike off at the platform on the corner of Main and 600 South.

From there he rode the bike three blocks west to Bluff Street and found himself right beside his destination. Ken's Cleaners was a small shop set at the south end of the block. The stucco finish was a pale bluish white, rather than plain white, and the door was set on the southwest corner of the building, looking out on the street corner, rather than in the middle of the building facing Bluff Street. Through the tinted thermal-conversion windows, Roget could only see the untended counter. He leaned the bike against the side of the building and then walked back eastward alongside it, flicking on the atmospheric sampler and tabbing the results so they'd be linked properly. Then, halfway back along the side of the building, he extended the microfilament used for air sampling and flicked it as high as he could, swinging it over the top of the low structure. He walked to the rear of the building and repeated the process.

Then he paused. He could hear a low mechanical rumbling, almost a groaning, coming from inside the back of the cleaners. Some sort of mechanical problem, he thought. He could feel the excess heat from the building. That much heat meant excess energy use or poor insulation or malfunctioning equipment or some combination of those factors. Those weren't his problems, for either his overt or covert job.

As he turned, he saw two older men standing in the thin band of shade cast by the building across the side street from him. Both wore white shirts—but long-sleeved—and dark trousers. He smiled politely, then turned and began to walk back toward Bluff Street.

". . . hecky-darn monitor . . . snooping round . . . worse than the DTs, if you ask me . . . tell by the all white . . . not really proper . . ."

". . . ChinoFeds ought to have more to do than bother small businesses . . ."

". . . bother everyone now and again . . . why they're ChinoFeds . . ."

ChinoFeds? Roget thought that epithet had vanished

a millennium ago, and his ancestry certainly had no Sinese in it. Even the apparently meticulous genealogy records kept on virtually all Noram citizens would have proved that. The briefings had mentioned rumors that the Saints had even kept tissue samples of prominent deceased Saints, but those had never been confirmed. And St. George certainly didn't look like a technology center, but more like it had been frozen in time a millennium ago.

Roget kept a pleasant expression on his face. What so many people refused to accept was that, when thousands of small businesses in thousands of towns and cities all exceeded the limits, the results on the environment could be significant. That attitude had been the principal cause of the deterioration of the old United States. Everyone had thought that they could question any authority and that they could do what they wanted because what they did didn't matter. In the end it had, and by then it had been too late.

He completed his readings and returned to the bike. He pedaled north in the bike lane for another three blocks, where he stopped in front of the next commercial establishment on the list—Santiorna's. The shop looked to cater to Saint women. While the fabrics on the mannequins were flashy enough, the cut of the garments, and especially the lengths of the skirts, were conservative. The other fact was that there were actual garments displayed, rather than holographic images. Was that because of the Saint culture . . . or because of the cost of power?

Roget knew that power costs were far higher in rural areas and in smaller towns and cities. The higher costs of power, indeed of living, were designed to reflect the true impact of development on the environment as well as to discourage movement from the metroplexes and contained locials. Location pricing and transportation costs of certain energy-intensive goods effectively limited their use away from the metroplexes and locials. By implementing that pricing and adding geometric pricing for incremental energy usage, as well as a few other regulatory and pricing devices, the Federation had minimized population migration. In effect, the more desirable the location, the higher the cost of living there and the fewer personal amenities effectively allowed, except at exorbitant costs. Federation citizens could have personal luxuries or the luxury of open space, but not both.

He set the bicycle in the corner stand and then walked toward the shop, checking the monitor. Unlike Ken's Cleaners, Santiorna's displayed no possible causes of excessive energy usage, even when he made his way to the end of the block and walked up the alley. He could sense eyes on him as he did so, but no one actually appeared. When he returned to Bluff Street and the front of the buildings, he saw two young women walking south toward him. When they saw the white monitor's uniform, they immediately stepped inside what looked to be a craft shop.

At that moment, Roget took another look at the business between the craft shop and the apparel outlet. DeseretData read the sign, with a design next to the name that incorporated two interlocked Ds. Why was the name familiar?

He nodded as he recalled. DeseretData was Brendan B. Smith's establishment. Just on an off chance that Smith might have something to do with the anomaly attributed to Santiorna's, Roget took out the monitor and tabbed in an entry for DeseretData. Then he scanned the front of the shop and used the air sampling microfilament. After that, he walked back around to the alley and took readings there.

He walked back to his bike, then paused as several small lorries drove silently by, followed by a brilliant yellow coupe that whined almost imperceptibly. He followed the coupe for all of a block, even as it pulled away from him, before he realized that he was getting hungry.

The iron grilles and pseudo-aged stucco of the Frontier Fort caught his eye. He angled the bike off the street, dismounted, and walked it through the drawn-back iron gates into the shaded courtyard. There was a rack that could hold four bikes. One other bike was locked in place. Roget set the bike there and walked to the door and then inside the restaurant. Inside was notably cooler, but not chill. The hum of conversation filled the space. Close to half of the twenty or so tables were taken. That surprised Roget because he'd heard no sound when he'd been out in the courtyard.

Good insulation, he decided.

The hostess was a smiling, slim, but weathered and older woman, dressed in an old American-style pioneer ankle-length black skirt and a high-necked cream lace blouse. "Just you, sir?"

Roget nodded.

"This way."

He followed her to a small table near the north wall. She handed him a printed menu. He hadn't ever seen one of those.

"We're out of the lamb, but there's a venison stew for the same price. Jessica will take your order."

Roget decided to try the stew and ordered it and a pale lager, almost absently, when the round-faced and blond Jessica arrived. Then, while he waited for the venison, he intensified his implants and listened to various conversations taking place.

". . . monitor . . . what's he doing here?"

". . . don't know . . . don't care . . ."

". . . this one's a young fellow . . . liked the other one . . ."

Roget wasn't all that young, but to the weathered older man, he probably looked that way.

"That's because you never saw him."

". . . young Joseph wants a Temple wedding . . ."

". . . problem with that?"

". . . Dad doesn't have a recommend . . ."

". . . his fault . . . think blessings come free . . ."

The venison wasn't bad, especially with the new potatoes, but for all his listening, Roget couldn't say that he'd picked up a hint of anything. He hadn't expected to, but one could always hope.

After he left the Frontier Fort, feeling refreshed and cooler, Roget pedaled to the nearest tram station, where he wheeled the bike onto the first car, folded it, and stowed it. Then he rode the tram to the town center station, where he changed to the east-west tram and let it take him back out to the Green Springs station.

The next two hours consisted of repeating his first round of monitoring of the Virgin River. Then he took the tram back to the town center station. From there he rode the bicycle north and uphill, crossing St. George Boulevard, turning two blocks west, and finally coming to a stop outside the first residence unit. It was actually a guesthouse called the Seven Wives Inn. To Roget, the name sounded more like an opera, something like *Bluebeard's Waiting Room,* a classic Grainger chamber work dating back to before the fall of the west, and one of the few still performed, perhaps because it had a certain atonality that appealed to the Sinese.

Unlike the stucco-walled stone or block dwellings that dominated St. George, the inn—or at least the original on which the now-ancient replica was based—had high gables and a sharply pitched roof with reddish-yellow brick walls . . . and more wood than Roget had seen anywhere else in St. George—even more than the replica of the house of the Great Prophet—set less than a hundred meters away at an angle across the old wide street. The Great Prophet's house had tall trees. That suggested that the Saint church organization had obtained waivers for the water necessary to keep them alive.

Roget set the bike carefully against the white picket fence and took out the monitoring unit. He finished the first scan and began the air monitoring.

A young man hurried out of the inn and toward Roget. "We just discovered a whole power network in the upper level. My wife turned it on inadvertently yesterday."

"One of the old cooling units?"

"Yes, sir. I turned it off this morning."

Roget nodded. "I'll still have to take readings. That's my job."

The man winced visibly. "I understand." Then he turned and walked slowly back into the inn.

As he completed his monitoring, Roget heard raised voices from inside the inn. That didn't surprise him either. Neither did several yaps from a dog, but they were too sharp to have come from a dachshund.

The second residence unit was a small dwelling up behind the historic opera house, not that far from the Seven Wives Inn. No one was there, and Roget completed the readings.

Before he headed to the remaining commercial sites, he decided to make a slight detour. According to what he'd discovered so far, the inn owned by Bensen Sorensen was only a block away. In less than five minutes he had come to a stop outside the white picket fence of

The Right Place. He tabbed in another entry and ran through the scanning and sampling. No one even looked out from the windows.

Then he pedaled downhill to the boulevard and eastward to the Deseret First Bank building and the row of shops to the south of it. The shop there that was on the list was vacant, but that didn't excuse the owner. Roget finished the readings. Then he had to pedal another block to where he monitored OldThings—an antique shop and antiquarian bookshop.

When he finished, Roget rode slowly back to the central tram station. There he waited for a good fifteen minutes before catching the eastbound tram. Once more, he wheeled the bike into the second car and folded and stowed it, and tried to cool off as he sat there for the journey back out to the Green Springs station—again.

He thought that several of the women in the front of the car might have been among those he'd seen leaving Green Springs when he'd first traveled there that morning. They didn't look as hot and as tired as he felt, and he still had another three sets of readings to take and ten klicks on the bike.

When he'd left the FSS that morning, Roget hadn't thought that the day would be that long. By the time he finished the last river readings and took the tram back to the town center station and then rode uphill to the FSS, it was approaching five. He wheeled the bike down to the supply office and got there at five before the hour.

"You cut it close," offered Caron Fueng.

"Long day."

"You look like it."

"That good?"

Fueng just smiled.

It was after five when Roget returned to the office.

Sung was gone, and the system was locked down. After unlocking it and keying his codes in, Roget took out the thin fiber cable and linked the monitor and the system. Then he waited while the analytics processed the data.

The first set of Virgin River readings showed a lower reading than the initial anomaly, but the second reading showed a thermal spike above ambient, while the third was lower than the second but clearly higher than the first. The system could not identify any probable cause, except "natural conditions, probably intermittent geothermal infusion." Some help that was, but if it happened to be natural, that wasn't something a monitor could do anything about.

Ken's Cleaners was definitely using excessive energy and emitting excessive heat, and a citation would go out, with a copy to the enforcement arm of the local patroller, once it was approved by Sung. The Seven Wives Inn's readings were normal. A single spike might only result in a warning, if that, in addition to a slight energy surcharge. The other residence was running a slight overage, and Sung would have to decide how to handle that.

The results from The Right Place were also intriguing. They showed that the inn wasn't exceeding any limits. In fact, the readings seemed low compared to the Seven Wives Inn and even the single small residence. Then, that just might mean that Sorensen hadn't had any recent tourists or pilgrims. On the other hand, the inn's exterior walls were of native sandstone, and thick stone and modern insulation might be a factor.

OldThings was borderline, but the vacant shop was running well above its limits.

The first unexpected reading came from those taken at Santiorna's. They showed nothing out of the ordinary. But . . . the monitoring information from DeseretData showed marked excessive energy radiation, but the system did not indicate any excessive energy usage.

Roget frowned. That seemed more than a little strange.

He shrugged and locked the system down again. He closed down the office. Then he stepped out into the corridor and ID-locked the door. He'd taken less than ten steps toward the front of the building when a figure backed out of a doorway and almost into him.

"Excuse me," he said politely, stepping aside.

"Oh . . ." The woman turned. She held a large box in her arms. Her eyes were wide, blue, and innocent, and her shoulder-length blond hair was unbound. Rather, it was held in place by a dark blue headband. "I'm sorry. I didn't think anyone was still around." She offered an embarrassed half-smile. "I'm Marni. Marni Sorensen."

"Keir Roget. E&W."

"You're the new field monitor, aren't you?"

"The same. And you?" Roget smiled politely, offering but a trace of warmth.

"I'm the junior fiscal compliance auditor."

"Quite a title. What does it really mean?"

"It means I ask the system if everyone is staying within their projected budget, and most of the time everyone is."

"No offense," Roget said with a laugh, "but how could they not?"

She grinned. "I didn't say that well, I guess. No one can spend more than their budget, but what if a section obligates 80 percent of its resources in the first 20 percent of the accounting period?"

"I see what you mean. But the system . . . ?"

"The system would flag anything that obvious, but what if it's 7 percent over a time period when it should be 5? Is that a trend or just the result of capital equipment replacement?"

Roget nodded.

"It's nice to see a new face, but if you would excuse me? I'm running a bit late."

"Go." Roget grinned sympathetically. "Don't let me keep you."

With an apologetic smile, she turned and walked quickly down the corridor.

Roget knew one thing. She wasn't running late. What he didn't know was whether that was just a polite way to excuse herself from a non-Saint or whether she had some other reason for brushing him off.

He took his time walking from the FSS building down to the town center tram station where he caught an eastbound and took it out to the station at 800 East. From there it was a five-block walk south to the apartment, a relatively new structure with twenty-one units that had been rebuilt on the site of a defunct university, located as many had once been on the basis of local politics and concealed vote pandering. Roget didn't care for the desert landscaping of the space around the central bloc of units, much as he appreciated its necessity. His unit was at the south end on the ground level, and that made it the hottest one. For that reason, among many, he definitely wanted to complete his assignment before full summer descended upon St. George.

He thumbed the scanner plate, then opened the door, his implants alert to possible intruders or energy concentrations. Although he sensed neither, he entered cautiously, glancing around the living room and the nook kitchen through the archway at one end. Then he checked the bedroom and attached fresher/shower.

Only then did he use the antisnooper to scan himself for spyware. The device didn't discover any. He took out his compact personal monitor and used the publink to run a check on Marni Sorensen. Most subs and mals didn't have the equipment or the software to decrypt Fed burstlinks.

He was somewhat surprised to find out that she had a doctorate in biology. He had also suspected she might be related distantly to Bensen Sorensen, not surprising when something like three hundred of the ten thousand–odd residents of St. George happened to be Sorensens. Saints had a proclivity for Scandinavian names—Jensen, Bensen, Swensen, Hansen, and more than a few others.

He was wrong. She was Bensen Sorensen's much younger sister. *That* was interesting, and disconcerting. Even so, there wasn't much he could do. Not yet. His instructions were clear enough. He was not to begin anything invasive out of his line of work for at least two weeks, nor to do anything that might call undue attention to himself.

He snorted at the last. Just being an outsider in St. George called undue attention on himself.

He checked for spyware again, but his antisnoop insisted he and the apartment were clean.

After showering, he changed into clean underwear and a white shirt and dark slacks. Then he walked up to St. George Boulevard and toward a restaurant he'd noted earlier—the Caravansary. Although the sun had dropped behind the bluff to the west of town, the air remained warm.

No one was waiting when he entered the Caravansary, and a solid-looking woman of indeterminate age merely nodded and gestured for him to follow her. As he did, Roget could see that, like most of the eating establishments in St. George, it was modest in size. There were no more than twenty tables set in a single L-shaped room. The lighting was muted and amber, imparting a sandy glow to the white plaster walls, on which were mounted, at irregular intervals, odd pieces of tack and other items meant to suggest desert, ranging from a faded and battered maroon fez to half of what must have been a camel saddle.

"The menu is on the table. Thereza will be with you shortly, sir."

"Thank you."

Roget settled into the chair that allowed him the wider view of the patrons and who might be coming or going. A small slate was set in a holder on the polished wooden table with pseudo rattan legs. On the slate were chalked the night's entrees: Lamb Marrakesh, Chicken Arabic, Mixed Kebabs, Rice Sansouci, and Brigand Lamb. None of the names meant anything to Roget.

"Sir?" Thereza was twentyish, blond, and offered an infectious smile at odds with the severe flowing brown dress and its wrist-length sleeves. "I'm Thereza, and I'll be your server. Everything on tonight's menu is available."

"Is there anything else available?"

Thereza looked at him. "You're new here, aren't you?"

"Does it show that much?" Roget grinned.

"Not that much. Most people who come here are regulars, except in full winter, when we get a few tourists and pilgrims. Most of them stay closer to the Temple. You're the only new face I've seen in weeks."

"There must be more newcomers than that."

"Not many. You have to have a job, or money, or family to relocate here."

"And it helps if you're a Saint?"

"Not to get a job. The Feds watch that. But most who aren't Saints leave sooner or later. Usually sooner."

Those who couldn't leave, Roget had been briefed, often ended up in rehab for substance excess . . . or as suicides. Outsiders had a high rate of depression in St. George.

"I could get you some sliced lamb with rice and gravy. That's not on the menu."

"Of the items on the menu, which is the best?"

"There's no best. They're all good. The Marrakesh is very spicy. The kabobs are tender but subtle . . ."

That translated to bland, Roget suspected.

". . . the Arabic is sweet, sour, and mildly spicy. The Sansouci is hot, and filled with diced lamb and vegetables, and the Brigand Lamb is my favorite."

"I'll try that."

"It comes with brown rice and sauce."

"Sauce on the side, please."

"That you'll have."

"Red wine?"

"The Davian or the Banff are both good."

Roget had never had the second. "I'll have the Banff."

Once Thereza had left, Roget turned up his implants to see what he could hear.

". . . haven't seen him before . . ."

"He has to be new. She spent too much time with him . . . flirts with all the handsome ones . . ."

". . . can you blame her . . . after all that last year?"

Roget wondered exactly what the speakers were talking about, but that couple returned to their food. He kept listening.

". . . council's going to petition the Federation regional administrator to release 100 hectares from the land bank . . ."

"The Feds won't do it . . . say we have more than enough land for the population . . ."

"Of course they do, but they're using the amount of land to limit in-migration. That policy keeps families from gathering . . ."

"Unless they're born here . . ."

"Half the fellows end up leaving . . . can't get decent jobs here, and the Feds won't hire many locals . . . heard the E&W monitor's job went to an outsider . . . pay's good, but you think any of our boys'd be considered? Be the same thing when Sung retires . . ."

In the end, Roget found the food acceptable, Thereza diverting, and the conversations he overheard uninformative, except in confirming what he had learned in his briefings before he had left Helena.

The evening was almost cool as Roget walked slowly back to his apartment. He wasn't certain that he looked forward to the weekend.

9

17 MARIS 1811 P. D.

Roget studied Lyvia Rholyn. While sitting, she was only ten centimeters shorter than he was. She had short legs and a long torso that resulted in a frame of slightly above average height. For earth, anyway. He hadn't seen more than a handful of people so far on Haze . . . or Dubiety, he reminded himself. Her shoulders were slightly broader than the Federation norm, as well. Her hair was straight and light brown, remarkable only for the silky fineness that became obvious when she turned her head suddenly, and possibly one of the reasons why the woman cut it short, barely long enough to reach the middle of her neck. She also seemed unbothered by the high humidity or by his study of her.

"Where are we headed, specifically?" he finally asked, blotting his forehead.

"Eventually to the MEC—the Ministry of Education and Culture. That will be tomorrow. Immediately, I'm taking you to a guesthouse near the main square in Skeptos. I assume you'd like to clean up, get a good meal, and a good night's sleep. After you clean up, I thought we could take a short walk to dinner, depending on your preference in cuisine. That would give you a feel for the city. Compared to Federation cities, I'm certain Skeptos is quite modest."

"You're not afraid I'll vanish?" He raised his eyebrows.

"You can try if you want. Your shipsuit isn't that outlandish, and you don't look that different from anyone here, although you're a trace taller than most men. But you have no link into anything, and the only way you can get food or anything else would be by some form of criminal activity. We don't use currency or coins. We do punish criminals, especially those who use weapons or threaten with them."

"More public service?"

"Some of it can be back-breaking hard labor. Since criminals have proved untrustworthy, they're also limited either personally or by locale."

"Prison camps?"

"Restricted hamlets is far more accurate."

Roget had doubts about the accuracy of that description. "So I should behave? Or else?"

"You can do as you wish. We're quite willing to provide you with much of the information you were dropped to obtain. At the proper time, you'll even be able to return to your ship with it."

Roget doubted that as well, even more strongly, but

she was right about the necessity of his playing along. For the moment. "Tell me more about Dubiety."

"Not until you've seen more."

"You've said that before."

"Verbal descriptions of places you haven't seen create the possibility of false and lasting preconceptions. In your case especially, we'd prefer not to create anything like that."

"Is everyone here a philosopher?"

"Hardly. Just those who are good at what they do."

Shortly, the subtrans slowed, coming to a stop. According to Roget's internals, they'd been traveling just over six minutes. Lyvia did not move.

"Where are we?"

"Avespoir. It's where the peninsula joins the mainland."

"How far from here to Skeptos?"

She frowned, as if mentally calculating. "A little over four hundred klicks."

Roget resigned himself to a good hour or more on the subtrans, perhaps several, then shifted his weight on the seat as three men entered the car. The tallest man wore shimmering dark blue trousers that were too loose to be tights, and far narrower than anything Roget had ever seen, despite the knife-edge front creases. His shirt was long-sleeved, pale blue, and equally tight-fitting with broad pointed collars that spread over a looser white vest.

The man in the middle wore something akin to a standard Federation singlesuit, but the fabric changed from a deep black toward vermilion as Roget watched. So did the man's boots. The third man wore a collarless, black tight shirt under a tailored burgundy jacket, fastened closed by a set of silver links, rather than by buttons. His high-heeled platform shoes were silver.

The three took the set of four seats behind Roget and continued talking animatedly. He listened intently. For several minutes, he understood nothing except a few stray words. Then more words made sense, including a phrase that sounded like "range of plasma-bounded energy opacity."

The subtrans decelerated for a minute before halting. The doors opened, and the three men left the subtrans, but two women got on. Both wore singlesuits of the kind that shifted color, except the lower legs of the taller woman's also turned transparent. The two talked so quickly that Roget understood not a single word. At the next stop, no one got off, but a rush of people boarded. Nine or ten, Roget thought.

Lyvia moved to sit beside Roget, and an older couple took the seat across from them. Both were fit and trim, and their skin was firm, their hair color apparently a natural brown for the man and an equally natural sandy-blond for the woman. Their age was obvious only in the fineness of their features and in the experience in their eyes. Both wore singlesuits, his silvered brown, and hers a silvered blue.

The couple exchanged several words, then addressed Roget and Lyvia.

"A very long trip and hike," Lyvia replied.

That was what Roget thought she said. He just nodded and smiled politely.

A few minutes later, the subtrans slowed, then stopped. The doors opened, and Lyvia stood. So did Roget. He lifted his pack and slung it over one shoulder, then followed Lyvia from the subtrans onto a larger concourse close to a hundred meters in length and toward one of two tunnels leading further upward. Lyvia was moving to the left tunnel, and Roget stayed close behind her.

A slender man in a black jacket and trousers glanced hard at Roget as the agent hurried to stay with Lyvia.

Roget checked the time. The trip from Avespoir to Skeptos had taken twenty minutes, but nine minutes had been for stops. Add another six minutes for acceleration and deceleration, although those were estimates, and the subtrans had covered the four hundred klicks in the equivalent of roughly fourteen minutes—figuring three additional minutes for speed changes. Something was wrong with his figures or the numbers Lyvia had provided. Seventeen hundred klicks an hour? Underground?

Roget drew abreast of his guide just before they started up the tunnel ramp, a good ten meters wide. "Four hundred klicks from Avespoir to Skeptos?"

"It's more like four hundred fifteen, actually."

"And a klick here is still a thousand meters?"

"So far as I know, it's never been anything else."

She could have been lying. Roget doubted it, and that had serious implications. Then, he had no illusions. He was supposed to reach those conclusions.

After some twenty meters, the tunnel joined another one, close to filled with men and women heading upward. Despite the number of people leaving the subtrans station, no one crowded anyone else. Still, Roget could sense the man in black not all that far behind him.

The air was markedly cooler than it had been in the tunnel when they emerged, and did not hold the semi-perfumed scent of the forest . . . but it was still humid.

"This is the central square of Skeptos," Lyvia said, stepping to one side of the walkway and stopping to offer a sweeping gesture that took in the open space, as well as the buildings surrounding it, although none looked to be more than thirty meters tall.

Roget let his eyes range over the square, merely an

expanse of deep green grass surrounded by four stone walks twenty meters wide. They stood close to one corner, the southwestern one, he judged, hoping he wasn't too disoriented by the lack of a distinct sky and no sun for direction. A single stone monument rose from the center, a round column some thirty-three meters high. Atop the column was a sphere of shifting silver gray haze. Narrower walkways led from each corner of the square to the circular raised stone platform around the column.

"The column?" he asked. "Some sort of memorial?"

"A representation of Dubiety."

Roget glanced around the square again. Beyond the perimeter walks were low buildings on all sides, low especially in comparison to those of Taiyuan, between which were the stone pedestrian ways that radiated from the corners of the square and from the middle of each side of the square. There was no provision for vehicular traffic or for airlifters of any sort.

"We need to get you settled. This way." Lyvia turned south and strode quickly along the wide walk, past what looked to be an eating establishment on the right.

"A restaurant?" asked Roget.

"Dorinique. It's very fashionable now. It's also good . . . and expensive."

"The more expensive restaurants and other establishments are the ones closer to the square, then?"

"Or to other subtrans stations. Not always, but usually."

"Isn't there any transport that's more . . . local?"

"Local transit is below the regional subtrans. Those were the people coming from the other tunnels."

Local transit was lower than the regional links? That definitely seemed odd to Roget, but he didn't ask, not yet.

They passed several other restaurants and a boutique that looked to cater to women. Overhead, the silver gray of the sky began to dim, just a touch, although there were no clouds below the haze. Roget noted that from outside of the shops on the street level there were no exterior indications of what might be housed in the upper levels of the buildings, but then, that was true in Federation cities as well.

The next shop caught his eye. "Finessa? A man's boutique?"

"Why not? In most species, the males are the ones who strive the most to display." Lyvia smiled. "Be careful with preconceptions here. My cousin Khevan—my mother's cousin, really—is the marketing manager for the twenty-odd shops of the group. He's also a former cliff ranger."

"Cliff ranger?"

"They deal with poachers and collectors in the mountain wilds. Very stressful and physical occupation."

"I got the impression you didn't have that sort of unruliness."

"All societies do. How one handles it is a fair measure of a civilization." Lyvia kept walking.

Roget's feet were getting sore, but he said nothing.

Six very long blocks later, Lyvia stopped before a two-story structure some thirty meters wide. The stone archway framing the door was trapezoidal. "This is the guesthouse. You might want to fix it in your mind." She turned and pushed open the door.

Roget followed her into a small antechamber. The door on the far side was closed. A single eye-level keypad was mounted on the wall. Above the keypad was a screen. She took the small tube attached to her belt and pointed it at the screen.

For a moment Roget sensed the faintest of energy emissions or emission reflections.

"The keypad is for the use of residents who are not linked or are unable to access services. You're one of them. The code is written down in your rooms."

The door hummed, then slid into a recess, revealing a small reception area where several chairs were grouped around a low table. The chairs were wooden armchairs but looked to have deep blue permanent cushioned seats similar to the yielding composite of the seats on the subtrans. All of the chairs were empty, and the top of the polished wooden table was bare as well.

"Are you coming?" asked Lyvia.

Roget responded by stepping through the door, which closed behind him. Except for the fleeting emissions involving the door screen, Roget had sensed no others, and still didn't, even inside the guesthouse.

Beyond the reception area was an open but railed circular ramp leading upward.

"You're on the second level." Lyvia started up.

Roget once more followed.

Halfway down the bare corridor off the ramp, illuminated by an amber light from the ceiling strips, similar to the sunlight filtering through the orbital shield arrays, she halted before the second door, again using the belt-linked tube to open it.

She stepped into a room some eight meters by four, with a window looking westward at another building. The view was clear, but Roget had observed the heavy tinting on the outside of all the windows they had passed and had no doubts he'd only see the tint from outside if he looked up from the wide walkway below. The chamber was sparsely furnished with a single couch flanked by two armchairs, all three pieces set around a low wooden table. On the left wall, less than a meter from the window that stretched almost from wall to wall, was a wooden desk set against the wall, with a chair of matching wood.

Lyvia walked to the desk, then turned. "There's a sitting room, a bed chamber and fresher, and a small kitchen with a standard replicator. Directions for the replicator and other systems and the code for your rooms and the guesthouse itself are here." She pointed to two sheets of paper on the desk. "The holojector controls are in the left desk drawer and the comm unit is in the right."

"Just like that?"

"I'm certain you can figure them out, and you'll learn more of what you came to find." She paused. "Oh . . . there are two singlesuits that should fit you in the bedroom closet."

"Should fit me?"

"They'll be close enough." She smiled. "You have internals for time. I'll meet you down in the reception area in forty minutes, and we'll go to dinner."

"Hours are the same here?"

"The hours are the same length, but there are only twenty-two." She walked back to the door, which opened for her, and left Roget standing in the middle of the sitting room as the door closed behind her.

He walked toward the door. It didn't open. He headed back to the desk and picked up the single sheet with the word "Codes" at the top. There was a single alphanumeric line: RogetW976A. Roget looked at it for a long moment. She'd never been out of his sight, and he'd never sensed any emissions or transmissions.

He took a deep breath of the heavy air. He smelled more of himself than anything else. Lyvia was definitely right. He needed a shower or the equivalent . . . and a good meal, preferably not from the replicator. He also needed to read all the directions.

But first he went to the keypad by the door and punched in the code.

The door opened. He nodded, stepping back into his temporary quarters and letting it close.

10

18 LIANYU 6744 F. E.

Roget slept late on Saturday. For him, late was eight, even in St. George.

After he roused himself and finally made his way to the kitchen side of the main room, he checked the menu on the replicator. Nothing looked all that appetizing, but he selected hot tea and eggs romanov, which fell within his caloric and energy budget. They turned out to be a very poor replication of the original concept, but he forced himself to eat most of them before sliding the remnants into the recycler. He wouldn't have them again, not from a cheap replicator with a limited ingredient basis.

Then he washed up and donned another white shirt and a fresh pair of dark slacks, since the heat limited anything to one wearing before cleaning, at least for him, and then headed out for a day of ostensible errands. He walked up 800 East to St. George Boulevard to catch the tram.

An older couple was already standing on the platform when Roget got there. The man was tanned and had brilliant white hair. The woman's hair was blond, as appeared to be the case with most Saint women. Roget couldn't help but wonder why the older men affected such silver white hair when standard hair treatments allowed people to retain their natural color throughout their lifetime at minimal cost.

"Good morning," he offered pleasantly.

"Morning," replied the man. "Must be new in town."

"Relatively," Roget admitted. "I'm Keir Roget."

"Mason Bradshaw . . . my wife, Leitha."

Leitha inclined her head politely.

"Pleasant weather we're having right now," said the man. "Enjoy it while you can." He turned as the tram pulled up to the platform, then stepped forward into the tram car once the doors slid open.

Leitha scuttled after him, every movement an apology.

Roget followed but took a seat farther back in the car.

Two young men hurried in after him and sat midway between him and the couple, but on the opposite side from Roget. For the short trip to the center station, none of the other four said more than a few words.

Once the tram came to a stop, Roget waited until the others exited, then took his time leaving. He paused at the top of the ramp leading down from the platform, looking southward at the single St. George branch of the Deseret First Bank, located on the southeast corner of Main and St. George Boulevard, just south across the boulevard from the electrotram central station platform. Like most financial institutions, DFB was global in scope. Unlike most that had originated out of the West-Euro culture, its clientele was largely based on sectarian affiliation—or in a place like St. George—local residence. Roget walked down the ramp, taking in the building, a two-story Navaho sandstone structure that, like much in St. George, was a replica of an earlier historic edifice, except for the solar panels. William Dane's office was there, but Roget doubted Dane would be in on a Saturday. Even so, given the screen-based banking services, no customer ever saw bank officers except by appointment. Roget didn't have a plausible reason for requesting one. Not yet, and his superiors would be less than pleased at any immediate obvious outreach.

Roget's first "errand" was to stop by the art gallery in History Square. In some places, local art galleries revealed more about a place than weeks of talking to locals might. In others, they were merely commercial outlets. He waited at the boulevard for several electrocoupes and a lorry to pass before he crossed, then turned west and crossed Main Street in turn, grateful for the single patch of clouds that momentarily blocked the bright desert sun.

The redstone-walled gallery was on the northeast corner, and the door and windows were trimmed in a deep green. The sign on the dark-tinted front window read Glen-David's. Roget opened the door and stepped inside, finding it comparatively cooler than most other shops. For a moment, he wondered why. Then it struck him. Certain establishments, like art galleries and medical facilities, had higher energy limits before geometric pricing kicked in.

"Good morning, sir." A silver-haired and slight man stepped forward. He smiled politely, but not warmly. "Are you looking for anything special?"

"No. I haven't been here before. Someone at work suggested I should." Roget returned the smile.

"You should indeed. We do have images or prints of most of what's on display. We can size them for whatever space needs you have."

"I'll keep that in mind."

"Just let me know if you need anything, sir."

Roget nodded politely, then turned his attention to the various works.

The art displayed was in a wide variety of media—hololight images, multishifts, pastels, watercolors, oils, and even a charcoal portrait. Most if not all of the subject matter was definitely local or Saint-derived. *The Flight of Nephi* was a multishift, an imposition/transformation of images flowing from that of a boy in ancient Israel to a man amid the jungles of Central America. *The Destruction of the Temple* was an angular and stark oil rendition of the Salt Lake Temple in the brilliant blue light of a focused nucleonic disrupter beam just at the moment before it turned to ashes and dust. That temple had never been rebuilt, not with the crater, now an extension of the Great Salt Lake, where much of the center city had been. *The Long Walk* was a pastel that depicted people in old American pioneer garb pushing carts along a trail flanked with prairie grass and bushes. Roget didn't doubt its general accuracy, even if he didn't know the historical context. One seemed slightly out of place, a portrait of a younger man in some sort of flight gear with a hazy combat aircraft that Roget did not recognize in the background. The card beside it read, "Original Not for Sale, images available." The portrait was good technically, but not outstanding. There was no indication who it depicted.

Then, there were the landscapes—Kolob Canyon, the Patriarchs, the Gorge—and the portraits. Some of the names were familiar, but most were not.

A handful were terrible. Most were good. Some were better than that. Few of them appealed to Roget, and only one was good enough for him to consider buying even as an image. He wouldn't ever have considered it, had someone described it to him. It was simply an oil of a small black dachshund sitting on the cushion of a blue velvet sofa. On one side was a knitted afghan of maroon and cream, disarrayed almost as if the dachshund had been sleeping under it and had just darted from it. The sun poured across her—the dog had to be female, although there were no obvious clues—from an unseen side window, and she looked expectantly out of the canvas, as if her master or mistress had just entered the room. Yet the skill—or love—of the artist was such that the dachshund was alive. She almost leapt out of the ancient canvas.

"The sunshine dog," Roget murmured, in spite of himself. He turned away and took several steps. Then he stopped and returned to study the painting again. He couldn't say why, but just looking at the image made him feel better.

After several moments, he shook his head and walked toward the front of the gallery where the proprietor sat behind a small console. "How much for an image of the sunshine dachshund?" Neither the original nor prints would do. Not as often as he would be shifted around.

For a moment, the proprietor frowned, as if he didn't understand why Roget would want the portrait of a small dog. "Full density image is 117 yuan, with tax."

"That's fine. I'll take it with me." Roget held his Cred-ID before the scanner, then tendered his datacard. "Do you know the dog's name?"

"I'd guess it was Hildegarde. That's what she said the title was—Hildegarde in the Sunlight."

"Thank you." Roget thumbed the scanner to authenticate the charges, then took back the datacard. "It's a good painting."

"It's not that expensive. You could have the original for six hundred."

Roget shook his head. He wished he could, but he

could take the image with him, and he couldn't take the original, and he'd end up having to give it away, and no one he knew would see what he saw.

After watching the proprietor load the image into his personal flash monitor, he smiled and left Glen-David's. Once outside in the warm sunlight, he walked uphill a block and turned west, stopping after about a hundred meters outside the picket fence surrounding the summer home of the Saints' great second Prophet and Revelator. It was closed, but he read the brass plate on the pedestal outside the gate. When he finished, he tried not to frown. According to the plate, the dwelling was the actual original and not a replica, as he had thought. When the first War of Confederation loomed, a dedicated group of Saints disassembled the dwelling and stored it in a hermetically sealed cave in the mountains to the northwest of St. George. When it was finally reconstructed, a nanitic covering was applied to the wood to prevent further deterioration.

Roget had his doubts about the explanation on the plate, for many reasons, but it wouldn't be wise to voice them. He turned and walked eastward in the direction of The Right Place. A slender blond woman was sweeping the sandstone slabs that constituted the walkway from the gate in the picket fence. Her back was to him as she swept around a redstone sculpture of a heavyset bearded man who wore a frontier-style coat. Roget assessed the sculpture as moderately good, but not outstanding.

The woman faced the front porch with its deep overhanging eaves and the low sandstone wall on each side of the stone steps up to the porch. Somehow, she looked familiar.

As he walked nearer, he recognized Marni Sorensen. There was no reason she shouldn't be sweeping the walk to the guesthouse of her brother, but it bothered him.

The front door opened. Another blonde stood there. "Marni! It's Tyler."

Marni did not look in Roget's direction, but hurried inside, barely stopping to lean the broom against the stone pillar on the left side at the top of the porch steps. The door closed with a *thunk* clearly audible to Roget.

Were energy/comm costs so high that the locals didn't even use direct personal links? Or were they privacy obsessed the way the survies were? Or was beautiful Marni part of the reason why he was in St. George?

While he took his time, Roget kept walking, past The Right Place and then downhill and back toward Main Street and the electrotram station. He waited in the shade, his eyes straying to the white of the old Temple and the western edge of the Genealogy Center, most of which had to be underground, until he could take the tram west to Bluff Street. From the station there he made his way south until he arrived at DeseretData, the only EES the directory listed in St. George. That was doubtless correct. Most people got their entertainment through direct-links, but there were always a few specialty and local shops for the material that didn't have enough of a customer base to pay net access charges or for material that didn't meet Federation standards, either technically or in terms of its content. Not that all that much content was banned, mainly prurient material aimed at underage children and direct or indirect religious or secular incitements to armed revolt, but there were always a few individuals who seemed to want to press the limits, no matter how loose they might be.

Even in fall, the day was warm, and Roget was glad to step inside the shop, although it wasn't that much cooler.

"Are you looking for anything in particular?" asked the fresh-faced young man seated on a high-backed stool behind the short and narrow counter just beside the door.

"Do you have sloads about the history of the area?"

"If you take the end screen and key in 'color country,' that will show most of what we have that's not on the FedNet."

"Thank you." Roget walked to the end wall console and flat screen and entered the keywords. He expected perhaps twenty sloads, all of them short. There were close to a thousand, some dating back three hundred years, another reminder that he was dealing with a culture that not only respected its history, but wallowed in it. On top of that, few of the sloads were short. It took him over an hour to select ten that he hoped would prove helpful—not about the history, which he knew, but about the slants and views of the local institutions that had scripted and produced them.

When he walked back to the front counter, it took a minute for the young man to look up from the screen in front of him. "Oh . . . yes?"

"You related to Brendan?"

"No, sir. Not really. Brother Smith is a friend of my parents. Did you find anything?"

"I left ten of them on the queue."

"Let me run the charges." After a moment, the clerk nodded. "If you want all ten sloads, it will be three hundred."

"I'll take them." Roget let the scanner take the Cred-ID codes, then added his thumbprint before handing over his flash monitor.

The clerk inserted it in the loader, then handed it back. "There you go, sir."

"Thank you."

On his way back from DeseretData, Roget stopped by the supply store—Smith's—where he picked up a replicator supply pak. He chose the full-range version, expensive as it was. The apartment replicator needed all the assistance it could get. He also picked up a few local apricots . . . three—at ten yuan each.

By the time he returned to his apartment, he had already decided which sload he'd scan first—*From Deseret to Federation District*. It purported to be a history of the area, produced almost a century ago. The production company was Deseret Documentary. The others were more recent, and all had been done in the local district by Saints.

Then he'd have to see exactly what steps he'd take next.

11

17 MARIS 1811 P. D.

Roget did enjoy the shower, although he hurried through it, and some of the toiletries supplied were not what he would have picked. As Lyvia had indicated, there were indeed two singlesuits, one in tasteful deep gray and one in dark green, as well as two pairs of underwear and socks as well, plus what looked to be short pajamas. Although his systems could detect no overt snoops built into the clothing, he had no doubts that they contained nano-level locators, and probably a great deal more.

More of concern was that the singlesuits fit so well that they seemed tailored to him personally. How could they have been? He hadn't detected any radiation or any active energy fields around him. Nor had he detected any direct comm links from Lyvia, and he hadn't been around any Dubietans except in the last five hours or so. All the little details of those hours were providing him with a picture whose outline he didn't like at all, and he'd scarcely begun to look at Skeptos and Dubiety.

He even half-wondered if Lyvia were some sort of private operator who'd picked him up on her own. After a moment, he dismissed that . . . mostly. She spoke Federation, and no one else seemed to. She'd known where his dropboat had landed, even something about his angle of descent through the orbital shields, and she'd addressed him immediately in Federation. If she could muster those kinds of resources as an individual . . . he had even bigger problems than he'd thought. And so did the Federation.

He left his temporary quarters with five minutes to spare, walking down the utilitarian upper hallway wearing the deep gray singlesuit and carrying inside it the small stunner. Besides the stunner, his boots were the only item of his own that he wore, but he hadn't cared for the almost slipperlike slip-ons that had been left in the closet of the bedroom. When he started down the circular ramp to the reception area, he saw that Lyvia had also changed. She wore a rich green and feminine one-piece suit, with a dark gray vest and dress boots that matched his singlesuit.

She waited until he reached the bottom of the ramp before speaking. "You like solid footware, I see."

"I always have."

"I can understand that. You look good in a dressy singlesuit." Both her mouth and her gray eyes smiled.

"Thank you. So do you." Roget inclined his head. "How do the locators in the singlesuit work?"

"I have no idea," she replied, "except that they're passive. No one but me knows where you are right now."

"That could change in a moment."

"It could. That's up to you." She paused. "What are you in the mood to have for dinner?"

"Something good, not excessively spicy, nor so subtle as to be boringly bland, and preferably something that you'd also enjoy. In short, I'm in your hands . . . as I've been all day." Roget kept his voice light and ironic.

Lyvia laughed. "You do have a sense of humor." She turned. "We'll go expensive."

Roget followed her out through the antechamber and into an evening under a sky that remained ever so faintly amber. Already he missed seeing stars in the heavens.

"I've confirmed reservations at Dorinique."

"That was on the central square, wasn't it?"

"Yes. We'll have a window table. That way you can watch the square."

Watching Lyvia was likely to be more interesting and practical, but there was no point in saying so. Roget slipped to her left and matched her steps, much less hurried than earlier.

The walkways were slightly more crowded than before, but Roget saw more couples, and their pace seemed more leisurely. The air was slightly cooler and comfortably humid, but barely so.

"Things are slower in the evening."

"They should be, don't you think?"

Roget hadn't thought about that. Taiyuan was far faster, Fort Greeley far more utilitarian and worn down, and St. George and Colorado Springs far slower, but Skeptos was a planetary capital. "Are there continental or regional capitals on Dubiety?"

"There are regional administrative centers, but we're not a republic with regional governments. That's an inefficiency that's no longer necessary."

No longer necessary?

There was something about the way the walkways and buildings were lit, but they had walked almost a full block before Roget realized exactly what it was. The light from the buildings or the almost invisible arching street lights didn't scatter. Nor did the pavement reflect it in the slightest. Yet the walkways were well-illuminated in a fashion that afforded no shadows for lurkers or those up to little good.

As they continued walking, Roget could hear a violin playing, cheerfully, rather than sounding lonely. He glanced toward the center of the square where a young woman stood on the low stone platform below the monument. He didn't see any form of amplifier or projector. "Buskers, yet?"

"No. Musicians apply for the privilege, and they're paid. If enough citizens register approval, they get a bonus. Sometimes it's considerable."

"What if people don't approve?"

"No one is allowed to play who isn't technically proficient."

"That sounds rather . . . restrictive," suggested Roget.

"We don't cater to unrestricted public taste. That panders to the lowest common denominator, and the more it's catered to, the lower it goes."

"Elitism, yet. What about popularity?"

"That's fine, but only when it's based on excellence."

"Great elitism, then," Roget said lightly.

"There's a great deal to be said for elitism, so long as it's only a barrier to incompetence and not to ability."

"An interesting way of putting it."

"What other way is there to put it?" Lyvia turned toward the door, which opened from both sides.

They walked inside, and the door closed.

A woman in a singlesuit with angled alternating stripes of white and black stood waiting. She wore a white sleeveless vest.

"Rholyn, two," Lyvia said.

"By the window, yes?"

Roget had to strain to make out even those simple words.

"Please. This is my friend's first trip to Skeptos."

"This way." The hostess turned and walked around a head-high partition. Behind it was a row of tables for two set against the window.

As Roget followed, his eyes and ears were caught by the four musicians playing on a small circular stage in the middle of the restaurant. He recognized the large keyboard instrument as an ancient acoustical piano— except it clearly wasn't ancient—while a tall woman played some sort of reed instrument. The two others played strings, a violin and a cello, he thought.

Roget took the seat facing the door, from where he could observe the comings and goings of patrons, once they stepped past the partition, and both the square and the restaurant. His eyes drifted back to the instrumentalists.

"You look surprised," observed Lyvia.

"Acoustical instruments? With all your technology?"

"Technology is a focused application. It doesn't do particularly well with the best forms of music, especially in dealing with overtones, because they're not always consistent, and they're not meant to be."

Rather than reply, Roget studied the table. The cloth covering it was pale green, but looked to be synthetic, as was the upholstery on the comfortable and supportive chairs. The cutlery, while curved slightly in a fashion he had not seen, was recognizably human. Each setting had a darker green cloth napkin, and a crystal tumbler and a matching goblet. To the left of the setting was a single shimmering sheet with writing on it—a menu.

The muted sounds of conversation and the continuing music seemed familiar, and yet unfamiliar, because Roget still understood few words and did not recognize any of the music. He was thankful that it was melodic and not driving.

Lyvia said nothing.

"You said that I was a friend," Roget finally spoke. "I'm glad you think of me in friendly terms."

"You haven't proved otherwise. I hope you don't."

"Courtesy as a conversion tool?"

"You're suggesting that Dubiety is an enemy of the Federation. Why? Have we done anything to harm you or the Federation? Besides leave the Federation behind more than a thousand years ago?"

Gently spoken as her words were, they brought Roget up sharply. "Are you? An enemy?"

"Have we sought you out? Attacked you? Sent agents down from warships to spy on your planets?"

"I wouldn't know," admitted Roget.

"We haven't, but I can't prove a negative." She smiled and picked up the menu. "We should order."

"Are you paying for this?"

"I'll be reimbursed. Have what you like. I imagine it's been some time since you had a truly fine dinner."

"That's true enough." He couldn't even remember when that might have been. He picked up the menu. He squinted, trying to decipher the words before he realized, belatedly, that the words were printed in old American script. While some of the spellings were unfamiliar, he could make out most of the fare descriptions. The entire menu was simple, listing four appetizers, three salads, two soups, and five entrees.

A young man appeared tableside, wearing the same type of striped singlesuit as the hostess had. "What would you like to drink?"

Roget actually understood the antique clipped words.

"I'll have an Espoiran red," Lyvia said.

"A pale lager, if you have it," Roget offered.

"Lager? Oh . . . pilsner. We have Cooran or Sanduk."

"The lighter one."

"Cooran." The server inclined his head. "Thank you." Then he was on his way toward the rear.

"You'll pick up the word patterns before long," said Lyvia.

"How did you learn Federation Stenglish?"

"I studied it, of course. It's broadcast all over the Galaxy."

Roget saw the server returning with a tray on which were a goblet and a chilled glass that looked like a cross between a tumbler and an overlarge champagne flute.

"Here you are, sera and ser."

"Thank you," replied Roget.

"Might I take your order?"

Roget ordered the Chicken Emorai, whatever that was, and a green salad with patacio nuts and a crumbled cheese. He thought Lyvia ordered some sort of beef in pastry.

Lyvia lifted her goblet. "To your enjoyment of dinner."

Roget inclined his head. "And to yours."

Her goblet held a pinkish vintage. Roget looked at it questioningly. "Red?"

"It tastes red, but there are some side effects of the shields, and we don't do artificial colorants in anything edible."

"How do the orbital shields work?"

"They deflect some solar radiation, transmit the majority, and reradiate the remainder. I don't know the physics behind their operation."

"Why are they there?"

"Dubiety is really too close to the sun. It was more like Venus until the terraforming."

"Ice asteroid and comet bombardment?"

"Among other techniques."

"Such as?" pressed Roget.

"High atmospheric bioengineering, nanitic heat dispersion . . . I don't know all of them."

"Why not just seek out a planet in a habitable zone?"

"At the time, that wasn't feasible."

"Why not?"

"There were traceability issues."

"From the Federation?"

"Who else?" She smiled wryly.

"We still found you."

"Much, much later, and that makes a difference."

"What sort of difference?"

A smile was the only answer he got.

"How long have the orbital shields been there?"

"Exactly . . ." she shrugged. "Today's date is 17 Maris 1811 P. D. That's 1,811 years since the first landing. The basic terraforming took something like two-thousand real-time years before that."

"Two thousand years before the landing eighteen hundred years ago, when you left the Federation less than two thousand years ago?"

"Give or take a hundred years."

Roget laughed. "That's quite a story."

"Time isn't what you think it is," Lyvia said mildly, stopping to take a sip of the pinkish wine.

There were two possibilities. Lyvia was lying. Or she was telling the truth. Roget didn't like either one. He didn't have any sense that she was lying. In fact, she seemed to be almost taunting him with the truth, but that could be because her lies were so outrageous. If she did happen to be telling the truth . . . then the Thomists possessed technology that posed an incredible threat to the Federation. But that raised yet another question— why hadn't they used it?

No human culture had ever failed to use superior force against a former enemy, if only as a coercive tool. But did the Dubietan technology provide enough of an edge against the obviously numerically greater Federation? When did numbers outweigh technology . . . or vice versa?

The entire restaurant seemed to swirl around Roget for a moment, but he knew that was just his own mind trying to deal with the surreality of the situation in which he found himself. He'd been dropped onto an unknown planet beneath a series of shields that were technically impossible, and he was having dinner in a fine restaurant, and he'd just been told that the culture had been founded some four thousand years before by refugees who had left the Federation barely less than two thousand years before.

The other possibility was that he was unconscious, and some alien intelligence was playing with his mind to such a degree that he just thought he was having dinner. That didn't make him feel any better because he was fully aware of the tastes, the smells, and the sounds. While Lyvia Rholyn was attractive to the eye and had a nice figure, she wasn't exactly his type. Any alien intelligence that could simulate all that and orbit a shield system in three layers was potentially deadly.

But . . . if it were that deadly . . . why bother to play with his mind at all?

He took a swallow of the Cooran.

The server reappeared with his salad and a thick creamlike soup for Lyvia.

Roget glanced out the window toward the square. A couple was walking toward them, and the woman had a leash in her hand. On the end of the leash was a small dog. Roget smiled. "That's the first dog I've seen."

"We had one when I was growing up."

Roget watched as the dog—seemingly a long-haired red dachshund, not short-haired and black and tan like Hildegarde or Muffin—made his way past Dorinique, almost strutting as he did. "Are pets less common?"

"Less common than what or where?" Lyvia raised her eyebrows.

Roget shrugged. "That's the only one I've seen." He took a bite of the salad, with a dark greenery that didn't taste that unfamiliar, for all its deep coloration. The nut fragments were good, but not a taste he recalled, and the cheese crumbles were similar to, but more tangy than, a blue cheese or gorgonzola.

Lyvia took several spoonfuls of her soup before replying. "They're expensive to license, and having one without a license can be a criminal offense."

"For a pet?"

"Animal companions require care, attention, and feeding. They can't speak for themselves, and that requires protection."

"I suppose you protect the wild animals as well."

"From people."

"What about food animals?"

"We don't have any, except for some chickens. All nonreplicated meat is tissue-cloned. It's less wasteful that way, and it's easier to balance the ecology."

"Oh . . ." The Federation had simply made natural meat horribly expensive. Most restaurants used high-level replicated protein.

"It also tastes better if it's cloned and grown properly, and uses less energy than replicator technology."

"I wouldn't think that energy was a problem for you."

For just an instant, a hint of surprise appeared in Lyvia's gray eyes. "Energy supply isn't the problem. Excessive use is. It disrupts the ecology and the climate. Any form of energy use creates heat somewhere along the line. Enough usage . . ." She shrugged.

Abruptly, Roget understood. "Dubiety's closeness to the sun."

"Exactly."

There was something there . . . but Roget couldn't quite grasp what it might be.

"How is your salad?"

"Quite good. Is it vat grown, too?"

"I wouldn't know. Some is free grown, and some is hydroponic. There are many mixed systems on Dubiety."

"As well as on other Thomist worlds?"

"You are persistent, you know?"

"That's what I'm here for."

"Leave those kinds of questions for tomorrow . . . if you can."

In the end, while he enjoyed the food and the company, he learned little more during the rest of dinner, except about the general geography and layout of Skeptos.

By the time Roget finished a small lemon tart, he was doing his best to stifle yawns and look attentive. Lyvia paid for the meal and ushered him back to the guest-house.

Once inside, she stopped at the reception area. "I'll pick you up for breakfast here at seven o'clock local. In case you oversleep, I'll have the comm buzz you a half hour before. After you eat, we'll head over to the MEC. You can bring the stunner you're carrying if it will make you feel better."

"You don't miss much."

"The idea is not to miss anything, Keir."

Roget smiled. That he understood, but he was so tired that he'd definitely missed more than he should have. "I'll see you in the morning."

She nodded, then turned and left.

Roget started up the ramp. Although he heard a door close on the second level, by the time he was at the top, the corridor was empty. He thought he could detect a faint fragrance, but that might have been his imagination. He paused. As he thought about it, Lyvia hadn't worn any noticeable fragrance or perfume, but he'd caught whiffs of scent from other women he'd passed. So it wasn't his sense of smell.

When he stopped outside his quarters, he had to think for a moment to recall his code before entering it. The door opened and he stepped inside, letting it close behind him. He studied the living area. Nothing looked any different. He walked into the bedchamber. The closet door was open. While they'd eaten, Roget's pale blue singlesuit and underclothes had been cleaned and hung in the closet, or folded and put on the open shelves on the right side, the one nearest the fresher. They also now held locators. Of that, he had no doubts.

He used his implants to trigger the camouflage, and the suit blended with the back of the closet. The power

readings registered full. He deactivated the camouflage.

After shaking his head, not sure he understood what
all that meant, he stood there for a long moment. There
wasn't any doubt that the Federation had set him up,
somehow, but for what? How could they not have known
a high-tech society existed beneath the Haze? Was he
just a probe to get a reaction? Or an excuse—when he
didn't return—for military action against Dubiety?

All he could do was play along and see what developed. He walked back to the living area and the corner
desk, retrieving the holojector controls and then picking
up the sheet of directions. He had to puzzle out the let-
ters, but those were mostly understandable, based on
old American, and that wasn't all that different from
Federation Stenglish.

So far as he could tell, the system offered access to
something like a hundred fixed program screens, plus
an ordering option that he couldn't use because he
didn't have a line of credit or system access or whatever.
He began to experiment but finally lowered the controls
in frustration.

For the most part, the characters in any of the dramas
or comedies, or whatever they were, talked too fast for
him to follow what they said. The news presentations
were somewhat better, but he lacked most of the local
referents for what he did understand to make much
sense. One "popular" science program dealt with
astronomy—and was far more clear . . . but told him
little. At first. Except that several of the images were of
the skies as they would have been seen from Dubiety—
and they were crystal clear. Were they a virtual creation, or did their technology allow them to see in or
around or through the orbital shields?

The holo projection was crisper than anything he'd

seen, even in Taiyuan. Yet his implants registered nothing. Could Lyvia have somehow disabled them? On an impulse, he walked into the projected image, and his detectors registered immediately. When he stepped out of the image, he could sense nothing.

How did they do it?

He collapsed the image and just sat down in the desk chair. Maybe if he got some sleep, things would make more sense in the morning. Maybe . . .

12

Roget's second week at the FSS continued just like the first had ended, except that the anomalies he investigated were all different—with one exception. The FSS system kept flagging the Virgin River anomaly. Roget had run a profile on the river readings going back a hundred years, and the thermal spike was well out of normal ranges. He'd taken more samples, and by Wednesday night he had located the general area of infusion as being close to where a dry rocky wash—Middleton wash—met the Virgin River.

According to the maps and history, the area to the north of Middleton wash had once been an intensely commercial shopping area. It had been partly slagged in the wars, then reclaimed and returned to something resembling the original topography, with several permitted low-impact exceptions. After more than a millennium, even in the desert climate, there were no overt signs of its ancient past. The wash itself had been dry on Wednesday. Roget still wondered if something buried beneath all that stone had come to life, if the natural geothermal systems had created a subterranean pathway down the wash, or if some other factor were involved. He couldn't help but wonder if it had anything to do with the death of his predecessor—whose body had been found on the other side of the Virgin River from the wash on the way to one of the cinder cones left from a prehistoric volcanic area.

Then, that could be coincidence, much as Roget didn't like to believe in or accept coincidences.

Thursday morning, Roget had his listing and schedule waiting for Sung.

The head monitor settled at the main screen, then spent almost ten minutes scanning various subscreens before turning his attention to Roget's proposed monitoring schedule. He finally turned. "Middleton wash? There's nothing there."

"There's nothing we can see, but that's where the thermal spike enters the river. I'd like to pin this down so that we can either find a human cause or identify it as natural with hard proof. I'm spending a lot of time checking that anomaly, and I don't want to still be doing it come summer."

Sung laughed. "All that exercise is good for you."

"It probably is. I just don't want it to be a waste of time."

"There's always something." The head monitor shook his head. "Go ahead. It can't hurt, and you're not swamped now."

"Thank you." Roget rose from his small console, turned, eased the bicycle away from the wall, and wheeled it toward the door. He'd given up on trying to check it in and out of supply and had signed it out for a month, leaving it in the corner of the office overnight.

The corridor outside was empty, although he half expected to run into Marni Sorensen, as he had several times over the last week. But then, that had usually been in the late afternoon when he'd just returned to the FSS building at the end of a long day, and they had never exchanged more than quick pleasantries.

Once past the building security gates and outside, he rode down to the main tram station where he waited a good fifteen minutes before the next tram arrived. After taking the tram out so far as the Red Hills station, the last stop before the final Green Springs station, Roget carried the bicycle from the tram and then unfolded it on the platform. He was the only one who got off. That was scarcely surprising since there were only a few houses on the east side of Red Cliffs Drive, and they were tiny and shabby, with the stucco more pink, from the years of bombardment by red sand, than white.

As was usual, the sky was clear, and the sun beat down on Roget as he pedaled less than a hundred meters northeast of the station. Once there, he discovered a narrow walking or biking trail running along the north side of the wash. He rode only a few meters down the trail before he dismounted and laid the bicycle at the side, then slowly clambered down over and between sandstone boulders and chunks of black lava. While he knew there were extensive lava beds in the area, the lava looked out of place along the wash, weathered as it appeared.

When he reached the bottom he surveyed the area, but all he saw was rock and red sand. He scuffed the sand with his boot heel, digging a small depression. He struck rock after some ten centimeters, and all the sand was dry. He walked downhill for another ten or fifteen meters and tried again, with the same result.

Climbing back uphill left him even hotter and sweatier, even with the cool-weave fabric of the white monitor's uniform. Before he raised the bike to resume riding, he blotted his forehead, then studied the north side of the wash. The red stone and sand looked as desolate as anywhere around and outside St. George proper.

After taking a swallow from his water bottle, he pedaled slowly and carefully down the trail for half a klick until he came to a side path leading uphill. He stopped. Less than fifty meters uphill on the winding path was a waist-high stone wall and an iron gate. Roget left the bicycle beside the trail and hiked up the path. As he neared the gate, he could see a long and low sandstone building farther uphill. The south-facing wall that extended from each side of the gate was of finished and polished black lava, so smooth that it looked like onyx, but the edges between the polished front and the mortar were rough and lavalike.

An iron sign on the gate read: DELBERT PARSENS, SCULPTOR. On the top of the posts on each side of the gate were figures sculpted out of hard red sandstone. On the left was a woman in a long flowing dress with an antique apron and wide collars, cradling an infant. On the right was a man in a waistcoat and trousers with his sleeves rolled up. The sculptures were so similar to the one on the stone pedestal outside The Right Place that Roget knew the same sculptor had to have done all three. Presumably, that was Parsens.

He opened the gate and stepped through the wall, then closed it behind him. He followed the path uphill. Even before he reached the building, Roget could hear the sound of a hammer and chisel echoing through the warm morning air. The path circled eastward around the low structure whose eaves were barely above Roget's head. The lower level looked to have been quarried out of the solid stone. At the east end of the building, at the top of three stone steps, he came to a doorway. A wooden sign in a niche cut out of the redstone wall to the left of the door announced: STUDIO OPEN. PLEASE COME IN.

Roget lifted the small sign and turned it over. The reverse read: STUDIO CLOSED. He replaced the sign as it had been. Then he looked to the north side of the building. A narrow road angled back toward Red Cliffs Drive.

The door squeaked as Roget pushed it open, but the sounds of hammer and chisel did not slow or stop. Once inside, he stood on a wide landing. In front of him was a ramp down to the long studio. A wiry blond man, stripped to the waist, looked up from the block of redstone, then lowered the hammer and chisel and waited.

Roget walked down the ramp.

"Do you want to commission something, or are you just looking?"

"Looking, I'm afraid. I didn't know your studio was even here."

"Even most folks in St. George don't know that, and my great uncle built it close to a hundred years ago." The clean-shaven sculptor's voice was soft. His blue eyes did not quite meet Roget's.

"I saw one of your statues somewhere . . . near the Prophet's house. At least, it looked like the ones on the gateposts."

"You must have seen the one outside The Right Place."

"You took this over from your great uncle?"

"His daughter Felicia. Been working here for twenty years or so since then."

"Where do you get the stone? Isn't it hard to come by?" Roget knew only a few quarries were permitted anywhere.

"I can cut stone on the east end of the property, and there's another quarry toward Silver Reef. Neither's the best, but I've got a limited permit here, and the Silver Reef quarry is one of the few permitted outside the protected and proscribed areas. I don't need many huge blanks. Most of the large blocks I do are for repairs and replacements, and those don't come along all that often these days. Once in a while I do a large sculpture, but mostly folks want smaller pieces."

"You do a fair number of . . . religious works." That was a calculated guess on Roget's part. "Are those mainly for local people?"

"Not necessarily local, but Saint-inspired," admitted Parsens.

"You were fortunate to be able to inherit this. I take it that you've made some improvements." Roget gestured at the heavily tinted windows on the south side of the studio.

"I've made some, but those windows were already here. Felicia was the one who really made the improvements." Parsens paused. "Could I interest you in one of the smaller pieces?" He gestured toward a glass-fronted case on the west end of the studio.

"You could interest me," Roget said, "but monitors get transferred a lot, and we don't get that big a weight allowance in moving. I tend to pick up projection print art. I did want to see your work, though." He nodded toward the roughed-out form beside the sculptor. "Might I ask?"

"It's a replica of an old work—John D. Lee. He was a rather controversial Saint during the founding period.

Not sure I would have chosen it, but," Parsens shrugged, "when it's a good commission, you do your best."

Roget could sense a certain unease, but not whether that was because of the subject of the commission or for other reasons. He didn't want to press. "I won't keep you, but I appreciate your time." He nodded, then turned and headed back up the stone ramp to the door.

As he walked back around to the path down to the wash trail, he studied the building closely. Although it wasn't obvious, there was a lower level, not under the studio, but under the western side. Yet it would have made more sense to have the lower level on the east where, with just a little work, obtaining natural light would have been easier.

Roget returned to the trail and his bicycle where he mounted and pedaled down along the wash, investigating the bottom at four other locations. All he found was dry sand and drier hard red sandstone. When he reached the Virgin River and the parkway, he took two measurements—one upstream of where Middleton wash joined the river, and one fifty meters downstream.

Then he went on to his other monitoring assignments. Again, he didn't get back to the FSS until after five. He wheeled the bike through the security gate and down the corridor to the office. He had to unlock the office and set the bicycle in a corner before he could unlock the system and upload his readings for the day.

The residential and commercial monitoring results were the usual mixture of false positives, probable mechanical failures, and carelessness. The thermal spike from the reading taken just downstream of Middleton wash was the most pronounced of any of the river readings taken over the past two weeks. The system offered a 64 percent probability that a geothermal plume of heated water was entering from beneath the stream bed, with a likely temperature of some thirty degrees, well above the river's twenty-degree norm.

A low-grade geothermal plume made perfect sense, since St. George was in fact situated in a geothermal basin. What bothered Roget was the lack of water anywhere else in the wash, and the fact that the plume appeared in midstream. Usually nature wasn't that tidy.

There wasn't anything that he could do about it, not yet. He'd talk it over with Sung in the morning. Even so, he had the feeling that Parsens had something to do with the situation. He finished up, including copying the data back to his own flash storage, then locked down the system.

A minute or so before quarter to six, he stepped out into the corridor . . . just in time to encounter Marni Sorensen again. The encounters couldn't have been coincidental.

"Good afternoon, Marni," said Roget.

"You did remember my name." Her smile was disarming.

"How could I forget when we keep meeting this way?"

"Oh . . . and do you have another way in mind?"

"We could try lunch some day . . . like tomorrow."

"You're never here."

"That's because I have no reason to be. If you give me a reason, I certainly will." He paused. "Lunch tomorrow?"

"I could do that."

"I'll meet you here."

She smiled. "I'll see you then, Keir." She stepped back into the office from which she had come. The door closed.

Roget nodded, then walked down the corridor to the security gate. She'd wanted him to initiate something.

The question was why, and he was afraid he knew, even if he couldn't prove it.

After he reached the apartment, he used his other personal monitor to run a search on Delbert Parsens. The results showed nothing out of the ordinary. That was what Roget had expected.

Then, to take his mind off Parsens and Marni, he transferred a copy of *Hildegarde in the Sunlight* to the image projector. It took almost a quarter hour before he decided on the right location and dimensions. He opted for a life-size image of Hildegarde. He knew it was an illusion, but the sunlight from the image seemed to spill into the apartment, and Hildegarde was better company than most as he ate his replicated dinner.

13

18 MARIS 1811 P. D.

Breakfast was in a small bistro around the corner from the guesthouse. Roget didn't see the name anywhere, and it wasn't on the menu. He wore the gray singlesuit, again with his heavy boots. He had French toast, strips of crispy bacon, orange slices, and a flavorful hot tea that any Sinese would have envied. Lyvia gave him a range of information about what was located where in Skeptos and little else. She wore a pale cranberry singlesuit with a deep gray sleeveless vest, one without the flashing light-threads, Roget noted. The faintest hint of a light fragrance drifted about her, but the scent was so light and fleeting that he'd never have noticed had he not been trying to detect it.

When they stepped out of the bistro, Roget was aware that the amber light filtering through the orbital shields seemed noticeably brighter than it had on previous days. "Variable star? Or variable shield translucency, for seasonal purposes?"

"Some of both," replied Lyvia.

"Did the original settlers know that?"

"They built the shield system with that in mind, I understand."

That was so like most of her answers, never quite complete or directly responding to his inquiries. Was that his problem in framing questions, her avoiding the thrust of his inquiries, or a little of both?

"We're headed back toward the central square. MEC is north of there," Lyvia said. "Just a few blocks."

As they walked northward, Roget could see a steady flow of pedestrians fanning out from the central square ahead of them. All sorts of differing clothes styles were present, from ancient ankle length skirts and long-sleeved blouses for women to shorts and formfitting shirts that left very little to the imagination. The same range was present on men, although Roget didn't see any togas or Mandarin-style robes, and more men seemed to opt for singlesuits, although the variety of colors and cuts, not to mention the light-threads, was considerable.

From the southwest corner of the square, Lyvia walked briskly past Dorinique.

"I see they're not open," said Roget.

"Just from noon to midnight. That's always bothered my cousin Clarya. She works nights, and she doesn't like starting out with a heavy meal. With her schedule, most days that's her only option if she wants to eat there. Besides, she says, who wants to spoil such exquisite—

and expensive—fare with the thought of work to follow?"

Roget laughed. He could understand that.

When they reached the northwest corner of the square,
Lyvia turned eastward until she reached the midpoint
of the square. There she gestured to her left at the wide
walkway north.

Roget had to take three quick steps to catch her, but
she did not say more until they reached the end of the
block.

"The building on the right holds the Ministry of
Transportation, and the one on the left is the Ministry
of Finance."

"Is your space force under transportation?" asked
Roget.

"Your question makes assumptions that I can't really
address."

"Can't or won't?"

"Does it really matter?"

"Not really," Roget admitted, keeping his voice
cheerful, although he couldn't help but feel frustrated.
He was in the middle of the capital city of a planet, and
for all the time he'd spent with Lyvia, he felt he didn't
know all that much more than he had a day earlier. That
wasn't entirely true, but it was definitely the way he felt.

As they neared the next corner where the walkways
intersected, Lyvia said, "The one on the left is the Ministry of Education and Culture."

The structure was a full five stories, a story above the
others around it. "What other ministries are in buildings that tall?" asked Roget.

"The Ministry of Science has about as much space,
and so does the Ministry of Environment."

"How many ministries are there?"

"That's it. We don't need any more. Some people think

that five is five too many. Probably most do, but that's just my opinion." Lyvia headed for the main entrance on the south side, pushed open the glass door, and walked into the entry hall. There were no guards—just a series of shimmering consoles as tall as a person, each set a good yard from the adjoining one. She stopped before the one on the right end.

"Lyvia Rholyn and Keir Roget. We have an appointment at eight thirty."

"Please enter your confirmation code."

Roget didn't see Lyvia do anything, but the console replied, "Please take ramp three to the third level. The door there will respond to your code. No other door will."

Roget accompanied Lyvia as she walked past the console toward the wall that held five doorways, each with a silver number above the stone square stone arch that held a shining steel door. The door slid open as they approached, then closed behind them. Illuminated as it was by amber piped light, the wide ramp with its gentle circular turns allowed them to ascend side by side.

At the third level, beside the door was a screen and keypad. Again, while Lyvia seemed to do nothing, and Roget's internals detected no energy flows, the door clicked, and she pushed it open. The two stepped out into a small reception area where several chairs were arranged in a semicircle that faced the wide window overlooking the east side of the building. The doors on both the south and north sides of the chamber were closed.

After a moment, Lyvia took one of the chairs in the middle and sat down. "It shouldn't be long."

Roget took the chair to her left. He grinned. "Even you organized Thomists make people wait."

"Not any longer than necessary." The words were in accented but clear Federation Stenglish. A tall sandy-haired woman stood in the now-open doorway on the south side of the chamber. She wore a silvery green single-suit with a dark green vest.

Roget stood. So did Lyvia.

"Agents Rholyn and Roget, this way, if you would."

Roget followed the two women along the corridor that slanted toward the middle of the building, past one closed door to the second door on the left, already open. The space held little more than a small circular wooden table, around which were four wooden armchairs. The window overlooked the north walkway from the central square.

The older woman closed the door and took the seat on the south side of the table.

Lyvia and Roget settled into the chairs facing her.

The woman looked directly at Roget. "I'm Selyni Hillis, and I'll be interviewing you for the Ministry of Education and Culture. This interview will be recorded."

"Interviewing? Education and Culture?" asked Roget.

"Why not an interrogation for a Ministry of Defense or War or a Dubietan Ministry of Security? Is that that you mean?" Hillis's laugh was surprisingly low and rough, yet not harsh. "Interview sounds so much better. Besides, interrogation implies either criminal behavior or a wartime situation, and to date, you've committed no crimes on Dubiety, and we're certainly not aware of a state of war. Should we be?"

"I'm not aware of any hostile action either undertaken or planned by the Federation," Roget replied.

"You'll pardon me if I don't find your words terribly reassuring," replied Hillis. "Your awareness is most likely ignorance. Not only does the Federation's left hand not know what the right is doing, but adjoining fingers are unaware of each other's actions."

"I can't help that. I only know what I know."

"What sort of ship dropped you?"

Roget shrugged. "A Federation ship."

Hillis shook her head. "You're not a green agent. You're probably an agent-captain or an agent-major. You know the class ship. So do we."

"Then you tell me," suggested Roget.

"A Federation light battlecruiser of the history class, most probably the *WuDing, MengTian,* or *DeGaulle.*"

Much as he had expected some accuracy, the identification of three cruisers of the same class brought Roget up sharply. Her response concerned Roget more than if Hillis had identified the *WuDing* directly. "Why do you even need to interview me? You know more about Federation naval vessels than I do, and you obviously trained Lyvia to deal with Federation scouts long before I even knew Dubiety existed."

"That may be, but what happens to you depends on you. That is, of course, true of all individuals in all situations." Hillis cleared her throat, gently. "When we learned that the Federation had located us, it seemed prudent to train a few individuals who would be able to make the first contact, as necessary."

"I only knew that Dubiety had been discovered just before I was dropped. You had to have known for years. How long have you known?"

"Two centuries or so."

Two centuries? "That seems unlikely as well as improbable. You knew the Federation had discovered you, and all you did was train people for contact?"

Hillis smiled. "I don't believe I ever said or intimated that."

"So you have a fleet hidden somewhere, ready to smash any Federation forces?"

"Such a fleet would be a terrible waste of energy and resources. We avoid that. We'd prefer just to be left alone. We're hoping you'll be as helpful as you can in assuring that outcome. It would certainly be best for all concerned."

"Why should I?"

"Look at it this way, Agent Roget. We knew that the Federation would attempt to insert an agent through the haze before finalizing its options. They operate according to well-laid plans, and they have for a millennium. We knew those agents would be predominantly male. Federation agents always are."

Roget frowned but did not speak.

"The Federation is a stable patriarchal culture. Techno-reinforced stability doesn't allow much change. It's the high-tech equivalent of the ancient water empires." Another smile followed.

"That suggests that the Federation has known about Dubiety for a time as well."

"That is highly likely, but I wouldn't claim to know what information is available to the Federation."

"You knew how the Federation would approach Dubiety."

"That was scarcely difficult. The Federation is predictable. We predicted five dropboats, and five were released. You can take my word for that or not."

Roget stiffened inside. "What about the other scouts?"

"We tracked five dropboats. One other made it through the shields. He's in Aithan. His landing site was somewhat more remote than yours. Sometime tomorrow morning, local time, he'll be interviewed, just as you are now."

"And I have your word for this? I can expect that,

sometime tomorrow, I'll be told that he's told you everything, and that there's no reason for me to withhold anything."

"That would certainly be your expectation. The conventional reasoning—and the Federation is nothing but conventional and oh-so-logical—is that we have no reason to keep you alive once you're no longer a source of information. Therefore, the less you tell us, the longer you have to live. If . . . if we were conventional, that might well be true."

"I'm glad to hear that you recognize that." Roget didn't bother to keep the irony out of his voice.

Abruptly, Hillis stood. "That's all for today. Lyvia will show you more of Skeptos and give you some more information on Dubiety."

Lyvia rose from the table, and after a moment so did Roget.

"So soon?" Almost before the words were out, Roget wished he hadn't said them.

"There's no point in continuing until you see more." Hillis nodded to Lyvia. "You can leave as you came in. Take him to the second level map room and then down to the new exhibit. Your codes will grant you both access."

Lyvia nodded.

Hillis smiled, then turned and left.

"What is her position?" asked Roget.

"Director of External Affairs."

"And what do those duties entail?"

"External Affairs. We need to go to the map room." Lyvia stepped away from the table and headed back up the corridor toward the reception area.

Roget could sense both displeasure and exasperation . . . and perhaps resignation. The thought of resignation bothered him.

From the reception area they descended one level. After passing through another door, another reception area, and then into a corridor that appeared identical to the one on the third level, they walked almost to the end, passing two men and a woman in singlesuits. All three nodded politely but did not address either Lyvia or Roget.

The map room appeared to be little more than a blank-walled, semicircular conference room with a table set forward of the flat rear wall and four chairs behind it. On the table was a small console roughly forty centimeters by twenty. Lyvia settled herself behind the console and touched it. The room darkened, and a map appeared on the circular wall.

Roget turned and began to study the map.

"This is the southern hemisphere, centered on the continent of Socrates," began Lyvia. "The area highlighted in the brighter golden light is the capital district . . . Skeptos in the center . . . to the left you can see the Machiavelli Peninsula." A point of light appeared. "That's about where you landed your dropboat and where I met you . . . there's Avespoir. . . . The next map is a topographic view of Socrates . . . next is Thula . . . northern hemisphere and farther to the west than Socrates . . . and to the east along the equator is the continent of Verite . . ."

"It's rather small."

"So is the truth."

Roget glanced sideways at Lyvia.

"Great illusions are always spun out of the smallest grains of truth," she said. "All empires and bureaucracies know that."

Roget continued to study the maps. From the planetary gravity—so close to T-norm as not to be that easily distinguishable, except at the end of a long day—and the maps, it appeared that Dubiety had slightly more land area than most Federation water-worlds and that it was older, with less tectonic activity and lower mountains and shallower seas.

After the maps came a series of real-time images of cities and towns. At least Lyvia assured him that they were real-time current images.

". . . Petra . . . in the hills of Cammora . . . Aknotan, overlooking Lake Theban . . . Solipsis . . . Zweifein . . . that's where Northern University is . . ."

Finally, the lighting came up, and the curved front wall blanked. Lyvia stood. "Now for the exhibit area."

"I can hardly wait." Roget's tone was ironic. "What exhibit are we going to view?"

"I'd rather not say."

"Whatever it is, you clearly want a reaction."

"Of course. We're providing you with information. It's only fair that you provide some for us."

"I'd be delighted."

Lyvia ignored his words and stepped from the map room and back out into the corridor.

Once more Roget accompanied Lyvia to the ramp, where they headed down, all the way to the level below the ground floor, although the ramp looked to descend two more levels below the one where they walked off. There was no reception area beyond the ramp door, just an antechamber with two corridors branching from it. Lyvia went right. They only walked ten meters before they reached another door, which opened as they approached.

Roget managed to keep abreast of Lyvia, even as he caught sight of his dropboat, or a remarkable reproduction. It sat on a low black dais in the middle of a large chamber.

Roget glanced around. He saw no obvious bay doors large enough to afford the dropboat passage. He also saw a simple placard in a stand before the dented and battered nose. He walked toward it and read:

Federation Dropboat [Model 3B, developed circa 6699 F. E. (1760 P. D.)] Used for dropping agents or couriers onto planetary surfaces in unfriendly locales or those without orbital elevators or normal orbital-attaining conveyances.

He turned to Lyvia. "How did you get it in here?"

"There are doors in the south wall, and the freight lifts are beyond that." She pointed her belt-tube, and the wall split and recessed on both sides, leaving a black-ness beyond.

Roget thought he could see two large tunnel mouths, both semicircles wide enough to encompass the drop-boat, before the wall resealed itself, leaving a seamless expanse. After a moment, he walked up onto the dais and stood next to the access hatch. He rapped on the hatch. The boat was solid, not a holo image as he had hoped. He touched it and used his internals to pulse the craft.

ID response accepted. Interrogative instructions?

"It's as you left it," Lyvia said from where she stood by the placard. "We did depower a few items. We pre-ferred that you not try anything suicidal. The self-destruct and control locks are inoperative."

Roget looked over the dropboat. It wasn't huge, but it still massed more than ten tonnes. The Thomists had located it, transported it something like two thousand klicks, if not more, in less than a local day, and casually deposited it in an "exhibit" area under the Ministry of

Education and Culture. Even if they had used air transport, that suggested, again, more than met the eye. Were his very perceptions being altered?

Why would any perception alteration even be necessary? Any human or alien culture that could do that would have no problem infiltrating and destroying the Federation from within. Or, at the very least, destroying all information on Haze/Dubiety within the Federation archives.

Finally, he stepped away from the dropboat. He smiled politely at Lyvia. "Where do we go from here?"

"I thought you might like to see the subtrans control center."

Roget stepped off the dais. "Lead on."

14

24 LIANYU 6744 F. E.

On Friday, Roget spent the morning walking around the center of St. George doing spot monitoring, something he was supposed to do at random at least twice a week. This was the first time he'd managed it since he'd begun the job.

Just before noon, he walked up past the tram station, checking the time. He was earlier than he'd thought. Instead of waiting around the monitoring office until he went to meet Marni, and getting trapped by Sung, or fielding the chief monitor's questions, he crossed the boulevard and then Main Street to get to the east side of

History Square. Glen-David's was open, and he stepped inside.

"Good day, sir," said a young woman.

"And to you." Roget didn't see the older proprietor.

"Can I help you with anything?"

"No, thank you." Roget smiled and moved toward the paintings and the few multis hung on the north wall. He kept looking, but the dachshund painting wasn't there. Finally, he walked back to the young woman. "There was an oil of a dachshund . . ."

"Oh . . . that." The woman looked embarrassed. "That was a terrible mistake. Someone bought an image, and Father almost sold him the original. They didn't realize . . ."

"An old master? Held in the family, and the heirs didn't realize it?" asked Roget.

"Not a master, but very valuable. The appraisal came back at over a hundred thousand yuan."

"It was a good painting." Roget grinned. "I bought the image."

"You're fortunate. It's never been made public. It dates back to before the wars."

"It's that old?"

"It was nanocoated less than a century after it was painted, Father thinks." She cleared her throat. "The owners would appreciate it if you held the image privately."

That suggested the painting was worth more than the appraisal, possibly far more, but Roget hadn't bought the image for gain, nor would he have bought the original for that reason. Because the image wouldn't ever have that much value, he did wonder why they wanted it held privately . . . unless ownership of the painting was in doubt. That wasn't his problem, and he certainly had no way of pursuing it, nor any interest in doing so. He just liked the image. "That shouldn't be a problem. I bought it for myself."

"Thank you, sir."

Roget couldn't help but smile as he left. He'd had better taste than he'd known.

He reached the door to the accounting office at one minute before noon.

Marni Sorensen stepped outside before he could open the door. She wore a long pale blue skirt and a deeper blue, short-sleeved, round-collared shirt. "You are punctual."

Roget inclined his head. "When I have a reason. You're a very good reason."

"You're also gallant."

"Shouldn't all men be? Shouldn't all women be charming?"

"The first perhaps. The second . . . I'll reserve my options there." She laughed.

"We do need to eat. Where would you recommend?" asked Roget.

"Have you been to the Lee House?"

Roget recalled seeing it, but it had looked less than promising. "No. I tried Lupe's, but my mouth burned all afternoon. I've been to the Caravansary and the Frontier Fort."

"They're small-town attempts at city cuisine. Do you want to try the Lee House? It's not far, and the food is better than the ambiance."

Ambiance? An unusual word for a small-town girl, except she was more than that. "I'll take your word for it." Roget smiled.

They walked side by side down the corridor, through the security gate, and out into an almost comfortable midday. High hazy clouds muted the desert sun as they started down 200 East.

"How was your morning?" asked Roget.

"The same as every other morning. Check yesterday's entries. Run projections against expenditures. Cross-check problem areas." Marni shrugged.

"You make it sound so fascinating." Roget kept the irony in his words light.

"I'm not interested in fascinating. Neither is the regional comptroller. Fascinating would mean some sort of budgeting disaster. What about your morning?"

"The monitoring equivalent of yours. Check the anomaly list. Work out the schedule. Then go out and do the random spot-monitoring so that I can have lunch with someone before I go out and take more readings in the afternoon to check the possible anomalies. Most of the anomalies will be either one-time ambient spikes or the results of mechanical failures that people haven't yet noticed, and they'll be upset when they discover the costs of deferring maintenance or overworking underengineered equipment."

"That's because equipment and energy are so expensive here. People try to get by on as little as possible."

"They could add soltaic cells."

She raised her eyebrows. "They're expensive. What good is all this sunshine if you can't afford soltaic panels? Most of the smaller businesses are stretched thin as it is. The panels are just too expensive, and they have to be replaced."

"Not that often."

"Any replacement is too often in a small town, and parts are sometimes as expensive as the original panel."

"That's because of the environmental costs of manufacture," Roget pointed out.

"Then why are the panels cheaper in Fort Greeley, Helena, or Colorado Springs? Or even in Topeka?"

"Transportation costs, I imagine."

She laughed. "You have an answer for everything."

The answer that Roget hadn't given, and that Marni hadn't voiced, was that the Federation made living in smaller and environmentally fragile communities almost prohibitively expensive, as well as uncomfortable. That was an understandable reaction to the excesses that had preceded the Wars of Confederation.

When they reached the John D. Lee House, Roget opened the door and held it for Marni before following her inside. The café was as unprepossessing as Roget recalled. An old battered wooden door with tinted windows so old that they were barely translucent was framed by two far wider windows that functioned better as mirrors. The entire café was no more than eight meters wide, with two lines of tables alternating with booths running back some ten meters. In a small open space in front of the door was a dark wooden stand. Both tables and booths were bare dark wood—or synthwood—covered with a hard transparent finish that revealed all the abuses the wood had taken over the years. Almost half the tables were taken, mostly by men, but there were several mixed groups, and even one table with three women.

"We just sit at any table that's vacant and set," Marni murmured, leading the way to the left and to a narrow wooden booth that could barely accommodate two, one on each side.

Roget gestured for her to take the front seat. That would allow him to watch whoever came in . . . or left.

Once he was seated, he looked around the booth, then saw the two menus—film-covered paper with a simple listing. He handed one to Marni.

"Thank you, kind sir." She barely glanced at it before saying, "I think I know what I want."

"You've been here often."

"There isn't that much choice in St. George, and it is

close to work and not too expensive. I don't come that often."

Roget smiled, then studied the menu, finally deciding on Southwestern chicken with Mex-rice.

An older woman in a long skirt and a short-sleeved gray blouse appeared. Her gray eyes were as washed-out as the blouse. "What'll you be having, Marni dear?"

"The Dutch-oven beef and potatoes. Lots of sauce. Water."

"You, sir?"

"Southwestern chicken and the Wasatch lager."

"Be right out." The woman stepped away, neither rushing nor dawdling toward the serving window at the back of the café.

After a moment, Marni said, "I sometimes have the chicken. It's not bad for a change."

Roget looked across the shiny but battered wood booth table at Marni. "You seem rather overqualified to be a finance clerk."

"It's about the best a university biology grad can get in St. George. You might notice that jobs aren't exactly plentiful here. I thought about trying to become a monitor, but I wasn't that interested in the kind of science you need to know."

"The kind of science? That's an odd way of putting it." Even as he said that, Roget wondered why she hadn't mentioned her advanced degrees.

"The kind of science that is as much environmental propaganda as science."

"The Federation does have a certain bias against excessive consumption."

"Only in Noram and Sudam . . . and Europe, what of it that's still livable. I've seen the holos and the figures for the Sinese sector. They aren't stinting in Taiyuan or Peiping or . . . lots of places."

Roget didn't point out that losers didn't often get to be choosers. "They're always looking for finance types. You could go there."

She shook her head. "My family's here. Besides, it wouldn't be the same." She paused. "Have you been there?"

"For training courses." That was understating matters, but true. "It's not bad. Different. Expensive on a monitor's pay. Very expensive."

"I don't see how you could stand it, having to spend so much, and especially being so close to so many people . . ." She shuddered.

"There's more privacy than you'd think. Most people just aren't interested in others. We'd like to think so, because we want to believe we matter to others."

"That's why I like it here. People share so much, and they do care."

"You're fortunate." Roget glanced around the café. "Who was John D. Lee?"

"He was an early pioneer."

"I never heard of him." Not before Del Parsens had mentioned Lee, anyway.

"That's not surprising. He was tried for murder after he led a troop against early U.S. government infiltrators posing as settlers passing through. He was executed because he was Brigham Young's adopted son, and the U.S. feds wanted to make an example out of him when they couldn't get to the Prophet."

"Oh." While he didn't know the history of the area in that kind of depth, Roget had some doubts. "An early Saint martyr."

"Of sorts."

At that moment, the serving woman returned with two plates, setting one before each of them and then returning with two glasses, one filled with water without ice and one empty and with an amber container. "There you go."

The lager was cold; the glass was cool, but not chilled. Roget poured the pale amber liquid into it but did not drink, waiting for Marni to sip her water or take a bite of her food.

She sipped the water first, then began to cut the beef, covered with a reddish-brown sauce. "I wonder if grass-fed meat tasted that different."

Roget shrugged. "Supposedly, high-end replicated beef is no different." He cut a thin slice of the chicken and then ate it, finding it moist and tangy.

"How would we know? There are only the control herds anymore."

"Maybe that's why I prefer chicken. It makes more sense to grow it than replicate it."

"How do you like it here?"

"It's better than the Fort," he said.

She nodded emphatically. "The Caravansary isn't bad, but you pay less here. You might try Vhasila's some time, too."

"What kind of food do they serve?"

"Old Mediterranean."

Roget took a swallow of the lager, then concentrated on his meal. He enjoyed the rice even more than the chicken and did not speak for a time. The lager was surprisingly good. He'd have to remember the brand, except it would doubtless be prohibitively expensive outside the region.

As he finished the last bits of rice and chicken, at the *clank* of crockery clashing, Roget glanced toward the rear of the café. There, a heavyset young man was clearing dishes from a table.

"Ernest isn't always as coordinated as he should be," observed Marni.

"Do you know everyone in town?"

"Most people do, after a while."

"Where else would be a good place to eat?"

She frowned, thinking, before replying, "I told you about Vhasila's, and the Desert Grille is good if you don't want another replicated breakfast."

The busboy stumbled, and the dish tub he carried jolted into Roget's shoulder.

"Sir . . . I'm sorry . . ."

Roget blinked. For a moment everything went black.

Then he was sitting at the table, as if nothing had happened.

"Keir . . . are you all right?" Marni's voice was urgent. "You looked so strange for a moment."

"I'm so sorry, sir," repeated Ernest.

"I'm fine," Roget said. He wasn't sure he was. His internal monitors indicated that he'd lost a full minute of consciousness, but there were no recognized toxins in his system. Not yet. He'd known Marni wasn't trustworthy, but he hadn't expected her to attack or do whatever in a public restaurant in the middle of the day. Still, he seemed to be all right. So far. Did he accuse her? He almost smiled. Of what? Even as a security agent he had to have *some* proof.

He took another swallow of the lager.

"You looked dizzy there for a moment," Marni said, guilelessly.

"I was. It could be that I got dehydrated."

"That can happen. Every so often, visitors wander out into the hills and die because they don't bring enough water."

"I'll remember that," he said dryly. Then he finished the last swallow of the lager. "I suppose we need to return to our various routines."

"That might be best. Adabelle will be getting nervous."

"Your superior?"

"She's been here forever. You hang on to good jobs here." Marni nodded toward the front of the café. "We pay at the stand."

Roget rose, checking his internal monitors again. Nothing. As he followed Marni toward the front of the café, their server hurried to the wooden stand.

"For both," Roget told the woman who had served them, "and 15 percent."

"Yes, sir."

Roget extended his CredID, checked the total appearing on the small screen, then thumbed the scanner.

Once they were outside, walking north on 200 East, Marni said, "You didn't have to pay, but thank you."

"You're welcome." Roget smiled. Paying for being attacked was something that hadn't happened before. He had the feeling it might not be the last time, assuming he survived. He was getting worried. Why didn't his system show whatever they'd done to him? What had they done? They couldn't have brain scanned him, not in a minute and without equipment.

"How long have you been working at the FSS?" he asked.

"Eight years."

"Do you think you'll stay?"

"With what else is available here, where else would I go?"

Roget nodded, although he sensed a certain falsity behind her words.

"What about you?"

"They don't like monitors to stay in one place too long." Nor security agents. "We're not supposed to get too close to too many people, and it's hard not to in places like St. George. In the cities . . ." He shrugged, noting a faint twinge in his upper right arm. Should he go to the local med-centre? He almost shook his head. His internals were better than the local diagnostics. They'd find nothing.

Neither spoke as they crossed St. George Boulevard.

When they finally reached the FSS building and the door to the accounting office, he stopped and smiled. "You're a very surprising woman."

"Any woman can be," she demurred.

"We'll have to have lunch again. It will be my choice."

"It's always the man's choice in the end," she replied lightly.

"That's what all women say."

"What else could we say?" She paused, then added, "I need to get back to work." She slipped into the accounting office.

Roget returned to the monitoring office, sitting down at his own console. He checked his internals again. So far, so good, but there was always the possibility of something delayed, and he needed to take care of that. He created a brief report on his personal monitor, including Marni Sorensen and the restaurant incident, then encrypted and burst sent it to his controller.

He hoped nothing would happen, but if it did . . . someone needed to know, and a report before something like a poisoning was a form of proof he hoped the Federation didn't need to follow up on. Then he stood and reclaimed the bicycle.

"Where are you off to now?" asked Sung.

"Another river reading. Then I'll check on the repair shop over on South Bluff."

"You're wasting your time on the river. It's got to be geothermal."

"I'm taking full water chem readings this time. That should tell me. Then I can compare them to the geothermal composition. If they come close to matching, you'll be right." He wheeled the bike out of the office and down the corridor.

From the FSS building he rode down to the tram station, where he folded the bike, boarded the tram, and rode out to the Red Cliffs station. Then he rode to the Middleton wash path and down it to the parkway, where he got off the bike and walked down to the river.

Roget took out the monitor, then flicked the sampler fiberline across the water, letting it sink and ride some before reeling it in.

After making sure that he had the data, he walked downstream to where there was a narrow footbridge over the river. He crossed and walked back upstream, but stopped short of a point opposite where he'd taken the first sample. He repeated the process, then reeled in the line and slipped the monitor back into its belt case.

He almost reached the bridge when a wave of dizziness washed over him. He staggered to the bridge and grasped the railing, steadying himself.

Then the blackness rose, blotting out everything.

15

Once they left the Ministry of Education and Culture, Lyvia walked straight toward the central square of Skeptos, striding past the building she had said housed the Ministry of Transportation.

"We're not going there?" asked Roget. "Isn't that the Transport Ministry?"

"No. That's just offices and the few administrators necessary to keep track of matters. You won't see anything useful there. We're going to the central subtrans center for all of Socrates. I would assume that you're interested in the technology and operation of our transport system."

"You assume correctly." As the amber outside light flickered slightly, Roget glanced skyward, but there were no clouds and no aircraft visible beneath the omnipresent gray haze, not that he expected aircraft any longer. "Do all towns and cities have access to subtrans?"

"Towns, cities, and villages. Either to a local system or a regional system, depending on a number of factors."

"Such as?"

"Distance and imputed total costs, for starters."

"What if the costs will always be prohibitive?"

"Then . . . there's no town, unless it's a protected recreational area like the Machiavelli Peninsula. The costs there are paid by taxes levied as a benefit on all inhabitants."

"Just like that?"

"No. The House of Tribunes had to approve it, as did the House of Denial."

"With a House of Denial, I'm surprised anything gets funded."

"Many things don't, but the worthwhile ones do, sooner or later. We don't exempt politicians from the libel, slander, and misrepresentation laws. In fact, the penalties are higher for them."

"And people run for office?" Roget's words came out sardonically.

"A different kind of people."

Were people really that different? Again, Roget had his doubts.

When they reached the walkway that ran along the northern edge of the square, Lyvia turned eastward. At the next corner she turned south. Before long, the two were descending the ramp down to the subtrans concourses.

Roget wondered where they were headed, because the tunnel was clearly leading down to the subtrans concourses, and he didn't see any other tunnels, and he didn't recall seeing any on the way into Skeptos. He assumed that there must be an entrance to wherever they were headed somewhere off the concourses. Instead, Lyvia walked to the side of the tunnel just short of the point where the larger tunnel for the local access joined the regional tunnel. There, she came to a halt. The section of one of the curved side panels where she stood looked slightly different to Roget, although he could have sworn it hadn't a moment before. As he approached, an oval area glowed, then slid aside.

"Come on," said Lyvia.

Roget stepped through the doorway with her, noting that almost no one looked in their direction. The metal sections closed, leaving them within a niche no more than three meters by two. After a moment, the back of the niche, also metallic composite, opened.

A muscular blocky man stood in the short arched tunnel, waiting for them, but how he had known when exactly to expect them, Roget didn't know, except that it had to be something Lyvia had done, even though he had sensed absolutely no communications and no energy flows.

The stocky man wore a singlesuit of royal blue, without a vest, and his dark hair was less than a centimeter long. "Welcome to the subtrans operations center, Agents Rholyn and Roget. I'm Tee Tayler. Please follow me." Although his words were heavily accented, Roget could understand them.

Less than thirty meters along the tunnel, Tayler turned through an archway on the left and led them into a chamber some ten meters wide and five deep. The only other person in the space was a woman seated behind a console set some three meters back from the wall—on which was displayed a floor-to-ceiling projected image.

Their escort gestured to the wall screen. "This provides an overview of the Socrates continental system, as well as the deep-tubes to Thula and to Patagonn."

Deep-tubes? Roget stepped closer. The map represented the continent. From what he could tell, there were three separate systems. The red lines represented local subtransit; the blue ones regional links; and the dark green ones the deep-tubes under the oceans. He mentally calculated. Assuming the map was to scale, Socrates was over nine thousand klicks from east to west at its greatest distance, and a good four from south to north.

"How much of the southern peninsula is ice-covered?"

"None of it," replied Lyvia. "Because of the shields, we get more even heat and light diffusion, and Dubiety's axial tilt is only about seven degrees."

"I know it's not transit, but . . . ocean stagnation?"

"We're closer to the sun, and the oceans are shallower," said Lyvia. "That provides more solar tidal movement than one might otherwise expect."

"But not enough for life to evolve originally."

"Life evolves everywhere that there's water or something that fulfills that function. It may or may not be large or intelligent . . . or it may be surprising." She pointed to the wallscreen. "Questions?"

Roget turned to the blocky man. "You have to be maintaining a vacuum in the tube tunnels." There was no other way that the subtrans could reach the velocities that Roget had calculated without a buildup of air that would stall or halt a high-speed tube train.

"Precisely. There is a slight leakage when the car doors open at each station, but we use that to cushion the stops."

"How?" asked Roget. "The tunnels look to be open."

"We create partial deceleration shields as the subtrans nears a station. They're an adaptation of space shields. After all, we're in a vacuum in both places. The stray atmosphere builds up against the shield, and we use the decel pressure to force the air through filters as a boost to the ventilation in the stations."

"What's the propulsion system?"

"Oh . . . it's just a grav-twist system set into a maglev, shield-contained, bottle effect."

"How do you manage to work that in a planetary gravity well?"

"That's why we have a completely integrated system," said Tayler. "It's actually locked into the planetary mass distribution."

Roget didn't see how that was possible, but then his physics background was fairly basic. Once more he was faced with the fact that the Thomists were doing something that the Federation either couldn't or hadn't. Whether they were doing it in the way they claimed or otherwise didn't make much difference from a practical point of view. They had subsurface transport as swift as most planetary air travel, and if one considered other factors, probably as fast, if not faster, in point-to-point passenger and freight delivery as any powered orbital or suborbital craft could manage. As deep as the tunnels were, they would be difficult to block or destroy with any normal weapons.

"What's the system capacity?"

"We can transit up to six cars in a given subtrans train. That's based on the size of the concourses, not on the system itself. We could easily run trains with twelve cars in an emergency, but it would take two stops at each destination to get the passengers or cargo out. Each local car will hold forty-two seated passengers with room for another twenty-eight without freight or crowding. So . . . say 350 a train. The regional and deep-tube cars are configured for thirty-two passengers, and two cars on each run are usually reserved for freight, except on holidays when we may only run one freighter. We also run six-car freight runs on off-times, and the system is designed so that we can run them to special freight concourses. Those are the green triangles on the system map."

"No separate freight system, then?"

"What would be the purpose? To waste resources?" asked Tayler, not quite scornfully.

"Are all the lines dual tube?"

"Yes." Tayler gestured to the system overview. "Also . . . you can see that every major city or large town can be reached from at least two other points on the system through redundant lines."

"That's quite an engineering feat." And a substantial resource commitment, noted Roget.

"It makes sense," Lyvia pointed out. "We don't worry about weather. The ecological effects are minimal, especially compared to the alternatives, and the materials used are impervious to just about anything. That doesn't count the shielding effect of the ground itself, and that's considerable, given the depth of the lines."

Lyvia was just confirming that the transit system could operate unhampered even under full-scale attack.

Abruptly, Tayler turned and walked toward the woman at the console.

Roget listened, although he couldn't catch every word of the low-voiced conversation in what seemed to be, he now recognized, a clipped and faster version of old American.

". . . car three on Principia alpha . . . field strength fluctuations . . . decel . . ."

". . . personnel at Matera . . . empty . . . run as a fiver . . . have Falcon station bring up a replacement . . ."

The woman nodded and Tayler returned. "Equipment replacement. Do you have any other questions?"

"What's the empty weight of a car?"

"Passenger cars are . . . roughly fifteen tonnes. A full freight car is three times that in length and weight. There are special cars that can carry three times the mass of a standard freighter."

"What's the mass the freight cars can carry . . ."

"How long is a car's service life . . ."

"What's the materials composition . . ."

Roget fired off as many questions as he could think of, and for close to a standard hour Tayler answered most of them.

Finally, Roget shrugged. "I think you've addressed everything I can think of."

Tayler smiled. "It's fair to say that I haven't had to recall so much in years. I'm surprised I remembered so much."

"Thank you." Roget inclined his head.

"I'll escort you out."

Despite Tayler's words, Lyvia and Roget walked back along the tunnel, followed by Tayler.

Once they were back in the subtrans tunnel, Lyvia turned to Roget. "Are you ready for something to eat?"

"That would be good." He wasn't particularly hungry, and that might have been because his system was anything but used to a twenty-two-hour day. He did want a chance to sit down and talk. "You pick the place."

Less than fifteen minutes later, they were seated in a small establishment off a walkway running north and south two blocks east of the central square. The decor inside Lucasan wasn't anything that Roget had ever seen. On the wall opposite their table were two crossed sabers, but their blades were not metal but shafts of light, one bluish white and one a sullen red. Occasionally, a burst of static issued from one saber or the other. Set on a pedestal between their table and the next was a cylinder set at a slight angle on tracked wheels with a domed top, its metallic finish in silver and blue.

Roget glanced toward the sabers.

"Nostalgia for a time that never was in a galaxy far, far away." Lyvia laughed softly. "At least we're honest about our nostalgia."

Roget didn't pretend to understand and picked up a menu, looking over the short list of unfamiliar names. At least written Dubietan was far easier to puzzle through than the spoken version.

"What do you suggest?" he finally asked.

"The Crepes Jedi are good. So is the Filet Leia."

In the end, Roget settled on Veal Mos Eisley, which seemed to have an interesting conglomeration of spices, and an amber Yoda Lager.

A server arrived, wearing an ancient and severe black and gray uniform of a type Roget had never seen, took their order, and returned almost immediately with their drinks.

Lyvia took a sip of something vaguely ruby in shade, before asking, "Why do you think you were chosen for this mission?"

Roget knew her words weren't as casual as their tone suggested. "I could guess, but I couldn't say that I really knew."

"It might be wise to guess." The faint and almost sad smile indicated her words were a suggestion and not a threat.

"I've had a fairly wide range of experience, both on- and off-planet, and in- and outsystem." He couldn't help but think about the hack/razor job required in his assignment on Khriastos station, which had amounted to being a cyber thief reinserting data deleted from the station's archives so that the Federation Finance Monitors could find it.

"What else?"

"What are you suggesting?" countered Roget.

"What is the cultural background of the average Federation Security Agent?"

"Our backgrounds vary." Even as he spoke, Roget saw where she was pointing him. "You're suggesting that . . . FSA Operations knew Dubiety had an AmerAnglo cultural foundation."

"Don't they send you where you'll fit in?"

"Or where we'll fit a role." Roget thought back to his mission in Taiyuan, where only an AmerAnglo would be considered "degraded" enough to deal in grayware. So degraded that no one had any problems with Sulynn's trying to kill him once she'd gotten what she wanted. Had that all been a setup for her next assignment? Roget wouldn't have been surprised.

"Ethnic stereotyping. A pity it hasn't gone away."

"You don't have to worry about that. From what I can see, everyone here is AmerAnglo descended."

"Not really. Everyone's light skinned, but that was a necessity. Otherwise, the genetics vary widely."

"The shields? Vitamin D?"

"Precisely."

The server returned with Roget's Veal Mos Eisley and Lyvia's Crepes Jedi, each accompanied by a small side salad of mixed greens, except that the greens—again—were almost blackish green. He took a small bite, but he didn't notice any great difference in taste from the "greener" salads he'd had on earth.

As they ate, Roget listened to the conversations around them. He was beginning to be able to catch words and phrases, but the total meaning of most exchanges eluded him.

"You'll pick it up." Lyvia finished the last sip of her drink. "What else would you like to see this afternoon?"

"What about the local spaceport . . . or orbital shuttle system?"

Lyvia smiled. "We can't. We don't have anything like that."

He didn't believe that, but there was no point in protesting. "All right. What about a manufacturing facility? Or a composite formulation mill? Surely you don't replicate everything, not as concerned as you all seem to be about the environmental costs."

After a moment, Lyvia nodded. "We can manage

that. Both, in fact. We'll start with the composite facility." She paused. "Are you done? Or would you like dessert?"

"I'm fine." Roget glanced around.

"I've already paid."

"Direct link?"

"Yes." Lyvia stood.

Roget did as well. "How do you manage that?"

"You mean, without stray radiation that your implants can detect? It's a very tight beam, a form of coherence that classical physicists said was impossible. Our scientists have been very good at doubting pronouncements of impossibility."

"Your whole society is impossible," he said with a laugh as they walked out of Lucasan.

"Magic is impossible, too, but an old Anglo scientist—I think he was a scientist, but maybe he was a writer— said that any sufficiently advanced science is indistinguishable from magic."

"How does this coherence work?" When Lyvia didn't answer and continued walking westward toward the central square, he added, "I know. It's not your field, and you don't intend to give me a simplistic and misleading reply."

"Exactly."

"I could use a few simplistic but misleading answers."

"You only think you could."

"Where are we going now?"

"We'll take the local subtrans south three stops to Coventral."

After they reached the southeast corner of the square, Roget was surprised at how long it took them to get down to the local concourse. Unlike the regional concourse, the local concourse was shaped like an L, with the north-south section a good fifteen meters below the east-west section and joined by another tunnel ramp. As far as appointments went, both sections of the local concourse looked almost the same in layout as did the regional one. When they stopped before an archway, waiting for a train, he asked, "Why are the local concourses so deep?"

"They all aren't, but it makes a certain sense here in Skeptos. That's because we get more regional travelers, and if they have luggage, it's easier for them. Also, it puts the local concourses on the same absolute level."

The concourse door opened, and Lyvia waited for a man and two women to leave before stepping through the archway. The local subtrans train had cars that looked to be the same dimensions as the regional subtrans, but the seats, if made of the same material, were slightly smaller and definitely closer together.

Since the car wasn't crowded, Roget sat across from Lyvia. "What about the agent on the other side of the world?"

"I haven't heard anything. I wouldn't. Not for a while. I'm assigned to you."

"What have you learned from me?"

"You're comparatively perceptive and well-integrated with your internal monitors and sensors." Lyvia's voice was low, barely carrying to Roget. "You represent a dangerous but passively aggressive culture that is looking for an excuse that will allow itself to justify an attack against Dubiety on almost any grounds. You're not entirely in sympathy with your own culture's objectives, and you were sent on this mission because your superiors feel that you need to understand the danger we represent and because if you don't return, the difficulty posed by the combination of your abilities and attitude will be resolved. If you do return, they will find some way to discredit or retire you. Or they might promote you to a comfortable but meaningless and powerless position."

"You're so encouraging."

"You asked." Lyvia glanced toward the doors as the train came to a stop.

One woman who had been sitting at the end of the car left. No one entered.

Neither Lyvia nor Roget spoke again until the train made the third stop.

"This is where we leave," said Lyvia.

Roget followed her out onto a nearly empty concourse and then up a tunnel ramp. About fifty meters up the ramp, the tunnel split, with a maroon tunnel curving to the left away from the standard gray and green tunnel. Lyvia took the maroon tunnel, and Roget kept pace with her. None of the half-dozen other passengers followed them.

"There aren't any signs or indications," Roget said.

"Haven't you noticed? We don't use them, except for places like restaurants in public spaces."

Roget hadn't, but as he thought about it, he realized that he hadn't seen any, except for the restaurants around the main square of Skeptos, and not even all of those had borne signs.

"Anyone who's linked to the commnet can find out where they want to go," Lyvia continued. "Posting signage is another waste of resources."

"I suppose everyone is linked."

"All except very young children and those few who have proven untrustworthy."

"And foreign agents."

"You're presumed untrustworthy. I don't think that's an unfair presumption, do you?" She smiled as she spoke.

"No. I can't dispute that."

After a less than ninety degree turn, the tunnel straightened, stretching ahead for what looked to be a good quarter klick.

"Do you people walk everywhere that the subtrans doesn't go?"

"Yes, except for people who are temporarily disabled. They can use individual powerchairs."

Before long, Roget saw an archway on the right side of the tunnel. As they walked nearer, a couple appeared and walked toward them at a good clip. They smiled and nodded as they passed. Roget returned the smile. "Are we taking the archway?"

"Yes. That's the entrance to CPInd."

Beyond the archway, outlined in maroon, was a narrower corridor that ended after twenty-odd meters at a shimmering metal composite door. Lyvia pointed her belt-tube. After a moment, the door split into two halves, each retracting into the wall. As soon as they were inside the squarish and empty chamber, the doors closed behind them.

Before Roget could say more, a door to his left opened, and a tall woman in a flowing red skirt and a skin-tight, black, short-sleeved top stepped through.

The angular woman studied Roget, then turned to Lyvia and spoke. "There isn't that much to see. The constitutors are sealed processors."

That was what Roget thought she said.

"He'll get an idea." Lyvia turned to him. "Did you understand her?"

"Something about not seeing much because the units are sealed?"

"Good. I told you it wouldn't take long."

Something about her tone bothered Roget, but he couldn't have said why.

They followed their guide down another ramp and out into a massive enclosed space, one large enough to hold several attack corvettes, Roget suspected. The constitutors, if that happened to be what they were, were shaped like rough half cylinders with annular rings set at unequal intervals, and with various large protuberances in other places. Each rose a good twenty meters above the floor and looked to be fifteen meters wide and a good hundred meters long. There were five, set side by side, with ten meters between each. At the far end of the chamber at the output end of each cylinder was a maglev freight car, one end opened and swung up. Two men guided the sheets of composite into the car.

Roget walked slowly along the side of the constitutor. Again, he could sense no energy emissions. Nor did he feel any heat radiating from the enormous machine.

Lyvia said nothing as he came to a stop near the end and watched the loading process.

Large as the chamber seemed at first sight, Roget realized that it was but a fraction the size of the works he'd seen outside Parachute years earlier—and far cleaner. The output rate was far greater as well.

Finally, he turned. "How do you do it?"

"It's standard molecular reassembly. Each unit handles a different type."

"You have, what, three of these for the planet?"

"Five actually, but one is always on standby."

Roget glanced back at the loading area as a freight maglev glided away, only to be replaced by another.

"Have you seen enough? There's not much else to see."

"How many people work here?"

Lyvia looked to the angular woman.

"Sixty-seven. Most are loaders."

"Why do you need human loaders?"

"They work better, and they're more flexible. Also, composite is hard on scanning perceptors."

"Why?"

The woman just shrugged.

Roget asked more questions, but most of the answers he got were either meaningless or consisted of shrugs.

"We need to go," Lyvia finally said. She turned to the woman. "Thank you."

"My pleasure and interest."

Once they were outside CPInd, Lyvia stepped through the maroon archway and turned right.

"We're not headed back toward the subtrans."

"No. We're going to take a private tube to MultOp."

"Is it subsurface as well?"

"Of course. When you insist that everything is underground and below much of the water table, it becomes easier to assure that there aren't any harmful emissions. We also insist on unified ventilation systems."

"So that the supervisors and owners breathe what everyone else does?"

"It works better that way."

"They could just move their administrative functions elsewhere."

"They could, but there's a heavy surtax on noninte-grated facilities, and that makes it hard to compete and stay in business."

"Do you people charge for everything you don't like?"

"No. Just those things that would otherwise harm people and the environment."

"What if people pay to pollute?"

"Some have. They haven't stayed in business long. They lost customers and employees because they had to pay more in production costs and because they had to pay the employees who stayed even more to keep them. Some people don't like buying from polluters, especially when their goods cost more."

The next archway from the maroon tunnel was on the left, and it was a bluish gray. After taking a short ramp and a left turn, Roget and Lyvia found themselves in a small concourse. The doors to a car that might hold twenty people were open. Once they stepped inside the private subtrans, the doors closed. Several minutes later, they opened onto a slightly larger blue gray concourse.

Roget stepped out alongside Lyvia. "What do they make here?"

"Everything. We don't operate along the old models. Basically, any manufacturer can fabricate anything once they receive the specs. Designers create prototypes or new versions, and all those are available on a royalty basis to any assembler."

"How does the assembler know if the specs work?"

"There aren't many single designers. They're businesses that have a number of designers and engineers. Designing is just part of what they do. They have the responsibility for product design and specifications . . . and the legal liability for them."

"So the designer really takes the place of the old multilateral, at least in terms of name identification or make or brand? And legal responsibility?"

Lyvia nodded.

The tour of MultOp was about as useful as the previous tour. Roget saw machines that essentially sprayed matter into predetermined shapes and colors . . . and functions. The finished products were covered in a thin biofoam and shipped.

As he watched the last stages of loading and shipping, a thought occurred to him, something that he should have picked up earlier. "How does all this get delivered?

People can't cart dining tables or anything else large home on the subtrans."

"There are freightways under the walkways in all towns and cities. Intelligent lorries take goods to the various buildings, or to common points in those places that allow individual dwellings. You can rent a delivery vehicle as needed, and some manufacturers or designers include local transport rental in the price." She rubbed her forehead. "You look hungry. I know I am. I'll answer any more questions you have about the day while we're eating. There's no place that's all that good out here. Do you mind if we head back to Skeptos?"

"No. How far south are we?"

"Twenty-one klicks."

Neither spoke except in pleasantries and short comments on the way back to Skeptos, but Roget did keep listening to the others on the regular subtrans train, which was far more crowded than it had been earlier. He was definitely understanding more, just enough to be even more frustrated.

Lyvia picked another restaurant within four blocks of the central square, except to the northeast. Classica was the almost invisible name on the tinted glass. Unlike Dorinique, it was small, and the decor was spare, with white plaster–finished walls and pale blue tile flooring. The table linens were a blue so deep that it was almost black.

Roget sank into the chair across from Lyvia. He was more than happy to order another lager, along with a chicken and broccoli feta pie and a Mediterranean salad. His eyes were burning slightly, but he didn't know whether that was some allergic reaction or just because he'd been straining to see and pick up anything that he could.

Once the lager arrived, he took several swallows before speaking. "What's the point of all this?"

"All what?"

"You show me around Skeptos. You give me a general idea of how your society works, but no details and
no real information. If you intend to let me report back
to the Federation, no one will believe me because I can
only provide generality after generality and my own
unsupported observations and calculations. If you don't
intend to let me return, why bother? I'll either be dead,
or I'll have plenty of time to learn."

"In time, and that will not be that long, we will provide you with proof. Proof that even senior security officers should find convincing."

Two salads appeared. Roget took a bite, discovering
that the brownish olives not only had pits, but were
strong and salty. Still, the tangy bite of the salad was
refreshing.

"What's the nature of that proof?"

"We'll send you off with a certain amount of documentation."

"You know the dropboat is in no shape to lift off, and
that would be so even if Dubiety didn't have orbital
shields."

"That has also been considered." Lyvia didn't look
up from her salad. "You will return."

The certainty in her voice wasn't totally reassuring.

As soon as they finished their salads, the server took
the plates away and presented their entrées.

Roget had no trouble eating every bite of the creamy
chicken and broccoli sandwiched between baked phyllo
sheets. As he waited for Lyvia to finish her skewers and
rice, he ventured another inquiry. "I've just assumed . . .
but do you have traditional marriages here?"

Lyvia frowned. "We have marriages and civil contracts and people who live together without either, and people who live alone. Some relationships are what you'd call traditional, and some aren't. We don't apply any stigma or prohibition to same-sex unions, if that's what you mean. All couples are treated the same. We do apply certain restrictions on those situations where more than two adults are involved in a relationship. History has shown such multiple unions do have a tendency not to carry their own weight in society."

"Restrictions? Such as?"

"If someone in that kind of relationship decides to have a child, someone has to post an educational and support bond."

"If they don't . . ."

"They can terminate the pregnancy, or they can be relocated into a situation where they can both work and have the child."

"Even you can't make everything work through economics."

"No . . . but mostly personal economics work. Some people always require the force of the state to behave and not to take criminal advantage of others."

"What about you?"

"What about me?" replied Lydia with an amused smile.

"Are you in some sort of . . . arrangement?"

"I have a partner. She and I have a daughter."

That explained more than a few things, Roget thought, including Lyvia's ease in maintaining a professional relationship and the very light fragrance that she used.

"Most arrangements here are still heterosexual," she went on. "That's the way human genes usually operate."

Lyvia stood, stifling a yawn. "I'd like to get home to see Aylicia."

"Then you should." Roget slipped from his chair.

They walked toward the front of Classica, and along the way Lyvia paid the bill with her belt-tube.

Once outside, Roget asked, "What about tomorrow?"

"I'll have to see what we can work out. I'll meet you for breakfast, the same as today."

Lyvia said little as she walked with him back to his guesthouse, and while Roget knew he should be finding out more, he discovered that he was too tired to press the issue. When he did reach his quarters, his feet ached, as did his shoulders. The shoulder pain had to be from the tension he'd only been peripherally aware of—at least, that was what he hoped.

But how could he not be tense when it was getting clearer and clearer that both the Federation and Dubiety were trying to use him? How could Dubiety be so aware of the Federation without the converse being true? Unless . . . Dubiety was more advanced than he'd even thought. Yet, if that were so, then the casual attitude of the colonel made no sense, unless he happened to be so arrogant that he and the Federation could not believe any splinter human culture might have surpassed Federation technology.

Roget could see permutations upon permutations.

Finally, he downloaded a duplicate of *Hildegarde in the Sunlight* to the quarters' system, amazed that the system actually accepted his flash memory, then adjusted the projection to the wall opposite the sofa. The dachshund he'd seen through the window the night before had reminded him. He sat down and looked at the familiar image of Hildegarde on the blue velvet sofa. He smiled.

"You've been in a lot of places, little girl," he murmured. "I'm not certain that you haven't learned more than I have. Especially here."

Hildegarde just continued to look at him expectantly, and that was fine with Roget as he leaned back and closed his eyes, trying to let his thoughts clear.

16

24 LIANYU 6744 F. E.

Roget stood in the high-roofed chamber. He glanced around but didn't recognize it . . . and yet, in some way, he did. There were small dark wooden desks arranged in a tiered semicircle. Most of the desks were occupied, primarily by men. A considerable proportion of those in the chamber were white haired. The ceiling was high and domed, and there were murals painted on the lower levels of the dome, just above the gallery where only a few people sat, looking down.

Why couldn't he make out the subjects of the murals? The light wasn't as bright as it could have been, but his eyesight was better than that. He squinted. It didn't help.

"A point of order has been raised against the motion to consider the amendment." The words boomed from somewhere, amplified.

Roget glanced toward the front of the dais opposite the middle of the tiered desk. A heavyset man with jowls sat at the single desk. He was the one who had spoken. Above and behind him on the wall was a large seal that featured an eagle. One claw held stylized thunderbolts. The other held some sort of branch.

"The amendment is germane. Under the rules, any amendment that references a specific clause in the bill . . ."

Roget's eyes flicked around the chamber. For some reason, he felt light-headed, and he put out a hand to steady himself on the nearest desk.

"Are you all right, Senator?" The young man who asked the question wore a dark jacket with a silver emblem in the lapel.

Something about the coat nagged at Roget. He couldn't say why. "I'm fine."

"Yes, sir." The young man moved away, as if relieved.

His feet seemed to turn him, and Roget found himself walking out of the chamber along an aisle between the evenly spaced desks. None of those at the desks looked up at him as he passed. Two women made a point of looking away.

He walked through an empty reception chamber or anteroom and then out a long colonnaded hall into another area where arched steel door frames were flanked by men in unfamiliar dark blue uniforms. He took the narrow exit space and made his way outside the building, where he stood between two massive marble columns at the top of a wide set of marble steps. Beyond the columns where he stood stretched others, holding up a long marble pediment above him. Below him stretched wide marble steps that descended and descended, finally ending at a wide concrete sidewalk.

People walked up and down the steps. Only a few looked in his direction, and they looked quickly away.

The sky overhead was dirty, covered in a haze of gray and brown. For all the haze, an orangish sun poured out heat. Sweat oozed from all over his body. After several moments, Roget walked down the marble steps. The stone felt gritty under his shoe soles, and the sun beat down on his uncovered head.

"Senator . . ." A young woman hurried toward him. She held a thin and angular microphone that she thrust at him. "Can you tell us the progress on the debate on the agreement proposed by Beijing?"

"Progress?" Roget laughed. "What progress? They want to take us over. We don't want to be taken over, but we don't want to pay the cost of independence . . . or of an effective military. Everyone wants someone else to pay, but now that you've taxed the upper middle class out of existence and driven the rich offshore, who's left to pay? You people have crucified anyone brave enough to explain that. There's no one left in there who has enough nerve to tell their constituents that . . . or to tell you." He pushed the microphone away and resumed walking down the marble steps.

Behind him there were murmurs.

". . . say he's lost it . . . coherent only some of the time . . ."

". . . why they keep electing him . . ."

". . . blaming us . . ."

Roget walked to the base of the steps and turned left on the sidewalk beside the empty asphalt drive and toward the low white buildings to the north beyond the trees at the end of the short expanse of green. Why couldn't they see it? Why was the obvious so impossible for them to understand? He felt so tired.

He reached inside his jacket for his phone. Except he wasn't wearing a jacket, and the phone had vanished. He needed to call . . .

Who was it that he needed to call? He couldn't remember. Why couldn't he remember?

Where was his jacket? He had been wearing a jacket. He couldn't go out into the chamber and speak on the floor without it. Where was it? He looked around. How could he have been so stupid as to have forgotten his jacket?

A blinding pain shot through his chest, and he staggered. His eyes watered. A moment of blackness washed over him . . . and passed.

When he could see again, the white marble buildings that had been less than a hundred yards before him swirled and melted into oddly shaped red stone. Some were only a few meters taller than he was. The green grass and trees had vanished, and he was walking on red sandy soil.

He stopped and glanced down at his chest. He was clad in a one-piece coverall of shimmering white. So white . . .

An institution? Had the administration had him committed? Carted off because he'd said too much? Or had they used national security as an excuse?

Roget blotted his forehead. How had it gotten so hot? He tried to swallow, then moisten his lips. They were dry and cracked.

He shook his head. It felt like it was splitting, and everything wavered around him. Where was he?

Something brushed his hip. He looked down at the white cylinder attached to his belt.

It was . . . he grasped for a name.

What was it?

His monitor! That was what it was. With that recognition, he looked around again, then reached down and grasped it. His eyes burned, and his fingers were clumsy, but he finally managed to get his position. He was nearly at the foot of Shinob, a good klick east of the Mill Creek wash and the Virgin River.

How had he gotten out here?

Dehydration. That must have been it. How could

he have been so stupid? He reached for the small water bottle at his belt on the left side. It was full. He drained it.

After several moments, his head seemed to clear, and he turned back west. He kept his steps measured as he followed the old and dusty trail back toward the Virgin River. He still didn't understand how he had gotten on the east side of the river. He'd only been at the bridge itself. At least he hadn't fallen in. He could have drowned, even in the shallow water, but his boots and his singlesuit showed no sign of dampness.

And what about the delusions about being called "Senator"? Or the marble buildings and the hazy sky? He knew he'd never been anywhere like that. He'd never seen buildings like those, nor had he seen a sky that polluted.

He knew about dehydration, but there had been nothing about delusions. Nothing at all.

He kept walking. No one was about to come after him any time soon, even in the comparatively mild midday heat of winter. He was just glad that he wouldn't be in St. George in full summer.

He hoped he wouldn't be.

He tried not to think about the dehydration delusion as he walked on. While it had seemed so real, it had been a delusion, hadn't it?

Or . . . his thoughts were still foggy . . . Something had happened. What? In a dingy café . . . that was it!

The Lee House. The lunch with Marni and the momentary blackout when the busboy had hit him with the tub of dishes, but what they had done must have been what gave him the delusion. He finally accessed his internal monitors, but they indicated no toxins, only borderline dehydration, and how had he gotten here?

Slowly, he recalled. He'd been taking a water chem reading . . .

He shook his head. He needed to get back to the bicycle and back to the FSS building, and he needed to drink more, as soon as he could. Dehydration . . . that had to be it. Didn't it?

17

19 MARIS 1811 P. D.

Roget woke earlier than he would have liked on Saturday, while it was still dark, or as dark as it ever seemed to get on Dubiety. He did have another thought, something he should have considered far earlier. Before he even dressed, this time wearing his own blue singlesuit, he walked into the main room of his quarters and began to search the holojector menu. If it accessed entertainment and other real-time material, there was always the possibility that it offered more.

After close to fifteen minutes, he located something called "Inquiries" and pulsed it.

"State your inquiry, please." The words seemed projected into his ears and nowhere else.

"Orbital shield system, functions and construction. Respond in Federation Stenglish." All the system could do was refuse to answer.

"Stenglish not an option." But the holojector did create an image of Dubiety, shown as a schematic cross-section of the planet. The molten core was somewhat smaller than Roget expected, and the planetary magnetic field depiction showed six poles, rather than two, and none of the three sets had anywhere close to the same orientation, nor did they correspond even approximately to geographic poles. The maximum field strength of each set was also at differing distances from the planetary surface. The fields generated by each looked to be more tightly focused than "normal" planetary mag-fields.

Roget grinned, if momentarily, until he realized that he could have discovered the inquiry aspect of the holojector/commnet earlier.

He did have to ask the system to repeat the explanation three times before he thought he had a general understanding of how the shields worked. Supposedly, each shield level was linked to a specific magnetic field, and the fields generated some sort of current or secondary field that created the orbital motion of the shield components.

When Roget couldn't get any more information on how the fields were structured or maintained or precisely how the orbital motion was accomplished, he tried another tack.

"Internal construction of each individual orbital unit?"

"Please restate your inquiry."

Between his nonexistent Dubietan old American and his use of simple words, it took close to a dozen attempts before the system projected another schematic. Each piece looked like a miniature modified lifting body, but that didn't make any sense because there was no atmosphere to speak of, not for aerodynamic purposes, at the orbital levels of even the lowest shield. The diagram showed a thin outer skin with what looked to be some sort of miniature devices along the inside of the rounded edges, but the system did not provide dimensions or details on the internal devices.

"No simplistic explanations on public comm? And that's not simplistic?" muttered Roget.

Next he made an inquiry on the subtrans. There was more detail there, including technical material on the placement of the magfield generators, but Roget was left with the definite sense that certain critical details were missing—such as how the Dubietans could generate enough power to power an entire transit network with trains moving at the speeds he'd calculated.

That led to an inquiry on planetary power generation. The system informed him that local power grids were generally supplied by fusion units, since fossil fuels, solar surface radiation, tidal, and geothermal technologies were all impractical. Planetary power was supplied by other means.

Planetary power? To what did that refer?

The only answer he got to that question and all sort of variations was that the information was unavailable due to the complexity involved.

"It's only complex when they don't want anyone to know the details," he murmured, not caring that his words were doubtless being transmitted and studied. After a moment, he realized something else. He couldn't have gotten as much comparable information off any Federation net.

He pushed those thoughts aside and inquired about communications specifics. The holojector showed him schematics on how all dwellings were linked by a form of fiber optics, but he couldn't get a description or much of anything on how they managed to transmit all kinds of radiation and energy without scatter.

Finally, after other even less fruitful searches, he put aside the holojector controls, cleaned up, and dressed. It was just after what passed for dawn when he left his quarters and walked along the upper hall and down the ramp to the reception area, looking for a door or some access to a lower level.

He found it in a niche beyond the ramp. It even opened as he neared, revealing a wide straight ramp headed down. At the base of the ramp, some eight meters below the ground floor, was a spacious open area and another wide corridor headed back in the direction of the front of the guesthouse.

He followed the corridor to another door, this one with a screen and keypad, which opened to his code. Beyond was another large antechamber, and to his left was what looked to be another code-accessed door. Roget ignored that for the moment and walked forward toward what he hoped was the door to the freightway. It opened as he approached.

Deciding on caution, he stood in the middle of the open door and studied the space beyond. It was simply an underground tunnel that looked to be the width of the walkway above. As he watched, a small lorry glided by silently, followed by another coming in the opposite direction and on the opposite side. Both had drivers, or loaders, or someone, sitting in the cab.

After a time, Roget stepped back into the large room—a receiving chamber, perhaps—and walked over to the screen and keypad on the side wall. Then he shrugged, stepped forward, and tapped in his guesthouse code.

A single off-key note chimed, followed by, "You have no deliveries in storage, Agent Roget. If you are expecting anything, please try later."

Roget nodded. While he hadn't actually observed the storage area, he had seen the freightways, and the response to his inquiry strongly suggested the truth of

Lyvia's descriptions. He had to use his code on the
other screen to reenter the guesthouse. Then he made
his way up to the reception area.

He waited less than ten minutes before Lyvia arrived.

"Good morning." He stood as he spoke.

"You're cheerful this morning."

"Would it do me any good if I weren't?"

"Probably not." There was no humor in her response.
Instead, Lyvia extended a small tube with a belt link.
"Here. There is a limited credit authorization on this.
You'll have to tell anywhere you use it that you'll need
to input your code manually. It's the same code as the
one you've been given for the guesthouse facilities. Using
the tube without a link is not common, but it's frequent
enough that no one is surprised."

"The poor?"

"No. It's usually for people who don't want their
identities known, or those whose assets are encumbered
by litigation, or those who have had ID difficulties."

"You actually have those sorts of problems? I thought
you'd solved everything through economics and regulations."

"Sarcasm doesn't become anyone, Keir, you especially."

He inclined his head. "If my attempts at levity have
offended you, I apologize. I am having a great deal of
difficulty in obtaining any meaningful information."

"I'm not at my best before breakfast," Lyvia replied.

"What about using this on the subtrans?" Roget held
up the tube.

"There's enough there for you to travel freely on the
local system, and that's the one area where you can just
point it at the black recorders and you don't need a code
authorization."

"I mean no offense, but how much is there on the

tube? I don't want to order meals or goods I—or your government—can't pay for." Roget used the clip to affix the tube to the waistband of the singlesuit.

"For now, there's a thousand dollars. The average meal at Dorinique is fifty, at a bistro perhaps fifteen to twenty. Local subtrans for you is a flat four dollars per entry."

"Why me?"

"The system adjusts for those who are linked. Those who aren't linked pay the average."

That made sense to Roget. "Why now?"

"It is Saturday, you know? And tomorrow is Sunday. More important, the Ministry wants you to explore Skeptos on your own. Security services don't listen to agents who are only on guided visits. I can't imagine those in the Federation are any different. Now . . . you can take me to breakfast."

"Where?"

"I thought we might try Veronique's." Lyvia turned and headed for the door to the outside walkway.

Roget found himself hurrying after her—again.

Veronique's was a small café four blocks west of the guesthouse and two south. Roget noted that Lyvia had picked where they ate so that he'd walked in every direction around the central square.

Once they were seated, Roget barely had time to look around the rear room with its plaster walls and pseudo-uncovered bricks that suggested an ancient French farmhouse, when the server arrived, smiling. Roget ordered something called eggs bernaise with tea. Lyvia asked for the breakfast crepes.

Once the server delivered the beverages, Lyvia took a long sip of her coffee, then looked at Roget. "I had some hard-copy maps printed for you because you can't link to the system and ask for directions. I'll give them to you after we finish. Just remember not to litter or try to force your way where you're not granted access. Since you're not linked to the commnet, you won't hear warnings or instructions."

"Is there anyplace I shouldn't go?" He took a sip of the tea.

"Anywhere that you're not granted access. Don't assume that's because we're keeping you from such places. They just may be private dwellings or places where the owners don't allow any strangers."

Roget nodded but wondered just how much access he would actually have.

The server returned and set a platter before him. The eggs bernaise turned out to be a pair of poached eggs, each set on top a half muffin, a slice of ham, another of a sharp cheese, then topped with a piquant sauce with tarragon.

Roget looked to Lyvia. "How much is real?"

"The eggs probably are, and the cheese started with replicated milk products, but the process after that was old style. The ham is high-level replicated."

"That's a lot of power going into replication," he observed.

"Less than the total would be for a fully agricultural society. Besides, the planetary ecology wouldn't take the strain of that much so-called natural farming. There are still areas that aren't much more than barren rock and sand, especially in Thula and Westria, and to a lesser degree in Verite."

Partly replicated or not, the dish was tasty, and Roget didn't leave any scraps. Neither did Lyvia.

"Are you finished?" she asked.

"Yes."

"Good. I promised Aylicia I wouldn't be too long." She rose from the table and slid a long envelope from the hidden thigh pocket of her singlesuit. "Here are the maps I promised. They're fairly high resolution."

Roget stood quickly and took the extended envelope. "Thank you."

"You need to pay," Lyvia reminded him.

"Gratuities?"

"They're very optional. Nothing for standard service. Ten percent for exceptional service."

"Five percent today?"

"Generous, but not out of line." A faint smile crossed her lips and vanished.

Roget walked toward the podium/payment station and the hostess standing there. "I'll need to enter my code manually."

"Of course, sir." She stepped away from the podium. "The total is on the screen here. Just use the pad on the side."

The transaction process was as simple as Lyvia had indicated it would be.

As they walked out of Veronique's, Lyvia glanced at Roget. "I'll meet you in the lobby of the Ministry of Education and Culture at ten on Monday morning. Director Hillis thought another interview and a briefing might be useful. Enjoy your weekend."

With those words she hurried away, leaving Roget standing on the walkway.

He had to admit that had a Thomist landed anywhere on earth, he or she wouldn't haven't been given funds, maps, and access, and allowed to explore, not at least without some form of escort. Still, the Dubietans could certainly keep track of him.

He looked over the maps, then shrugged and folded them back into the envelope, slipping it into a thigh pocket. He might as well wander at first. He turned and began walking. He covered another four long blocks westward past a mixture of small shops, bistros, and unmarked buildings, before he came to an expanse of green that he judged to be a klick square. Evergreens of a type he'd never seen before, with long soft blackish-green needles, marked the perimeter of the park, if that was indeed what it was. All of them ranged in height from four meters to six at most. He walked through the pewter-colored metallic archway between the evergreens. Ahead, the path split.

Roget took the left branch, leading toward a circular grassy field where children, ten or eleven years old, he thought, were playing a game of some sort on what looked to be a circular grassy field. They carried short lengths of a metal shaft ending in an oval mesh frame. There was a single post in the middle of the field, and four narrow open cones branched from the post at a height of five meters.

Half the players wore silver jerseys, and half wore a shimmering purple. Both teams contained girls and boys, it seemed, and the object of the game appeared to be to use the mesh-sticks to fling a yellow ball into one of the cones on the post.

Roget followed the path up a slight slope to where several benches were located. Grass sloped down to the field some thirty meters away. A few handfuls of adults, both men and women, stood around the edge of the field, but the benches were empty. Roget seated himself and began to watch the players. After a time, some aspects of the game became clearer. Narrow strips of the grass had been colored to show four circles. The first circle was red and ran around the post some three meters out. No player crossed that line, nor the other red line, the farthest one, some thirty meters out. The other lines were a brilliant yellow, at ten meters, and a brilliant blue at twenty.

A whistle shrilled as one player smacked another's arm with his stick. Immediately, the smacker left the game and stood in a yellow box just outside the perimeter.

"Are any of them yours?"

Roget frowned momentarily—not at the friendly tone, but because he had understood the words and because they had definitely not been in Stenglish. He turned to the older man, wearing old-style black trousers and a black shirt with a shimmering gray vest, who stood at the end of the bench and smiled. "No. Just watching."

"They're worth watching."

Roget nodded. He didn't want to say much, aware as he was that, while his understanding was better, his speech certainly remained alien.

"To be young again, and carefree." The man shook his head, then walked eastward in the general direction of the central square.

After the man left, Roget stood, then continued to follow the path as it wound toward a set of gardens bounded by a rough wall of black stone, behind which were more of the dark evergreens. As he followed the path through the opening in the wall, he could see that most of the plants were not the green of earth, but either a paler green or of a green so dark that it was almost black, like much of the lettuce in the salads he'd had on Dubiety. Less than a third of the plants were flowering. The blooms were, again, either on the pale side or very dark. One striking flower was a purple black trumpet with gold-fringed blossom ends. He'd never seen anything like it before.

He bent forward and sniffed. The fragrance was lily-like, if not exactly, with a hint of gardenia. Then he straightened and continued through the garden. He

walked another thirty meters along the garden path
when he saw a pale-leafed plant that was wilted and
desiccated, either dying or dead. For some reason, the
dying plant struck him, but he kept walking. Another
thought struck him. He hadn't seen any butterflies. He
turned back to the garden.

Deliberately, he inspected the first flowering plant at
the end of the garden. It had a variation on traditional
earth flowering plants—stamen, pistil, and pollen. So
did the second. The third had tiny blue flowers, but as
he studied it, he heard the faintest whirring, and an
insect—more like a tiny hummingbird—appeared, flit-
ting from flower to flower.

Roget resumed his walk.

Beyond the garden on the southwest side of the path,
he neared another game of the same sort, but the players were clearly older, and there were more adults ring-
ing the field or pitch or whatever it was called.

A path ran around the park, just inside the evergreen
hedge. Roget hadn't noticed it before, but what called it
to his attention were two women running in long easy
strides. Both wore but minimal clothing—skin-tight,
low-cut briefs and minimal breast bands—and none of
the men standing around the game even turned their
heads.

Roget was definitely distracted, enough so that he
walked right into one of the benches, cracking his upper shin on the seat. He winced, then bent and rubbed
the spot gently.

After a moment, he straightened and continued
walking.

By the end of the day, as he walked back toward the
guesthouse, he had covered close to twenty klicks of
walkways through and around the center of Skeptos.
He'd eaten a meal hardly passable at a tiny café without

a name, and a slightly better one at a place called Calderones, where the servers all had their hair tinted purple. He hadn't asked about it, not trusting his command of old American.

He had seen a section of the city where there were individual dwellings, but, elegant as they appeared from without, they were comparatively modest in size, the largest being but two stories and encompassing perhaps six hundred square meters at most. He'd also seen small multiple dwellings that, while not decrepit, verged on shabbiness, or what passed for it on Dubiety, and where teenage males lounged on the corners.

He'd walked through three other parks and entered a natatorium with a gallery, where some sort of competition was taking place involving boys and girls of all ages. What he had not seen was anything that looked like an industrial or production facility. He had passed buildings and grounds that looked to be schools, although he did not see anyone there, except a few children playing, with an adult or two nearby.

When he trudged up the guesthouse ramp, well after dark, he was exhausted. Once he entered his quarters, he resolved that he would use the subtrans on Sunday to widen his explorations. Even so, as he sank into the sofa in the main chamber, he almost didn't want to consider the implications of what he had seen. During the entire day, he had neither heard nor seen any form of aircraft. Nor had he encountered anyone or anything who looked like a police officer or a patroller, or an E&W monitor. He had seen people of all ages, and even those with significant variations in their physical features, although none were extremely dark skinned, possibly because lighter skin was a biological necessity under the orbital shields, and . . . most important, he had understood almost every word he had heard spoken.

He couldn't help but wonder if the Thomists were doing something to his perceptions . . . or if his entire thought processes were being manipulated by some alien intelligence.

Yet his feet ached, and the place where he'd cracked his shin was definitely sore and probably bruised. His internals matched what he had sensed and felt, and even his physical condition. He had tasted food, some of it barely palatable. He had smelled the flowers, heard children playing, and seen all manner of buildings and dwellings.

Either way, he reflected . . . he was in trouble.

18

25 LIANYU 6744 F. E.

Once he'd returned to the FSS on Friday afternoon, Roget had explained his early return because of a bout of dehydration. Sung had given him a lecture and let it go at that. Roget had thought about sending another encrypted linkburst report to his controller, then decided against it. He didn't want either dehydration or delusions on his record. He had kept monitoring his internals, but once he'd increased his fluid levels, they continued to indicate he was normal.

Even so, on Saturday morning, Roget slept until close to ten. When he finally woke, he realized just how exhausted he'd been the night before. When he was alert enough to check, he found that his internal monitors indicated that he was in good shape. But then, they hadn't given him any warning on the dehydration/ delusion induced by whatever charming Marni and her compatriot had done. His shoulder wasn't sore, but he thought he could see the faintest hint of a circular patch of redness in his upper arm. That would fit with some sort of nanojector, but why were there no other signs? And what had Marni had in mind? She wasn't the type to do something without a purpose.

After eating a leisurely, if not particularly appetizing, replicated breakfast, cleaning up, and dressing, Roget carried a case from the bedroom out to the main area. There he laid out the gear he had available on the table that doubled as desk and eating space. When he finished, he glanced toward the projection to his right. He couldn't help smiling at the little black dachshund with the tannish brown patches over her eyes. "You are something, Hildegarde."

He knew that the dachshund was only an image, but who else could he talk to in St. George? Besides, she did remind him of Muffin.

"You made a lot of people happy, I'd bet, little dog."

Hildegarde didn't answer, but Roget imagined that she bounced a little and wagged her tail as he turned from the image to the gear on the table. He finally decided on the wrist dart gun, a waist-pak that contained various tools designed for circumventing security systems and locks, and, just for emergencies, a small explosive and incendiary device. He had been in St. George for two weeks. That meant he no longer was restricted to mere observation, and he was getting tired of being a target.

Once he arranged the gear, he went back to the bedroom closet and ran a check on the nightsuit, a dark gray, long-sleeved singlesuit. When activated, the special threads and sensors created the image of whatever was behind the suit—from all angles. If Roget slipped the hood over his head and face, even in bright light, he merged with the background, and in darkness, he was close to invisible.

The next step was to use his personal monitor to access certain information and dig out what he could about his putative targets for the evenings ahead. That would take more than a little time.

By the time twilight had begun to creep eastward from the western bluffs across the town, Roget had discovered quite a bit more to put with what he'd already discovered. The women's clothing shop Santiorna's was owned by Julienna Young, the sister of one Brendan B. Smith. While interlocking family ownerships were not uncommon in smaller towns, when energy anomalies occurred involving two properties side by side and when one of those properties was owned by someone already flagged by a Federation agent—a dead agent—Roget thought that was carrying coincidence a bit too far.

In addition, William Dane, Bensen Sorensen, and Brendan Smith had all been classmates at Deseret University, and Smith's father had been a director of Deseret First Bank at the time Dane had been transferred from the Elko branch of the bank to St. George . . . and the elder Smith still was a director, from what Roget could determine. The only one who seemed to have no direct links to the other three on the initial listing Roget had received was Mitchell Leavitt—except that financial dealings usually touched everyone in a town as small as St. George. Leavitt, the collateralizer, had held a second deed of trust on the property owned by one

Delbert Parsens, and Parsens had done the sculpture outside The Right Place, Bensen Sorensen's guesthouse. The deed of trust had been released three years earlier for one thousand yuan and "other considerations of value."

Was that too tenuous a connection? Was it just another example of small-town financial incest, so to speak? Or a lead to something larger? One way or another, Roget needed to find out, and that would take some on-site investigating, beginning with Deseret-Data.

He donned the nightsuit, along with matching dark gray boots, but left the fine mesh hood tucked inside the collar. Then he looked toward Hildegarde. "I'll see you later, little dog."

Wearing the unactivated nightsuit that looked like a casual gray singlesuit, remarkable only for its plainness, Roget left his apartment and walked up 800 East to the tram station. He and two youths, who barely looked in his direction, were the only ones to board the westbound tram. At the main station, Roget transferred to a southbound car, which he took to the 300 South platform. That left him a three-block walk to Bluff Street.

The evening was slightly cooler, and he could hear the occasional buzz of insects. He only saw one older couple on the other side of the street, and they had waved and then continued onward.

A block short of Bluff, when he could see no one nearby and in the shadow of an ancient mulberry tree, he activated the nightsuit and eased the hood over his head. Then he walked the last block to the corner where Santiorna's was located. The shop was dark, and Roget's detector showed no energy emissions at all. Next door, to the north of the clothing boutique, DeseretData had closed, but the lights were still on inside.

Roget walked back along the side of the boutique, but his equipment and monitors detected nothing. Then he slipped up the alley to the rear of DeseretData. Even there, his detector showed no energy emissions whatsoever. Roget moved to the building's energy monitoring box and focused the detector there. Only a slight energy flow was apparent, and there should have been more. Roget glanced down at the alley surface, lightly covered with the red sand that was everywhere. Something caught his eye. He turned, but it was only a cat skulking away. He looked back at the alley surface again.

There was something . . .

He bent down and brushed the sand away. Under the thin layer of sandy grit in the alley were old bricks. Roget looked closer. The bricks were indeed old, but their spacing was perfect, and old bricks in alleys didn't stay perfect for very long. In fact, the bricks along the entire rear of DeseretData had been replaced recently, probably within the last year or so, out to a good two meters from the rear wall.

Roget brought the energy detector to bear on the bricks. Beneath them was the faintest hint of energy flows. As he sensed, rather than heard, voices, he straightened and stepped farther into the shadows.

The rear door opened, and the young man who had answered Roget's questions when he had bought the infosloads stepped out, then looked back into the shop. "You sure you don't need any help, sir?"

"No. I won't be long," came a voice from inside.

"Nine on Monday, sir?"

"A few minutes before. Don't be late."

"No, sir."

Once the young man closed the door and hurried down the alley toward the cross street, Roget stepped back and studied the thick roofing tiles, noting the lines of mortar at each corner of the rear roof. Even for St. George, the tiles were thick, thicker than necessary even for solar tiles. . . . He nodded. They were industrial solar tiles, soltaic cells designed to produce and store electric power. While there was no direct prohibition of their use, tiles like those were extremely expensive, far too costly for a small EES in St. George. Yet, from what he'd discovered earlier, DeseretData was drawing a full quota of power from the grid, and it shouldn't have needed that much with the soltaic array set up on the shop roof.

He walked back along the alley. From what he could determine, Santiorna's also had soltaic tiles across its entire roof. By clambering up on top of a sealed recycling bin, Roget managed to trace the almost hidden connectors that linked the roof grid of the boutique to that of DeseretData. Again, that wasn't proof of anything—except that someone was using a great deal more power than was being registered or monitored. In itself, that certainly wasn't illegal.

He eased himself back down to the alley.

A faint click and then a flash of light that vanished alerted Roget, who flattened himself against the rear wall of Santiorna's. A tall blond man—presumably Brendan B. Smith himself—stepped out of the rear door, locking it, and then sending an energy pulse upward toward the eaves. Immediately, a low-level ambient motion and mass detector field cloaked the two buildings. Roget backed away quickly, slipping to the far side of the alley.

Smith frowned and looked down at a device in his hand. He glanced around, then stepped back several paces from the rear door. Then he nodded, slipped the system controller into a belt holder, and began to walk down the alley.

Roget remained motionless until Smith was well out of sight. He hadn't expected that DeseretData would have such a sophisticated system. Why would a mere EES local outlet need it . . . unless it was more than just an EES? Then he moved silently toward the rear door, stopping well short of the detection field. He took out his monitor and called up the field diagnostic functions.

Even with his equipment, it took Roget almost half an hour before he managed to create a diverter field, and another fifteen minutes to bypass the rear lock circuits. Then he had to pick the mechanical lock as well. The more he had to do, the more convinced he was that whatever Brendan Smith was doing was something Smith didn't want anyone to know about, particularly the Federation.

Once Roget was inside, he slipped on a pair of flat night goggles, and the narrow backroom of the shop turned shades of pale green. He began to search for a doorway or some access to a lower level, although neither was apparent. Eventually, he found a sliding panel at the side of what looked to be a closet. Behind it was a wooden circular staircase down to a basement. Roget took it, if carefully.

The lower level contained three microfabrication units—ancient but effective molecular fabricators. Their presence definitely explained the power requirements of the building. Roget moved to the first, but the fabrication bay was empty, as were those of the second and third machines. A short workbench was set against the south wall, and several objects had been laid out there.

Roget bent down to see them more clearly, then swallowed. While not fully assembled, the pieces definitely looked like an old-style pistol, except for the barrel, which was a dark solid material flanked by two thin metal rods, each of which terminated a fraction of a centimeter short of the end of the solid barrel. The grip had not been fitted, but inside the frame were the mounting and leads for a quick discharge capacitor. Roget was standing over a device that looked suspiciously like an antique narrow-beam nerve shredder.

There was something about the basement walls. They were all dark and metallic. Although he couldn't tell for sure, he thought they were covered with lead sheets nanocoated with something to keep the lead from getting into the air. The last thing he noted was the heavy vault door set in the east wall of the basement. He wasn't about to try to open that, not with the equipment he carried, but he was more than willing to bet that behind the heavy vault door lay an armory of some sort.

He made his way back up the circular staircase, then closed the sliding panel.

His internal sensors registered the change in energy fields. Someone had deactivated the outside security system. While he thought he'd bypassed all the alarms, there was always the possibility of another system, a totally passive one.

Roget slipped to the rear wall and then dropped into a squat, facing the door. He waited. After almost five minutes, the door opened.

Nerve-shredder blasts swept the back room even before the man stepped inside, and Roget flattened himself against the floor and rear wall. Despite his position, one bolt slashed Roget's right leg. Sheer agony slammed up his leg and spinal column, and it took all his concentration to keep still and wait for the man—Smith—to step fully through the rear door.

Roget fired a dart.

Smith looked blankly at the narrow penetrator protruding from his chest, then tried to grab for it, but his fingers slipped away as his body began to convulse. The nerve shredder dropped from his other hand.

Roget inched forward toward the paralyzed man, trying to get an impression of who or what, if anyone, remained outside. Just short of the still half-open door, he began to pick up signs of two other men, also with nerve shredders, standing outside, well back from the rear entrance. One wore goggles—heat/motion detectors.

There was no way for Roget to cross the open distance without getting hit by the shredders, especially with one leg burning and numb. He eased awkwardly into a standing position and opened the waist-pak. Out came the explosive device. Step by step, he made his way back to the closet and the sliding panel, which he eased open before he tossed the device down into the basement.

Then he hurried—as quickly as he could—out of the back room and into the front room, circling so that he would not be in the line of fire from the two men outside. He waited . . . and waited, keeping low so that he could not be silhouetted against the growing glow from the fire that was beginning to reach up the wooden staircase into the back room.

He slowly moved until he was positioned beside the front door, one hand on the heavy stool that sat beside the processing console.

Behind and around him the entire building shuddered, and the floor shivered, buckling upward in the back room. More flames began to lick upward in the rearward section of the building. He could sense one of the men behind the building rushing toward the rear door, hopefully to reclaim Smith.

All sorts of nanomists began to flood the premises, along with water from an old-style fire sprinkler system, but the oils and chemicals in the supply bins of the microfabbing equipment in the basement had begun to feed the flames, and with some of them supplying oxygen, the fire continued to grow.

Because the heat was getting oppressive, even as low as he was to the floor, Roget finally slammed the stool through the glass of the door. The rush of air offered a moment of respite before the fire intensified. Roget took a deep breath, then began to clamber through the lower part of the front door where the glass had been. A handful of people had gathered on the far side of Bluff Street, but Roget judged that his nightsuit would blur him enough against the shifting light created by the fire that his exit from the building would not be that noticeable.

The toe of his boot on his injured leg caught on the metal rim of the door, and he had to use his free hand to help lever his barely responsive leg high enough to free his foot. Even so, if anyone saw his figure, no one yelled or said anything as he limped slowly and painfully up Bluff Street. Behind him the sound of klaxons and sirens rose, and fire lorries and local patrollers converged on the burning building that held DeseretData.

It took Roget almost an hour to reach his apartment, by foot and slowly, because he didn't want any record on the tram system of where he'd been. From there, he immediately burst-sent a message to his controller, explaining the probable armory behind and beneath the smoldering ruins of DeseretData, as well as the microfabbing equipment and nerve shredders, and an explanation that the discharges from the devices used by the three men had apparently set the fire. He wasn't about to report that he had, and neither the colonel nor his controller would have wanted that in a report.

Within minutes, a response arrived. Roget read over it, his eyes picking out the key phrases.

> ... incendiary results unfortunate but understandable ... will alert local authorities and request complete inventory of weapons discovered ... federal inspector will arrive within hours to cordon area ... remain in current status ... do not contact inspector ... As necessary ... authorization to use all force required against those involved ...

That might be, but Roget was in no shape to use force against anyone, or do much more, for the moment and for at least several hours, until the worst of the nerve pain in his leg subsided.

He also wasn't in the least happy with the wording that suggested the fire was unfortunate. Without it, he'd most likely be dead or captured by the locals as an intruder, and the FSA certainly wouldn't have been happy about that—except that he'd have been disavowed, with no records remaining to show his affiliation, and he'd have ended up relocated and brain-damped, if not worse.

19

Monday morning, Roget was awake early. Sunday had been a more detailed repeat of Saturday, except that he'd used the subtrans to visit the areas around five other local stations. While the geography varied somewhat, and the architecture more than a little, the similarities were overwhelming. He saw no sign of industrial facilities anywhere on the surface, but he'd found more than a few tunnels from the subtrans ramps that led to archways that didn't open to him. There were parks and schools and shopping districts—and no wheeled surface transport, except for two powered chairs used by individuals who looked to have acute leg problems. He'd sweated through the humidity and observed happy people, sad people, laughing and crying children, and not a single individual in what looked to be a uniform. There were few overt signs of old age, but that was to be expected in an advanced society. There were also somewhat fewer children than he would have expected, which suggested a comparatively stable population—something rare in a society without apparent overt control measures. While he'd worn his camouflage-equipped blue shipsuit both Saturday and Sunday, there had been no place and no reason to use it, but he'd felt more comfortable having its capabilities.

When he finished breakfast Monday at the nameless bistro where he and Lyvia had eaten on Saturday, he took his time walking to the square and then north to the Ministry of Education and Culture. He was early enough that he saw a constant flow of men and women in roughly equal proportions leaving the central square—but not nearly so many as he would have expected in a capital city.

Surprisingly to him, there was a chill and brisk wind, as if fall or even winter were on the way. How could that be, given the redistribution of solar radiation by the orbital shields and the minimal axial tilt of the planet?

Lyvia was waiting inside the Ministry of Education and Culture. She wore a deep blue singlesuit with a short cream vest. "You look better in the green than the blue or gray."

"The gray and blue both need cleaning. I'm not used to the humidity here. Is everywhere on Dubiety as damp as Skeptos or the Machiavelli Peninsula?"

"The general humidity level depends on the altitude. People who have trouble with it often move to the Anasazi Plateau in the west of Thula. The altitude there is around two thousand meters. Some people think that Chaco is a charming town, with all the native stone. Andoya isn't bad either. They're both quiet, though. Very quiet compared to Skeptos or even Avespoir."

"It's colder today," Roget observed.

"That's not surprising. We're headed into fall."

"But the shields . . . ?"

"Dubiety's orbit is elliptical enough that the change in total radiation makes a difference. We don't have hemispherical seasonal differences but planetwide seasons. It's fall everywhere at the same time. Oh, there are local variations, usually because of altitude and proximity to the oceans, and when it does get colder in the mountains, we have stronger winds." She gestured toward the doors that led to the ramps. "Shall we go? I imagine Director Hillis is waiting."

The fact that she spoke in old American reminded Roget, and he asked, "What sort of technology have you aimed at me so that I've been able to understand people better? I assume it's been in my sleep."

Lyvia nodded. "It's easier that way."

"What is it?"

"A linguistics booster. You only needed a little help. Stenglish differs from old American more in cadence and pronunciation than in terms of basic vocabulary."

"How does it work?"

"I have no idea, except that similar technology has been around for a long while, even in the Federation. Or it used to be." Without waiting for a reply, she turned and headed for the ramp doors.

The implication of her last five words bothered Roget, but he took three quick steps and caught up with her. He didn't say anything until she paused at the third level before the door opened.

"What about the other scout?"

"I have no idea. Director Hillis could tell you." Lyvia stepped through the door, turned to her left, and headed through the reception area, past a young-faced man who looked up abruptly as the two agents swept past him.

If Hillis would tell, thought Roget, and if what she said could be trusted . . .

Selyni Hillis stood waiting by the door to the very same conference room where Roget had first met her. "Please come in. We need to cover some matters quickly."

Roget and Lyvia had barely stepped into the conference room when Hillis closed the door and pointed to a bound volume set beside a blue case that was roughly five centimeters thick and eight centimeters on a side. Both rested in the middle of the conference table. "The Federation places a great emphasis on hard evidence.

These briefing packets contain information printed on nearly-indestructible film sheets that can be washed and sterilized. In addition, the case contains the same information, as well as a great deal more, in link-insets compatible with Federation systems, including the portable versions that can be operated independently of ship systems."

"They won't let anything like that onto a Federation ship," Roget pointed out.

"We're aware of that. That's why the information is set out in multiple formats. It can be read from the drop-boat, run through whatever filters you think necessary, and transmitted from there. If someone is particularly suspicious, it can be read aloud and transcribed, or scanned with your own equipment and retransmitted."

"Is the technique for language implantation in there?" Roget gestured toward the case and bound volume.

Selyni Hillis smiled. "We're not about to spend time reinventing what the Federation has lost or buried."

"Then what will you offer them?"

"Why don't you read the material and see? That's why it's here." Hillis took the chair closest to the door.

Roget took the chair that put his back to the window, sat down, and reached for the bound volume. He opened it. The first inside page was blank. The second was a table of contents.

The first chapter heading read "Planetary Radiation Shields." Roget flipped to the first page of that section and read a page, then a second. He couldn't say that he understood everything, or even that it was technically correct, but it purported to contain the theory and specifications for designing a shield like the ones around Dubiety.

He looked up. "Assuming this is correct and not

technical double-talk, why would you give this to the Federation?"

"It's not double-talk, and we do have our reasons."

Roget went back to the table of contents. The second heading read "Pseudo-Event-Horizon T-D Transposition." He tried to read that section, but all he could glean from it was that it purported to be another form of interstellar jump drive. The next section dealt with a form of anomalous composite with radiation-damping properties. The next section was a proof of some sort that he could make no sense of at all, except for the title, "Trans-Temporal Entropic Reversal."

He looked up. "If I understand any of this, you're offering technology, or technological insights that the Federation doesn't have."

"Or has and has chosen not to employ. We're not exactly privy to what the High Council or the FSA has decided."

"I don't see the linguistic technology here, but you'll give them technology they don't have?"

"That's an interesting choice of words, Agent Roget. Let's just say that in the interests of friendship and a willingness to avoid conflict, we'll offer potentially useful technology." Hillis smiled.

"What's to keep a Federation fleet from just showing up and taking whatever they want?" he countered.

"We would hope that the Federation would read and consider our offerings first. That's why we'll be sending you back with the material. Our technical staff has been working on your dropboat over the weekend, and they believe they'll have both boats ready to launch for your return by Thursday, Friday at the latest."

"Exactly how am I supposed to get through your orbital screens?" asked Roget.

"We do have ways, but that is one matter that we'll

keep to ourselves for now. I trust you do understand that."

If there actually happened to be such a way, he could see why they wouldn't be interested in revealing it. He was more worried that he was just being set up for what amounted to a suicide launch. But . . . if that were the case . . . again, why the elaborate charade? And if it weren't a charade . . .

"Why don't you just defy the Federation?"

"We believe in offering first," replied Hillis. "In technological societies, all conflicts cost more than they recover, even for the winner."

"Historically, that hasn't seemed to matter."

Hillis shrugged. "We hope that the Federation has learned something from that history. We have."

"You seem to think that—"

"What we think is irrelevant to what the Federation will do. What the Federation thinks is what matters. Your job as an agent is to provide information. Your job as a human being is to provide insight and persuasion. Also, we'd like you to return to the *WuDing* in one piece. We'd prefer not to give the Federation any unnecessary excuses for stupid actions."

"I'm just one agent." Roget paused. "I'd be interested to know how the other scout is faring."

"He isn't as adaptable as you. He attempted to attack a number of people. He's been restrained until he can be returned to the *WuDing*—or whatever Federation ship will handle your recovery."

"You're sending us both back? How thoughtful." Roget knew he shouldn't have been so sarcastic, but it was a measure of his frustration—and something else he couldn't immediately identify.

"You don't want to return to your beloved Federation?" Hillis's words matched Roget's almost perfectly in the degree of sarcasm. She turned to Lyvia. "He should see Manor Farm Cottages. Today might be best."

For just a moment, distaste flitted across Lyvia's eyes. At least Roget suspected it was distaste. Whether Lyvia found another escort duty distasteful or whether she found going to Manor Farm Cottages unpleasant, he didn't know, but either was possible.

"Might I ask what these cottages are for?"

"You'll understand when you see them. If you have questions after you do, Lyvia will certainly be able to answer them. We'll meet again tomorrow sometime." Hillis turned to Lyvia. "You know where to reach me."

"Yes, Director."

"That will be all for now." Hillis stood. "Good day."

As he rose, Roget's first thought was that he still didn't understand the almost disjointed interview/interrogation system the Thomists were employing. Was it merely to get him into a room where they could upset or confuse him and then use technology to pull thoughts and information out of his mind? But why would they go to all the trouble of putting together an information package and then design it so that its contents could be received without any Trojan horses? Or did the very words themselves constitute something like that? And then there had been the words about not giving the Federation any excuse for stupid actions. Had that really been the point of sending agent scouts in the first place? Certainly, the FSA had done that before, as Roget well knew . . . personally.

"We can go," Lyvia said quietly.

Roget followed her out along the corridor and down the ramp to the main level. Then she headed through the building foyer for the walkway leading to the central square. Her steps were long and deliberate. Once they were outside, Roget drew alongside her. He got the definite impression that she was less than pleased with the assignment the director had ordered.

"How long will this take?"

"Several hours, at the least."

"Where are we headed?"

"The regional subtrans in the square." Her words were cool and clipped.

Roget decided not to say more, not for the moment. In fact, he said nothing at all until they were seated side by side in a half-filled car on the regional subtrans line heading northward out of Skeptos.

"How many stops before we get off?"

"It's the second stop."

Roget sat quietly through the first stop and rose when Lyvia did at the second. From his internals, he calculated that the travel time had been approximately eleven minutes. When they stepped out onto the underground concourse, they were the only ones. Lyvia marched toward the ramp, and Roget matched her step for step.

"We're close to three hundred klicks from Skeptos," he ventured.

"There's a reason for that. The cottages are purposely isolated, except by subtrans. You'll see why."

"You people never explain anything before the fact," Roget observed.

"That's not true. We explain whatever we can. Some things have to be experienced or observed for the explanation to make sense, and trying to explain them before the fact just creates false impressions and preconceptions."

Roget couldn't help but wonder if overwhelming people with experiences that they were unprepared for did exactly the same thing but saw no reason for voicing the point, not given Lyvia's attitude.

When they emerged from the subtrans tunnel and

ramp, Roget noted that there was but a single walkway leading due north out of a low circular grassy vale, totally without trees. At least Roget thought the walkway led north, but without a visible sun and with his questions about just how precise his internal monitors were, his directional senses were as likely to be assumptions as totally accurate. Beyond the grassy depression were trees in all directions, as if the subtrans station had been set in the midst of a vast forest.

"Can you tell me why the cottages are located in such an isolated locale?"

"For safety purposes," replied Lyvia. "You'll see."

"How far do we have to walk?"

"It's four klicks to the outskirts of the cottages."

The forest held more deciduous trees than had the one on the peninsula, and the air was even more humid. The underlying scents mixed a richness with dampness, but without the hint of sweetness that had bothered Roget. "There aren't any butterflies here."

"No. Their absence makes balancing the ecology more difficult, but it's necessary."

"Is that because it's not that deep . . . literally?"

"There is an indigenous subsurface microbial ecology, but it never evolved beyond that, and it's not hostile. Not any more hostile than any bacterial or microbial ecology anyway, and there are some interesting things going on there. It's more a problem of balancing with people in a way that makes sense practically and economically. We've opted away from truffles, for example. If they eventually develop, that's fine, but introducing that kind of gourmet and economic temptation is just asking for trouble."

Roget kept asking about the ecology as they walked, because that was an area where Lyvia was willing to talk, and information, any information, was better than no information. Besides, he could deduce some things from what she did say.

The forest ended abruptly, as if a line had been drawn, and a good klick ahead, Roget saw a series of low dwellings—cottages, in fact. Somewhere in the distance, the forest resumed, but the cleared area that held the cottages looked to be a rough oval about three klicks across. The cottage walls looked to be of local stone, and the roofs of something resembling slate, although Roget wouldn't have been surprised if it had been some form of composite.

"There are the Manor Farm Cottages, and there's the security station." Lyvia pointed.

Ahead on the right side of the path stood a single dwelling, separated from those farther north by a good hundred meters of open grassy ground.

"That's the first security establishment you've pointed out."

"It's been the only one to point out," she replied.

As they neared the security cottage, a muscular man wearing a short-sleeved yellow singlesuit stepped out of the dwelling and stood on the front stoop, waiting for them.

"How many security agents are there here?"

"I'd imagine just a few, either a couple or a pair of partners. They're really here to deal with outsiders or illnesses or accidents."

"Agent Rholyn, you're expected. I'm Mattias Singh." The black-haired man smiled, then turned to Roget. "What you see in and around the cottages may be disturbing. Please keep in mind that no one there can physically touch anyone else without suffering. It would be for the best if you did not touch them either."

Roget nodded.

"Take your time, and see what you need to see, Agent Rholyn."

"Thank you." Lyvia's voice was pleasant but cool.

Less than fifty meters past the cottage, Roget's internals registered a low-level energy field of some sort. Even without his monitors, he could sense something, a low sound that raised the hair on the back of his neck, but it passed after he'd taken another dozen steps.

Off to his left, a gray-bearded man wearing brown trousers and little else ran across the grass away from the cottages, then collapsed in a heap. Roget stopped and watched. The gray-beard rolled over, then crawled back toward the cottages before slowly standing. Then he again ran away from the cottages, as if trying to escape, before he crumpled onto the grass once more.

Roget turned to Lyvia.

"There's a subsonic fence around the cottage area. Didn't you sense it? All of those restrained here experience agonizing pain if they even approach it. Sometimes some of them will crawl halfway in and become so paralyzed with pain that they can't move. That's one of the things that Mattias or his partner have to watch for."

"Can't anyone else . . ." Roget broke off his question. The immobilizing nature of the pain and the fact that none of the inmates could touch another supplied him with the answer to his uncompleted inquiry.

As Roget and Lyvia neared the first line of cottages, a woman wearing antique hoop skirts with her hair piled into a conical shape that looked like the tip of an ancient artillery shell waddled toward them. "I dare say that you be visitors, and unwelcome you are. Please cease and desist, and depart henceforth."

"We'll depart soon enough." Roget didn't want to

walk over her, but she was blocking the middle of the walkway, and he took another step.

She scuttled back. "Begone, evil one."

On the side porch of the next cottage, a painfully thin woman sat rocking on a makeshift rocker. Her eyes were fixed on the porch railing, even as she rocked herself methodically.

Roget blinked. A man hurried toward them, wearing a Federation shipsuit.

"You're not one of them, are you? I can see the difference. We're all prisoners here. Can you tell the Federation about us? Please! Anyone who's different they lock up here, and they say we're maladjusted, but we're not. I've been here years and years. I just want to go home. Please. I don't belong here. I really don't."

Roget couldn't help but stop, but when he looked more closely at the shipsuit, he could see that it was well-sewn but poorly designed, and with insignia and devices he'd never seen and that mixed officer and enlisted emblems.

"You have to tell them. You have to get help."

Roget looked at Lyvia.

She smiled sadly.

"You're no Fed! You're one of them. You're just trying to trick us . . ." Tears ran from the corners of the man's eyes, and he turned away.

Roget moved on.

"Come to the circus . . . come to the play, for all the world's a play, and the play's the thing . . ." Those words came from a thin-faced man who sat on a stool before a small table at the west side of the walkway, under an open window to a cottage. His fingers flicked out oversized cards onto the polished but battered wood surface. "I can call up Madame Sosotris for you, or even Tiresias . . . for you, sir, are the hanged man. You may not know it, but, that, you are . . . and you will return to your people, an alien people who clutch alien gods . . ."

Roget repressed a shiver. Mad as the man clearly was, Roget might well end up a hanged man, figuratively, of course, if dead all the same.

A woman of indeterminate age sat on the ground, leaning back against the wall of the next cottage, her feet splayed across dirt that might once have been a flower bed. She just giggled, then giggled again.

An odor of rancidness and outright filth crept more tightly around Roget the deeper he and Lyvia walked into the cottages.

"Doesn't anyone take care of them?" he asked in a low voice.

"Why? They've chosen not to be taken care of. We keep the replicators full and the houses functional. They can go to the clinic if they choose, or not, as they please. None of them is of exceptionally poor intelligence. All of them have chosen to remain here, and they did so while their minds were stabilized. We used to do stabilization once every five years and ask again, but the results were the same."

Everywhere Roget looked was madness, from glittering bright eyes to dull or vacant ones. What the inhabitants of Manor Farm Cottages wore ranged from almost any kind of clothing Roget had ever seen to nothing at all. Those who wore nothing tended to be painfully thin.

Abruptly, Lyvia turned to Roget. "You've seen enough. We need to head back to Skeptos. I'd like to pick up Aylicia before it's too late."

"That's fine with me." It certainly was, because it hadn't been Roget's idea to visit the cottages. Besides, both the sights and odors were beginning to get to him.

Lyvia turned. "We can go back this way. It's the other

main walkway. That way, you can see a different view of more of the same." Her voice remained cool.

Roget frowned as he neared another cottage. The stones of the walls glistened. The windows sparkled, and the trim was even painted. An angular man was scrubbing the stones of the north wall of the small dwelling vigorously. He didn't look up or sideways as Lyvia and Roget walked by. Roget had the feeling that his scrubbing was what had polished the stones. He wondered how many years it had taken.

In an open grassy area to his left, Roget turned to watch a gray-haired woman running, holding a string with a small kite attached. Even at full speed, the woman could barely keep the little kite airborne.

Roget said nothing more. He just kept watching and walking until he and Lyvia were on the path away from the cottages and had passed the subsonic barrier.

"Now you've seen the Manor Farm Cottages."

"How can anyone do that? How can you?"

"It's their choice."

"That's no choice," snapped Roget.

"No . . . they have a choice. They can ask for personality modification or guided re-memory emphasis. All of them have rejected that. They claim that they wouldn't be themselves."

"Isn't that true?"

"Absolutely," Lyvia agreed. "But the people that they are as themselves make choices that impact violently and adversely on others, occasionally fatally, and individual freedom must always stop well short of other people's persons."

"So you'd turn them into automatons . . ."—he struggled for the word—". . . zombies, the living dead."

"They're very much alive. Not particularly sane, but

definitely alive. Medicating or adjusting them might turn them into zombies, though."

"And you can't do anything better than this? There has to be a better way."

"Sometimes there isn't. There are limits to what one can do to the human brain," Lyvia replied. "Are you running around screaming that we're evil monsters who won't share our technology? Even if you feel that way?"

"Of course not."

"Exactly. Even you choose to behave civilly in a situation where you feel under threat. If they choose to live in what amounts to an animal farm . . . that's their choice," Lyvia replied. "We don't feel obligated, beyond the basic necessities, to coddle those who are unwilling to make decisions that allow them to function in society. We don't believe that we should have to spend huge amounts of resources keeping people who won't act responsibly comfortable and in better situations than those who work. Unlike some societies, we require accountability and real choices."

"What sort of choice is that?" He gestured back toward the cottages.

"It's a real choice."

"Why don't you just . . . adjust them?"

"Without their consent? And then where would it stop?" asked Lyvia. "Once you give governments the power to adjust people and their perceptions, you're on the road to empire and ruin. Throughout history, societies have forced unfree choices on people. We don't force the choices; we just insist on the consequences of those choices falling on the choosers—except when it's clear that there isn't the mental capacity to choose. There are very few people to whom that applies, and they're handled far more gently and warmly."

"What about the lack of emotional capacity?"

She gestured back toward Manor Farm. "They end up in cottages like these and they remain there for life . . . or until they decide they want to change."

"That's . . . cruel."

"Is it? All choices involve change," she said patiently. "These people wish to hurt others in one way or another, either by refusing to take responsibility for their actions or taking emotional or physical pleasure in inflicting abuse. That's not acceptable."

"What about those who seek adventure, the thrill of danger? Do you imprison their minds as well?"

Lyvia smiled. "No. Just as there is always another dynasty, so to speak, there are always frontiers, and we let them seek such—just not on Dubiety."

"What do you mean by 'another dynasty'?"

"Isn't it obvious? In stable empires, the rulers change. If matters get too bad, another family or group usurps power, and matters go on mostly as before. Societies that have frontiers tend to be more stable in the center because the adventure-and-danger seekers gravitate toward the frontiers, as do the antisocial or the less advantaged."

"How many of your well-adjusted citizens know about places . . . like these?"

"Every last one of them over the age of eighteen. It's called the Omelas requirement. I don't know the origin of the term, but it means that they have to see that, while all choices are possible, they all have repercussions, and that even in the best of societies, the greatest cruelty is freedom of choice. A society that eliminates all misery eliminates true choice and freedom."

"The great freedom to be miserable." Roget didn't hide the sarcasm.

"Without it, there is no joy." After a moment, she gestured behind them. "Do you think I really wanted to bring you here? That I enjoyed this?"

Roget was silent.

20

26 LIANYU 6744 F. E.

Roget did get some sleep on Saturday night and early Sunday morning, but he still woke with a headache— and a very sore leg. He could move his leg, and that would have to do. A very hot shower helped get rid of the headache and eased the soreness in his leg somewhat. As he hurried through a marginally palatable and fully replicated breakfast, he considered what he needed to do . . . and what the Saint dissidents might do— although he had no doubt that they thought they were patriots or idealists or true believers, something along those lines.

One possibility was that none of the conspirators would do anything and, if questioned, claim that Smith had been operating on his own. The other was that they'd attempt to remove any additional evidence located elsewhere. Roget was betting on the second, and that was another reason why he was up early on Sunday.

He sponged and wiped off the nightsuit as well as he could, then donned it. He did not power it up. That would come later. While it wouldn't be as effective in daylight, its background matching provided excellent camouflage during the day, especially inside and when he wasn't moving, and that might come in useful. Then he reloaded the wrist-dart, still with just paralyzing darts rather than the lethal variety, and gathered his equipment together. Within ten minutes he was out of the apartment, walking up 800 East to the tram station, where he waited ten minutes before he took the next eastbound. He was one of three people in the entire car, and the other two were Sudam men who seemed to be dozing.

Once he left the Red Cliffs station, and he was the only one who got off there, he walked to the path down Middleton wash, through the gate to Delbert Parsens's studio, and up the path and around to the east side of the building. The sign in the outside niche read STUDIO CLOSED. That didn't surprise Roget. He'd discovered that most Saint establishments were closed on Sunday, as they had been traditionally for centuries, if not longer.

He stepped into the shadows of the entrance at the top of the stone steps and powered up the nightsuit, then eased the mesh hood over his face. Roget could sense the energies of the building's security system, but it was on standby, suggesting that people were inside, for all that the studio area looked empty. The door was locked, but only manually, and it took but a few moments with his picks before Roget was inside. He locked the door behind himself, replaced the picks in his waist-pak, and moved slowly down the long gradual ramp from the entrance into the main studio, keeping close to the walls and display cases to his right.

No one was in the studio. Roget glanced at the block of redstone Parsens had been working earlier but didn't see that the sculptor had made that much progress on the John D. Lee statue. He continued through the studio

and up a short and narrow ramp to the older section of
the building. The staircase to the lower level wasn't
concealed at all, but lay behind a partly open door off
the old main foyer of the building. Roget could sense
energies below, as well as hear the murmur of voices
that grew louder as he eased down the steps. At the bottom was a small foyer and an open door to the right.
The room there was empty, but was set up as a small
lecture hall or classroom.

From where were the voices coming?

Then he realized that the mirror at the rear of the
lower foyer wasn't anything of the sort, but a reflective
holo screen. He started to ease his head through the
screen near the edge, fighting the disorientation, and
found himself looking at a closet. To his right was a
side panel, barely ajar. He stepped into the closet, then
peered through the narrow opening in the sliding side
panel.

Beyond it was a long chamber, and along one side
were piping and what looked to be antique heat concen-
trators and generators. Beyond them was an array of
more modern and large flash capacitors. As Roget had
suspected, a small geothermal power plant lay under
the studio, most probably the source of the thermal discharge to the Virgin River.

Roget couldn't see that much beyond the three men
who sat around an old table, except that there was a
solid wooden wall on the west end of the chamber. That
didn't mean there wasn't another hidden doorway or
passage, not the way the Saint conspirators seemed to
favor them. After a moment he recognized two of the
three—Parsens and Sorensen. The third looked like the
single image of William Dane he'd been able to find.

Roget listened.

". . . tried the antidotes with Brendan, but by the time we could get to him he was already gone . . ."

Antidotes? Roget had made sure that his wrist-dart had only used paralytic darts, not combat darts that immediately shocked the nervous system into a fatal shutdown. Had Smith had allergies? But if he had, why had the others been prepared with an antidote . . . unless they were waiting for a security raid?

"Mitchell . . . he said he'd be here later. Something came up in his ward . . ."

"Something always comes up in his ward, especially if there's anything possibly inconvenient to do . . . or decide . . . unless he knows someone else will do it . . ."

"ChinoFed has to be the new E&W monitor . . . no one else new in town . . ."

". . . early thirties and a temp appointment . . . says FSA to me . . ."

". . . could be a deep agent they activated . . ."

". . . wouldn't have two of them here. They don't think we're that big a problem . . ."

"No . . . just think that the only good Danite is a dead Danite . . ."

Danites? It took a moment before Roget recalled the religious terrorist organization that had been agitating for local regional rule, based on "cultural differences."

"They'll see."

"They might see too soon. They got Brendan, and Tyler says that there's a Federation inspector at Deseret-Data already with a military escort. They've found the armory."

"Not everything was there."

"Enough, and enough for proof."

"Only against Brendan."

". . . won't stop them . . ."

"Do we move everything out of here?"

"Where do we move it? And why? Except for some personal weapons . . ."

"The FSA can claim anything they find is illegal. You know that . . ."

"Too bad Marni's stuff doesn't always work . . ."

". . . converts some . . ."

Converts some? Chemical conversion? There was no way that could work. In any case, Roget didn't dare wait too long, and he'd heard enough. He lifted his arm and fired the first dart, then the second. Both Sorensen and Parsens were convulsing before Dane leapt to his feet and whirled toward the panel door, his hand reaching for the nerve shredder on the table.

It took Roget two darts to get a clean shot, but Dane struggled, then collapsed.

Roget pushed aside the panel and hurried toward the fallen men. All three were twitching, and Sorensen began to gasp.

Antidotes? Roget searched Sorensen quickly but couldn't find anything resembling an inhaler, a syringe, or an injector. He moved to Dane, but found nothing there. Parsens had an injector of some sort, and Roget immediately pressed it against Sorensen's bare neck.

Slowly, the gasping stopped—except both other men had begun to wheeze. Abruptly, Parsens shuddered and stopped breathing. Then, so did Dane.

Roget stood, slowly.

Had all of them been death-sensitized to Federation paralytics? Why? So they couldn't reveal the extent of the conspiracy or the underground—the Danites? He turned toward the west wall . . . too late.

"I wouldn't move if I were you."

Roget finished turning, slowly, to face the speaker, standing before an open door on the west end of the underground room. The one side of the door matched the paneling, one reason why Roget hadn't noticed it.

Marni Sorensen stood there, wearing motion-detecting goggles, with a nerve shredder trained on him. "Stay right there, Keir. You may be in a camosuit, but there's no one else quite so tall as you in town."

"I wouldn't think of moving. But I do have a question for you before you shred me. What was that business with the false memory?"

"It wasn't false. It's just a chunk of memory. Not yours, but one picked to give you a chance to understand. To learn what's really important in life. At worse, it would disorient you. We would have preferred that you understood. Live converts are far better than dead FSA infiltrators."

The whole idea of memories inserted into his brain chilled Roget, but he couldn't dwell on that. Not at the moment. "Whatever it was, it killed an innocent photographer . . ." That was a guess on Roget's part.

"He had the same chance you did. To understand—"

"And become an unwilling convert?" Another guess on Roget's part.

"It doesn't work that way. It just opens you to understand. He was another Federation spy who couldn't understand . . ."

"He was just an observer."

"*Just* an observer? Like you're just an E&W monitor." Her laugh was short and harsh. "It really is too bad you won't get to relive the rest of the memories. You might understand, then, you traitor . . ."

"Traitor to what . . . ?"

"I couldn't expect you to be loyal to Deseret, but you could have been loyal to the United States . . ."

"There hasn't been a United States in more than a thousand years," Roget protested.

"That's right. That's because of cowardly traitors like you, knuckling under to the Sinese to keep yourselves comfortable . . ."

"What's back in the other room, besides more geo-thermal power units?"

"It doesn't matter." She lifted the barrel of the nerve shredder fractionally, so that it pointed directly at his chest.

Roget stretched his arms slightly, bringing them forward just slightly. "What's the point? You've already killed one Federation agent, and you're about to kill another. For what? You don't have the funds or the resources to take on the Federation. Your hidden armory is already under Federation control."

"You don't understand, do you? Faith and knowledge will always triumph. It takes both. The United States thought will and skill and knowledge was enough. It wasn't. The Republic of Faith and the Islamists thought faith was sufficient. It wasn't."

"Marni . . ." Roget said quietly. "No one else is coming. The Danites will lose. You won't get rescued."

"Neither will you. The Federation's weakness is that it doesn't ever send enough operatives to handle situations. You're more expendable than I am." Marni Sorensen smiled coolly as she kept the nerve shredder pointed at his midsection.

Roget almost felt sorry for her . . . and her ignorance. "That's its strength as well." He stretched, swinging his arms together and locking his fingers.

The dart took her in the eye, and she stood there, shivering, trying to press the stud on the shredder before it slipped from her fingers and *clunked* dully on the crimson carpet.

". . . you still have to live with the memories . . . understand . . . you will . . ." She shuddered, then collapsed into a heap, twitching.

Roget hurried toward her, then bent down and rifled through her singlesuit, searching for an injector that might hold an antidote. There wasn't one. He rushed through the open hidden doorway to the room from which she had come—and halted. The south side of the long chamber was filled with equipment, including more microfabbers and other devices he didn't immediately recognize, but the north side was bright and spotless . . . and looked like a small but equipment-intensive laboratory of some sort. Roget hurried through the laboratory, opening drawers, cabinets, and cases, but amid all the equipment, while he saw a case of unused and unopened injectors, he didn't see, or couldn't find, anything that resembled a loaded injector.

By the time he returned, empty-handed, Marni was dead.

Roget looked down at her still form, then shook his head.

He checked Bensen Sorensen, but the innkeeper and Danite was still breathing. Roget used a pair of restraints on Sorensen's hands and feet, although the dart wasn't likely to wear off before the Federation inspector appeared.

Then he walked upstairs and out to the studio, where he used the comm system and his personal monitor to burst-send an urgent report.

The reply was immediate:

Inspector and team on the way. Vacate and do not break cover.

Roget slipped his monitor back into its case, then moved toward the door. Marni had been the only one who'd actually seen him, if in the nightsuit, but his cover was still broken, no matter what his controller said. Still, he wasn't about to argue. Not where he was.

He hurried back out through the sliding panel, leaving

it open, and up the stairs, and then to the studio and up the ramp.

Likely as not, more than a few members of the Saint Quorum and Presidency would end up vanishing over the weeks and months ahead. Then again, they might not, but they weren't his problem. Despite what had just happened, he wasn't an eliminator . . . unless he was threatened. He was just the one who uncovered the problems and started the resolution.

He told himself that again as he opened the door at the east end of Parsens's studio, then stepped outside, leaving it unlocked this time.

He took three steps out into the full morning sunlight before a wave—or a cloud—of dizziness brought him to a halt, the red rocks and stones to the east of him swirling like solid red clouds.

He staggered backward, then sat down on the bottom step, just before the blackness rose up and drowned him.

21

21 MARIS 1811 P. D.

That Monday night, Roget sat on the sofa in his guest-house quarters, sipping what amounted to barely drinkable formulated lager. He looked at the projection of Hildegarde. The cheerful little dachshund helped lighten his mood . . . a little.

"All you have to worry about is being loved and fed, little dog . . ."

Hildegarde continued to look expectantly out from the projection.

"That's the thing about dogs. You're always happy to see the ones you love, no matter what, and that's definitely not true of people." Roget knew that Muffin, his childhood companion, had been that way, but he'd been too young to fully appreciate her faithfulness and affection until long after she died. Was Hildegarde a way of reminding him? Quite possibly, but even from the projection, he could tell that Hildegarde was different from Muffin. There was a hint of seriousness, determination . . .

He laughed. Much as he enjoyed the projection, he was also projecting what he felt. As his soft laugh died away in the lowered lights, he turned his thoughts from dogs to his own situation.

He still hadn't learned what the colonel really wanted, even if he would never directly request it—and that was a military assessment of Dubiety. Not that Roget hadn't tried to find out more, but the entire Dubietan society made discovering and accurately assessing industrial, technological, and military capabilities difficult. He would have wagered that his estimations were accurate, but estimations didn't matter to the FSA, not when the Mandarins wanted hard facts and evidence, as bureaucracies always did. His lack of such hard information would, of course, provide a perfect rationale for instituting military action against Dubiety, and that was most likely what the Federation wanted. What empire wanted rivals that might surpass it?

The danger was that such rivals might already have surpassed it and that the Federation would refuse to see it. Like Midas of Lydia, for whom the oracles foretold the fall of a great empire, except it was his own.

Roget shook his head, thinking back over the day.

Once he and Lyvia had returned to Skeptos, she had taken her leave, right at the central square, and he had roamed through the city, heading more into the eastern sections, where he had found differing architectural styles, and a whole section that might have been lifted, if modernized, out of ancient Crete—at least as the archeological renderings he'd seen had depicted the ancient Minoan civilization.

Along the way, he had also discovered an opera house, featuring *The Wonder Age,* a work he'd never heard of, not surprisingly, and an art museum, with a wide range of work, all of it seemingly good, if not great. He'd gravitated to the paintings, especially nautical scenes, and to one deep-space painting, depicting a huge ovoid craft, partly eclipsed by an asteroid, with a small grayish silvery sphere in the distant background. The color of the sphere was wrong for it to be Dubiety, as viewed from farther out in the solar system, unless the artist had taken liberties, which certainly wasn't unlikely, but Roget hadn't gotten that feeling.

While it was difficult to determine the absolute size of the featureless ovoid spacecraft, a comparison to the detailed features of the asteroid suggested that the ovoid was far larger than any Federation battlecruiser and perhaps even as large as a small nickel-iron asteroid. Was it a planoforming craft? But if it happened to be, where had it been built, and where were the facilities for constructing it? And where was it now? The other aspect was the gallery in which the painting appeared. Everything else there was completely verifiably factual, scenes on Dubiety. There was even a scene of a cottage similar to those at Manor Farm Cottages, where a half-clad old woman sat in partial shade looking at a chessboard, while a bearded man wearing a formal jacket over a tattered singlesuit looked blankly beyond her from the other side of a table holding half-eaten food.

He had not seen anything like *Hildegarde in the Sunshine,* and that had pleased him, he had to admit.

He and Lyvia were scheduled to meet again with Selyni Hillis on Tuesday morning. Roget couldn't say that he was looking forward to it, although he couldn't have said why. Certainly he'd been treated with courtesy and given the freedom to go wherever he wanted— within certain limits. The problem was that he'd found little direct evidence of Dubiety's technical or military capabilities within those limits. There were more than a few indirect indicators, such as the engineering and speed of the regional subtrans trains, the quiet sophistication of the planetary economic system and its ability to function as a social control, the capability of the Dubietans to focus energy so tightly that virtually no stray radiation escaped anywhere—not to mention the orbital shields of the planet itself.

What these all signified—if his interpretations were correct—didn't bode all that well for his mission, the Federation, and Roget himself. But . . . they weren't proof either, and Roget had learned that the Federation tended to value hard proof, even proof that led to the wrong conclusions over accurate intuitive speculation— and that was without considering the hidden, or not-so-hidden, agendas.

Dubiety certainly wasn't all that it seemed. The carnivorous butterflies had been one indication, and the Manor Farm Cottages were another, both horrifying in more than one respect. The whole issue of choice nagged at him. The Dubietans seemed to have adopted an almost hands-off attitude—or one of minimal care—for those in their society who refused or who were unable to live by their society's standards. Yet . . . all societies needed some way to deal with sociopaths and worse. And he couldn't argue, not strongly anyway, against the idea that the antisocial and irresponsible shouldn't live comfortably on the efforts of others or against the premise that meddling with people's minds against their will was unacceptable. But they conditioned the inhabitants of the cottages against touching others, and that was certainly meddling.

The odors had bothered him, as well, and he definitely wasn't sure about the validity of the Omelas idea that the freedom of choice always created some misery. But then, didn't every society create misery? Wasn't the question only what kind of misery? And for whom?

The Federation didn't have cottages like those at Manor Farm, but it also didn't tolerate those who didn't accept the rules—and many of those dissenters died, and the rest certainly didn't end up with the best of lives, especially with the way the Federation conditioned them. With what Roget had seen during his years with the FSA, he'd never been sure that the Federation had had many better options for social control, given the range of human nature, passions, and beliefs. Yet the Dubietans had seemingly found a way to handle those without patrollers visible everywhere, but was that just because beneath their velvet-gloved surface lay an even more effective iron fist or an even more silent version of the FSA?

Or had they found a way to use technology and economics less disruptively?

He shook his head. He felt as though his thoughts were spinning in circles.

Finally, he looked back to the projected image. "After all these years, I still wonder about your mistress,

Hildegarde. She must have been quite someone for you to look for her so expectantly . . ."

Hildegarde didn't answer. She never had, but that didn't matter. Roget still smiled.

22

26 LIANYU 6744 F. E.

"Did I hear the mermaids singing each to each, as if I dared to wear white flannel trousers and walk upon the beach?"

"Not until human voices wake you," replied a warm and slightly husky voice.

"What?" Roget blinked. He sat at a table set with glittering silver cutlery. Crystal water and wine goblets stood just beyond the three knives and the gold and black rimmed white bone china before him. The wine in the goblet was dark red, or looked to be in dim light, and the table linens were brilliant white. The light was soft, from a single candle in a crystal holder.

Across from him at the table for two a woman smiled. Her mahogany red hair barely touched the collar of the pale green blouse that complemented the darker green jacket. She wore earrings, Roget realized, and her ears were pierced, something he'd not seen in years. There was the faintest trace of a warm smile on lips that were neither too full nor too thin.

"Your mind is wandering again," the woman said.

"You misquote the old poets when you're someplace else in your thoughts. What political chicanery or legislative legerdemain are you concocting now?"

Roget wanted to protest that he had nothing of the sort in mind. Instead, he replied, "Merely an amendment to allow for greater local religious autonomy for the states."

"Merely?"

"So long as everyone's rights are protected, why should those who believe in nothing be allowed to dictate what those who believe differently can say in public places? Freedom of speech should work two ways, shouldn't it?"

"For all your parliamentary and political expertise, Joseph, I'd like to believe that you're still that young missionary trying to convert the faithless and provide a testimony for those who believe in the irrationality of reason rather than in the irrationality of God."

Joseph? Roget knew he wasn't Joseph, but the words still came out of his mouth. "You, Susannah? You'd *like* to believe?" He smiled warmly. "You of all people know who I am. You always have."

"The nonbelievers won't support it. You know that."

"I do know that."

"Then it's a gesture, a mere political move to solidify your support among the Believers."

"Is that really so bad? They need someone behind whom they can unite."

"They're already behind you. Who else do they have?"

"If I don't remind them, now and again, they lose total faith in the political system."

"You're more worried that they'll lose faith in you, I think." The woman smiled sadly, then took a sip from her wine goblet. "Isn't it late for gestures?"

Roget knew she was almost as old as he was, yet

there was a beauty, and a melancholy behind the bright and yet deep green eyes. "If we're being frank . . . yes. But gestures are all I have left. The Believers want a return to a strong and Christian nation, but they'll sacrifice strength to hold off the atheist onslaught on religious expression. The atheists want neither a strong faith nor a strong nation, but one where commerce is king and where anything and everything has a price . . . and where the price for national economic and military strength is too high." He shrugged. "I've said that for years, and I've fought for rebuilding our military, especially the Navy. You know I have. What has it accomplished? Until the Democrats retook the House and Senate, I managed to stave off the worst. Now . . ." He let the silence speak.

"I would have liked things to have worked out differently," she said.

"You know how I feel about you."

"I know what you say."

"Then I'll do a riff on old Tom . . . if we became lovers in more than spirit, that love would die, because where we would be would be what we are not . . ."

Her laugh was short, and both warm and bitter at the same time. "You've been charming enough that I've even accepted the modern equivalent of courtly love for all these years, all because you can be so poetic, you old raven."

"Ah, yes . . . the raven ascending flames the air, for there are no doves in Hell . . . or in Washington where all are consumed by flame or fire."

"Or fire," she added. "Why is it, as you once said, that the end of all exploring is to find one's self where one began?"

"I only repeated what old Tom said more than a century ago."

"Oh . . . yes . . . the most erudite war hero, the noble Senator Joseph Tanner, who is adept with both his words and those of others."

"These days, dear lady, words are all that I have left, and sometimes, precious few of them. Occasionally, they suffice to gain me the votes to plug a hole or two in the dike of our foundering republic."

"Oh . . . Joseph . . . why . . . why did it come to this?"

"What else could we have done? How else should I have presumed."

"That is not what I meant, at all." The words of her reply were coolly ironic.

"I know that, too." Roget reached for the wine goblet, taking it and then raising it. "To you, dear one. I have so enjoyed these dinners. They're one of the few pleasures I have left."

As he saw the pain in the woman's eyes, Roget thought he should say something, anything, any small word of comfort. But he was mute. He struggled again to force the smallest word of warmth.

With that struggle, the blackness swirled around him, and phrases, strange phrases, rushed through his thoughts.

". . . to lead you to an overwhelming question . . ."

". . . the art of preparing a face to meet other faces . . ."

". . . not a hero, nor meant to be . . ."

". . . the knowledge, the wisdom, and the faith we have lost in gaining information . . ."

". . . continue the fight against darkness in air and fire, in words and deeds . . ."

A cold chill froze Roget's forehead, and he opened his eyes. He lay on the sofa in his own apartment in St. George, looking up at a junior security monitor. A cold compress rested across his forehead.

"He's awake, Inspector Hwang, sir."

An inspector? Roget slowly struggled into a sitting position, awkwardly catching the compress.

A solid black-haired man in the uniform of a Federal inspector walked toward Roget. "Don't try to get up, Agent-Captain Roget."

"Yes, sir."

The inspector pulled one of the straight-backed chairs from the table and turned it to face Roget. He sat down. "You were found unconscious by the door to that sculptor's studio. How did that happen?" Hwang's voice was calm, neither sympathetic nor critical.

"I couldn't say, sir, except that it might be an after-effect of whatever the Danites injected me with in the restaurant on Friday."

"You let that happen?"

"Yes, sir. As I reported on Friday, I didn't expect the entire restaurant staff to be Danite sympathizers. I hadn't done anything except my cover duties as an E&W monitor, but they apparently knew who I was from the beginning."

"We've discovered that," Hwang said dryly. "Why were the three in the studio dead?"

"They all had some sort of suicide implant as a reaction to paralytic darts. They carried antidotes, but they'd tried to use them last night on Smith—he was the one who died in the EES shop—and I could only find one injector, and that was the one I used on Sorensen."

The inspector nodded. "He suffered considerable brain trauma. We may not get much from him either. He'll end up in a low-function security colony."

Roget had the feeling that he'd botched just about everything.

"You smoked out this cell, and that's what single agents are supposed to do. You even saved us the trouble of dealing with most of them."

"I overheard them saying that there are more, all over old Deseret."

"There always have been. There probably always will be. True Believers never understand the need for secular rationality. That's one of the reasons why there's a Federation Security Agency." Hwang paused. "Your cover is gone, and you've got medical problems. We'll send you to Cheyenne for rehab and recovery. Don't worry about anything but recovering."

"Yes, sir."

"I've sent for a lorry to take you and your personal effects out to the local airfield for air-evac. It should be here before long. There will be two guards outside until you leave."

"Thank you, sir."

Hwang nodded, then rose.

After the inspector and the junior monitor left, Roget couldn't help but wonder how he could not worry. The memory sequence had been so real . . . so very real.

Joseph Tanner—had Tanner been real? That was certainly something Roget could research. But then, what if the senator had been real? What did that mean? How had Marni ever captured those memories? Would Roget ever be able to escape the memory flashbacks? But then, there had been something about memory selection . . . but how?

There were so many questions he'd not had a chance to think through . . . so many.

He swallowed, sitting on the couch, not knowing when his transport might arrive. His eyes flicked to the projection of Hildegarde, still looking up expectantly. Just looking at the small black-and-tan dachshund helped, even if Roget couldn't have said why.

23

Nine in the morning, local Skeptos time on Tuesday, found Roget and Lyvia seated around the same conference table where they had been the day before, with Roget again facing Director Hillis.

"How was your visit to Manor Farm cottages?" asked Hillis.

"Instructive and depressing," replied Roget.

"Why did you find it depressing?"

"How could one not?" countered Roget. "With all those dysfunctional individuals whom you've left with no hope?"

"They are provided with comfortable quarters, ample food, medical attention if they'll only seek it out, clean clothing if they choose to wear it, full incoming communications, not to mention considerable freedom to move about. What else, exactly, would you suggest that would not result in harm to other innocents?"

"What about curing them?"

"We cure those where, first, it is possible, and second, where they wish it. Those in the cottages have chronic conditions where any treatment would impair their intelligence."

There was no argument to the conditions stated by Hillis, not one with which Roget would have been comfortable or could support logically.

"You, Agent Roget, are afflicted with the old American illusion that insists, when you are faced with a difficult set of choices, all of which result in unpleasant outcomes, that there must be a better way. It's always useful to explore the possibilities, and even to give them a trial, but it's also bullheaded stupidity to insist that there must be a better way if you and other intelligent individuals cannot find such a way."

"How do you know there isn't a better way?"

"From what you've seen of Dubiety, if we'd discovered one, don't you think we'd have tried it? Do you really think that any one of us likes the cottages?"

Roget had seen Lyvia's reactions, and he had to admit that Hillis's words also sounded truthful. Somehow, that also bothered him, but more than a few things about Dubiety concerned him, and every day there seemed to be something else. "So when will you reveal to me your awesome military prowess so that I can report to my superiors that the Federation should leave you well enough alone?"

"Even if we showed you a battle fleet twice the size of any Federation fleet, they would not take your word for it. We will be allowing you to return with documentation and descriptions of technology the Federation does not have, and I will wager that it will be dismissed as irrelevant, insignificant, or a complete fabrication."

"So what's the point of allowing me to return?"

"I think we've already shown you that," replied the director, "if you will just think about it. I won't spell it out, because your superiors would then believe that you will have parroted our words." She rose and looked to Lyvia. "Perhaps a tour of the capitol building would help."

"Yes, Director." Lyvia stood, almost wearily.

Roget stood and inclined his head politely.

Selyni Hillis nodded. "Tomorrow at nine thirty." Then she left the conference room.

Roget waited for Lyvia to lead the way to wherever the capitol was, although from his recollections of the maps Lyvia had provided, he thought it was north of the central square as much as a klick, if not farther.

Lyvia said nothing until they were outside the ministry building. Then she stopped and fastened her jacket against the chill wind before she spoke. "The capitol is about ten blocks north. We can walk back to the square . . ."

"I'd just as soon walk if that's all right with you," he replied. "If it's not too cold."

"I'd prefer walking." Lyvia started out.

Roget matched her quick steps.

After two blocks, he had to admit that he was happy to have his jacket, which had vanished from his pack and then reappeared in his guesthouse closet when the gray singlesuit had been returned and cleaned. He wondered what had been added that had taken the extra time.

"The capitol isn't exactly in the center of Skeptos," he finally said.

"There's no reason for it to be. It has its own local subtrans station under the plaza."

"Was it planned that way?"

"It was."

"How many tribunes are there?"

"Two hundred and one, and the representation is by population in geographically cohesive districts. We don't allow gerrymandering."

"And those in the House of Denial? What are they called?"

"Popularly, they're the deniers. Technically, each has the title of reviewer. There are usually around fifty, but the number can vary. The limits are no less than forty and no more than fifty-nine. No reviewer can serve more than five years without remaining out of office for the same time."

Roget didn't pretend to understand how the Dubietans made a system like theirs work, but, from what he'd seen, it seemed to . . . at least for them.

Two blocks north of the Ministry of Education and Culture, the officelike buildings gave way to structures much more like the guesthouse where Roget was lodged, but sections of the ground level right off the walkways were given over to various shops. One featured a range of athletic gear, and he saw a display of the basket-sticks, similar to lacrosse sticks, that he'd observed in the games in the parks over the weekend.

Then, after they walked past a two-level apartment-style dwelling, there were no more buildings immediately before them.

"There's the capitol and the square," announced Lyvia, stopping and gesturing at the green-tinged marble structure set on a low rise in the middle of grass, knee-high hedges, and gardens. The square looked to be half a klick on a side, with the capitol a low two-story structure some hundred meters across the front and half that in depth. The only adornment was a low silvery dome in the middle, topped by the silvery hazy sphere that represented Dubiety. Three sets of pale green marble steps rose from a wide but narrow plaza. "The center steps are to the Judiciary, the ones to the left are to the House of Tribunes, and those to the right are to the House of Denial."

Roget saw only a handful of people on the plaza below the building, and all those were in the center, below the steps to the Judiciary, several of whom emerged from circular stone kiosks that doubtless were where the tunnels emerged from the subtrans.

Lyvia led the way toward the plaza, following a wide

but winding stone path through the gardens that generally angled in the direction of the House of Tribunes.
Most of the flowers had wilted or dried up, and those
that had not looked as if they would not last all that long.
The amber light that filtered through the orbital shields
seemed less intense as well.

"How much colder does it get?" he asked.

"It stays close to freezing for around six weeks in
winter, but you'll be gone before that happens. Then
we'll be into spring, and that is long and chill but not
freezing."

Roget hoped that meant he'd be on his way back to
the *WuDing,* rather than permanently gone.

The west end of the Plaza was empty except for them,
as were the green-tinted marble steps leading up to the
simple arch that was slightly trapezoidal. The south
facade of the capitol had no columns, no ornate decora-
tions, just sheet walls of marble, interspersed with long
narrow windows. At the top of the steps was a set of
greenish translucent doors that opened as they approached. Inside was a foyer stretching a mere ten meters on each side of the doors and extending back six
meters or so. On the north side of the foyer were two
sets of double doors, wooden doors, rather than the
translucent automatic ones.

Roget glanced around, but he saw no one in the foyer.

"This way." Lyvia walked toward the right-hand
doorway. The old-style wooden door actually had brass
handles. She pulled on the handle, and the door swung
toward her. Inside the chamber, the lights flashed on.
She left the door open until Roget took it when she
walked inside.

As he released the door, letting it swing closed, Roget
followed her into the chamber, a half-amphitheater with
true wooden desks set on tiered daises, all facing a

raised podium. Behind the podium was a holo projection—a starscape of some sort. Roget moistened his lips as he studied it. He couldn't be absolutely certain, but the image appeared to have been captured from orbit above Dubiety facing outsystem. It was a true image, not exaggerated, because there was only one disk, and that was tiny, most probably the nearer of the three outer gas giants.

Most government assemblies featured flags, or seals, or symbols designed to create a sense of unity and/or patriotism. The only decoration in the House of Delegates was a vast projected hologram of the endless universe. Otherwise, all the walls were bare.

"Is that the only hologram projected?" he asked.

"There are three others, but they're all starscapes. Each is from a different quadrant of Dubiety's orbit. They change seasonally."

"This is the winter one, then?"

Lyvia nodded.

Roget continued to survey the chamber before finally speaking. "This whole part of the building's empty."

"Both ends are," replied Lyvia. "Neither House is in session. The Judiciary operates year-round."

"What about staff?"

"The Tribunes don't have official staff. Each has a small office on the upper or lower levels. It's just large enough for them."

"Are any of them around?"

"I couldn't say for certain, but I'd judge not. Anyone who has a problem with existing law or wants to propose legislation can comlink those problems or suggestions to their representative. That doesn't require that they be here."

"No one wants to meet face-to-face?"

"They very well might, but it's frowned upon, and in certain cases cause for dismissal from office."

"What?" Roget had trouble believing that. Dismissal for meeting with citizens and constituents? And she had called the Dubietan government representative?

"The right to personal representation is highly over-rated, not to mention one of the greatest contributors to corruption in governments that are theoretically demo-cratic and/or representative."

"If you wouldn't mind explaining that point . . ."

"You don't see why?" Lyvia's voice was tart.

"No. I don't. How can someone possibly represent a group or a district or whatever without being able to meet with them?"

"First, anyone who is eligible for election has to have lived in the same area with those they represent for at least ten years, and no one can be elected to the House of Tribunes who is less than forty-five. We don't much care for representatives who haven't been successful in some-thing else first. Second, anyone can petition them and send them concerns. They just can't do it face-to-face."

"And image-to-image is different?"

"All images are recorded. Permanently."

Roget began to see where the explanation was headed. "Subject to recall?"

"Subject to examination by the House of Denial and by any concerned citizen."

"But some people don't present themselves well when it's not in person. They need to have physical feed-back."

"For what? To play on the emotions of the represen-tative? To influence by other than the merits of their position? To override careful judgment with an upwell-ing of sincerity?" The scorn in her voice was biting. "Or worse, to offer or suggest indirect favoritism? Or an out-and-out bribe?"

"How do people know what their constituents are thinking? Do they have to rely on polls or surveys?"

"Polls and surveys are prohibited."

That was another shock to Roget. "And you think you allow freedom of expression?"

"Anyone can say anything that's truthful to anyone through any commnet and in any public venue. You might remember that. They just can't contact others on an organized basis and ask what those others think. That also applies to debates and discussions in any governmental forum."

"That doesn't sound exactly like representative government."

"It's very representative, Keir. It's a systematized way of avoiding political mob rule where government bases its actions on what people think they want rather than on the best judgment of the representative."

"What about businesses? Can they survey the public to see what people want to buy? Or is that prohibited as well?"

"No. They have to offer the best they can and learn from their experiences. We try to reward leadership, not followship. We're not interested in following the lemminglike path that doomed the old United States and most of the Euro-derived so-called democracies." Lyvia paused, then asked, "Have you seen enough here?"

With only an empty chamber before him, Roget had. He nodded.

Lyvia led the way back out and then around the front foyer and toward the rear of the building before turning to her right into a wide corridor leading toward the middle of the capitol.

Roget looked down the corridor, presumably to the Judiciary. "Are we going to see the justices?"

"We can walk down there and see what's in progress. Visitors aren't allowed in the chambers, but whatever is happening in the chamber is projected out into the main foyer. The same is true of the House of Tribunes and the House of Denial."

"Aren't you concerned that someone might present a false record of the proceedings or the debates?"

"With seven political parties and a very enthusiastic crop of attorneys who would love to seize the assets of anyone who did that? It's rather unlikely. Also," she added, "distortion or falsification of records of government proceedings is one of the few offenses that can merit a death sentence."

"But not murder?"

"Corruption of government kills and abuses everyone, and it's always for personal or professional gain, not for social improvement. In any case, we have very few murders," Lyvia said dryly. "Murder and child abuse are among the few offenses that result in a sentence of permanent alterations to brain functioning."

"And some of those in Manor Farm Cottages are there for that reason?"

"Possibly. There are some who cannot function in society after such treatment." Lydia resumed walking toward the Judiciary chamber.

Roget studied the corridor that seemed vaguely familiar, totally unfamiliar as it was, walking several meters before a wash of blackness swept over him. He took an unsteady step, then blinked. When he opened his eyes, the corridor was different.

Fluted columns lined both sides, and it was narrower, and the ceiling lower. The floor was a mixture of a reddish stone and one of grayish white, both highly polished. He stood in the middle of a group of people, all very young. Beside him was a tall and willowy brunette girl.

"Another explanation," she murmured, her eyes flicking to the front of the group where a fresh-faced guide had stopped.

"This corridor is known as Statuary Hall. That is because of all the sculptures that have been placed here over the years. . . ."

Roget/Tanner took in the guide's words as his eyes drifted from statue to statue. He recognized one or two, but most were unfamiliar, although he probably would recognize their names from American history.

"Joe . . ." whispered the youth to Roget's right, "Cari said you got your call. When do you leave?"

"In May just after the end of the semester."

"Where are you going?"

Roget—or Tanner—didn't want to answer that question. He just smiled. "Wherever they send me."

"You must know . . ."

Roget/Tanner shrugged. "It doesn't matter." Except it did. That he did know. He'd hoped for a mission somewhere in the Far East, but he was going to Peru. His parents had said that the country was like southern Utah, with red hills and mountains, but the Andes were far more imposing than places like the Wasatch Range or even Brian Head or Cedar Breaks. He'd wanted to improve his Mandarin, but it appeared that he'd just have to learn Spanish as well.

"This way," announced the guide, as the tour resumed.

"You could be a senator someday, Joseph," suggested the brunette in a low voice.

"I'm more interested in being a pilot, Cari."

"I suppose I could get used to being married to a pilot."

Roget/Tanner managed not to gape. He and Cari had dated, but he'd never tried anything serious, and he certainly hadn't proposed. How could he, with a mission coming up, three more years of college, and, if he were fortunate, flight training after that?

"You'll be more than a pilot. I know that."

"You know more than I do." His eyes drifted to the small rotunda ahead.

He could feel dizziness creeping up over him . . .

Roget found himself sitting on a stone bench. To his right and across the foyer was a holo showing a justice in a gray robe behind a judicial podium, looking down at a woman in a formal singlesuit and black jacket.

". . . did the defendant ever provide you with any evidence about the accuracy of the assertion in the prospectus . . ."

"Keir?" Lyvia's voice was strained.

That surprised him. "Yes. I'm . . . here." He'd almost said that he was back.

"You walked down the corridor as if no one were around you, and you were saying things about being a pilot."

"Flashbacks," he admitted. He wasn't about to admit that they weren't his flashbacks, not exactly. "It happens sometimes."

"And they sent you to Dubiety?"

"FSA doesn't know."

"Or they don't care."

That was certainly possible. "I couldn't say."

"Are you all right?"

"I'm fine. They don't happen often, sometimes not for years."

"When you're under stress, I'd imagine," Lyvia probed.

"Not even that, necessarily."

She nodded, not in agreement, but as if she had heard what he had said.

What was it about the Dubietan capitol? Or was it just that it *was* a capitol, and the first time he'd seen it?

"We should get you something to eat. A low blood sugar doesn't help."

"That might be good." He was hungry. He was also worried. He hadn't had a memory flashback in years, not since deep-space small-craft training, as he recalled. Dreams, yes, but not daytime flashbacks.

24

28 LIANYU 6744 F. E.

By the time Roget was escorted out of the unmarked Federation flitter at the FAF base outside Cheyenne, it was late on Sunday afternoon, and the two Air Force senior rankers were most insistent that he check into the medical facility immediately. Roget did . . . and then spent an uneventful evening and a restless night. On Monday he was ushered from medical test to medical test. None of the results were conveyed to him, and he had a quiet dinner in the officers' dining room. He slept somewhat better on Monday night, but not enough better that he didn't have vaguely uneasy dreams that he could not remember when he woke.

At nine thirty on Tuesday, two FSA guards appeared

and "requested" that he accompany them in an un-marked electrocar to the base security building. He did, and at almost precisely ten hundred he was escorted into a large office that held a large, plain, and impres-sive desk without a visible console, and three chairs set before the desk. The walls were plain, doubtless to en-able projections. Sitting behind the desk was a silver-haired Sinese in a colonel's uniform.

"Agent-Captain . . . please sit down." The colonel's voice was pleasant, almost musical. "You've had a rather trying month, it appears."

"I'm fine, sir."

The colonel smiled politely. "That's what the results of your medical tests show. You've recovered com-pletely from the injuries of your previous assignment. Outside of a few abrasions and bruises, your body shows no signs of further abuse." The colonel paused. "According to the medical staff, there is no apparent physical reason why you should have been found un-conscious outside the sculptor's studio, but the read-ings from your internals and the medical personnel present confirm that your consciousness had indeed been affected."

In short, Roget thought, the doctors had confirmed that he hadn't been faking, and they were all worried.

"Do you have any thoughts about this, Agent-Captain?"

Roget's internals could sense the various energy flows around the room, and he had no doubts that every bit of interrogation and surveillance technology known to the FSA was trained on him. "Yes, sir. I do."

"Please proceed to offer those thoughts."

"As I reported earlier, I was injected with an unknown substance by the Sorensen woman. Shortly thereafter, I suffered extreme dehydration and disorientation. I would surmise that the efforts involved in resolving the situation in St. George triggered a follow-up episode. Since I have experienced no additional symptoms, and since the medical tests, from what you suggested, sir, apparently indicated no remaining unknown substances in my system, it would appear to me that it's unlikely that there will be future occurrences."

The colonel nodded. "Your report suggested that this Danite terrorist organization might pose a regional threat to the Federation. I would be interested in why you think so—beyond the reasons you stated in your reports."

"I don't know that I have reasons beyond what I reported, sir. The terrorists seemed almost contemptuous of the Federation, as if we had no idea what we were up against. The fact that I could be assaulted with relatively sophisticated medical techniques openly in a public restaurant also suggests a wide degree of at least tacit public support."

The colonel's laugh was soft, short, and scornful. "The Agency has been aware of the Danites for many years. They meet and plot and think we know nothing, and so long as they do nothing, we allow them to have their secrets. When they do something, as they did in St. George, we act, as you did, and for a number of years thereafter they decide that meetings and muttered words in hidden rooms amount to rebellion. Then they attempt to act, and once more fail. It is predictable. It has been so for centuries."

"The Sorensen woman was a Federation employee," ventured Roget.

"All her communications were monitored. We thought they might use her as a lure. Did they not do just that?"

"I was aware that she had ulterior motives from the first, sir, as my reports indicated."

"As you should have been and were and as has been the case for generations. They seem to think that we see nothing and hear nothing when everything is seen and heard." The colonel paused. "You reported on the geothermal power units, but your report was less detailed on the chamber adjoining the one where you observed the terrorists. Can you elaborate on your report?"

"I hurried through it. I was trying to find an injector that might have held an antidote. It looked like a combination of a small manufacturing operation and a laboratory. The facility under DeseretData was used to fabricate nerve shredders, but I couldn't determine what the equipment beneath the sculptor's building was used for. The lab looked more like a very professional medical facility. As I reported, Marni Sorensen had told me she had a background in biology." He didn't mention her doctorate because he wanted to see how the colonel responded or avoided dealing with that fact. "When I reported in, I was told to vacate immediately. So I didn't go back and make a more thorough investigation."

"Her background didn't deal with biological terrorism, and she would have known any number of agents that might have disrupted your system without registering on your internals. She would not have needed a laboratory so elaborate for that. It would appear that either someone else had to have been involved or that she had some other project of value to the Danites. Would you have any idea who or what those might be, Agent Roget?"

"No, sir. None of those I investigated had that kind of background, not that I could determine."

"A pity. We will find them. We always do." The colonel paused. "After consulting with the medical staff, we have decided that you will be granted three weeks' convalescent leave. You will report back here for medical tests three weeks from Thursday. If those tests indicate that you are fully recovered, you'll be posted to your new assignment. If not, but it appears that you will recover, you will be temporarily assigned to analysis."

"Yes, sir."

"That will be all, Agent-Captain. You are free to leave the base at your convenience. If you choose to spend any or all of your leave here, you may request a room in the officers' quarters. If you wish to spend time elsewhere, you're authorized to receive the government travel rates at any lodging establishment, but the cost is your responsibility."

Roget stood. "Thank you, sir."

"Thank you. You managed to keep a messy situation relatively quiet. All the people of St. George know is that a fire brought an inspector and several people vanished. That's enough to keep them looking over their shoulders." The colonel looked down at the desk.

Roget inclined his head politely, then left the office, closing the door quietly.

The only person outside was the colonel's assistant, an older woman who said politely, "Good day, Agent-Captain."

As he walked from the security building to wait for a shuttle outside, he considered his options. Three weeks' convalescent leave. He frowned. His sister lived in the Fort Greeley complex that had grown up after the re-duction of Denver, and that wasn't all that far from Cheyenne on the maglev. He'd have to see if he could visit there for a few days, not that he'd impose on her for a bed, but he hadn't seen her in several years, not since she and Wallace had moved to Fort Greeley because he'd been posted away from Noram and couldn't justify the expense of transoceanic travel. He wouldn't stay that long because he didn't want to spend too much of his pay on lodging.

First, though, he wanted to do some research after he checked out of the medical center.

He had to wait almost a quarter hour for the shuttle, and it was another quarter hour before he was back at the base medical facility. By the time he collected his few personal items and authorized the various bureaucratic acknowledgments and releases, another hour elapsed.

Finally, some two hours later, he was settled into a small room in the officers' quarters, using his monitor to access the commnet. His first inquiry was for Joseph Tanner.

The response was close to immediate. While there were almost a hundred entries, none of the living Tanners, or those who had died in the last century, fit his criteria. When he eliminated them, just three remained, and only one fit his criteria. It was comparatively short.

Joseph Jared Tanner, Senator, United States of America 2039–2127 A.D., reputedly a former naval military pilot who was known as an opponent of "excessive" social programs and a staunch opponent of global federation . . . instrumental in the temporary resurgence of U.S. military forces before the Wars of Confederation . . .

That was it. Roget still smiled. Joseph Tanner had been real. His smile faded when he thought about how few Joseph Tanners remained in the records once they died. Fame—even remembrance—was indeed fleeting.

His next inquiry was on Marni Sorensen. Interestingly enough, there was but a single entry matching her name.

Marni Carpenter Sorensen, (3162 F. E.–) B.S., M.S., Deseret University, Ph.D., University of California–Davis. Coauthor, "RNA, 'Junk' Matter, and Memory Retention," *Noram Medical Journal* . . .

Following her name was a listing of articles and publications, but the last was dated some five years earlier. Given the delays caused by peer review and editorial matters, that suggested she had stopped researching and publishing when she'd returned to St. George. He frowned. She'd stopped publishing, but not researching. He also wouldn't have been surprised to learn that she'd contacted some of Tanner's descendants. Had she also obtained the basis of what she had used on him from Tanner descendants? Or from Saint genealogical tissue samples? He would have bet on one of those and given odds. But he wasn't about to say anything, because he'd either end up out of the FSA and being a medical guinea pig somewhere . . . or worse.

Was that why the major had dismissed Marni so cavalierly? While it might have been because he couldn't believe a woman was that brilliant, or because he hadn't been told the full extent of what had been going on in the laboratory, it was far more likely that the FSA didn't want it known, even among agents, exactly what she had been doing.

And that suggested . . . ? Did the FSA already have the ability to extract and process memories for reimplantation? Were they already using it? Perhaps in the low-function relocation communities?

Roget repressed a shudder. There wasn't much he could do about it if the Agency were doing that, but it was definitely something he needed to keep in mind. Even so, one way or the other, he had no doubts that Marni had been the source of his "flashback memories," although he doubted that he'd ever know for certain whether her research had resulted in an implantation of genetic-based memories or "merely" gene-based suggestions of memories that his own brain had reprocessed into coherence.

He could see why the Saints were interested in her work, though, especially if it rendered people more susceptible to being supportive of the Saints . . . or even made them likely to convert. He could also see, scientifically important as that research might be, why neither the Federation nor the Saints would want to make it public. He certainly was in no position to inquire more directly than he had. Even so, he'd likely face more questions about his inquiries. But he'd had to know. And now that he knew . . . there wasn't a thing he could do about it.

25

23 MARIS 1811 P. D.

Roget had gone back to the capitol for an hour on Tuesday by himself after he and Lyvia had eaten lunch. Once there, he had watched and listened to the Judiciary proceedings, but he didn't see anything out of the ordinary. The case itself dealt with the issue of misrepresenting a product, as depicted on a fictional drama. The plaintiff contended that, regardless of whether the drama represented a series of fictional events, the defendant had used the setting of the drama to overrepresent the product's capabilities, with the active collusion and support of the designing firm, and that was an actionable event under the law, and the designing firm that had supplied the product was liable for damages.

Roget was shaking his head, figuratively, when he left the Judiciary, because the case wasn't something that he would even have considered. Yet it made perfect sense under the system Lyvia had described, and again, that bothered him.

Later that afternoon, he visited a series of art galleries on the south side of Skeptos, but while he saw all types of art—except art forms such as multis that required continuous energy output—he didn't see any other depictions of spacecraft, or any kind of aircraft. He did see depictions of sailing craft and something that looked like a human-powered submersible, as well as several scenes of mountain or highland villages with snow. One was even captioned *Winter in Chaco*.

He ate alone but decided on Dorinique, although he had to walk around the square several times before they could seat him. He only saw one dog, if from a distance, but it wasn't even a dachshund.

On Wednesday morning he was in the lobby of the MEC building by quarter past nine, and he waited for a good ten minutes before Lyvia appeared. They walked up to the third level and to the conference room with little more conversation than polite necessities.

Director Hillis walked in and came right to the point.

"Agent Roget, your dropboat will be ready for launch tomorrow. After breakfast Agent Rholyn will escort you to the . . . transport facility. You're expected there at eleven hundred—noon local. That will require your leaving Skeptos at about nine."

"What about the documentation?"

"It's already aboard the dropboat. You'll have time to check it after you reach the facility."

"The other agent?"

"He's already there. Given his mental state, it's questionable as to whether he'll be of much use to the Federation, but removal from Dubiety and the strain it created within him might allow personal restabilization. It will also make it slightly more difficult for the Federation to use his absence as a provocation."

With three other agents perishing in the attempt to land, would one make a difference? And why would Dubiety create that much strain on an agent? "Was he exposed to anything markedly different from what I was?"

"No. In fact, he saw far less before he became totally unstable and uncontrollable. That is understandable, however, since his background is Sinese."

"Did you apply greater distortion to his perceptions?"

"We have not attempted to distort either your perceptions or his," replied Hillis calmly. "What would be the point? It's against our beliefs, and once you return to Federation jurisdiction, any such meddling would be apparent."

"It's not likely that they'll believe me, you know?"

"That depends on you, doesn't it?"

"And on them and on whatever you send back with me," Roget added.

"The documentation will be there, as will other evidence if you choose to take it."

"You're being awfully casual about all this. You're the first splinter culture the Federation has encountered."

"The first of which you're aware." A wry smile appeared. "I also wouldn't say that we're casual. Weren't you met with someone prepared to talk to you? Haven't we attempted to show you how Dubiety operates? No . . . we're anything but casual. 'Resigned' might be a better term. Hopeful, but resigned. The Federation is rather set in its ways."

"Are you suggesting that they've hidden or destroyed other cultures?"

"I'm not suggesting anything. Remember, we're Thomists. I'm certain you know the origin of the name."

Roget did—a takeoff on the idea of Doubting Thomas.

"We well may be the first splinter culture the Federation has encountered. We may not be. We can't speak for that which is beyond what we know. Neither can you. Not accurately."

"I stand corrected." He kept his voice wry.

"I have two last observations for you to keep in mind."

Roget waited.

"First, the longer a culture or society exists without external pressures or conflicts and the more successful it is in maintaining its institutions unchanged, the more likely the slightest pressure, even the pressure of knowledge, is likely to result in unplanned change. Second, the speed of technological development is directly proportional to the true effectiveness of education and markets and to the amount of resources behind the discovery and dissemination of knowledge, as well as being inversely retarded by the degree of governmental control and regulation." The Director turned her eyes to Lyvia. "It occurs to me that Agent Roget has not seen any background on the planoforming of Dubiety. The Natural History Museum."

Lyvia nodded.

Hillis stood, smiling. "I won't see you again before you lift off to return to the *WuDing*. I do wish you the best. Whether you believe us or not, you, as an individual, are welcome here."

"Even if the Federation takes over?"

"One way or another, that is unlikely."

"One way or another?"

"We didn't leave the Federation to have it chase us down and incorporate us again. The Federation didn't look for us for centuries without a very definite agenda."

"You're suggesting . . ." Roget didn't want to voice the actual words.

"No. I've told you. We're opposed to war, but we will do what's necessary. We'd prefer an agreement in which both sides respect the other's systems and agree not to meddle."

"Just how do you expect to make that work?"

"We'll see how the Federation acts first. Remember, we've done nothing aggressive." She paused. "I don't know that it would help, but you might suggest they inquire into the events of 6556 F. E., and the disappearance of Federation Exploratory Force Three. Or possibly that your High Command review any stellar maps that might exist of this area in the year 4245 F. E. It might reveal something, Major, if they're wise enough to understand what they see."

Roget stiffened slightly. He'd never mentioned his rank, or rank-equivalent.

"Now . . . I think you really should see the museum." Selyni Hillis inclined her head, then slipped from the conference room.

"Keir . . ." Lyvia's voice was calm but surprisingly gentle.

Roget accompanied her out of the conference room, down the ramps, and through the lobby.

Outside, the wind had picked up, and with the ever-present humidity, the day was definitely chill and raw.

"Is the museum the only thing on the day's schedule?" Roget finally asked as they walked southward toward the main square.

"That's it," replied Lyvia. "After that, you can wander as you like. I'll meet you tomorrow at quarter to eight for breakfast. Bring your pack and anything you'd like to take with you back to the *WuDing*."

"I haven't exactly gathered souvenirs," Roget said. "By the way, exactly where is this museum?"

"Some six blocks straight south from the main square."

"Natural history? I didn't think Dubiety had that much *natural* history."

"Isn't whether you call history natural or unnatural merely a matter of viewpoint?" replied Lyvia. "Whatever your perspective, I think you'll find the museum of some interest."

Roget thought about asking why, then dismissed the idea, knowing what her answer would be. "Is there anything else you think I should see? After the museum?"

"If you haven't done so, you ought to sit in public places and just watch the people."

Roget almost laughed. He'd done a great deal of that already, even though he knew that the colonel couldn't have cared less about what Roget observed about the conduct of everyday life on Dubiety. Instead, he just smiled politely and kept walking.

Before long they were past the central square and then, after passing a line of clothing shops, Roget could see what could only be the museum. It was anything but imposing—merely a squarish two-story stone-walled structure that looked somewhat older than the buildings flanking it. The door toward which Lyvia and Roget walked was trapezoidal. Roget had the feeling that the trapezoidal doorways were more likely to be used on older buildings, but he decided against stating that observation. The milky-green door split, and both sides slid open as the two neared. Immediately inside the doors, which closed behind them, was a modest foyer, four meters by five, with a hallway to the right and another to the left.

"To the right," said Lyvia. "That's where we'll begin. There are a series of short time-lapse visuals with explanations."

Roget followed her to the first exhibit—a projection into a niche, which immediately displayed an image once they stopped. The image was of a planet with a thick swirling atmosphere. Roget watched and listened . . .

". . . Dubiety . . . as initially discovered . . . Venerian in general composition, but with a solidifying core more terrestrial, if smaller . . . planoforming began almost four thousand years ago with upper atmospheric bioseeding . . ."

Purplish dots appeared on the swirling atmosphere.

". . . less than a hundred years later, the process of bombarding Dubiety with ice comets commenced . . ."

Roget watched the initial time-lapse illustration, then followed Lyvia to the second niche.

". . . concurrent with midlevel atmospheric biotransformations, core reenergization was commenced using a variant on the trans-temporal entropic reversal process. Several transfer ships and crews were lost initially because of unforeseen temporal schisms . . ."

Temporal schisms and entropic reversal? Was the museum just a setup for him?

Three exhibits later, when he walked around the next corner, he saw a line of young people walking out through a set of double doors within the building. He looked to Lyvia.

"That's the theater. The museum runs a consolidated program and seminar for students."

"Do they have to know the physics for trans-temporal entropic reversal?"

"No. Just the basic application principles. The physics is beyond most scientists."

"Why are you giving it to the Federation?"

"We're not giving the applications—just the theory. They'll have to develop the applications themselves. That's if they have the insight and the will. Let's move to the next presentation . . ."

Roget was more than a little discouraged when he left the museum almost two hours later. The various presentations and explanations had made it very clear that the Dubietans—or a far larger Thomist culture—most likely had developed something suspiciously close to time travel, or time and distance travel. From what he could tell, it was practical only for the transfer of large masses and entailed massive quantities of energy, which they generated from a process he understood not at all, but which required conditions of most considerable pressure and heat—such as a planetary core.

Exactly how was he going to explain that? Or prove it? Or even provide some examples by which the Federation could investigate the possibility? Was any of it true? Or had he been guided through a total deception?

The other thing that nagged at him was that perhaps the Dubietans had even more applications than he'd been shown.

What he'd observed was disturbing enough. He'd measured travel times and distances. He'd experienced full sensory perceptions. So . . . those facts tended to suggest that either the Dubietans had the ability to replicate totally all sensory and intellectual inputs or the technology that they claimed or exhibited was in fact real. Neither possibility cheered Roget in the slightest.

In the damp and misty air outside the museum, Lyvia looked to Roget. "You look rather down, Keir."

"That's a fair assessment. In my position, you would be as well. Exactly how can I prove what I've seen and can't explain?"

"Believe me. We'll be able to help greatly with proof. Whether the Federation will accept the implications is another question." Lyvia smiled brightly. "I'll see you in the morning." With that, she turned and walked away.

Roget walked slowly back to the central square. While the wind had subsided to a slight breeze, the misty air was still raw and chill. Even so, he settled himself on one of the benches next to the walkway, just trying—again—to make sense out of the day.

From somewhere near in the square came the sound of a stringed instrument. He turned his head. Standing on the raised stone dais around the central monument was a woman with silver gray hair, playing an overlarge violin—no, a viola.

Roget began to listen more closely.

Finally, after almost an hour, the violist stopped and began to place her instrument in its case. Roget rose, somewhat stiffly, and walked toward the violist. She closed the case and lifted it, then paused as she saw him approach.

"I wanted to thank you," he said. "That's all I can do."

She inclined her head. "You are most welcome."

"You play elsewhere?"

"I'm second chair in the Skeptos Orchestra."

"And you like to play here?"

"Some of the members of the orchestra apply to play

in the square." A mischievous smile followed her words. "Some think it's beneath them. I like to play in both venues."

"Why here?"

"You get to reach out to people as individuals. Half the people who attend concerts do it for other reasons. Here, anyone who stops to listen really wants to hear what you play."

"I can see that."

She frowned. "You're not from around here. Patagonn? Or the unsettled part of Thula?"

"Farther than that." Roget smiled. "Why did you decide to become a musician?"

"Why does anyone decide anything? Because it was what I wanted to do. I kept at it because I had the talent. I might have kept at it, even without the talent, but then, I wouldn't be playing here, would I?" She smiled politely. "If you would excuse me . . ."

Roget stepped back. "Of course. But . . . thank you."

"You're welcome." She walked along the walk to the northeast.

Roget watched her for a moment, then turned slowly in the direction of the guesthouse.

26

Roget arrived at the maglev station in Cheyenne at seven fifteen Thursday night. Even using a priority transportation code, he hadn't been able to get a seat on the maglev until the Thursday night train leaving at eight ten. While Meira had assured him that there wouldn't be any problem in his stopping by their apartment once he arrived in Fort Greeley, Roget still worried about arriving so late.

His codes were good for a window seat against a rear bulkhead at the back of the coach, but it was under a vent, and the faint mixed odor of ozone and hot oil was annoying. So was the additional odor of synthcheese and overcooked chips, but what regional public transport in Noram didn't smell of stinky cheese and chips? The stiff old polycloth of the seat crackled every time Roget shifted his weight, and the older Sudam woman who had the aisle seat frowned at every crackle, as if somehow Roget were deliberately trying to keep her awake.

Two seats farther forward sat two young Sudams in the rear-facing seats. Roget could tell they were looking him over, and he intensified his hearing.

". . . leave him alone . . ."

". . . big, but he doesn't look so tough . . ."

". . . Marshan caught the readouts . . . priority codes for that seat . . . traveling alone . . . means combat specialist or security agent . . ."

". . . so what?"

". . . guys like that . . . break you in pieces . . ."

The two Sudams turned their eyes toward a pair of hard-faced women, then looked away.

The hour on the maglev seemed far longer by the time Roget swung his small bag out of the overhead when the train stopped at Central Station in Fort Greeley. Given what he'd heard from the two seated across from him, he waited until most passengers were off the train before stepping out onto the platform and then making his way toward the tunnel leading to the electrotram station.

The vaulted waiting hall that served all the platforms was dimly lit, but Roget suspected it would have been dim in midday and even on that handful of days when the wind blew enough so that the sun shone unhampered by the miasma created by too many people at too high an altitude for too many centuries, even with relatively clean power sources.

"Personal soltaic cells, cheaper here than anywhere!" called out a thin, scraggly-bearded youth.

"Commcards . . . less than ten yuan a minute . . ."

"The best in personal servicing . . ."

Roget sidestepped a would-be lifter, then unbalanced him, leaving him to totter into a muscular man in the desert camouflage of a merc's uniform, who slammed the unfortunate to the composite tile. There was always a market for mercs in the chaos of Afrique where Federation control was limited to destroying large concentrations of anything, but primarily of soldiers or weapons.

Roget kept moving, his senses and internals alert to anything moving toward him, but he reached the eastbound tram platform without incident. According to the directions Meira had sent him, all he had to do was take the local tram east for three stops and then walk

south along 100 Fourth for three blocks to the Willis-
D'Almeida.

As large as Fort Greeley was—a good three million–
plus people, close to 90 percent of those in the Federation District that encompassed all of old Colorado and
half of old Wyoming—the trams ran frequently. Roget
waited less than five minutes but kept an agent's scan
going the whole time.

Even at close to nine thirty at night, once he was on
the tram, he had to stand, but he did manage to slip into
a corner where it would be difficult for lifters. Ten minutes later, he stepped out onto another platform, this
one older and synthbrick-walled, a style that had graced
midlevel condo areas a century before. Two older
women, not gray-haired but excessively careful in their
steps, left the tram by the same door as Roget, as did a
couple with two children, a boy and a girl who looked
to be twins, one of the few exceptions to taxation sur-
charges on families with more than one child.

Once he walked down the steps and onto the well-
lighted walkway, flanking 100 Fourth on the west side,
Roget was careful to stay in the center. A couple walked
swiftly past him, each carrying a half-staff, one of the
more popular self-defense weapons allowed by the Federation. Each capped end held an immobilizing jolt, and
the staff was sturdy enough to inflict major structural
damage to an immobilized or stunned assailant. Neither the man nor the woman gave Roget more than a
passing glance.

The first block south of the tram station held a market
complex, but it had already closed, and Roget could see
cleaning personnel inside. Three young men paced
around one of the entrances, glancing toward it now and
again but not toward the walkway or the passing pedestrians. Roget's sister's condo was in the block ahead, on

the third level, opposite the recreation area and park. Despite the late fall chill, Roget could see several volleyball games in progress and a soccer game on the main field. He shook his head. He'd never been that enthused about team sports.

The fifth-story Willis-D'Almeida was neat from the outside, and seemingly well maintained, but from the off-tan shade of the snythbrick facade, it probably dated back more than a century. All the security lights were functioning, although several flickered as Roget climbed the outside steps to the third level and then made his way along the wide balcony to the front door of unit thirty-three. There he pressed the buzzer.

Brighter lights flared around him, and his internals caught the energy from the low-grade scanner even before he noticed the faint hum of the unit.

The door opened.

"Keir!" Meira stepped back. "You're here. Come on in."

Roget stepped inside, and his sister quickly closed and locked the door, reactivating the security system as she did.

"Where's Wallace?" asked Roget, setting his bag down beside the door.

"He's on the night shift. The pay's better, and he's here when Neomi gets home from school. Let me get Neomi. It's really past her bedtime, but she wanted to see her uncle. She's talked about your coming ever since you let me know."

As Meira headed for Neomi's bedroom, Roget glanced around the main room, a space a good six meters by four, but with a couch and two worn brownish tan armchairs at one end and a table with four chairs at the other. He could see a narrow kitchen beyond the table. The short hallway taken by Meira at the other end of the main room led to two small bedrooms and a fresher. While the condo's living area was larger than the room he had in officers' quarters in Cheyenne, it certainly wasn't much larger than the apartment he'd had in his brief stay in St. George, and Meira had to share the space with Wallace and Neomi.

Meira returned, holding the hand of a dark-haired and gray-eyed girl who looked up at Roget sleepily.

"Uncle Keir?"

"That's me." Roget squatted so that his face was almost level with Neomi's. "It's been a while since I last saw you."

"A long time." Neomi yawned.

Roget straightened.

Meira led Neomi over to the couch, where she seated her daughter and then settled beside her. Roget took the nearer armchair. It squeaked as he sat down.

"How was your trip?"

"The maglev was like always . . . crowded and stinky, but Cheyenne's close enough that it took less than an hour."

"Where are you headed next?"

Roget shrugged. "They don't tell me until I report for my briefing after I get off leave."

"Can you say where you've been?"

"Let's just say it was hot and dry."

"That describes about half the world these days," she replied.

"And everyone speaks Stenglish."

"Everyone? That might limit it to a third of the world."

"It was definitely in a dry third of the world." Roget laughed softly. It was better not to reveal anything if he didn't have to.

"Do you use an assumed name?"

"I haven't had to so far. I'm just listed in all the

databases as a Federation Information Specialist, along with the thousands of others. Most of them are Federation Information Specialists. I can do that job." *And quite a few others as well.*

"Is there anything you can tell us?"

Roget laughed. "Where's your holojector?"

Meira pointed to a square cube on the small end table beside her. "There."

Roget copied the image of Hildegarde to Meira's system, frowning as he could feel and sense the heat. The holojector was probably on its last legs, but it did project Hildegarde's image out from the blank section of the wall reserved for just that.

"Don't tell me you managed to get a dog?"

"No. That's an image of a painting. You can see how good it is. I was walking through a gallery, and I saw it. The actual painting was for sale for something like seven hundred yuan. If I had a normal job I would have bought it, but I liked it enough to buy an image. When I visited the gallery later, the painting was gone. It had been put up for sale by heirs before they realized its value and its antiquity. It was worth over twenty thousand." Roget deliberately low-balled the value, knowing what Meira's reaction would be.

"You should have bought it." Meira's voice was cool. "At the least, you could have sold it back. The fools."

"Pretty doggy," said Neomi.

"Couldn't you have bought it?"

"I knew it was good, but not that good," Roget replied. "If I had, I'd have bought it and worked out something."

"It is a good painting," said Meira. "You've always had a fondness for dachshunds. I hated the way Muffin followed you."

"She was a good dog," Roget said.

"She was friendly to everyone, but she loved you."

"She liked everyone." Roget didn't mention that it might have been because he'd been the one to play with her and let her sleep at the foot of his narrow bed. "Anyway, I thought it was interesting that I ran across such a valuable painting, and it was a dachshund." He collapsed the holo image.

"That's all you can tell me?"

Roget nodded. "It's a requirement and better that way."

"You always kept everything to yourself," Meira continued, almost as if Roget had not said that he couldn't say more. "I sometimes think that Muffin was the only one you talked to."

"That could be. Father was always using anything I said against me. Mother . . ." Roget shrugged.

"You're still rebelling against them, even after what happened . . ." Meira's eyes brightened.

"No. I gave that up years ago, even before that." Roget didn't want to get into recriminations. It certainly hadn't been his fault that they'd been killed in the great southern hurricane of 6741 that had destroyed what had been left of Baton Rouge. The Federation hadn't been about to spend billions of yuan on land being eaten away by the sea, especially not in Noram. "But I have thought about childish rebellion, Meira."

"Oh?"

"We react, one way or another, to the circumstances that existed when we were growing up, but so did our parents, and those in their generation. Usually, at the time when we were children, they couldn't do much, but as they got older they did their best to change things."

"My, aren't you being generous now?"

"When people try to change things, it can be bad or good," Roget pointed out. "All I'm saying is that they did the best they knew how."

"With the Federation restrictions, no one can do much, not unless you've got billions, and words are cheap." Her words held an edge. "You must be doing well after all these years."

"I'm still the same rank. I get a bit more pay for seniority."

"Doesn't it bother you that the Sinese get preference, no matter what they say?"

"I can only do the best I can do. What about you? How are things here?"

"I did get a half-time position with the local health outreach organization. They can always use trained nurses or medics. They say I can go full-time once Neomi is in school all day. She goes to the children's center here in the afternoon, but . . . going all day would cost more than I could make. Since Wallace is the night maintenance director at the university, we have staff family privileges, and that does help." She shook her head. "We lost so much in the hurricane . . . we'll probably never recover it all. Coming here was all we could do. What real choice did we have?"

Neomi yawned.

"I do need to put her to bed."

Roget stood. "You probably need sleep as well. I thought maybe I could take you all out to dinner tomorrow."

"That would be nice . . . and appreciated. If you could make it early, sixish, Wallace could enjoy it without rushing off."

"If you'd like to pick a place . . . ?"

"CindeeLee's!" burst in Neomi.

"We can talk about it later." A wry expression crossed

Meira's face. "Oh . . . I forgot to tell you. You can stay with us . . ."

"No, there's no need to inconvenience you. I have a room at the Palais, and the Federation's paying for it." That wasn't true, but he didn't want Meira to feel guilty. She had enough problems as it was.

"We had a dinner there once, a banquet, actually," said Meira. "We couldn't have afforded it if we hadn't been guests."

The Palais was far from the most expensive hotel in Fort Greeley. Roget knew that. "I'll call you, and you need to put my niece to bed."

"It might be better, this late . . . You can get an electrocab at the kiosk on the main level."

And safer, thought Roget, although neither of them uttered that thought. "Thank you."

He walked to the door of the condo, picking up his bag from where he had left it by the door. Then he turned and smiled. "It's good to see you."

"You, too, Keir."

The balcony walkway was deserted as he made his way to the central stairs and down to the main level to the kiosk. There was actually a cab waiting.

As he sat in the rear seat on the way to the Palais, he reflected, yet again, on the possible reasons why he and Meira had never been all that close. Had it been that she resented him and the extra costs their parents had borne to have a second child? Or just that they were so different? The health outreach job was so like his sister—trying to care for everyone. Roget had the feeling that, no matter how hard you tried, there were some people beyond help.

Societies had to have rules, too, and rules that applied to everyone. He couldn't help but think about Marni and her collaborators. They'd wanted a Saint-ruled world—or at least their corner of it ruled by Saint principles. But that was what had led to the Wars of Confederation and the iron crackdown that had followed. When every group's principles were different, and every group was willing to fight to the death for those principles, you couldn't have a civilization. You could only have warfare, rebellion, and chaos.

If he had to be honest with himself, Roget didn't agree 100 percent with all the Federation laws and policies, but . . . what was the alternative? As Meira had asked, what choices did any of them have?

Still . . . Meira had looked so tired. At least he could offer dinner and slip some credits into her account on the pretense that they were to be used for Neomi. They would be, but that would free some money for Meira. He hoped.

27

24 MARIS 1811 P. D.

After an early breakfast at yet another unnamed bistro, Roget and Lyvia walked four blocks to the central square, where they made their way down to the regional subtrans concourse. Roget had donned his original pale blue shipsuit, although he wore the outer jacket over it, but with the variety of attire in Skeptos, he certainly wasn't wearing anything nearly as outlandish as some of those they passed on the ramp heading down to the concourse.

As they stood waiting in front of the leftmost green translucent door of the eastbound side of the concourse, Roget asked, "How many stops?"

"Just two."

"How long?"

"Forty standard minutes or so."

That meant a trip of around eight hundred klicks. From what Roget recalled, that would have put them in the middle of flatlands between two mountain ranges and north of a large inland lake. There was a city near there, but he couldn't recall the name and didn't want to dig the maps Lyvia had given him out of his pack.

The subtrans doors opened, and Roget carried his pack into the train. There were few enough passengers that Lyvia sat across from him, and he put his pack in the seat adjoining his. The doors closed.

"Are you nervous?" she asked.

"Not about the subtrans. Later . . . wouldn't you be?" he countered.

"I thought Federation pilots had nerves of steel, or composite or something," she said with a smile.

"They might. I'm an agent first, and a pilot second."

"That's what the Director thought."

"What else does she think?"

"That would only be speculation on my part."

"I'm certain that some things aren't speculation."

"You're fond of dogs, and you've never had a deep relationship with anyone. You don't quite fit the Federation mold. That's why you're both useful and not totally trusted . . ."

Roget realized that Lyvia was speaking in old American, and he was having no trouble at all following her.

"It's also why you're still sane and the other agent isn't."

"Dubiety isn't *that* strange."

Lyvia laughed.

After a moment, so did Roget.

Superficially, he realized, the differences weren't that great, but beneath that superficial similarity was a huge gap. "Did the other agent slowly lose it, the more he saw?"

"I never saw any reports."

The way she said the words suggested to Roget that she thought so.

Before long, the subtrans glided to a stop. Three people from the back of the car got off. A man wearing an orange vest over a brilliant flame-green singlesuit towed a wheeled case that rumbled slightly. No one entered their car, and the doors closed.

"That was Knossos. We'll be getting off at Rhodes."

"Are all the towns and cities in Socrates named after something Greek?"

"No, but a disproportionate number are."

"The original skeptics?"

"Probably not. Just the first with enough power and confidence to write their doubts down. Even so, there were enough conformists in ancient Greece that they ended up forcing Socrates to suicide."

Roget wondered if there might be a village or town called Hemlock, but didn't ask. He still could help thinking about the last words the director had offered . . . about events two and twenty-five centuries earlier. They'd been almost tossed off, as if they were absolute and yet as if whatever the Federation found would be disregarded.

When they disembarked at Rhodes, so did some twenty young men and women, mostly from other cars. Only a handful of men and women were waiting to board.

"Just wait a moment," Lyvia said.

Roget slung his pack over his shoulder and stood there.

Only when the concourse appeared empty did Lyvia turn and walk to the end away from the ramp leading up to the surface. At the end of the concourse, as they neared, a section of the wall slid open, revealing a narrow ramp. The hidden doorway closed silently behind them.

The ramp led straight down for a good hundred meters, then ended in a small foyer. On the right side was a single set of translucent doors of the same type used in the subtrans concourses, except that these were a dull yet deep red—the first of that color Roget had seen. This time Lyvia used her belt-tube and the doors opened, revealing a much smaller conveyance, almost a large capsule with but four seats, two on each side facing each other. All four seats were a deep green without trim.

Lyvia gestured and Roget stepped inside, taking a seat and putting his pack on the one beside him. Lyvia settled across from him, and the doors closed.

Roget studied the capsule, deciding from the lack of wear and its compactness that it was not used heavily. He could sense that they were descending. Descending? To reach a launch site that would send his dropboat into space?

Roget shrugged. That made about as much sense as anything had on Dubiety.

When the tube capsule came to a halt and the narrow door slid open, he asked, "How deep are we?"

"Deep enough."

From what his internal sensors registered with the change in air pressure, Roget guessed that they had dropped a good klick, if not more, but that estimation was rough, not an exact calculation because he didn't know all the variables. He followed Lyvia out into a small foyer whose metallic walls glistened like brushed pewter. Opposite the doors to the tube capsule was a metal framed archway.

The archway door split open. Each side of the door was almost a meter thick, and he walked swiftly through after Lyvia. Two guards—stationed behind energy screens—watched as Lyvia and Roget stepped through the heavy metal and composite doors. For the first time, Roget did sense energy emissions and scanning. Another closed archway stood behind and between the pair of guards.

"This is where I leave you." She smiled. Warmly, Roget realized. "Good luck."

"Thank you." Roget unclipped the belt-tube. "I suppose I should give this back to you."

"You can take it with you," Lyvia said. "It's another piece of evidence." She smiled. "Besides, if you ever do come back, you can still use the credits."

Roget shook his head. "They'll want the evidence."

"It doesn't matter. The credits are registered in your name."

"If I don't come back, give them to Aylicia, if you can."

"Thank you." She turned and walked back through the still-open archway from the tube capsule. It closed.

"Major . . ." offered one of the guards. "The technicians are waiting."

Roget looked back toward the second archway, now open. After a moment, he said, "Thank you," and stepped through the archway.

On the other side waited a man in a white singlesuit, standing in another featureless and high-ceilinged foyer. "Major Roget, this way."

Roget nodded and followed the other along the wide

corridor. In a way, he felt more comfortable—wherever he was—because the installation had the definite feel of a military operation.

The technician turned into the second doorway on the left, the first one that was open. A series of wide lockers lined one wall, and a bench was set back from them. An open archway led into another chamber, which looked to hold freshers and toilets or the equivalent.

At the end of the bench was a frame holding a suit similar to the pressure suit Roget had worn on his descent through the orbital shields. The suit was a lighter shade of blue than his had been, almost white. He set his bag down on the end of the bench.

The technician pointed. "That's a deep-space pressure suit. Yours was too degraded, and we didn't bother trying to figure out how to repair it. We modified the neck-ring so that it is compatible with the standard Federation helmet. That was for comm compatibility. We checked the seal against your helmet, and it's perfect. Your helmet is in the dropboat." He pointed to a flat bag on the end of the bench nearest the suit. "There's an emergency suit there with a quick-seal hood, in case you can't get to a full suit. You might consider taking it. Of course, it's only got about an hour of oxygen, but that's usually enough for us to get to people in our operations."

"Thank you." Roget didn't know what else to say.

Roget studied the emergency pressure suit, then paused as he noted the red triangle on the waistband of the suit. "What's this?" He pointed.

"That's an emergency beacon. Press and hold for several seconds. Not that I expect you'd want pickup from us." The technician laughed. "I'll be outside when you're ready, and I'll escort you to the . . . launch chamber."

Within moments, Roget was alone. Launch chamber? Possibly klicks below ground? And he was standing in a locker room that held a good twenty lockers. He reached forward to the nearest locker. It was locked, unsurprisingly.

Finally, he took off his jacket and folded it, setting it on the bench. Then he began to don the replacement pressure suit—far easier to get into than the one he had used before, yet he had the feeling it might well be more durable. The seals literally melded into a seamless fabric.

Once he had the suit on, he bent to retrieve his own pack. Then he paused as he saw the flat package on the bench. The tech's observations were as close to an absolute recommendation as he'd gotten. He picked up the pack and felt it, then scanned it. A Trojan horse?

He shook his head. Why would they bother? They could have turned the entire dropboat into that. Besides, it was another piece of evidence. Finally, he slipped the flat package into his pack, rearranging items so that the pressure suit was on the bottom and his jacket was on the top. Then he closed the pack, slung it over one shoulder, and headed out of the locker room.

The tech was waiting in the corridor.

"This way, Major."

Roget walked beside the tech toward the end of the corridor and another metal girded archway with a closed set of doors. "Is this the only launch center?"

"It's best that I don't answer that, Major."

"Can you tell me what entity operates it? It seems . . . military."

"When you deal with massive force, any organization needs discipline. In that respect, we're no different."

Roget couldn't argue with that, but before he could frame another question they reached the archway, and

the doors opened. He and the tech stepped into a huge
domed and circular composite-lined chamber more
than two hundred meters across. The apex of the dome
was at least two hundred meters above.

A dropboat rested in a massive cradle in the middle
of the chamber. The floor was polished and perfectly
level, but the cradle was centered in a circle of amber
composite so large that the cradle and boat looked almost lost, yet the gray area outside the circle was far
larger. Protruding slightly from the mouth of a tunnel to
Roget's right was a second cradle with another Federation dropboat.

"You'll be in the first boat, Major. The second boat is
slaved to yours. Don't make any course or power cor-
rections until Drop four is in formation on you. The
slave relay won't work until it's in position. But any
power or course changes you make will be copied precisely by Drop four. Someone will probably have to do
a maglock or a tow on it once you get close to whatever
ship they want you to rendezvous with."

"The other agent?"

"He's . . . very erratic. We're going to keep you two
apart because he's stable for the moment. We just want
to get you both back in one piece." The tech walked directly toward the cradle. "His comm is also blocked,
except for the links to our control, but he won't know it
until after launch."

"And mine?"

"Yours is open all the way. You'll see."

Roget certainly hoped so.

As they neared the cradle and the dropboat, Roget
saw a portable ladder set at the side, arching over the
cradle and leading to the dropboat's hatch. The tech
stopped at the bottom. "Once you're inside we'll roll the
ladder back. Except for the cradle and the boat, the

space inside the circle has to be absolutely clear. Do you have any last questions?"

"How long will the launch take?"

"Less than ten minutes once you've finished your checklist and are ready. After you finish your checklist, control will contact you, and we'll orient the cradle. Make certain you're fully restrained."

"I can do that." Roget smiled.

"Best of luck, Major."

"Thank you." Roget climbed the ladder, carrying his pack. The hull was a different color in several places although the metal or composite the Dubietans had used melded into the original exterior seamlessly, except for the difference in shading. The hatch was open, and he had no trouble entering the dropboat. He could tell immediately that extensive repairs had been undertaken internally, not because of patches or oil or dirt, but because the entire interior looked almost new. Shaking his head, he stowed his pack in the tiny bunk cubicle behind the pilot's couch and then inspected the interior.

Once he finished his interior inspection and settled himself before the controls, Roget donned his pressure helmet, linked to the craft's systems, then went through the predrop checklist, hoping that it would cover what was needed for whatever kind of launch the Dubietans used.

He went through the checklist twice. If he could trust the linkage and the reports, all systems were green, and all power reserves were at one hundred. He ran another set of diagnostics, but the secondaries confirmed the primary reports. He knew he hated trusting in what he didn't understand, but, yet again, he had to put his trust in the Thomists. *Do you really have any choice?*

He didn't, but it seemed, in retrospect, that he'd had few enough in his life.

Dropboat three, this is Magna Launch Control, communications check. The words were crystal clear. They were also in old American.

Control, this is three. Loud and clear.

Interrogative restrained and ready to launch.

Restrained and ready to launch, Magna Control.

Stand by for cradle orientation.

Standing by.

No sound penetrated the dropboat, but Roget could feel the cradle and the boat moving smoothly and then coming to a stop, nose up, perhaps thirty degrees.

Cradle orientation complete and verified. Stand by for launch.

Ready for launch this time, Control. Roget pushed out of his mind the impossibility of a planetary launch from deep underground and waited.

Good luck, Major.

Roget had no idea what to expect, but what happened next was totally unanticipated—blackness through which he could see nothing while he felt pressure, barely two gees, if that, followed by a lifting of the blackness, weightlessness, and by readings on all of his instruments showing that he was in space.

He didn't have time to think about the impossibility of what had just happened.

Where was he? Roget scanned the screens. Dubiety/Haze was well insystem from him, and he could discern a good thirty Federation ships directly in front of him on his present courseline and solar inclination. Thirty? There had only been five when he'd been dropped nine days before. Only nine days? In some respects, it felt far longer.

He ran another set of checks, but all his systems were green, and he was on an interception course for the center of the Federation formation. Even his closing speed was within the parameters that would allow phase deceleration. His power was still just below 100 percent.

He checked for the other dropboat, but Drop four was nowhere around.

"They have to move the cradle," he murmured, forcing himself to wait . . . and wait.

Then, his screens blinked, and abruptly, he could see Drop four at his one seventy at a range of three klicks. Inside the pressure suit, he shivered. The Dubietans had launch-projected two dropboats something like a million klicks and set them within three klicks of each other?

"Frig . . ." he murmured. He cleared his throat, then transmitted, *WD-Con, this is Drop three, returning. Estimate CPA in one five. Drop four is incapacitated and slaved to three. Four will need maglock or tow.*

Drop three, say again.

Roget repeated his transmission.

Stet, Drop three. Stand by for further instructions.

Roget continued on course toward the Federation fleet, noting that he had been launched directly at the *WuDing*. He didn't know of any Federation system that could have achieved that kind of accuracy—let alone have launched a dropboat through a chunk of the planetary mantle. Clearly, they could have literally launched a torp or explosives to materialize inside any of the Federation ships. They hadn't. That raised again the question of exactly what the Thomists had in mind. From what he'd seen, the Federation didn't have any technology that matched the best of what he'd seen on Dubiety. He'd questioned more than a few times whether he'd seen what he'd thought he'd seen, but now that he was returning—assuming he wasn't imagining that as well—it was appearing more and more likely that he had indeed seen what he recalled.

Drop three, maintain course. Zee one will rendez-

*vous. I say again. Maintain course. Zee one will man-
age link and dock.*

*Stet. Maintaining course this time. Will await in-
structions from Zee one.*

Within two standard minutes, the EDI screen indicated a ship accelerating away from the fleet on an in-
tercept course. The parameters indicated that the ship
was an attack corvette.

Roget smiled. No one wanted his dropboat anywhere
close to the main body of the fleet. That suggested the
colonel hadn't expected anyone to return . . . or perhaps
not the manner of his return.

Another minute passed, then another.

*Drop three, this is ZeeControl. Interrogative power
for decel.*

ZeeCon, power adequate for phased decel. He had to
assume that the same would be true for Drop four.

Three, request ID this time.

Roget pulsed the transponder. The return link identified the oncoming ship as the *ZengYi*, one of the newer
attack corvettes.

Several minutes more passed.

*Three, maneuver to link. Maneuver to link. Leave
your lock closed for examination and possible decon-
tamination.*

*ZeeCon, Drop three. Understand maneuver to link.
Will leave lock sealed for decon.*

That's affirmative, three.

As he maneuvered the dropboat toward the *ZengYi*,
Roget realized he did have more significant proofs than
he'd thought. First . . . the Dubietans had literally hurled
or transposed his dropboat from somewhere beneath
the planetary surface . . . and literally dumped him
right in front of the Federation ships. He also had a different pressure suit, not to mention the documentation

sent by the Dubietans and the repairs to the dropboat. He even had city and local maps printed on local paper or the equivalent that should reveal something.

Yet Director Hillis and the others had seemed to think that no amount of proof would suffice to deter the Federation from attacking or attempting to annex Dubiety in some form.

Roget feared that they might be right, but he'd have to see.

28

21 DONGYU 6744 F. E.

In the end, Roget only spent three days in Fort Greeley, and another two at the Estes Park nature reserve, expensive as it was, before he returned to the Federation base in Cheyenne. As he'd anticipated, Meira had protested his giving her credits but did eventually accept them for Neomi. As he'd also expected, Wallace was polite and reserved, as he always had been to Roget.

The remaining nine days of his leave were long, but he really didn't want to spend credits like water on hotels and resorts. So he read, rested, and tried not to think too deeply about his last mission—and the possibility of more memory flashes—and what might await him on his next assignment.

He also spent more than a little time talking to Hildegarde, but only to the image on his flash and only when he was somewhere alone, away from Federation buildings, and not likely to be snooped. He had no doubts that all officers' rooms were fully monitored.

Finally, after another full day of tests at the FAF medical center, he was back at the FSA building at Cheyenne base, sitting across from the same unnamed colonel who had debriefed him after the St. George mission.

"Agent-Captain Roget, you're in good shape, according to medical. There don't seem to be any lasting physiological effects from the events of your last assignment."

"Yes, sir." Roget still worried about the false memories. The first he'd ascribed to dehydration. And then, especially after Marni's dying words, the second memory-flash had hit hard. Still, he hadn't had another episode, and he sincerely hoped he wouldn't have. For all their probing, doctors hadn't found any sign of anything wrong with him, thankfully. That didn't mean everything was resolved. Roget just knew he'd have to cope . . . somehow.

The colonel smiled.

Roget distrusted the expression, even as he returned the smile.

"You did some research immediately after you were debriefed. Some rather interesting research. Tell me about it, Agent-Captain."

"Yes, sir. I was curious. One of the Danites muttered something about a Joseph Tanner. I'd never heard the name, and I wondered what he'd meant."

"You didn't put that in your report."

"I should have, but I didn't remember that until later. At the time, I was much more concerned about trying to find a way to keep them alive so that they could be questioned. After that, as you may recall, the dehydration left me a bit disoriented. All I could find about Tanner was a historical reference." That was certainly true, although the colonel obviously knew what Roget had found, but Roget wasn't about to make that point. "Do you think he might have been one of the founders of the Danites, sir?"

"That's rather unlikely. The Danites date back to the original Deseret, before it was conquered by the old Americans."

"I didn't realize that, sir." Roget tried to sound properly chastened, hoping that would divert the senior officer.

The colonel looked coolly at Roget. Roget returned the look calmly, but without challenge.

"And the woman?"

"I was thinking she might have some connection with Tanner, in some way. She didn't, not from what I could determine. I do wonder why a biologist would walk away from a university position."

"Cults can do peculiar things to people, especially to women."

Roget nodded. "I did see that in St. George."

The colonel waited a moment before speaking. "It's a most unpleasant aspect of those who don't understand the benefits of the Federation."

Another warning, thought Roget.

"In view of your situation," continued the colonel, "your next assignment is particularly appropriate. We're going to send you outsystem. This has advantages and disadvantages for you. One advantage is that you've been approved for promotion to major. Another is that the assignment will broaden your experience base. The disadvantage is that you'll spend six months to a year in intensive training learning to fly various small orbital craft. Since you're already a trained atmospheric pilot, it shouldn't be too difficult a transition, and flight status also includes incentive pay. Another disadvantage is that there is often some time dilation, particularly in fleet-related assignments. You have no close family, and you work better alone. That combination makes you an ideal candidate for several assignments once you finish your additional training."

Roget felt a chill deep inside. Outsystem attachment to the Federation Interstellar Service was where FSA sent expendable agents. "I wouldn't know, sir, but it sounds interesting."

"I'm certain you'll enjoy these assignments far more than you would in spending years in data analysis as a permanent captain, Agent-Major Roget." The colonel smiled politely.

Data analysis wasn't a choice; it was a veiled death sentence, if not by disappearance when everyone had forgotten him, then by sheer boredom, or by bankruptcy and/or extreme poverty by being forced to live in the Taiyuan area on a captain's stipend.

"When do I start . . . and where, sir?"

"I thought you'd like the opportunity, Major. You'll leave on Saturday for Xichang. There you will undergo a three-week indoctrination into FIS customs and procedures and be fitted for equipment. Certain internals will also have to be reconfigured for space applications. Then you'll be sent to Ceres station. That's where the IS trains its small-craft pilots. You'll also be brought up to speed on deep-space station systems and datanets, as well as a few other technical applications."

If the FSA wanted to spend that many yuan on providing him with such intensive additional training, Roget reflected, it was likely that future missions might be highly risky but not necessarily suicidal. The FSA mandarins still had to justify their expenditures to the Council.

Besides, what realistic choices did he have?

29

While Roget had waited inside the dropboat, his outer hull had been tested, inspected, prodded, and probed with every device known to the Federation—or so it had seemed. Then they had started in probing within, still from outside the dropboat, accessing all data and scanning the interior of his craft. An exterior physical inspection of the dropboat hull and systems followed. Hours later, he had been allowed into the corvette's loading lock, where he'd been scanned, remotely, along with all of his gear, and all of the documentation he had brought back. Then he'd had to strip and be inspected once more. He'd been allowed to dress in his shipsuit, but the Dubietan pressure suit and his helmet remained behind.

Once he'd been cleared onboard the corvette, he'd been immediately escorted into the small squarish comm room off the corvette's tiny ops bay, where he had been left by himself. The consoles were all locked and on remote, and so quiet was the space that he could hear his own breathing. He could also smell his own sweat, not from fear, but from the heat and the time waiting in a pressure suit. A large water bottle sat in a holder on the right side of the console bay. Roget took a long swallow, then sat waiting, knowing that all manner of scanners and the like were trained on him. His eyes dropped to his pack, still holding the emergency ship-suit in its packet. The maps had been removed, but not his personal items and clothing. While the pack had been scanned, no one had removed the shipsuit. Was it transparent to Federation scanners? Or had the techs merely considered it as a shipsuit?

Abruptly, the image of Colonel Tian appeared, sitting behind his console on the *WuDing*. "Greetings, Major. Welcome back. You appear to have weathered your landing and the time on Haze."

"Yes, sir."

"Tell me what happened. Begin just before your drop-boat reached the orbital shield. Please take your time. No detail is unimportant."

Roget had doubts about that, but replied, "Yes, sir. The orientation imparted by my initial course allowed insertion in the same orbital pattern as the upper orbital shield, but I had to increase my relative speed considerably . . ." From there, Roget continued through his rocky descent and landing and his time on Dubiety. He had to stop more than a few times for water, and he was hoarse and raspy when he finally finished his summary.

Colonel Tian gave a last nod but did not say anything immediately.

Roget understood. The colonel was getting the interpretation of all the data obtained from observing Roget.

Finally, the colonel did speak. "Your physiological workup indicates that you have been in a gravity well that matches that observed of Haze. Since there has been no indication of any mass large enough to generate artificial gravity anywhere else near here, it does appear likely that you have indeed been on the planetary surface. Likewise, you have been physically active, and your hair samples and tissue analyses indicate exposure to a T-type world, but one with a similar but differing ecology." The colonel paused. "Those results suggest that you were physically present and active on

Haze, since replicating those results otherwise would require an extremely advanced technology at variance with what we have observed. Also, the sample distribution supports your presence on-planet."

The fact that the colonel continued to use "Haze" in speaking of Dubiety suggested his own doubts about Roget's account, but Roget merely replied dispassionately, "My own observations suggested that counterfeiting my experiences would have been difficult."

"But not necessarily impossible."

"Anything is possible to a sufficiently advanced technology, sir."

"To their technology?"

"I don't believe that they went to that extreme, sir, but there are certain aspects of their technology that appear unique, as I have mentioned."

"Which do you think are most unique?"

"The high-speed subtrans system is one, both its operating speed and its extent, especially the deep tubes between continents. Their ability to communicate without any stray radiation is another. The ability to create multiple artificial magnetic poles with enough power and variance to use to control the levels of orbital shields is a third."

"The first two are mere adaptations of existing Federation technology. Why do you find them so unique, Major?"

"The amount of additional resources and effort required to construct them suggests that there well may be other reasons for their use and existence."

"And what might those be, do you think?"

"I have no idea, sir. But the Dubietans I met seemed very pragmatic."

"It seems less than pragmatic to return any agents, especially one in a disoriented state."

"I doubt they do anything without a reason, sir."

"Nor do I, Major. Why do you think they returned you?"

"To show good will. To demonstrate that they could." *To warn you.* "To suggest they have advanced technology."

"That is certainly what they would wish you—and us—to believe. If they have such, why not use it in a way that leaves no doubt?"

"They claim that they do not wish to be the ones to offer any hostile action against the Federation or any action that might be perceived as hostile."

"A most convenient excuse not to show their supposed advanced technology."

"Sir . . . it would seem to me that the course line and velocity with which my dropboat was returned suggests an advanced technology. So do the orbital shields. So do the repairs to the dropboats."

"Comparable technology, Major, not advanced technology."

"Begging your pardon, sir, but I've not seen any Federation technology that is comparable to that."

"Begging your pardon, Major, how would you know?" The colonel's tone was flat.

Roget decided to offer another approach. "The Dubietans also stated that no amount of proof would convince the Federation if it were not disposed to be convinced."

"Did they say that in so many words, Major?"

"They were somewhat more blunt. They sent the technology documentation. They rebuilt the dropboat, and they returned me, and they suggested that the Federation would find none of that convincing." Roget could see that the Dubietans had read the colonel correctly.

Colonel Tian's image looked blandly at Roget. "The

diagnostics on the dropboat and the tracking of your return course indicate that you didn't lift off from Haze at all."

Roget repressed a sigh. "In fact, I did. Rather the Dubietans launched me—"

"Exactly how did they launch you?"

"From a rather elaborate cradle in the middle of their launch complex, as I indicated."

"Are you still convinced this launch complex was underground? Are you certain that wasn't another illusion?"

Roget let the illusion reference pass. He'd never said anything was an illusion. "I traveled there by their tube system. My internals indicated we descended quite a bit to get there. I would think that the dropboat recorders would have provided details."

"Nothing shows on the datacorders between the time of your landing and the time, within a few nanoseconds, when your dropboat appeared on the farscreens and EDIs of various Federation vessels."

That meant the dropboat had recorded his landing. "Then we have a record of the planetary parameters."

"If they can be trusted," replied Tian.

"They match what I've reported and what your analyses already show."

"And how do you know that?"

"Because, sir, you would have told me if they had not, and you would have dismissed all that I have reported far sooner. I would also guess that there is no evidence at all of tampering with the recording systems of either dropboat."

The faintest hint of a frown appeared on the colonel's face but vanished immediately. "Oh . . . and what might that indicate?"

"That they have a very advanced technology. If they

did not tamper with the data, then what I have said bears that out, and if they did, and we cannot detect it, then they also have advanced technology."

"You are rather adamant about that, Major."

"I know what I saw, sir. I also know what I brought back and how I returned to the *ZengYi*. Has anyone had a chance to study the documentation the Dubietans sent?"

"We don't have a science team here, Major. The engineers are looking over what's been scanned to us. We're not about to datalink."

The Federation had known about Dubiety . . . and they hadn't dispatched a single scientist with the *WuDing*? "Supposedly, the data can be read on an independent system."

"That may be, Major, but the *ZengYi* doesn't have that kind of equipment, and I'm not about to risk anything like that onboard a capital ship."

Roget could understand that, but he didn't understand why a portable console couldn't be transferred to the corvette . . . unless the colonel wasn't all that interested in the data.

Another series of questions followed, in which the colonel repeated and rephrased earlier inquiries. Then came yet another set of rephrasings.

Roget kept his answers shorter and more factual the second and third times he replied to the variations on the same questions, especially since the colonel clearly wasn't interested in knowing what Roget thought, only what he could prove.

Finally, Tian cleared his throat. "For the present you will remain on board the *ZengYi*. I would caution you not to speak to anyone else about the specifics of your mission. I trust you understand, Major."

"Yes, sir." *You don't want anyone to know what*

might be down there, especially if you're going to try to destroy it.

The colonel's image vanished.

Within moments, the hatch to the tiny comm room opened, and a Federation lieutenant stood there. "Major . . . we're a bit cramped, but there's a spare bunk in the exec's stateroom . . . if you'd like to rest."

Roget rose, picking up the pack at his feet. "I would, thank you. It's been a long day." But not nearly so long as those ahead of him, he feared.

The executive officer's stateroom was all of ten meters down the main upper deck passageway. There, Roget stretched out on the narrow upper bunk but did not really sleep, lying there in a worried doze. He was more than glad to sit up when the hatch opened, but he barely remembered to keep his head down before he almost rammed it into the overhead.

"Major, Jess Uhuru," offered the dark-skinned Federation captain. "I'm the exec here. I just wanted to let you know that the wardroom is open. We didn't know what sort of schedule you've been on."

"Thank you." Roget swung his feet over the side of the bunk and then dropped to the deck. "I'm sorry to intrude on your space, Captain."

"We're happy to be able to accommodate you, sir. It's not often that anyone gets to see an FSA officer who's survived a hostile planet."

"It wasn't that hard once I landed. Their orbital shields are rough, but they're not hostile down there." *Not yet.* Roget paused. "What about the pilot of the other dropboat?"

Uhuru shook his head. "He's sedated and restrained in sickbay. He started raving about all of us just being tools of the creatures down below." After a moment, he asked, "Are they really alien down there?"

"They appear quite human, but they have a very different way of looking at things." That was accurate enough. "It can be very upsetting." Roget followed the exec out into the narrow passageway.

"Here comes the commander, sir." Uhuru stepped back.

A squarish major appeared in the passageway. He smiled broadly. "Major, Kiang Khuo. We're glad to see you made it back."

"Thank you. I'm sorry about being parked here."

"That's not a problem. We can handle an additional officer or two. Beyond that . . . let's just say that it gets cozier than anyone would like." The *ZengYi*'s commander gestured toward the open hatch to the wardroom mess, less than five meters aft from where he stood.

Roget made his way along the passage and into the officers' wardroom, compact like everything else aboard a corvette, a space some five meters long and slightly less than four wide, with narrow chairs that barely fit the four officers already seated. He took the seat to the right of the commander, who seated himself at the head of the table. Uhuru sat across from Roget.

Khuo served himself from the platter in front of him, then nodded to Roget. "Replicated sesame stuff, but at least the galley was overhauled just before we broke orbit. Last deployment . . . we won't go into that." He shook his head.

Roget took a moderate helping of the sauced meat, then of the sticky rice. "Did you come out with the *WuDing,* or were you with the follow-up fleet?"

"We were here from the beginning. We were the escort on the scoutships that did the drops. Have to say it was something watching all of you. One minute you were on the screens, and the next the gray haze swallowed you all—except the last dropboat. Poor bastard.

He just exploded when he hit the gray." Khuo looked to Roget. "Was there a trick to it?"

"I just checked the relative motion. We didn't drop fast enough." Roget shrugged. "Had to goose the drop-boat to keep from getting run down."

"Run down?"

"Oh . . . the shields are millions of chunks of grayish stuff all orbiting at pretty high speed."

"What kind of chunks?" asked a young lieutenant at the end of the table.

"That's all I can say about it right now," Roget replied.

"Major . . . you seem to have the Security types concerned," offered Uhuru.

"They're often concerned," Roget replied. "That's their job."

"We couldn't pick up any track of your dropboat," said the exec. "Then you were on the screens. Did the Thomists—they are Thomists, aren't they—somehow shield you?"

"So far as I know, they didn't. They repaired the dropboat and launched me back on a return course." While Tian had told Roget to say nothing, the officers of the *ZengYi* had already observed more than he'd said.

"How did you get so close without any trace?" pressed the young lieutenant.

"I don't know how they accomplished that," Roget replied.

"But—"

"Lieutenant . . ." Commander Khuo's voice was quiet but firm.

"They're still analyzing the data and the materials I brought back," Roget said. "They might offer some answers. Until they do, I suspect, I'm likely to be your guest."

"How did you end up in outsystem security?" asked the commander, clearly signaling a change in wardroom conversation.

"FSA decided I was the type of agent who worked better alone and on challenging projects," Roget replied.

"I think that might equate to resourceful and expendable," suggested the commander.

Roget had long since come to that conclusion, but he just smiled. "We do what we can."

"That's all any of us can."

"What do you think will happen . . . with Haze?" asked the exec.

"What the fleet marshal—or anyone—least expects," Roget replied. "I don't know what that will be, but the Dubietans are surprising in their predictability."

"Surprising in their predictability?" The commander raised his eyebrows.

"What they do is extremely predictable in hindsight, but unexpected in its applications. That's all I can say." And more than the colonel would have wished, even if Roget hadn't revealed anything directly. He took a sip of the tea.

It wasn't bad, but it tasted flat, especially compared to the food on Dubiety.

30

Three pilots with fresh deep-space, small-craft certifications sat in the low gravity of the Belt Control operations office opposite a senior Federation Interstellar Service major. The major was speaking. Roget was one of the pilots listening intently.

"All three of you have excelled in your training. That is to be expected. Also expected, before you are dispatched to your next duty station, you have a proficiency flight. Call it a postgraduate assignment." The senior major looked over the three pilots. "The other name for it is 'the squirrel run.'"

Roget had heard of the squirrel runs through certain sections of the belt. Despite the best efforts of the Federation Interstellar Service, independent operators, often piratical, still tended to pop up—or be discovered or rediscovered among the smaller bodies scattered through the Asteroid Belt, or the Oort Cloud, or the Kuiper Belt. Most of these tended to die off, literally, because they'd escaped the Federation's outsystem control with too little equipment, but there were some who persisted . . . and some who raided outsystem mining outposts for hard-to-get technology or supplies when their own failed or were exhausted. The unofficial Federation policy was to leave well enough alone unless the belt colony appeared to be prosperous and growing, or unless the unapproved colonists had turned to piracy.

Not so benign neglect, thought Roget.

Lieutenant Castaneda exchanged looks with Lieutenant Braun, but neither spoke.

"Is this a pirate colony, sir, or an unapproved one?" asked Roget.

"Does it matter, Major? Orders are orders."

"Yes, sir. It does matter. A pirate colony is more likely to have amassed various arms and armament systems. An established and unapproved colony will be heavily dug in and fortified but is likely to have older weapons systems."

The senior major nodded. "It is older and unapproved *and* a pirate colony. You will carry a full range of armament. You are not to attempt any rescues, regardless of possible distress calls, because this colony has used that ruse to capture vessels and savage others for their equipment and supplies."

"Yes, sir." Roget appreciated that information. He would have wagered it wasn't laid out that bluntly in the official briefing materials.

"Major Roget will be the flight leader. Briefing consoles five, seven, and nine are reserved for you and will respond only to your IDs. You have two hours before you're to report to the attack boat locks. That is all."

The three stood.

"Best of luck, gentlemen."

Once the three were outside the ops section in the main wide corridor beneath the surface of Ceres, Lieutenant Castaneda glanced at Lieutenant Braun. Then both looked to Roget.

"Squirrel run, sir?"

"Think of tree rodents. They're hard to find in a forest. They duck in and out of things, and when they have a ship, they can circle around an asteroid or a chunk of rock as fast as you can, just like a squirrel around a trunk. They can dig in deep, so deep that all you can do is seal the entrance, and if they survive, they'll just dig out somewhere else. That's unless you take in really massive weapons and fragment the rock that holds the whole colony—and then FIS gets hell because you've scattered all sorts of missiles across the system that will have to be tracked to make sure that they don't impact other installations."

"What's the point, then, sir?"

"To keep the squirrel population down and wary," replied Roget dryly. "And to give all new pilots a solid idea of their limitations." He walked with long and low strides along the blue-walled corridor that led to the ready room—and the briefing consoles.

The two lieutenants followed.

A good standard hour later, Roget was fully suited and standing in the surface lock, ready to enter the needleboat he'd been assigned. He pulsed his ID and authorization code to the lock receptor, and the bar on the lock plate turned green. Then he twisted the wheel through three full turns—all locks on the station that could open to vacuum had manual wheels—before again pressing the plate. The lock opened, revealing the closed outer lock of the combat needleboat.

Roget pulsed his authorization codes and the outer lock door of the needleboat opened.

Once he'd closed the outer station lock door and then stepped into the needleboat, sealing it behind him, Roget began his preflight in the cramped needleboat lock. A good fifteen minutes later, he settled into the pilot's couch, where he linked to the boat's systems. His preflight check had revealed that the needleboat was one of the newer ones, and fully armed—not one of the worn and tired craft usually assigned to student pilots. The tiny single cabin area was also clean and the replicator fully stocked for a full four weeks, although the mission was scheduled to last slightly less than two weeks.

He took his time with the full system checks. Finally, he pulsed the others.

Digger two, Digger three, this is Digger one. Interrogative status.

One, two here, status green. Ready to launch.

Digger one, three is ready to launch.

Roget nodded, then pulsed, *BeltCon, this is Digger one. Digger flight ready for departure and launch.*

Digger flight, this is BeltCon. Cleared to linear this time. Quadrant Orange is your departure lane.

BeltCon, Digger lead, understand cleared to linear. Orange Quadrant. Digger flight delocking this time. Roget switched to tactical. *Digger flight, delock this time. Form on me.*

Digger lead, Digger two, stet.

Digger three here, stet.

Roget released the maglocks on both sides of the needleboat and used a burst of steering jets to ease it up from the docking cradle and toward the intake chute for the orange quadrant linear accelerator.

Orange Control, Digger one, approaching intake.

One . . . cleared to enter and take position.

Roget checked his suit and all the connectors, then the system integrity indicators before he used the steering jets to ease the needleboat over the accelerator's magnetic cradle.

Orange Control, Digger one, in position this time.

Stet, One . . . stand by for lock-in.

Standing by.

Roget felt the needleboat drop, and a dull *clunk* echoed through the hull, a sound that Roget felt as much as he heard as he checked his suit once more.

Outbound velocity wasn't limited by the linear accelerator's capabilities, but by the design limits of the needleboats—and their pilots—as well as the need to decelerate at the destination, particularly if the destination didn't have a mag-grav attenuator net. No pirate colony had that. But because the force of the linear accelerator could stress the needleboats and possibly cause a pressure loss, all pilots were fully suited for launch.

Digger one, locked in cradle. Interrogative ready for launch.

Roget ran a last set of checks. *Orange Control, Digger one, ready for launch.*

A wall of blackness pressed Roget back into the pilot's couch, an inexorable pressure that seemed to last forever before releasing him to the light gravity of the needleboat, set internally at one-third T-norm. Most of the training boats didn't have internal gravitics, but gravitic control systems were required for any flight lasting more than four standard hours, and most training hops were far shorter than that.

He checked the EDI as the accelerator launched Digger two and then Digger three.

Digger flight, close on me.

Digger lead, two here, closing this time.

Lead, three here, closing.

Digger flight, understand closure. Run systems checks this time.

Once Roget verified the integrity and pressure of the needleboat, and his outbound course, Roget removed his helmet, slipping it into the overhead rack where he could reach it immediately if the boat lost pressure.

Now all he had to do was endure six days of boredom before he and the others reached their target.

31

Another day passed with more medical tests and screenings before Roget was transported to the *Wu-Ding*. Once there, he was subjected to even more tests, and his pack was thoroughly screened as well, although no one actually opened it. Roget didn't bother to point out that shortcoming. After all the tests, he was escorted to the stateroom he'd occupied once he'd been revived on the way inbound to Dubiety. He was told to wait there.

Since he had left the dropboat, Roget had not been allowed near any screens or instruments that would have updated him on what the Federation fleet was doing. Even so, he had no doubts that they were preparing for some sort of strike against Dubiety. He also had no doubt that such a strike would be catastrophic—and not for the Dubietans. Of course, he couldn't *prove* that, not to the colonel's satisfaction and probably not to his own.

He didn't even look inside his pack, since he was certainly under observation, nor did he call up the flash image of Hildegarde.

Three hours later, two ship marines arrived and escorted him forward to see Colonel Tian.

Once Roget stood inside the small space off the operations bay, the colonel looked up from where he sat behind the folded-down console and motioned to the other chair. "Good afternoon, Major."

Roget's internals confirmed that it was late afternoon

Federation baseline time, but how good the day was happened to be another question. "Good afternoon, sir."

"You're one of the two who were able to return. Or allowed to return." Tian's voice was as emotionless as ever. "According to what you said the Thomists told you, only one other dropboat made it through the haze. Do you believe them?"

"My dropboat was badly damaged," Roget pointed out. "The commanding officer of the *ZengYi* confirmed that dropboat five disintegrated immediately upon reaching the outer orbital shell. It's almost a certainty that the other two suffered great damage and were destroyed in the middle layers. I don't see that the Dubietans would have anything to gain by lying about their fate."

"You trust these . . . aliens too much, Major. I would have expected better from you."

"I don't trust them at all, sir, except where I can verify for myself what may have happened."

"You dismiss rather lightly that your perceptions may have been . . . affected."

"I did think, sir, and I continue to think about whether everything I saw or felt had been mentally induced." Roget smiled, ironically. "The more that has occurred, the less I think that is likely."

"That is a most interesting conclusion. Would you care to explain why you think it so unlikely?"

"Any society that could launch a dropboat with the velocity and accuracy with which I was returned, not to mention the ability to repair the dropboat and create the material for the pressure suit I wore, as well as create the orbital shields, would have little difficulty in dealing with the ships you've gathered. Therefore, what exactly would be the point of going to all the trouble of inducing all that detail, especially with the depth of sensation. If they do not have the technology that I have seen and whose results our ships have documented, then they have the ability to change the perceptions of all of us, as well as affect our instrumentation. Therefore, they either have the ability to do that or they have the advanced technology. In either case, attacking or angering them is unwise."

"Oh? You were planetside some nine days, and you know their psychology and strategies so intimately?"

"I'm not talking about psychology, sir, but about technical capabilities." Roget paused, just briefly. "Have you had a chance to go over what I brought back?"

"I've gone over your reports and the materials you brought back. All of them are quite unbelievable."

"That may be, sir. It's also what happened." Roget kept his voice level.

"No. It is what you believe happened. Whether what you believe is what actually occurred is another question. Have you considered that?"

"Yes, sir." Roget laughed softly. "I considered it almost every day, if not every hour." *Why doesn't he want to understand?*

"And you don't think your thoughts were manipulated?"

"Everyone's thoughts are influenced by what they observe, or what they think they observe, sir. While I was planetside, I was fully aware of the complete range of human senses and sensations. Also, the Dubietans were not hesitant to suggest that they believed that they were essentially going through the motions in letting me see what I did and in sending back the materials that they did. You've tested me every way you can. Didn't the tests show I was planetside?"

"Isotope analysis of your hair indicates you were somewhere earthlike, yet very different. There were too few contaminants for you to be on a human-industrialized world capable of the kind of technology that could create orbital shields and high-speed launching facilities."

"Sir, given their emphasis on environmental costs, such a world wouldn't have a high level of contaminants."

"No human civilization has yet managed that degree of environmental control. Just how likely is it that an isolated world could do so?"

Roget had the strong feeling that Dubiety wasn't that isolated, but, again, all he had to go on was inference from what Hillis and Lyvia had said, and Tian wasn't about to take inference as proof. Not when he wouldn't take what proof there was and logic. "And the devices? How do you explain them if they don't have a high-technology capability?"

"Interesting, but hardly convincing. One projects a modulated form of energy that doesn't scatter."

"They apply that everywhere. There's not even light-scatter from streetlights, and my internals wouldn't pick up anything."

"Oh? There are other possibilities."

"What? Such as the fact that I was somehow mind-controlled from the moment of touchdown? That they're totally alien and planetbound because of other factors? That they fed everything I thought I experienced into me? I thought of those. If that's so, then they're no danger. At most, all the Federation would have to do would be to avoid Dubiety."

"That is not a possibility."

"All they're suggesting is that they be left alone."

"That is not possible," repeated Tian.

"Why not, if I might ask, sir?"

"You may ask. I will even tell you." The colonel

leaned back ever so slightly in his chair. "Some three thousand years ago on earth, there was an ocean admiral named Zheng He. This admiral commanded the largest fleet in history. In terms of numbers of vessels, it may have been the largest ever. It dominated earth's oceans for three decades, until a rebel uprising led to the creation of a new emperor—Hongwu. Hongwu burned the great fleet and turned China away from the world. Why did he do this? Because the fleet only explored and destroyed. It never provided any significant gain to China, and the harsh conditions of the time only led to the conclusion that the fleet was useless and a drain on the people. That is the first lesson."

Roget waited.

"The second lesson concerns the relationship between the ancient United States and the Tojoite Japanese Empire. Japan had closed itself off to the world, much as China had. But when the emperor was forced to open Japan to American traders at cannon point, the Japanese embarked on nearly a century of frantic industrialization and modernization. In the end, they attacked and destroyed much of China and invaded and occupied all the American lands west of the Hawaiian Islands. For years the entire world was at war. In the end, the Tojoites lost, but the devastation blighted the world for more than a century and led to the eventual fall of old America. That is the second lesson."

By his choice of those examples, Colonel Tian was obviously suggesting that the Federation Interstellar Service was to be used for far more than mere exploration and that any isolated world posed a potential threat that the Federation could not ignore.

"There are other examples from history, sir," suggested Roget.

"They are not from our history and are therefore less

applicable." The colonel's eyes hardened. "What else did you learn about their technology, if anything?"

"I detailed all that I could determine, sir, and brought back all that I could."

"You provided little of technical value, Major."

"I supplied you with maps, with a detailed description of the structure of their industry and transport systems, as well as how their communications are structured."

"*You* provided not one word about how this technology operates."

"I brought back a small transmitter, the technical material that documents how the orbital shields work, how some other transport systems may be possible . . ."

"I had the chief engineer study the material. He says that's all technical gobbledygook. There's no way that it could work as you say it can. Nor can the so-called transmitter."

Roget realized, abruptly, that there had been not one word about the language implantation technology. In his report, he had definitely mentioned what Director Hillis said about that being a technology that the Federation already developed. Yet the colonel had avoided asking about it. Because it had been suppressed and was being used covertly by the FSA and other security types? For more than language training? He wouldn't get an answer if he asked. Either Tian didn't know or wouldn't say. But he could try another approach. "Sir . . . how old is this solar system?"

The colonel frowned.

"According to my original briefing materials, it's considerably older than the Sol system, yet Dubiety has a molten core, a core supposedly reenergized by their technology. If you can measure the planetary magnetic fields, you'll find three sets of magnetic axes—all offset to each other. Those fields have something to do with the structure and operation of the three levels of orbital shields. To me, sir, that suggests that their technology is anything but gobbledygook."

The colonel frowned. "We've already established that the magnetic field is odd, but many planets have different or off-angled fields."

"Three separate fields, sir? I doubt that."

"Doubts are not facts, Major."

"Sir . . . I am an agent, not a scientist or a theoretical physicist. I was never allowed more than limited access to their commnet, nor to any written material that might explain how they have accomplished what they have, except for what I brought back. Even so, I am a trained observer, and what I saw suggests great caution in dealing with the Dubietans."

"Tell me." The colonel's voice was soft. "What do you think that they have accomplished?"

"They have built a subsurface transport system that is faster and more reliable than any planetary air or surface or subsurface transport system in the Federation, and far more effectively designed and operated than any system we have. They have created a layered orbital shield system that selectively admits solar radiation, keeps the planet from being observed by any form of energy, and would probably destroy most vessels trying to land on the surface. They have developed a tight-beam directional broadcast technology that radiates virtually no stray radiation yet allows all citizens commnet access. They have structured their society in a way that makes most continuing or habitual criminal activity extremely difficult, if not impossible. They can launch a dropboat at high velocity and with greater accuracy than any current Federation technology, and they can do so unobserved. Finally, they have some way of observing the Federation, and they have been doing so for centuries."

"Yet they allowed you to depart?"

"They helped me. The dropboat was badly damaged on the descent. You can tell that from the repairs. They wanted me to return. Why else would they go to all that trouble?"

"The techs have examined the dropboat. They can discern repairs, but no spy gear and no explosives or weapons."

"I assume they brought it into the engineering bays and totally disassembled it," said Roget mildly.

"That was unnecessary and unwise. All necessary inspection could be carried out with the craft on tether."

Since the dropboat wasn't exactly a great military threat, given its minuscule size compared to the *Wu-Ding* and the armament and shields of the battlecruiser, Tian had to be more concerned about possible nano-snoops.

"And what is the nature of the repairs?" asked Roget.

"They're comparable to Federation standards."

Roget suspected the repairs were far better, and that the colonel wasn't about to admit that.

"Is there anything else, Major?"

"One thing, sir. Dubietan Director Hillis suggested that you make an inquiry into the events of 6556 F. E. and the disappearance of Federation Exploratory Force Three. She also suggested that High Command review any stellar maps that might exist of this area in the year 4245 F. E."

"That's almost a thousand years before the Federation was even space faring."

"Send a ship twenty-five hundred light years away and record what it sees," suggested Roget.

"We scarcely have time or resources for such."

But you and the Federation have enough to start a conflict that will cost far more. "It wouldn't take that long."

"I'm sure they suggested that. It would buy time."

"They didn't suggest anything except looking at maps."

"I'm certain you believe that, Major." The colonel offered a cold smile. "That would be in their interests."

"That may be, sir, but there are unresolved observations about Dubiety. I would suggest looking into those dates before taking any action."

"We look into everything, Major. We look at the facts, especially."

Only selectively. But wasn't that an all-too-human trait?

"You may go, Major. For the time being, I strongly suggest you confine yourself to the wardroom, the exercise spaces, and your quarters."

"Yes, sir." Roget wanted to shake his head, but there wasn't even much point in that. Instead, he inclined his head politely and rose. The colonel had made up his mind—or it had been made up for him before the *WuDing* had set out for the Dubiety system.

32

After five days alone in the needleboat, the last thirty-odd hours on decel, Roget was restless but worried about what sort of reception might await them at the target destination. He hadn't gotten all that much sleep, either. Despite the vast distances between asteroids and the other ancient debris in the Belt, the needle's speed and course had resulted in the detector's alerting him a good twenty times, usually just after he'd dozed off. By the time he'd made course changes and regrouped the flight, he was awake, and getting back to sleep was difficult.

He considered the situation. According to the briefing materials, the pirates had raided the mining storage and consolidation outpost off Themis just after a solar slow-boat had arrived. They'd discovered and disabled almost all of the tracking devices in the cargo—except several of a newer design. Using those, the FIS had tracked the pirates to the pair of asteroids that was Roget's destination—less than an hour away. Given the raid, the FIS had decided that the pirate colony had been far too disruptive, but not enough to warrant fleet action, given the costs. Also, a needleboat flight had far more chance of making an initial attack unnoticed.

For a while yet, there was nothing Roget could do except wait.

He used his belt flash to project the image of Hildegarde just out from the side bulkhead, so close that he could have reached out and touched her—had she actually been there. The little black dachshund with the tan oval patches above her eyes gazed at him, as expectantly as ever. Just looking at the projected image of the ancient oil painting seemed to relax Roget, far more than viewing one of the scores of holodramas stored in the needleboat's entertainment files. Even the incongruity of seeing Hildegarde sitting on an ancient blue velvet sofa and a hand-knitted maroon and cream afghan, with the entire scene framed by plasticoated metal bulkheads, didn't bother him.

"It doesn't bother you either, does it, little girl?" he murmured.

Hildegarde just kept looking at him, expectantly.

Roget left Hildegarde perched on her sofa in midair above his right shoulder as he checked the needle's course and the data assimilation on the target.

Although the two asteroids revolved around each other, the tracking signalers and the energy indications made it clear that the target was the larger body—an irregular chunk of rock shaped roughly like an elongated potato some eight klicks long and three in diameter at the thickest part, one bulbous end. The needleboat instruments confirmed the briefing materials—that the target asteroid was half-nickel and half solid, stony basaltic material, the larger bulbous end being the metallic part. From the stray energy emanations picked up by his instruments, Roget pegged the "colony" as being located in the middle of what loosely might be termed the larger bulbous polar area.

The EDI showed only diffuse energy, barely above ambient. That wasn't surprising. While a pirate colony that had survived for any length of time had to have several fusactors, they would be placed where virtually all heat and energy would be used and trapped within the nickel-iron core of the asteroid.

Another twenty minutes passed before Roget collapsed the holo image, returning Hildegarde to her electronic kennel, so to speak, and squared himself before the controls. He donned his helmet, although he hoped that he wouldn't end up with integrity damage after the mission. A week's return in a suit would be sheer hell.

Like any FIS flight, the three needles would attack from widely divergent approach angles because pirate colonies were always energy limited, and a split approach required them to fragment their defenses or to ignore one or more of the attackers.

Digger flight, Digger one. Commence separation this time.

Digger one, two here, stet.

Digger three, stet.

The basic strategy Roget intended to employ was the reverse of the squirrel defense. Because the pirates/unauthorized colonists had to be dug in fairly deeply, the needleboats could appear, fire torps, and cross any area covered by defensive systems quickly enough that it would be difficult to track and acquire the attackers. The downside of the strategy was that the number of such passes was limited because the asteroid was too small for the needles to establish tight orbits and all passes had to be fully powered.

Roget's first pass would target a source of energy emanations—generally comm equipment or the colony's scanners. With luck, that would limit the pirates' ability to focus on the FIS needles.

Digger one will lead. Commencing run this time.
Stet.

The two other needles would follow his pass, but not from the same approach angle. Digger two would slip past the companion asteroid, while three would come in from an approximate reverse of Roget's pass. Roget doubted that the pirates had the equipment or the power to maintain a full sky scan. Most didn't . . . but there were always exceptions to everything, and unexpected exceptions could cause casualties.

The asteroid swelled in the screen projections before Roget.

Power at fifteen. Target lock-on, confirmed the needle's targeting system.

Fire one. Retarget to target two.

Roget waited just an instant before the system confirmed its lock on a pile of rock that held a ghostly rectangular shape—most probably a concealed launch or recovery tube and lock.

Fire two.

The screens indicated torp one's impact on target— and the pirate energy emanations died away.

An energy flash alerted Roget, but even before he or his systems could react, a pirate torp was halfway toward the needle. Within instants, it had fragmented into a cone of smaller missiles. Roget increased power, but he could see that the edge of the missile cone would impact his shields.

At the last possible moment, he diverted all available power into the needle's shields.

Even so, the small ship shuddered as the hail of solid-iron missiles pummeled its shields. Iron at even moderate speed was hard on shields. The pirates had one great advantage—lots of iron—and one disadvantage—a lack of power with which to propel it at more than a single incoming craft at a time.

Digger two, three . . . be advised target launching mass driver torps with iron missile cone.

Stet, Digger lead.

The needleboat's tracking system had flagged the source of the launch—another tube hidden almost a klick from the now-incapacitated comm array—and he relayed it to Digger two and three. Before his system had a chance to determine the location of the scanner arrays that the pirates had to be using to target the Federation needle boats, Roget was beyond the curved section of the asteroid where he'd begun his attack.

The backside showed no energy sources, and no torps rose from the basaltic surface.

Roget shifted his course and eased the needle behind the companion asteroid before readying the third and fourth torps and moving into position behind the third needleboat.

Digger three, will tail-chase you.

Stet.

Roget hung back slightly as Digger three angled toward the pirate installation, instructing the targeting system to search for the energy burst of the mass driver that was flinging the crude torps at them.

Target located, the system noted.

Fire three.

Digger lead, two here. Shields amber.

Two, break off attack. Stand off this time.

Stet.

Good, thought Roget. There was no point for two to risk getting turned into scattered mass and energy. Not yet, anyway.

A flare of energy spurted from the asteroid's surface.

Digger three, note last impact. Mass driver shaft. Target that impact on next pass.

Stet, Digger lead.

Roget fired his fourth torp at the mass driver shaft, but he was far enough past the target area that the asteroid's bulk blocked his detectors. He'd have to wait for the next pass to see how much damage they'd been able to inflict.

He swung the needle into another powered turn, one that would bring him back over the area of the installations, but at almost ninety degrees to his last pass. No sense in being predictable. The pirates might have something else waiting.

Digger lead, impact on target. Impact on target.

Stet. Coming in for last pass this time.

Once he was clear of the bulge of the asteroid, Roget zeroed in on the target display. Digger three's torps, following his, had opened a small crater in the uneven surface. Roget could see a roughly circular tube at one end of the crater. One advantage of attacking a low-gravity installation was that the debris tended to get blown clear, rather than just piling up in the crater.

The moment he had lock-on, he fired a single torp.

The torp ran true, vanishing into the circular opening. Then a wide semicircle of the basaltic surface buckled. Dust spurted everywhere, as did stone fragments.

Roget cleared the area well before stone fragments flew outward across what had been his flight path.

Digger flight, stand clear of target area this time.

Three, standing clear.

Two, clear.

Roget slowed his needle and swung into a turn that would carry him back over the target area. He expected dust to be hanging over the area because the asteroid was so small that its gravity was minuscule. Instead, the scanners revealed scattered areas of dust and other clear areas where dust plumes were already klicks out from the surface. For a moment, he didn't understand why. Then he swallowed. The last torp had done enough damage that the integrity of much, if not most, of the subsurface installation had been breached, and the release of the internal atmosphere had created those lanes of clearer space, even if the distinction between clarity and dust was so slight that only the scanners could pick it up.

The surface was far more uneven than before, but that and three small craters were the only outward indications of the destruction created by the three needle-boats.

Record and document, Roget ordered the system.

Recording.

Roget checked the scanners and all the instruments, but outside of fast-fading residual heat, there was no sign of life below, and certainly no energy emissions.

Digger flight, report status.

Digger lead, two here, shields amber, all other systems green. Four torps remaining.

Digger lead, three, all systems green, no torps.

That was to be expected, since Roget had pulled two off the attack when his shields had gone amber.

Once the system announced, *Documentation complete,* Roget called up the nav system, then eased the needle away from the pair of asteroids.

Digger three, take station on my quarter. Digger two, close up and trail our shields.

Two closing up this time.

Roget nodded. That positioning would at least minimize the strain on two's shields for the long return flight to Ceres station. There was always the chance of debris of various sorts, perhaps even debris that they had recently created, or debris that dated back billions of years. Either way, impacting it without shields, or with damaged shields, was not something good for a needle-boat—or its pilot.

Recommended return course set. Please approve, requested the system.

Roget checked, then cross-checked it. *Digger flight, sending return course this time.*

Digger two, stet.

Digger three, stet.

Digger flight, turn to return course this time.

Stet. Both other pilots responded as one.

Commence return course, Roget ordered the system.

Only when the needleboat was on the return course did Roget lean back in the pilot's couch and remove his helmet.

Had some of those in the colony survived? Roget had no way of knowing, and no ability to verify whether there were survivors or not. Even if there were survivors, life would be grim and most likely short—even if they had another functioning fusactor shielded deep within the asteroid. Power was vital but not necessarily sufficient, especially on a basalt-nickel-iron rock without much in the way of ice.

Why had the pirate colonists attacked the slow-boat at Themis? If they hadn't, Roget doubted that Belt Control would have sent out a three-needleboat flight for a two-week-plus mission, not with the equipment and costs involved.

Yet, he reminded himself, how else could those on the asteroid have gotten equipment? No one would sell it to them. What other choice had they had, except to surrender and beg for mercy? Mercy, in a relocation camp after marooning and leaving the slow-boat crew to die?

Earth hadn't been big enough, in the end, for many conflicting cultures and views. Would the same prove true of the solar system? Or the galaxy? Or did the problem lie in the Federation's views? That didn't necessarily follow, either, since there had been rebels and outcasts long before the Federation, and even old America had been founded by rebels.

Was there an answer?

Roget looked to the controls, not really seeing the readouts before him.

33

27 MARIS 1811 P. D.

Roget lay stretched out on his bunk, his eyes open, wearing the same coverall he'd worn on his descent to Dubiety, with its still mostly undischarged capacitors. While he'd been waiting for the inevitable, he'd thought about projecting Hildegarde into the narrow space between the bunk and the bulkhead flanking the hatch, but he'd decided against it. His internals were operating normally, if not even better than usual, aboard the *WuDing,* and he could easily sense all the snooping and scanning gear focused on him. If the colonel had a record of him viewing—or talking to—the image of a centuries-old painting of a dachshund, that would be grounds enough for immediate confinement in the brig as mentally unstable . . . and that would make what he had to do even more difficult.

His eyes flicked toward the stateroom hatch—little more than a composite door, as were most quarters' hatches, for all the imported nautical terminology and the remote electronic lock that had not yet been activated. He smiled, faintly, and went back to waiting.

Less than twenty minutes later, the annunciators blared.

"All hands to battle stations. All hands to battle stations." *All hands to battle stations*.

Almost simultaneously, the stateroom door locked itself.

Roget had expected both. Certainly, Colonel Tian would wish him contained while the *WuDing* led the attack against Dubiety.

With his first moves, Roget slipped the heavy, flat bag that held the Dubietan emergency pressure suit out of his pack and up inside his nightsuit coverall. Then he powered up the concealment features of the nightsuit and pulled the hood over his head. Moving to the stateroom door, he slipped two tools from the flat container inside his waistband. In less than a minute, he was out in the passageway, empty because it was in officers' country. He closed and locked the door behind him, deliberately but swiftly, and stowed the small tools.

Could he get to one of the airlocks aft of midships before the *WuDing* provoked the Dubietans into action? That was likely, since the *WuDing* and the Federation fleet didn't have the advantage of the Dubietan technology.

Moving quickly, he headed aft toward the first ladder. At the top of the ladder he flattened himself against the wall. Two ship's marines rushed up the ladder and past him in the direction of his former stateroom, proving the usefulness of the camouflage suit against the pale blue of the bulkheads.

He swung down two levels of the ladder and headed outboard, moving to one of the maintenance ways that he didn't think was snooped as thoroughly as all the main passageways were. He made it down almost to the outer ring, where the maintenance way ended, before he sensed another pair of marines. He eased open the maintenance hatch, just a crack, but the marines were not yet in sight. So he swung the hatch inward, then used the heavy hinges as an aid to wiggle upward and to wedge himself into the narrow overhead, hoping he didn't have to wait too long. The camosuit blended into the dark blue.

Roget waited, easing out one of the narrow picks from his waistband.

In less than a handful of minutes, he heard voices.

"Sensors say he's here somewhere."

To your right somewhere . . . hard to get readings down there.

"There's an open maintenance hatch."

Check behind it.

One of the marines stood before the hatch, looking down it, a heavy shocker in hand.

Roget flicked the pick as far back up the maintenance way as he could.

Clink.

"He's got to be up there by that niche." The first marine charged through the hatch and toward the sound.

The second stepped inside the hatch and halted.

That made it all too clear that the marines hadn't been in any kind of real combat or fight for all too long. Roget struck, coming down with his left boot squarely into the marine's eye and nose at an angle that slammed the hapless man into the solid bulkhead. The marine did not move, although Roget sensed rather than saw that, because he kept moving, swinging himself out through the hatch, then flattening himself against the main passageway bulkhead, on the side opposite the hatch hinges.

"Carteon!" The second marine whirled, then moved quickly back down the maintenance way. As he peered through the hatch, Roget moved, yanking him forward so that his boots caught on the hatch lip, then dropping him. In another quick movement, he had the marine's shocker. He used it on both marines, then grabbed the unused weapon from the first marine.

Holding the shocker in one hand, Roget sprinted to the next ladder aft and swung down. He stopped halfway down, moving slowly so that the camosuit would not blur. Less than ten meters away was the hatch that was the entrance to the midships maintenance bay. Also less than ten meters away stood two crewmen in combat space armor, but without helmets, guarding the hatch that led to the maintenance area and the lower midships locks. Both men held heavy-duty shockers.

Roget eased forward a step at a time, keeping the shocker on the side away from the guards and hoping the camosuit was blending the weapon into the blueness of the bulkheads. He didn't have that much time, not before more marines with heat-imaging units reached him, but he needed to get closer to use the weapon.

"You see something?" murmured one guard. "Down there a ways?"

"All I see is blue and more blue."

In the moment that both crewmen were not looking directly at Roget, he took two steps and froze. He was almost close enough. Almost.

"Spray the—"

Roget darted forward and fired.

"—passageway!"

The second crewman got off a shot, and Roget's right arm erupted in flaming agony. His entire body shivered, almost uncontrollably. Both crewmen were down, but Roget could hear more marines thundering down the ladders.

He pressed the hatch-access stud. The big hatch began to open. The maintenance area beyond the hatch went dark, as did the passageway behind him where the fallen guards lay. Roget jumped through the hatch just before it closed in response to the power cutoff.

He staggered against the nearest bulkhead, and at the impact his arm flared into more agony. Going to night-sight didn't help Roget because he wasn't in low-light conditions, but in no light.

The colonel hadn't cut power to the area to blind Roget, but to disable any equipment he thought that Roget might try to use. The power loss also meant Roget would have to find the emergency personnel lock in the dark and operate it manually.

Roget smiled. If . . . if he could remember the location, the power cut might be to his advantage because without power there were no snoops . . . and the emergency locks were designed to be opened manually—especially for times when there was no ship's power.

He forced himself to concentrate, despite the lines of nerve flame running up and down his right arm, then began to move toward the aft side of the maintenance bay. While it felt as though it took hours to find the emergency lock, it was less than a minute according to his internal systems.

Although the lock wheel turned easily, it took several minutes before he was able to rotate it enough times left-handed to open the inner-lock door. He swung the heavy door toward himself, wincing momentarily as the emergency-lock lighting struck his dark-adjusted eyes. Once he was inside the lock itself, he had to repeat the process to close the inner door. He couldn't vent the lock chamber without the inner door being closed, and without venting, there was no way he could swing the outer door into the chamber even after he'd rotated the wheel to the open position.

At that moment, power returned to the area, and that

meant the marines would be after him in moments. As he'd recalled, there was a broomstick racked beside the outer door. There was also a soft emergency pressure suit with an equally soft helmet—a poopysuit. He checked the broomstick propellant, then winced. Less than 20 percent. Not much margin for error. He pulled on the poopysuit, except for the helmet. Poopysuits usually held less than an hour of oxygen, if that, but the indicator showed forty minutes, and that should suffice.

While he'd thought to vent the lock last, he changed his mind, donned the helmet and sealed, then twisted the lock vent open immediately. That way the marines wouldn't be able to open the inner-lock door. Then he went to work turning the outer-lock wheel—again left-handed and even more clumsily in the heavy suit gauntlets.

Once he had the lock open, he grabbed the broomstick in his left hand and eased out into vacuum, forcing his almost-numb right hand to hold to the recessed grab-bar outside the lock.

With the disorientation of weightlessness, several moments passed before he finally located the tether—aft of the largest maintenance lock. His dropboat was still linked to the tether, and fortunately, not all that far from the rear of the large maintenance lock.

Abruptly, the tether separated from the dropboat, and a quick blast of gas from the tether pushed the dropboat outward. The colonel definitely didn't want Roget getting to the dropboat.

Roget straddled the broomstick and aimed it and himself at the dropboat's lock, giving both gas jets a solid jolt and hoping that his aim was good. If he missed, he was as good as dead . . . and not immediately. He hadn't planned to be in vacuum for more than a few minutes in the poopysuit. The emergency suits didn't have much

insulation, and if he missed the boat, whether he'd as-
phyxiate or freeze first would be the only question left
to ponder, and probably not for that long, because he
couldn't reach the distress alarm in the Dubietan emergency suit without breathing vacuum.

He pulsed the broomstick's left gas jet just momentarily, correcting his course more to the right. After a
moment, he could see that he was closing on the empty
dropboat. He forced himself not to use the jets more. If
he came in too hard, the absorber wouldn't handle the
jolt, and the mag-grip wouldn't hold.

Another minute passed, and he was within ten meters
of the dropboat. He glanced to his left. So far, he and
the dropboat had only slid back fifty meters along the
WuDing's hull, and separated less than twenty. That
was good because that left him too close to the battlecruiser for the colonel to deploy weapons against him or
the dropboat.

The mag-grip on the end of the broomstick hit one of
the patches repaired by the Dubietans. While the recoil
absorber took up most of the shock, the mag-grip began
to slide sideways.

"Shit!" muttered Roget. Just his luck they'd used a
non-metallic composite.

The mag-grip skidded along the dropboat's hull, but
finally grabbed onto the metallic composite above and
aft of the lock. Roget inched his way up the broomstick
until he managed to grab the recessed handle next to
the lock access panel. Holding on with his injured hand
was painful, but he needed the other hand to manipulate the lock controls, while keeping his legs wrapped
around the broomstick.

Once he had the outer lock open, he shifted grips, then
eased himself and the broomstick partly inside. Eventu-

ally he managed to get everything into the lock and close it behind him. His entire body was shaking.

When the lock was pressured, he stripped off the poopysuit, awkwardly opened the inner lock hatch, and tossed the emergency suit into the tiny bunk cubicle behind the control couch, before scrambling into position enough to power up the controls. Then he pulled the Dubietan emergency suit from under his coverall and out of its film wrapper. There were instructions—very brief and clear. He followed them in donning the suit up to the point of activation. That had to wait.

Next he strapped himself into the couch and checked the systems.

Power levels were as he'd left them—roughly 40 percent. That *might* get him close to Dubiety, but he wasn't about to try it yet. He'd ride along with the course vector and velocity already imparted by the *WuDing*. He was gambling on the fact that, so long as he did nothing detectable, the colonel would not be able to persuade the *WuDing*'s commander to use the drives for more separation in order to turn weapons on the dropboat.

Three minutes passed, then four. Suddenly the *WuDing*'s shields contracted, leaving the dropboat outside them, then expanded, pushing the dropboat away from the battlecruiser and effectively adding a ninety-degree vector to the battlecruiser's—and the small craft's—previous course. Roget swallowed but still did not activate the drives, just letting the dropboat angle away from the *WuDing* on a course that was inclined downward and at about 280 degrees relative to the battlecruiser's course toward Dubiety.

The slight downward velocity would soon carry the dropboat below the Federation formation. Despite the chill in the dropboat, so much so that his breath was steam, Roget was sweating. The hardest part of any operation, especially this one, was sitting tight and waiting.

He scanned the EDI. The Federation fleet was moving at a steady but almost stately pace toward Dubiety, one designed to save power for the weapons that whatever marshal was commanding would soon be unleashing against Dubiety.

Soon? He ran a quick calculation and came up with almost a standard hour before the fleet would be in position to bring everything to bear. Where would he and drop three be in an hour?

He ran another set of calculations. The results were as he feared. If he did nothing, he'd be too far below Dubiety. He reset the parameters and tried again.

If . . . if he could get away with a thirty-second max angled drive blast in the next few minutes, he'd stay within what he *thought* would be the Dubietan operational envelope, but still far enough from the fleet by the time he was in range of the Dubietan technology to avoid being an easy target for any of the Federation ships. Being in that Dubietan envelope would make him vulnerable to whatever the Thomists might do, but he hoped what he planned would resolve that difficulty.

Thoughts, guesses, and hopes. That's all you've got left. He pushed that thought away. He'd have had less than that if he'd remained aboard the *WuDing. No doubt about that at all. None.*

Once again he waited, letting the seconds tick away until the last possible moment before triggering the corrective drive blasts. His eyes flicked to the EDI, wondering if any of the Federation ships would waste a torp on him.

No one fired.

He'd hoped for that, basing his judgment on three things. First, he wasn't on a direct course to Dubiety.

Second, the colonel might well believe that if the Federation succeeded, they could let him drift forever or capture him at leisure. And third, the dropboat had no weapons of any sort and posed little direct threat to any Federation ship.

When the dropboat's drive cut out, Roget checked his course and the EDI again. No torps, and he was headed into the edge of the envelope he'd calculated. Once more, all he could do was wait.

As the minutes ticked away, he kept checking the readouts, but nothing changed except that the fleet—and dropboat three—edged closer and closer to the silver grayish sphere that was Dubiety.

After twenty minutes, the EDI signaled a disturbance, but not from Dubiety. Rather the instruments were suggesting a large energy source coming from outsystem. More Federation ships? Was that the reason for the stately progress of the Federation fleet? Waiting for reinforcements to join up? All that for a single planet?

Because the dropboat's EDI was anything but specific for that distance, Roget kept studying his instruments and worrying. It was almost ten minutes later before his EDI—far less accurate than detectors in the capital ships—gathered enough information. Roget just looked at what appeared on the screen before him. What his instruments registered was not possible.

A single vessel sped insystem, and that ship had to embody more than a hundred times the mass and energy of the largest battlecruiser ever built by the Federation. Roget's eyes flicked from the outsystem screen to the insystem screen, but he saw no change in the speed or course of the Federation vessels.

At that moment, Roget remembered the painting in the museum in Skeptos—an oil painting depicting a ship the size of an asteroid. Was that what his EDI was picking up? Was it real? Or some sort of electronic illusion? But how could the Thomists counterfeit the impression of all that energy?

From the lack of response from the Federation ships, clearly the marshal in command of the attack force believed the vessel showing on the EDI screens was an illusion or a decoy. Roget's guts tightened, telling him they didn't believe it was an illusion of any sort.

He still wasn't within the Dubietan operating sphere. His lips twisted. For all he knew, he might be, but he was assuming that sphere only extended as far as they had been able to launch the dropship. Besides, even the rearmost of the Federation ships was far enough from the dropship that a torp launched at Roget had no certainty of hitting—or inflicting damage.

Roget kept waiting, his attention split between the two screens, watching as the massive Thomist vessel neared. Then he swallowed again because energy flared against what had to be the shields of the Thomist ship. The EDI energy levels indicated that whatever had been in the way of the Thomist dreadnought had not been something insignificant, perhaps even a small asteroid. Whatever it had been, it was gone as if it had never been, with no apparent effect on the monster craft.

The Thomist vessel was still well away from Roget and his dropboat when the EDI registered something like an energy cocoon encircling the largest of the trailing Federation warships. The *ZengYi,* Roget thought, a large attack corvette, the one that had met him. One moment, the energy cocoon and the *ZengYi* were there. The next, they were not.

Roget winced. The crew of the corvette hadn't deserved that. They'd just been following orders, and they hadn't even fired a weapon.

But they would have. Roget knew that, but he still wished it hadn't been the *ZengYi*.

The Federation fleet still did nothing. Not that the marshal could have, because the monster Thomist ship was well out of torp range.

Then something flared from the *WuDing* toward the silver haze of Dubiety—a planet-scouring missile with a modified light-drive. Moments after launch, the missile vanished.

Roget activated the dropboat's drive, pouring full power into propulsion and adjusting his course. He couldn't wait any longer. He had to get as close to Dubiety as possible. The marshal and the Federation vessels weren't about to worry about him and his tiny dropboat. Not with what they faced.

His attention went back to the two EDI screens.

Another energy cocoon formed around a cruiser—the *DeGaulle*. This time the ship's commander applied full power. Roget could tell that from the rapid rise in energy intensity. But nothing happened. The ship did not accelerate, and the energy cocoon only brightened—until both the *DeGaulle* and the cocoon vanished from the EDI.

Two more of the energy cocoons followed, enveloping two corvettes and disappearing them as well.

Roget glanced at the upper corner of the EDI. An energy glow had begun to surround Dubiety itself. Things like that weren't supposed to happen, but, unlike the colonel, Roget wasn't about to argue with what appeared to be reality. As he watched another cocoon of energy encircle another Federation ship, this time most likely the *Shihuangdi,* Roget unstrapped himself from the pilot's couch and scrambled the scant few meters aft to the airlock, where he opened the inner hatch and hurried into the chamber.

Did he want to do what he felt was his only chance?

No. But watching the Federation fleet vanish, ship by ship, was like . . . *Like the last twist of the knife?*

Absently, as he closed the inner airlock door and then pulled the hood of the Dubietan emergency pressure suit over his head and sealed it, he wondered from where that thought had come. He pushed that question away and vented the lock chamber, then let the automatics open the outer lock.

As the hatch opened, he grasped the broomstick and then kicked himself and it out into the vacuum. Nothing seemed to move, not the points of light that were planets, nor the small disk that was Dubiety. He glanced down at the ship, then up and beyond. His eyes picked out a small greenish white disk—the Thomist ship.

He slowly straddled the broomstick and pointed it at Dubiety, not that it would carry him any fraction of the distance toward the hazy planet, and flicked on the gas jets. With what the Thomists were doing to the Federation fleet, the farther he got from the dropboat, the better.

Only after eleven minutes, when the jets gave out, did he press the large distress stud on the front of the emergency pressure suit.

As a certain chill began to creep over him, another set of words whispered through his thoughts.

. . . consign him to the darkness that lies beyond all darkness, to the blackness so deep that it has no shade, for out of the void came he, and into it will the return be . . .

34

The inbound trip back toward Ceres station had been long and boring, but that was the way space travel was. All interplanetary or insystem travel seemed longer because suspension cradles weren't often used and because more than a few FIS missions were single-pilot.

Roget checked the distance again. Another two hours remained until Digger flight reached the accelerator's grav net and they could begin the exterior-assisted decel. Without the magnetograv decel, they would have had to spend another two to three days for decel on the return leg, and he'd been cooped up in the needle far too long as it was. Like the accelerator, the decel net was harder on the needles. It also required a mass base, such as a moon or a large asteroid, and the environmental purists claimed that the continued use of the system had significantly changed Ceres's orbit. Roget had no idea whether the claims were true, but he didn't see that it would matter much one way or another. Ceres was big enough that the changes wouldn't go unnoticed and far enough away from anything but other asteroids that it shouldn't make that much difference.

As he sat and waited out the last hour or so of the mission, Roget couldn't help but think about the pirate colonists. Had they wanted to stay outside the Federation so much that they were willing to risk everything? How could anyone take such risks?

He almost laughed. The squirrel run had been almost as much of a risk. A little larger pirate torp or a slight variation in course, and Castaneda might not now be with them. The same could have been true of himself, he acknowledged. Any mission against comparable weapons was dangerous, and even missions against militarily inferior opponents carried risk.

Was the Federation that unbearable? There was no point in thinking about that, not when he didn't have any real alternatives.

Before him, the board shimmered, then somehow changed. In front of him, where the farscreens and displays had been, was a wraparound canopy, and on the lower section were projected displays. Roget/Tanner blinked, but the clear, wraparound canopy did not change. The clarity didn't help much, not in the darkness outside the aircraft.

His eyes kept a continual scan across the heads-up display and on the destination, the ultratanker *Deep Resource,* bound for Long Beach. While the tanker held something like six million barrels, even with all the green fuel sources that the United States had developed, that still amounted to just one day's oil imports—and that was with thirty dollar a gallon gasoline and power rationing.

A short burst of static was followed by a transmission. "Blackbolt lead, do not engage unless attacked. I say again. Do not engage unless attacked."

"Bolt Control," Roget/Tanner replied, "understand negative on engagement unless attacked."

There was no response, and Roget did not key another transmission. His eyes were on the RRD display, which showed two ships—high-speed SEVs from their speed—closing from the west on the big tanker. If Ops hadn't wanted him to keep the SEVs from diverting or sinking the tanker, why was he leading a flight out some four hundred miles east of Luzon in the middle of the night?

Because they want you to stop the interception with plausible deniability. Roget understood that all too well. He also understood that, at the moment, the good old USA needed every tanker it could get, at least until the Colorado shale projects were fully up and running.

He checked the RRD again.

Roget/Tanner had "official" orders not to attack the Chinese SEVs, but that didn't mean he couldn't warn them off in a way that would allow the tanker to continue onward toward its destination. Behind the night-visor, he moistened his lips. Then he linked to the fire-control computer.

After a moment, he nodded. It just might work.

"Bolt two, Bolt three, Bolt lead going down for flyby and recon. Hold position." He eased the stick forward and the AF-76 Raven screamed downward through the thin cloud layer. He leveled off at two thousand, headed directly toward the nearer SEV.

He switched to the CF, the common ship frequency. "Unidentified vessels, you are nearing hazardous waters. Approaching the *Deep Resource* may endanger your ship. I say again. You are nearing hazardous waters. Approaching the *Deep Resource* may endanger your ship."

"Unidentified aircraft, you are within Federation airspace. Bear off."

Roget snorted. The ChinoFeds claimed almost all the airspace in Westpac beyond Midway and Johnston Atoll, even if they didn't usually aggressively patrol more than three hundred miles eastward from their various "protectorates." Australia had fallen, as much a victim to global warming and drought as to the Chino-Feds, and so far Japan had held out, alone, but with a century of falling birthrates and economic difficulties, how much longer the Japanese could remain independent was yet another question.

"Blackbolt lead, two scrammers inbound. ETA in five."

That was all Roget needed—hostiles with greater speed.

"Bolt two and Bolt three, hostiles inbound. Stand by to take all measures for self-defense." What that really meant was to use the advanced standard hand missiles against the scrammers at the slightest provocation.

Roget adjusted the target setting. *Just a patch of water,* he told himself. *Just a patch of water.*

Target destination has no identified target. Confirm launch, requested Roget's targeting system.

Roget flicked his thumb over the glowing green stud on the stick and pressed down firmly.

As soon as the first missile was away, Roget turned the Raven slightly south, not that he needed it, and checked the second SEV.

Target destination has no identified target. Confirm launch, repeated the targeting system.

Roget pressed the green light a second time. Confirmation wasn't needed when the system had a target lock-on, but Roget couldn't do that. Not in this situation. The software and satellite systems would confirm that he had not fired at either SEV. Not that the ChinoFeds or the cowards in Washington would be happy, but Roget had just followed orders to warn off the Chinese vessels.

He watched the RRD as the first missile plowed into the water just in front of the high-speed surface effect ship, leaving a temporary crater in the water, just enough to allow the heavily armed vessel to plunge forward, losing its air cushion and steerage, not to mention its engines, as it nosed into the water and waves surged over the bow, all the way up to the bridge.

Roget grinned momentarily, waiting for the second missile impact.

The effect was the same for the second SES.

Bolt lead, Bolt two. Scrammers in range.

Bolt two, Bolt three. Defense permitted this time. I say again. Defense permitted this time.

He watched the RRD as four standard hand missiles flew from the other two Ravens toward the incoming scrammers. Neither CF aircraft clearly expected the navy pilots to launch first, because in moments debris was sifting downward.

Roget eased the stick back, edging power up, and the Raven rose through the cloud layer.

Bolt flight, form on me.

Roger.

Roger, Bolt lead.

Both SEVs were dead in the water, disabled if not sinking, and the skies were clear except for the three navy birds headed back to the all-too-old and tired *Reagan*. And the *Deep Resource* was on course for Long Beach and a fuel-starved United States of America.

Blackbolt lead, interrogative status? The transmission was faint, but clear.

Like everything that the navy has, thought Roget. *Two unknown vessels apparently suffering mechanical damage. Resource vessel on course. No other aircraft in sight.* Let Ops sort that one out.

Understand no other aircraft in sight.

That's affirmative this time.

Report approach.

Bolt Control, will report approach.

Roget/Tanner checked the RRD, but the skies remained clear—for the moment and the mission.

Once more darkness swirled and one kind of blackness replaced another, and the night-visor vanished, replaced by the screens before Roget.

Roget shook his head. While he'd had short memory flashbacks during his training, they had been brief, almost momentary. This one had seemed far longer. Why? Because Tanner had been an atmospheric combat pilot?

In what little information he'd discovered about Tanner, there had been nothing about his attacking Federation aircraft . . . and Roget certainly hadn't read anything about the Federation's efforts to sink or divert oil tankers to energy starve the old American republic. All the histories just mentioned that excessive reliance on offshore energy sources had been a factor in the fall of old America.

Again, he reminded himself, he'd just have to cope. Telling anyone would cost him everything.

. . . *interrogative status* . . . The partial and garbled transmission brought Roget up short. He and the other two needleboats had to have been crossing some sort of systemic energy flux or dead zone.

BeltCon, Digger lead, returning this time. Estimate one five to approach perimeter.

Digger lead, understand one five to approach. Interrogative comm status.

BeltCon, comm is green. Transit of dead area. Comm is green.

Digger lead, report approach.

He could report his flight's approach. That he could do, even as he pondered how the ancient Americans had handled the unauthorized destruction of two aircraft and the disabling, if not the sinking, of two Chinese Federation warships.

Not for the first time, he also wondered again just how Marni Sorensen had managed to select the "memories" of an ancient hero that would resonate with him. Or had she injected him with snippets of memory from Tanner that his own mind had interpreted and expanded? How much really was Tanner and how much came from him? And did those memories make him part Tanner? Would he ever know?

35

27 MARIS 1811 P. D.

Darkness and cold swirled around Roget, and sounds he could not hear clashed and merged into a symphony he had not composed, a life he had not led, a path he had not followed . . . and yet had. From the darkness, he emerged into an even more immediate coldness.

Where Roget stood was chill, mainly because a torrent of cold air poured down on him from somewhere, cooling the sweat in his short silver white hair. He blinked as the lights around him intensified. All around him people were talking, generally in low and intense tones, and he found himself nodding to something he had not heard.

A slender young man in a navy blue blazer and a white shirt dashed up and stopped short of Roget.

"Sir . . . St. George is coming in . . . coming in big. That should do it."

Do what? Roget did not even try to verbalize the question, belatedly realizing he was remembering yet another bit of Tanner's past.

"Joe! You can talk to them all now. It's about time . . ." came another voice from behind Roget/Tanner.

"Past time . . . they've been waiting hours," said someone else.

". . . didn't go off and leave people, like some . . . waiting here with everyone else . . . why he'll win . . ."

". . . indeed, now, there will be time to wonder if I dare . . ." Roget's words were to a tall and slender brunette woman, standing beside him. "After all this, Cari . . ."

She smiled sympathetically and warmly and said, "Go ahead. This is what you wanted, Joe . . . it's your moment."

"It's yours, too. I wouldn't be here without you," he replied. "April isn't the cruelest month. November is."

"You'd be here, dear, even if I weren't. Nothing could have stopped you."

"It wouldn't have meant much without you."

"You'd have found someone. You're too good to be alone."

He started to reply, but behind him a chant rose, swelling like thunder, or the cymbals of an unseen orchestra.

"Go! Go! Go! . . . Go . . . for . . . Joe! Go! Go! Go! We want Joe!"

Roget/Tanner glanced over his shoulder toward the crowd.

"You'd better talk to them before they shout down the roof," suggested Cari.

"No, Mrs. Tanner . . . he needs someone to do a proper intro." Mike Penndrake stepped up to the couple. "He just can't walk out there. They expect someone to tell them how special he is and how special they are."

Penndrake's sweaty square face looked more greasy than exercised, Tanner thought, but he nodded. "Make it short, Mike."

"As short as I can." Penndrake offered a wide smile, the kind that was all too common among political operatives, Tanner/Roget had come to learn. Then he turned and stepped up to the podium and the small microphone, which he picked up. He tapped it several times, and the crowd's murmurs and the chanting died away.

"Welcome to Tanner election headquarters, such as it is."

Laughs rippled across the crowd.

"In just a moment, you'll all be hearing from the man you all supported, the man you came to see. I'd just like to remind you, not that you need any reminding, that from the day he was born, all through school, this man has lived an exemplary life. At a time when patriotism was often equated with stupidity and treason, he put his life and his career on the line. He stood off an entire ChinoFed force to assure fuel supplies for America. He was wounded three times in the Westpac War, and each time, he came back and flew again. If we'd had more men like Joe Tanner, all the Pacific would still be an American ocean, and Japan would be our ally and not a ChinoFed fiefdom." Penndrake paused, just for an instant. "Now . . . for the good news. We just got the results from St. George . . . and Joe Tanner is the new senator from the great state of Utah! I give you Joe Tanner, a genuine war hero who knows the cost of war and the price of peace . . . a man for the times ahead."

With a broad smile Penndrake stepped back and gestured toward Tanner/Roget.

The gymnasium erupted once more in cheers and whistles.

Roget/Tanner turned from Cari and stepped forward to stand behind the battered wooden podium. He smiled and looked back to his left where Cari stood, her face thinner than it had once been, but still holding the quiet supporting enthusiasm that she'd always offered.

As Tanner waited for the cheering to die down, smiling warmly, he surveyed those in the crowd, many of them older and graying, others looking scarcely old enough to be adults, trying to let everyone know that they were welcome. His eyes dropped slightly to the group standing on the floor just below the stage and podium. The stylish redhead stood there, looking up at him, her deep green eyes bright.

Susannah appeared far younger than when Roget/Tanner had last encountered her . . . or remembered her.

Tanner smiled directly at her, then raised his head and cleared his throat. "I can't tell you how much everything that all of you have done means to me. A year ago, no one gave us a thought, and without all of you, every last one of you, we wouldn't have had a chance. I don't want to kid any of you, nor mislead you. This is a great victory, but it's only the first battle in a long fight to reclaim our heritage. For too long, those in power in Washington have strangled our industry and technology with meaningless regulations that neither improved our economy nor our environment. They squandered billions on weapons technology that did not work and refused to fund what did. They exported jobs while watering down education so that all too many of our children struggled to compete in a global economy. They bailed out multinational financial corporations while bankrupting average citizens . . ." Tanner/Roget held up a hand for silence. "I've said all this before, and you listened, and you acted, and you all gathered behind us . . . and that's what this great country of ours needs more than ever—the will and effort of determined people like you who make real and meaningful change possible. Thank you! Thank you, each and every one of you . . ."

Tanner/Roget lowered his head for a moment, then raised his eyes and looked out at the crowd cheering in the antique gymnasium . . .

Streamers fluttered from the high ceiling, and lights strobed and flashed . . . and the sounds all died away into a deep silence.

A different kind of chill encased Roget, one that did not let him move hands or feet, or even his eyes.

"You'll be all right."

Roget heard the words, and the voice was familiar, but he couldn't identify the speaker before another kind of blackness, warmer, more comforting, swept over him.

36

Roget opened his eyes, wondering if he could even move. He was lying flat on his back. He blinked. That was good. Then his eyes took in the overhead, a pale green. He started to take a deep breath, then stopped. His chest and lungs hurt. So did his legs, and his head ached and throbbed. He closed his eyes. That didn't help with the headache. So he opened them and studied the ceiling again. At least it wasn't blue. At least he wasn't in a Federation sickbay or brig.

Slowly, he turned his head.

He lay on a bed in a small room. Beside the bed he could see a bedside table and a chair. The room had no windows, and the door was the translucent green type he'd seen only on Dubiety. An acrid smell hovered around him. It took him a moment to realize that he—his sweat—was the source of the odor.

Since he doubted that the scene he beheld was any form of an afterlife, someone had rescued him, and his rescuers were presumably the Dubietans. He could only hope that he didn't end up in some place like Manor Farms, although that would be better than what had awaited him with the Federation. About that he had absolutely no doubts, not with the way the colonel had treated him at the end.

But why did everything hurt?

The door split, and the two translucent green sides slid back. Selyni Hillis stepped through it. Roget struggled into a sitting position in the bed, trying not to wince as he did, and trying to ignore the intensification of the headache. He closed his eyes again. That didn't help any more than it had the first time, and he forced himself to look at the director.

Hillis dropped into the chair. "Pardon me, but it's been a very long several days."

Roget managed the slightest nod. More than that and he had the feeling his head would fall off. He knew it wouldn't, but it felt that way.

"Where am I?" he asked, his voice raspy.

"In the med-center of the translation complex."

"Translation complex?" blurted Roget.

"What you thought was a launch complex, where we sent you and the other dropboat back to the *WuDing*."

"Oh . . . thank you for rescuing me."

"You're welcome." She offered a wry smile. "It took a while to get to you, and the recovery was rough on you. We will extract some payment for that."

Roget waited. He didn't want to ask. But Hillis didn't volunteer more. He finally asked, "What did you have in mind? For repayment?"

"Nothing physically that onerous. We'd just like your detailed memoirs and observations about the Federation. You can write or record them over several years, but it would be best to start while your memories are fresh."

"And?"

"That's just for the rescue. You'll still have to find an occupation. We'll talk about that later."

"What happened?"

"You must have seen, didn't you? The dropboat was functioning enough to split from the *WuDing*. I'm surprised that they let you depart."

"They didn't have that in mind," Roget admitted. "It took a little effort, and some luck."

"That part of your memoirs will be very popular, I'm certain."

"You'd . . . make them public?"

"That's the general idea. Anything the government says, even on Dubiety, especially on Dubiety, is regarded with a certain skepticism. You might even get a bit of continuing income from them."

"You didn't tell me what happened," Roget reminded her.

"What did you observe?" she countered.

"The Federation ships vanished. The huge dreadnought—it was your ship, wasn't it?—it destroyed them one by one."

Hillis shook her head. "We didn't destroy any of them."

"Then what did you do? I saw them vanish. It was your ship, wasn't it?" Roget asked again.

"One of ours."

"It wrapped energy around the Federation ships, and they disappeared."

"They did. We didn't destroy them. We translated them to the far side of the Galaxy. They might end up close to each other. They might not. Some might end up in a solar corona somewhere, or in the gravitational hold of a gas giant, although the odds are very much against that. We don't have that fine a control over those kind of distances. They'll just have to do what they can wherever they end up. Some of them might survive to build colonies . . . if they decide to create instead of trying to dominate."

Hillis could have been lying to him, but Roget didn't think so. There was a factual weariness behind her words.

"Won't the Federation just send another fleet?"

"They could. It wouldn't be very bright. This is the

third one in two centuries. You should have gathered that from what we told you."

"But . . . why do they keep doing it?"

"Conditioned reflex. They've absorbed everything—they think—by waiting and patiently trying again. It will be another century, assuming the Federation lasts that long, before they can amass enough resources to replace the ships they lost."

Roget understood that. The Federation Mandarins couldn't afford to let it be known that a mere Thomist colony had wiped out an entire fleet in moments without suffering any losses. That would have undermined the Federation far too much because its order was supported by the illusion of absolute knowledge, power, and control.

"You don't think the Federation will last that long?"

Hillis shrugged. "It's hard to say. They lost a tremendous resource investment when they lost those thirty-three ships, and that's a significant drain that will fall mostly on earth. Sooner or later, some seemingly smaller event like that will trigger its fall." She paused, then added, "On the other hand, we did them a favor because they generally place potential troublemakers in the exploratory fleets, carefully spread around, or in fleets like the one that tried to attack. Some of the junior officers are those who think too deeply. That's how dynasties and empires survive, by keeping the able, the discontented, and the ambitious at a distance. The problem on old earth has always been that those on the frontiers turned back on the center."

Roget thought about his own earlier "squirrel run." "They don't allow rebels and troublemakers on earth or anywhere in the solar system."

"The Federation will take longer to fall, and it will

fall farther," predicted Hillis. "Civilization as such might not even survive."

"But you send your own troublemakers out."

"We don't try to destroy them. We give them ships and resources. It solves their problems, and it solves ours. It's also a very good way of ensuring the survival of the human race, although there are some philosophers who question the ethicality of such survival, and of foisting off such aggressiveness on the rest of the galaxy."

"Has anyone found other intelligence?"

"We've found ruins and data, nothing more. It's a very big galaxy, and civilizations don't last all that long in the galactic perspective."

"That dreadnought . . . did that come . . . ?"

"Some of the ideas behind it, but the Ryleni never left their home system." Hillis paused, then said, "Now . . . I have a question for you. Why did you cast yourself into space? Couldn't you see that we were removing the Federation ships one at a time? You didn't need to do that." A smile hovered in Director Selyni Hillis's eyes, but not on her lips.

Roget had asked himself that before he had stepped out of the dropboat's airlock. "Because I had faith that you could pick me up, and because I wanted you to know that I was choosing to leave the Federation behind. I wasn't certain that you'd know that without some sort of . . . grand gesture. I didn't know how else to make that clear, and I thought you were destroying the Federation ships. Call it a statement of intent, backed by skepticism and worry."

"Skepticism and worry . . ." A soft laugh followed the words. "You're a Thomist at heart, I think." She shook her head. "You did make your intent clear. So clear that you also caused some difficulty and consternation." She paused for a moment. "That was quite literally a leap of faith."

"I'm not that kind of Believer."

"We knew that. Still . . . there is a time for proof and a time for belief—not in the supernatural, but in what one knows exists, even if he cannot fully explain it." Hillis smiled. "Faith in accomplishments and faith in others is far more solid than faith in gods who have never passed the test of proof of their existence."

"How could one ever really know?" Roget asked dryly, stifling a cough he knew would hurt.

"One cannot ever definitively prove that a god or a being does not exist. That is not possible, but time has proven that, if such a being exists, he or she or it does not interfere in our lives for either good or evil. That should be sufficient for any thinking being."

"For some it is not."

"I said 'any thinking being.' "

Roget smiled wryly at the correction before asking, "Where's Lyvia?"

"In Skeptos."

"Did she really dislike me that much?" He felt so tired, and all he'd done was to ask a few questions.

"No."

"She just didn't like me that much. Is that it?"

"Let us just say that you impressed her enough that she did her duty."

Roget nodded, holding back and swallowing a yawn. He had questions, so many questions, and he asked the next one that came to mind. "Some of that data in the information package . . . it might have gotten back to the Federation. Doesn't that worry you?"

"We hoped it would. That was one of the reasons for sending it back to the *WuDing* with you."

"Was the information false?"

"Oh, no. It was all absolutely accurate and technically correct."

"You wanted the Federation to have it? Why?"

"Think about it." Hillis smiled. "If you can't figure it out by the time you leave Skeptos, I'll tell you. But I don't think I'll need to."

Leave Skeptos? "I don't want to end up in something like the Manor Farm Cottages or whatever else . . ."

Hillis shook her head. "You're too well adjusted for that. If you want to, we can train you for a position as a balance coordinator. You have all the necessary background knowledge. Before all that long, there will be a vacancy in Andoya. That's in Thula, and it's a pleasant place. It's a bit cooler there than Skeptos, but I imagine you'd prefer it that way."

Roget wasn't about to commit, not without knowing more. He stifled another yawn. "What's a balance coordinator?"

"The coordinators work to balance the environmental, energy, radiation, and other impacts in a region. By now, you should know how important that is for us."

"Because the shields insulate both ways?"

"Exactly." Director Hillis rose from the chair. "You need some more sleep. You're barely able to stay awake. It's not that often that someone recovers from near anoxia and close to terminal frostbite."

Had he been that close to death?

"Not quite," replied Hillis, clearly reading his face, "but it will make a great story when enough time has passed. We'll talk about what training you'll need when you feel better, assuming you're agreeable."

Roget eased himself back down onto the bed, then turned toward Hillis, who had almost reached the door.

"Hildegarde . . . my flash . . . the image?"

"The extreme cold destroyed the storage in your belt

flash monitor. But we saved all the images you called up at the guesthouse in Skeptos, and they're waiting for you." Another smile crossed her face. "You won't need her for all that long, except as a reminder. Now . . . get some sleep."

They did have the image of Hildegarde. They did.

He closed his eyes.

EPILOGUE

Roget couldn't help but smile as he strode toward the nature walk on the west end of the hill beyond the conapt complex where he'd settled temporarily. He was learning the business of being a balance coordinator from the woman who had held the position for nearly two decades, a very hands-on proposition, and he found that he was enjoying it. He also enjoyed Andoya.

The worst of the frosts had lifted, as Lyvia had predicted months earlier, and the cool, but not-too-cool, spring in the highlands of Thula was definitely to his liking.

As he passed through the two stone pillars marking the beginning of the walk, he heard a sound he hadn't in years—a certain deep bark. Just one bark.

At that sound, Roget turned. He couldn't help but smile as he saw the black and tan dachshund leading her owner toward the pillars that marked the start of the nature walk circling through the low hills. Standing there, he waited until the dachshund and her owner neared before speaking.

"She's beautiful." Roget thought he'd spoken correctly. He squatted to get a better look at the dachshund, then extended his hand, letting the dog sniff it. After a moment, he stroked her head gently. "You are special, aren't you?"

The dachshund wagged her tail, and the woman laughed.

Roget stroked the dachshund once more before straightening. The dog's owner was, he realized, most attractive with mahogany red hair cut longer than most Dubietan women. It even brushed the collar of her pale green blouse. She wore a darker green scarf as well, both shades of green set off by her piercing green eyes. Yet she was older, perhaps even close to his own age.

"I'm sorry," he apologized. "It's just . . ."

"Do you have a dachsie?"

Roget shook his head. "Not now. I have . . ." He shook his head again. "It would be hard to explain."

"You're that Federation agent, aren't you? Or you were." Her voice was amused.

"I'm afraid I was. I didn't mean to bother you. It's just that . . ."

"Freya likes you. She's more careful with most strangers. She only barked once."

"Oh . . . I should introduce myself, other than as a former Federation agent. I'm Keir Roget. I'm training as a balance coordinator here." He wondered if her name might be Susannah, but that would have been too much of a coincidence.

"Emmelyn Shannon." Her eyes met his.

Roget wondered what she saw.

"Emmelyn . . . I like that." Abruptly, he laughed, embarrassed. "I'm sorry. It's not my place to approve or disapprove. I'm so sorry."

Her laugh was soft, amused but not cutting.

"Might I walk with you and Freya?"

"With Freya and me, I think. You didn't even look at me. You saw her first."

Roget laughed again, in relief. "I did. She reminds me of another dachshund who meant a great deal to me. She still does. Her name was Hildegarde."

"A very proper name for a dachshund."

"So is Freya." Roget glanced down.

Freya looked up expectantly, with almost the same expression that the ancient artist had captured in the portrait of Hildegarde.

"She does like you." Emmelyn laughed softly again, a sound somehow familiar.

"I hope so." Roget squatted and stroked Freya's head and neck again, enjoying the feel of her smooth coat under his fingers. Finally, he stood.

He smiled at Emmelyn. "You don't mind, do you?"

"I'd only have minded if you'd ignored her." She flicked the lead gently, and Freya set out down the bark-mulched path, confident that the two would follow.

As he walked beside Emmelyn, Roget glanced sideways. Emmelyn had to be special. With a dachshund like Freya, how could it be otherwise?